She poled over to the porch landing and blinked into the lamplight. The open door was an invitation — from a place that had lately suffered murder and invasion.

Fool to go in there. Fool to come this far, Altair.

She bumped into the landing and caught a tie ring with her bare hands, letting the pole end fall in the well and the rest lie aslant across the deck rim. Muscles strained, the way of the boat fighting back; sore joints protested. She braced bare feet, snatched the rope through and made fast.

Then she stepped across to that stone porch, climbed the single step, and walked into the lighted stone hall.

The door swung to, kicked from behind it. She spun and staggered to a quick freeze, facing a man with a knife, as another door crashed open and poured armed men into the hall at her other side....

C. J. CHERRYH

Angel with the Sword

VGSF

VGSF is an imprint of Victor Gollancz Ltd
14 Henrietta Street, London WC2E 8QJ

First published in Great Britain 1987
by Victor Gollancz Ltd

First VGSF edition 1987

Copyright © 1985 by C. J. Cherryh

Maps by Pat Tobin

British Library Cataloguing in Publication Data
Cherryh, C.J.
    Angel with the sword.
    I. Title
    813'.54[F]   PS3553.H358

ISBN 0-575-04009-2

Printed and bound in Great Britain
by Richard Clay (The Chaucer Press) Ltd, Bungay, Suffolk

Angel with the Sword

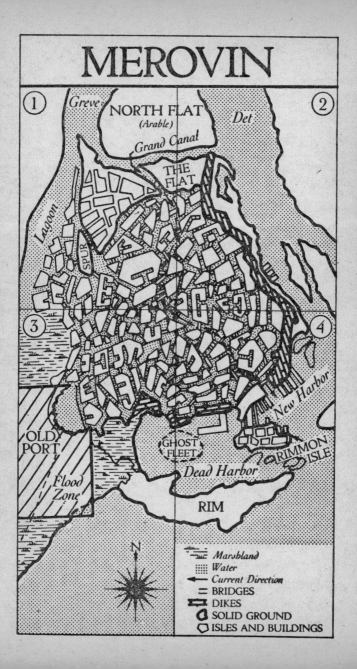

Table
of Contents

Chapter 1

NOW in all the world there were above a hundred cities; which was a good deal better world than the Ancestors had left. There was the heptapolis of the Chattalen strung up and down the Black Sea like a line of black pearls; and there was the prosperous river-land of Nev Hettek, which sent its boats chugging down the great Det to the Sundance Sea. There were settlements near the strange ruins of Nex. Wherever human stubbornness could find a toehold, trade went; and the world, which was named Merovin on the charts, got along as best it could, poised between the sure knowledge that outworld humanity had no interest in it and the eternal hope that the inhuman sharrh had no use for it, present or future. Certainly the sharrh had no intention of letting Merovin's scattered inhabitants off the planet and into space.

So the world—it was only in the religious context the inhabitants ever called it Merovin—managed for itself, these hundred cities descended from humans too stubborn to quit the world when the human-sharrh treaty demanded the removal of the colony; descended from colonists clever enough to have hidden out from the search teams; and tough enough to have survived the Scouring which took out the tech. The sharrh ignored Merovin's inhabitants thereafter. (Though there were rumors that there were sharrh onworld who had not kept *their* side of the treaty.) The uproar and the commotion died down; the human fugitives came out of the hills, rebuilt their ruins and begat offspring. And twenty generations of descendants cursed them for absolute fools.

Twenty generations of descendants built the hundred
cities, and lived in them; and knew of a heartdeep certainty
that elsewhere in the universe humankind fared a great
deal better than humankind did anywhere on Merovin. The
stars shone overhead like paradise unattainable and Merovans
lived and died under them with the knowledge that the
heavens were as wide as their own lives were limited.
Thanks be to the Ancestors. Who were fools

Now there *were* wonders on Merovin. Even the most
sullen and despairing soul admitted a certain majesty in the
Misty Mountains and the green rolling Sundance; in the
fabled Desert of Gems or (with a shudder) the remote
sharrh ruins of Kevogi and Nex. There was a moon to
inspire romantics—*the* Moon, it was called, and two more
bits of moon, which Merovans named the Dogs, that
chased the Moon through the heavens. There were cities
like Susain, where mines made wealth. There were trading
centers like Kasparl, that teemed with strangers from rivers
and from caravans. Merovin had its bright spots.

But in all the world of a hundred human cities there was
likely no worse place than Merovingen of the thousand
bridges, which was six hundred fifty years old and still
working on its decay.

Of all the ill luck of the Ancestors, Merovingen had
been the worst. First city in the world. The spaceport—
well, the Ancestors knew what had come of *that*. And, in
the Ancestors' ineffable wisdom, Merovingen had been
situated on the Det, for the anticipated trade that would
come down the river on cheap barges to be lifted offworld
from the spaceport.

Well, trade did come down the Det, though the spaceport grew up with grass and brush. But the earthquake that
had leveled luckless Soghon upriver (which was to be
Merovingen's main contact-point with the interior) also
shifted the course of the Det so that it largely inundated
Merovingen. Merovingen thrust itself up desperately on
pilings and built bridges and went on growing up and up
and sideways on the flooded ruin of former buildings,
despite fever and the slow rising of the river (or the
inexorable sinking of Merovingen's pilings, there was de-

bate which was the case). Merovingen lived, which was its own misfortune, just well enough not to die.

It was a wonder of sorts itself from a distance, like a ruined gray-board pier all built up with towers, a fanciful profusion of windowed wooden spires as if it were all one building. (It nearly was, so closely it crouched over the canals which had replaced other modes of transportation.) It truly had a thousand bridges—a mad three-tiered web of catwalks and air-bridges, bridges joining balconies, bridges joining bridges, stairs joining level to level, so that houses and shops and manufacturies jostled one another for the least hour of sunlight, excepting the lofts and towers which were *the* place to live if one were doomed to live in Merovingen. The towers caught the breezes (and the storms); while the lowermost inhabitants lived in perpetual readiness to move their belongings out come flood. And the whole creaked and groaned in the winds, or to the push of the tide up the shallow harbor and into the canals; or (one feared) the settling of the whole mass of the city another fraction into oblivion. That was Merovingen-above.

Below the city moved a dark demimonde of barges and bargemen, skips and poleboats and whatever craft could negotiate the web of canals and the largely unregulated overhang of Merovingen's bridges. Down in the watery depth of the city existed the lowest of levels, the foundations of buildings in the last stages of shoring-up before they too sank and became part of the underbracings below the mud—little nooks of shops and taverns that catered to the desperate, who would add their bones someday to the underbracings. It was a place of disappearances. Lives came and went transitory as the boats which flitted like black ghosts in and out among the bridge pilings, through some sunlit patch open all the way to the sky, then gone again, silent and untraceable in the web. A life went out, a body slid beneath the water, and no one noticed. Or if someone did, there was nowhere to file the complaint. There was a governor: Iosef Alesandr Kalugin was his name; but no one got that far, and mostly it meant there was a rich somebody who sat atop the pile along with other rich somebodies, who could buy a lot of deaths, and cared little for one more.

So Merovingen got along as the world did. Its marvelous appearance was best appreciated at distance, say, the upwind side of the present bay. Or from the sea beyond the Rim. Closer and one could smell the wind as it rotted there, old Merovingen building its mazy bridgeways with the disdain of latter-day Merovingians for coherent plans of all sorts. It festered on its shallow sidestream and failed harbor, praise the Ancestors for their foresight. It stank. It was the haven of pirates and the desperate and outcast of other cities.

But the majority of unfortunates just happened to be born there.

Altair Jones was one such—poling along through Merovingen's black waterways and under its bridges and along its rare open canals for whatever small freight she could run on her patched-together skip, much of which had been deck-planking on the old *Det Star* till her boilers blew and sent her fifty two crew and eight hundred nine passengers to their reward. Altair Jones was a lanky, long-limbed seventeen-odd; or sixteen: she forgot, and her mother had left her nothing but a battered boat, the clothes on her back and an Adventist name, the latter of which did her no great service in a city mostly Revenantist. Barefoot, in ragged breeches and a river-runner's cap drawn low on black hair above a dusky tanned face, she was beyond looking like the boy she had pretended to be before she filled out; but you would know if you ever caught her eyes that you were looking at someone who would hole your boat or your barrels if you gave her reason; and that years after the offense; and with you sleeping sound aboard and all unsuspecting. There were easier pickings on the river than Jones. People got that impression early-on. You dealt with Jones business-like and you knew your cargo might get where it was going if you had a barrel or two to carry. And if you were an honest canaler you'd ask Jones to watch your boat and goods while you took a stint ashore. And it would stay unbothered. When she went ashore, her skip left under someone's guard, she carried a knife and a barrel-hook, which were only the tools of her trade, but river-rats and canalers had ways of using the latter that made the townsfolk of the bridges shiver and the ruffians of the mazy walkways think twice: canalmen were never rich pickings and one shout of Ware, hey! would bring every water-rat within earshot into the melee, with their hooks and their knives unsheathed.

Not that there were not scoundrels and cutthroats among canalmen. There were; and bodies quietly slipped into the Det's bay, and boats got robbed, particularly little boats of partnerless canalers who found themselves up some dark bywater with retreat cut off from either end. But Jones was too canny for that. She handled her skip mostly without the ancient little motor, which worked only fitfully at best; she used the pole and the hook, worked in and out the traffic of high day with a deft shift of bare foot and shove of the pole that sped her through tight spots, but she took no chances by night: she left the deep nooks to the combines and the gangs that ran them and did her night tie-up usually by the Hightown Bridge, wherever she could find a spot at the fringes of the other canal-folk, an ungainly midnight collection of ramshackle craft, some real fishing boats off the Det and out of the harbor, overnighted on a supply trip; mostly canaler-craft; some skiffs or hired-poleboats or smallish barges and numerous skips like her own.

She fished a bit in her idle hours—for eels, mostly; the canals were noxious, but the channel in the harbor was still wholesome, and when things were truly slow and after storms when the sea was boiling into the Dead Harbor and onto the marsh and the Port Flat, she nursed the lame motor out round the Rimwash, built a fire of driftwood on the beach to stake out her territory, and fished and combed the Sundance shingle for what the tide washed in, which was sometimes nets and sometimes line and now and again a bit of plank or a rare shell to dicker with or a bit of canvas to trade or sell.

And regularly, the only regular trade she had, she would pole up to the back door of taverns here and there, where she would buy up a few barrels; it was up the canalside steps and knock at the back and the potboy would unchain the barrels and sell them off for the few pennies she had; she would resell them to old Hafiz the brewer up the canal and haul a freight of beer and whiskey back again. So the trade went, not much pay and late hours, but it was bread to go with the river eels.

And now and again, at Moghi's tavern by the Fishmarket Stairs, her first and best customer, there was a different sort of trade, a few barrels of very fine brandy to take down-canal to Hafiz with the empties. How *that* got to Moghi was a good question, coming from high up the Det as it did, or even from the Chattalen. But Hafiz had his uptown clients and when that fine brandy went *down* the canal, a big load of Hafiz' best beer came *up* it, and a bit of real coin came her way at either end.

Tonight might be one of those nights, since there was a Nev Hettek riverboat warped into port Detside, and that meant illicit goods filtering into Merovingen-under-the-bridges, same as it meant fine goods uptown. Altair Jones scented possibilities.

So she came in the dead of night, poling lazily past the gathering of barges at the Hightown Bridge as if she were looking for a mooring-spot, and then going on the Grand Canal under the pilings of the Fishmarket Stairs, where a winding set of steps came down from the triple bridgeways of Merovingen-above. The high board buildings went up level upon level above; catwalks laced the space between them, all silvery gray in the moonlight; and Fishmarket Bridge crossed the canal, on stout pilings that stood like a watery black forest by one of the few solid bits of rock in Merovingen. And tangled amid it all, the back porches of a second-hand store, a spicery, a bakery, and Moghi's dilapidated tavern, where the light of a porch-lantern danced on the waters and invited approach despite barred, shuttered windows and closed door.

There at that corner of Moghi's porch, Altair snagged a convenient piling and looped the tie-rope around, the current carrying the skip up against Moghi's porch ladder, an unobtrusive and rickety span of nailed boards. But when

her ears caught a flurry of footsteps on boards, above the
slap and ripple of the canal water, she stopped with her
hand on the ladder; and her sharp eyes, scanning up and
about, caught a move in the moonlight up amongst the
back and forth lacery of the Stair, up along the nether tier
of the triple bridge.

Men in cloaks. She froze right as she was, hugging her
skip to that piling and keeping low by that lamplit porch,
because there was more than one kind of vermin that
skulked about the bridges of nightbound Merovingen. She
pulled her cap-brim down low to shade her eyes from any
glimmer of Moghi's porch lantern, and held the rope tight
to keep the boat from swinging and bumping against the
porch. A shiver set into her muscles, which was the cold
and the strain on her arms.

There were maybe a half-dozen of them, all dark-cloaked,
out on that bridge not so far above. She heard the mutter
of their voices as they came to the rail. Up to no good, it
was very sure. Sometimes smugglers dealt with Moghi, on
business they wanted private—that was one kind of trouble. But these looked like something else, all cloaked and
hooded and hunched over some weight they carried together to that rail.

Something pale gleamed among them, fitful glimmering; it shone like a body then, suddenly airborne in the
night, and hit the black water with a splash that threw
water on her. Altair sucked in her breath, huddled tight
against the piling as the laughter drifted down to her;
another shiver got to her taut muscles, and the current tried
to take the boat this way and that, but she resisted it with a
steady pull of her arms.

"See him?" one asked, faintly, above her head.

"No," said another. "That's done 'im."

The figures went away then, a flicker of shadow among
the railings, and the thump of leather-shod soles up the
Fishmarket Stair. Sound diminished. Trouble left the river-
side and ascended to Merovingen-above, maybe where it
had come from in the first place. And not a thing stirred
from Moghi's.

Altair let go the piling; the skip bumped and bumped

again in the water-motion, and she fumbled at the tie-rope
with cold fingers. No barrels tonight, by the Ancestors.
Not a crack would Moghi's porch door open right now,
not to any knocking, if they had wind of that, but there
were other doors Moghi's bullylads might stir from if they
heard that trouble, and she had no wish to be caught in
explanations. She jerked loose, coiled the rope, anxious to
be away.

Something splashed out of time with the water. She
squinted outward. A disturbance broke the ripple-pattern
near the pilings of the high bridge's southward jut, a trick
of the eyes—no, again, again. Whatever, whoever they
had flung in had floated. She froze stock still, cursed to
herself and swayed to the motion of the water that was
pushing on that floating body too, taking it and her loose
boat the same way, beside the webwork of Fishmarket, in
the shifting glimmer of the moon and Moghi's reflected
porchlight. Black pilings of the high bridge drifted by. A
ripple-spot emerged and ebbed in the black-shining water
where it caught Moghi's porchlight.

Something struggled there. Death did not attract her.
But a struggle for life—that deserved audience, at least.
Deserved curiosity. Or some kind of human sympathy.

A gleam of white, then, a splash in the dark. Not
wave-motion. The water slapped the pilings out of time to
that sound. She ran out the pole as silently as she could
and probed the water at middle depth.

A hand broke the surface. Broke it again near the boat,
fingers reaching up a piling, failing as they found no
purchase.

She got down on her knees on the slats at the sloping
prow and probed with the pole down by that piling, not
wanting to do that at all, no; what someone threw in the
canal was *their* business. But this lonely battle was persistent, horrid, down in Old Det's dark bowels. Old Det had
eaten something that went down hard: and being water-rat,
Altair was on the side of the something and not greedy
black Old Det.

Give it a chance, poke it up, make it fight.

Fool, another small voice said in her skull. They might

not be unwitnessed. There were the bridges. The killers had gone that way, into the high town. They might be looking down on her this very moment.

Others might be watching. Moghi's folk. Or shore-siders who would *sell* information to worse places; or sell a soul, having learned the relative value of souls and bread on waterside.

The pole hit something yielding, deep-down against the bottom. Something dragged at it below the water, gripped it, began to climb up it—

She took in her breath and shoved the pole hard against the stony bottom, taking the boat back, but that something came along with the pole, making it drag. The water splashed at the bow, a white hand shot up and closed at the rim right by her knees. She snatched at the barrelhook at her belt and watched in mute horror as the fingers began to lose their grip and slip away.

Hook that hand and she might hold him sure. And cripple a man for life. Hook was safe. That pitiful reach up might be a trick, a trap, a drowning man could pull her under that black water and kill them both.

The fingers slipped free. She grabbed that vanishing hand with her bare fingers and pulled, let go the barrelhook and grabbed it with both hands, braced her bare feet and hauled up and back, standing, balancing the stern-heavy boat against the dead weight. A man's limp body came up over the edge, one arm and head and shoulder before she ran out of pull.

It was a body all-over pale even to the hair, a young and well-made body draped precariously over the bow of her skip, which was a vast waste to have feeding the fishes and the eels, even if he was what he probably was, some poor debtor or someone afoul of the gangs. Some gang member, very much the likeliest, and the sensible thing was to let him slide right back down amongst the fishes and the pilings.

She stayed braced that way a long several gasps for breath, holding on to his slippery wrist with the boat bobbing and rocking. Then she trod down on his hand,

knelt on his back and hauled the other arm out before he
could slide back in. Both arms this time.

Pull.

Damn. Damn. Damn fool.

She did not want to be a murderer. Or a party to
murder. And by not drifting past she had suddenly gotten
to that kind of choice.

She fell hard onto the bottom-slats, thump!, bruising her
backside, and scraped the rest of his body up onto the rim,
right up to where it would hurt, which was enough for him
to stay aboard and for her to let go of, and altogether
enough charity for a stranger. But she caught her breath
and worked forward, with a rocking of the boat, knelt
down over his back and fished one leg up by main force,
heaved and hauled him into a limp, sodden knot on the
slats.

The drag his trailing body had given the skip was gone.
The boat spun slowly, hit a piling and slewed again, slow
shifting perspective through the timbers. She worked over
him, knees bruised on the slats, knelt astraddle this human
flotsam and leaned with all her might on his back, squeez-
ing the water out, push and push and push, one, two,
while he spasmed and the water came up out of his gut and
into the bilge. The skip drifted and bumped and thumped
its way along, every thump a bruise on something she
valued more than this drowned, hopeless nothing. She
swore on the edge of every breath. Damn fool. Bang my
boat up. Damn you falling into my canal. Not my fault.
Blame *them*. What'd I do to owe you this? (Thump.)
Damn.

A moment of moonlight then as the skip drifted between
bridges and overhangs. Push and back, push and back. She
let the skip drift and spin and kept it up, no time to stop.
Dammit, dammit, dammit . . . "Dammit, breathe, dammit."

He *was* breathing. She felt him choke and falter, water
coming up; and kept leaning on him and swearing at him
and gasping and swearing, until his hands began a febrile
movement and the boat swept into the eddy off Ventani
Pier. She started the rhythm again, because the vomiting
became too much to let him breathe steadily. Push and

shove when he choked, till he heaved it up and got another half-liquid suck of air down his throat.

Bang, broadside onto the timbers of the pier with a shock that popped her teeth together. Old Det was lively when the tide was turning. Push and let be. Push and let be, until the gasps got smaller and equaled her own. *Thump*, against another piling, and a dizzy spin into moon-light toward the dreaming clutter of night-tied boats at Hanging Bridge.

She let him breathe on his own then. He lay with his face sideways on the deck-slats, where he had twisted trying to breathe and now just rested, his sides working hard for what air would come. His face shone with waxen pallor, a fine face, now that the strangled look had left him, a beautiful dead-looking face, profile against the skip's rough boards; she realized suddenly she was sitting on the handsomest naked man she had ever looked on, and him dying the way all pretty things died the river got its black hands on.

Fever if not the drowning. He had drunk too much of it.

Her mother had gone that way. She had saved kittens out of Old Det's waters. And once a toddler barge-wash knocked off a boat deck. None of them had lived.

Damn. This one too. Dammitall.

He breathed. She felt a spasm, another weak heave of his gut, but this time his hands dragged toward leverage and he tried to move. She rolled aside onto her haunches as he made an effort to get himself farther up onto the dry grating and move his knees out of the bilge—one knee on the slats, and she tried to pull, but got nowhere against his weight. He lay there panting and coughing and then tried again as if he were the only one involved in this, as if he felt nothing, knew nothing but that cold water at one extremity of his body and solid wood in front of him. He got the one knee up, lost it, got it forward again and hunched his arms under him. They went into bridge shadow, drifted perilously toward a cluster of night-moored canalers. She got up and used the pole, and used it continuously for a few moments because the Grand Canal ran perversely awry where the flow from the Snake came into it, by

Hanging Bridge; she averted collision, and kept traveling, imagining curious eyes among boats moored along the shore, watchers among the homeless on the bridge, herself with a naked man lying pale as a seastar on her skip.

She poled along then, past Mantovan, beneath its bridge, past Delaree and Ramseyhead, there on the rim of the moonlight where the Grand Canal gave out onto the Channel, and a few big barges had snugged into the wharves for the night, waiting loading tomorrow.

Safe company, those barges. Quiet company. The big black sides hove up like walls, the waves lapped and splashed to tide-draw; and a little skip glided along under the wharf unnoticed—here the drowsing hulk of a fisher-craft, its nets up like gossamer wings against the night sky; here another barge, and another, a deep friendly forest of pilings and mooring-lines like vines in the dark. Yonder a Falkenaer ship rode in deep harbor, masts and rigging webbed against a lowering moon, among the lesser bulk of coasters and Det-barges. There Rimmon Isle bulked, the lights of its landing agleam, the towers in shadow at this hour.

The sweat ran on her sides, beneath the oversized sweater; sweat ran down her temples beneath the band of the cap, despite the nighttime chill. She found a likely place on the edge of moonlit water and whipped the weighted line around a piling, warped in and made a secure hitch, this side and the other, and dropped down on her haunches, trembling. She removed her cap, wiped the sweat with her arm.

Her passenger had gotten onto the dry slats, and lay sprawled, one foot still in the bilge. So he had life in him enough to care for cold and wet. Part of her wished he had gasped his last and just lain there to be rolled back into the canal where he would be no more bother to anyone; and part of her said she ought to quietly heave him now; while a third small part of her mind just sat still waiting to see whether she might not have to take a barrelhook to him after all when he waked. But until then she was not obliged to become a killer, which she was prepared to be, which she had determined long ago she had to be, to stay alive in Merovingen-below.

Tonight, perhaps. The boat drifted and swayed on the currents that surged among the harbor pilings. Almost out of her territory. Almost. They were beyond the Dike. Beyond this point the deep currents began. And beyond this point no boat could go by pole, except beneath the pilings that led out past Rimmon bridges to the Dead Wharf and the Ghost Fleet and the marsh. She sat there panting and letting the sweat dry in the wind and waited for something, his move, her recovery, it was uncertain what.

He made feverish small movements, and still lay there with his eyes open and maybe not seeing her at all, except as a lump of shadow.

So she did not have to think about the barrelhook. He would die before morning. Very likely he would, of the shock and the cold. Like the kittens. Like the Gentry toddler. A body did that, betrayed itself by letting go when it had fought its way all the way back from this much shock. Now surely fever would set in. And the cold would take him. The river gave up very little, and maybe his skull was cracked. There were black marks all over his pale body, bloody scratches, the shadows of bruises. One leg bled a dark trail into the bilge. He blinked finally, blinked yet again, a shadowy flutter of half-open eyes.

"You're on my boat," she said, if he should wonder where he was. Another blink. He lay there a long moment with no more movement than that and and his breathing. He was not shivering. And that meant he was still dying, only slower.

"*I*," he said. "I—"

He might live till sunrise. If he did, he had a chance in the hot sun, in its baking warmth. If it were not so long till dawn. Everything was against him. The hour. The canal-water he had drunk.

"You want to live?"

"Uhhhn."

"You hear me?"

"Uhhhn."

"There's a blanket in the hidey. Right ahead of you.
You want it, you get inside. Straight on."

He stirred a hand, an arm, as if reaching in that direction were enough; and then the other arm, and a knee, and
he edged himself a little forward. Again. Slow hitches. He
managed a harder shove, and made it with his arms under
his belly this time, as if his gut hurt, which it must. He
stopped finally. She got the pole and jabbed him in the
side, the way she touched dead things in the canal, to get
them out of her way. "Move."

He moved. She had not thought he would this time. He
crawled inside the halfdeck shelter, all excepting his feet,
and stopped, not a care that he would be freezing. Nothing. She had a man going to die among her belongings,
right in there in a crawlspace where a dead weight was
going to be difficult to get out, and she sat out here with
her teeth chattering from fright.

Fool. Dump him in. Give him to the fish tonight instead
of tomorrow, that's what you ought to do. He's just going
to die, is all. Too many people could have seen you. Some
might know you. If Moghi gets wind of you and this
trouble at his door—

But after a long time of imagining that villainy she
locked her arms between her knees, and rocked and thought
and rocked and thought without any shape to her thinking:
mist-thoughts, the Revenantists called it, nowhere thinking, back to past lives and past deeds that damned a soul to
Merovin instead of the stars; and double-damned a soul to
Merovingen; and three times damned it to the hell of
Merovingen-below.

The Revenantists promised at least no worse place. Which
thought failed to cheer her. Mist-thoughts led in circles,
and came back to self-preservation. *That* was the law in
hell.

Until a fool intervened in others' business and got a load
of karma for it; and a dying man on her hands; and nothing
for it but to sit and wait; or do something to help him,
because he had no strength or wit to wrap himself in the
blanket in the hidey.

She stowed the barrelhook in a coil of rope and put her

knife beside it: her mother's first rule—Don't you get in no wrestling-match with no man. You knife 'im later, hear? and you *do* that, too, hear? Don't you never threaten. You just do it. If it takes you twenty years. World's got enough bastards. Take 'em out as you find 'em.

Her mother *had* killed a man. Maybe more than one, her mother had said. None of your business. Ain't a thing to talk on. It's something you just do when you got to and if you go talking about it you're asking his friends for more trouble. Who needs more trouble? They don't want it 'less they're crazy. You don't. —But old Seb don't like me much. I tell you why. It was his brother I killed. Watch him. If he ever crosses you, you're a fool if you don't get him.

Seb was dead now. Someone else did him. Her mother had died first. Altair had no feuds of her own that she knew of. She was a fool to take one on. But her mother had never reproached her about skimming kittens out of the Det. Only when she had pulled the Gentry boy out of the canal, when she came back all wet and shivering onto the boat from the other mother's thanking her (she had dived deep for him, had gone all the way to Det's dark bottom)—You drink any of that? her mother had said, eyes white-edged with anger. Damn fool. And slapped her in the face.

She was days figuring out it was love. And fright. She had been twelve and her mother's moods used to scare her. But maybe the Revenantists were right and it was mist-thinking, and her mother saw into her own future. Her mother died of that water, in high summer when it was most dangerous. Died without telling her essential things. Like who her father was. Or whether it was that man she had killed.

She had never told her how a woman dealt with getting a man onto her boat without having him get out of line and thinking he could take it over; and she had no idea at all whether she was a fool for saying no when men made her offers. She didn't want to kill anybody. She didn't want to make a fatal mistake. She didn't know what the right and wrong of things were—she knew well enough *how* it was to have a lover: a lot of things happened on barges right under the eye of God and everybody, on hot nights when the hidey was too hot. But her mother never had a man she ever saw. Her mother muttered ugly things when men shouted invitations. And Altair Jones pretended she was Retribution's son, not her daughter, as long as her mother lived. That was her mother's idea. And she did her bathing at night and wore loose clothes after she began to have breasts. She gave up some of the cautions after she showed too much, which was when she was twelve and after her mother died; but habits were hard, they were very hard. And she was a fool now. And scared.

And guilty, in a confused way, not sure whether it was a betrayal of her mother she contemplated, or something her mother would have looked at like her skimming up a struggling kitten and just hoping one would live, finally— Break your heart, her mother would say with a shake of her head. Poor thing's gone, Altair.

And she: *Mama*. Flatly. Never saying what ached inside her; snuffling back her tears when another thing died in her hands. So there was herself and her mother alone on the boat and never another living thing to touch. She saw cats in the rich houses, scampering through the balcony-gardens. She caught a feral cat once the year after her mother died, and it was so crazy it leapt into the Grand and swam for shore. She let it go; it had bitten her half a dozen times, and the bites went bad. She had imagined it would be soft to touch and would take to boat life. It would kitten and she would have kittens to sell to rich shore folk and do well for herself. But it was a shore creature. And her hand and her whole arm swelled. After that she had a chance to get a tame cat off a poleboatman—he wanted her, she wanted the cat. But in the end she got scared, that we would get what he wanted and then maybe kill her and rob her: he was a back-canaler and maybe stole that cat from rich customers—who knew?

So she gave up on cats. Slowly gave up on chance-taking. And men.

Till she got, in a confused way, step by step, to be a fool for something else floating down the canal.

Well, she said to herself this night—she talked to herself now and again, in her head, in her mother's voice—well, you finally got a man on your boat, didn't you, same as the damn kittens. Or maybe like that ingrate cat. And you got yourself a problem, don't you, Altair? What you going to do? Huh? Let him die?

He ain't any harm the way he is. Hasn't got a chance, the damn fool, without I do something.

So she stirred herself and she crawled into that shelter and heaved and hauled the blanket out from under him and over both of them, because she knew what it was when water-chill had gotten into one's bones. —"Tuck your feet up, fool, get all of you inside."

He moved. She tried to get her arms about his damp, cold body and keep the blanket snug, but he was too heavy to get an arm under; she pillowed his head on her arm and put herself up against him as close as she could get. The cold went from him to her, until the shivering started, great racking tremors that knotted him up for minutes on end until the last strength went out of him.

Then he was still.

That's the end of it, she thought. Out of strength. Fever comes now.

Rain-chill, winter-chill, river-chill: but there was a way to make a body warm. Her mother had done it for her; she had kept the sick kittens close against her heart, trying the same. And it was *not* the same as her mother and the kittens; but it was dark inside the hidey; and he was clean, Ancestors knew, clean as old Det let anybody be; and more, he was dying, not going to tell anybody or snigger about it later.

It was selfish, more than anything, just for herself, scraps, which wouldn't hurt anything, and wouldn't go anywhere, since he was dying. The last living thing she had touched, really touched and held, was five years ago, when her mother was alive. So it was selfish; and perhaps every wicked act put the Retribution further away; but every good one brought it closer—so maybe what she did to make him easy balanced the wickedness in her mind.

Damn. It won't hurt. It might help.

She flung her arms up and wormed out of her sweater, undid her breeches and worked out of them too, till she could get her bare skin next to his full length—no great thrill: he was cold as a day-old fish. But she rubbed him till her arms ached and hugged him against her and bled the heat of her exertion into him, and did it again when she had caught her breath. He came to in the midst of this and started shivering again, which made him hard to hold on to, but she kept working—nothing sensual in the business at all: it was a fight that she kept up, chafe his skin till she had to rest and warm him with her sweat and do it again till finally either she was chilled or he was warm as she was. She gave a great sigh when she realized that; she put her arms about that human warmth and snuggled in without a twinge of guilt.

So she would dream about him after he had gone into the water and fish swam in and out the sockets of his eyes and picked the last little memory out of his brain who he had been, or why he had died; but he would not haunt her for it. Her mother had, for a while; until she came in a dream and cursed her gently the way she had when she snuffled over the kittens. Damn fool, Altair. Damn fool. Everything dies. Old Det gets it all. Love life and cuss death and be as good as you can.

She drew a great breath and gave a long sigh, relaxing further, inside as well as out. She made up memories for her bit of flotsam. He was a rich merchant's son, fallen on hard times. He had come downriver and met misfortune.

His father and his mother would send searchers. But they would be too late. They would find a trinket or two in the markets. His bones would lie at the harbor bottom, under the keels of the moving ships. She would stand on the quay and watch the fine foreigners come ashore and she would hold the secret they wanted, a little canalrat would hold the secret all to herself and watch them in their fine clothes and their jewels offering rewards for the recovery of this rich man.

But he had come to her with never a thing, and she could not prove her claim to rescue. So there was no good to tell; and dangerous anyway, to meddle in the affairs of rich merchants. There would be the smugglers and the brigands and the gangs after the rich men left. *They* were the law on the river and in the harbor and in the canals of Merovingen. And the collection of fish-picked bones down there in the mire of the Det was already considerable. She had no wish to join them. Hence her silence.

Their ship would steam back upriver, the rich relatives uncomforted.

She held him close and let him sleep, so that the life would go out of him that gentle way the way it went out of drownling kittens and birds that fell in the winter ice, just quietly, on a breath. She would roll him overboard in the morning, slip, splash. Her secret. The closest secret almost-event in her life, when she had *almost* saved a rich man's son and *almost* had a lover.

Somewhen she fell asleep and woke in an unfamiliar tangle of male limbs. A gentle snoring had waked her. The snoring stopped. He had a hand on her breast—her knee was tucked up against him somewhere embarrassing. She held still. He shifted a leg and nestled closer there in the sightless black of the shelter, his head burrowed against her bare shoulder. Then she lay there with her heart pounding, thinking whether to get up or not to get up, and since she had to wonder about it, it seemed all too much effort to escape a man who was, well, if not dead, at least not in a way to make himself a nuisance by morning. He was only warm, and different, and temporarily all her own in a way no one but her mother had ever been.

Merovingen was out to take, that was all: body, soul, life and property if a woman was once fool enough to give up that line that said No; and fool enough ever to share that little portion of the world that a pole and a boathook and the habit of sleeping lightly could keep solitary and safe from men bent on mischief and murder.

So, well—once. Maybe once, for a few days when he got well, if he got well; and *then* put him off somewhere. On her terms. And let him do what was natural for a man the gangs were after, which was get on the first boat up the Det and keep going.

Far away from Merovingen. So he would never talk,

one way or the other. So he was a safe kind of lover. She
mulled that over in her mind and came to that conclusion.
He had no grudge against her. He had every motive to stay
out of sight and let her get him to some destination; and if
he looked like he had designs, well, then, she would pick
that up: she was good at reading intentions. Then it was
the boathook for him—or she would find out who his
enemies were and give him to them if he looked to turn
ugly. If he made any threat to take her boat.

Now that she had come this far she suddenly knew all
sorts of ways to get a man off her boat. Like wait till he
was asleep and do for him. Or hail a fellow like One-Eye
Mergeser and start a fight; or a dozen strategems she could
think of, if things went wrong.

But they would not. He was not like that. He had a
gentle way about him, even if he was asleep. He would be
grateful, for a few days, in the strange nowhen that had
cast this pretty bit of flotsam up onto her boat.

Old Det gave a gift, that was what.

A lover from a past life?

Only if the Revenantists were right.

She doubted it.

One got what one took in this life. Her mother told her
so.

Chapter 2

SHE waked again in that close, unfamiliar warmth—chagrined: she had not meant to sleep so long or so soundly. But her passenger was still warm without feeling fever-warm; healthily sweating, in fact, with the closeness, as the first stir of activity came in the dark outside the hidey, and some coaster out in the harbor churned up a wake with its engine as it beat along toward the shallow channel to the sea. Getting an early start on the world.

The sweaty warmth against her stirred, burrowed closer and snuggled down with a sigh as if a woman's arms were part of his ordinary sleep. Or he was awake and damn well knew where his hands and his face were. She wriggled aside and out of the shelter, searching up her clothes as she went; and sat outside with the fresh wind chilling her skin and the gentle rocking of the boat all part of a strange, still-black morning, there beneath the wharves.

She ran a hand through her hair, found it itchy and none so nice. Her clothes were not as bad: she had washed them three days gone; but she was sweated and hated to get into them. She never minded a few days unbathed: weather sometimes set in with a chill that discouraged bathing, and she was alone on her boat; in fact she cultivated a certain griminess—too clean and a woman looked like she was looking, which invited all sorts of trouble. She made a spitting sound in self-disgust, not at the dirt, but at the silliness that made her care for a day; for once—well, not to be thought dirty. *He* was not; he was clean-shaven, without even a stubble, she recalled, until this morning when she had felt his chin against her shoulder—

(So he went fresh-shaven to his murder—A woman? Had he been meeting with some lover? But those black-hooded skulkers had had no look of someone's outraged kinfolk.)

—a fastidious man, at least. If there had been dirt on him the canal had left only its own fishy stink, which passed for clean in Merovingen-below. So could she be— fastidious when she wanted to be.

She had soap. She found the little cake of lye and lard and slipped over the side of the boat in the safe halflight before dawn, bobbed up again treading water in the gentle slap and toss of the chop. No danger of drift. She scrubbed her hair not once but twice and three times, and scrubbed herself with the white froth floating away on the waters beneath the pilings, while the sun came up enough to give a little rust color to the peeling paint of the boat-side.

And just as she surfaced from her final ducking she found herself staring up at a pale, very live face peering over the rim of the boat.

So there she was, with a naked man on her boat above her and herself at decided disadvantage down in the cold water. "Get back," she said, sharp and hostile. "Back." Thinking if he should turn surly there were still ways, and the knife and the hook for him, and the bones at the bottom of the bay. She glared up at him and bobbed there. Flung a splash of water up at him. "Back."

That seemed to wake his wits. He moved backward in some haste and retreated up a few feet toward the bow as she glared at him, elbows on the rim. He did not look threatening, rather dazed as a man might be who came back from the dead stark naked on a crisp morning.

She pitched the soap into its bucket and gave him a hard, misgiving look just to be sure he stayed put. He had settled as he could, knee tucked up and side-ways. So she glared again, gave one great duck and heave and came up over the edge, slithered aboard in a wash of water and sat down and snatched after her clothes, dropped them all into her lap fast, and struggled into her sweater without a pause to dry her hair or to towel off. Pants next, quickly. She got up and hauled, not fool enough to turn her back in modesty. She just fixed him with her eye and glared to show she was in no way embarrassed and that he had only tentative welcome on her boat.

He stared. Not like the dirty boys that spied on the barges from the bridges; and hooted and called down insults, imagining they saw more than they did. He stared as if a naked woman was a holy and unexpected wonder to him, while the boat swayed in the chop a passing coaster kicked up; he sat leaning on his hands and swaying too, with the boat-motion.

He was so damn nice-looking. Her heart did a curious little quickening and she felt—warm. And oddly safe and unembarrassed and expansively content with what she had done. Reckless. Ancestors, she was not wont to be so soft-headed. But maybe it was natural that people took chances when they were in love. Like shooting the Det Bore when it came, though it tipped boats and took the unskilled; it was that kind of feeling, heart thumping, everything aslide and uncertain and by-the-Ancestors alive.

"My name's Jones," she said. "Altair Jones. This is my boat." And when he did not respond to that: "I've decided," she said, "you can be my lover."

He blinked and got a wary look, slid a bit back till his back hit the wood of the far side. In one heartbeat she was dismayed; in the next felt the fool; and in the third she knew for certain that she was. A man had a right to say no. She never heard of one who was inclined to, unless— Maybe he liked men, that was all. Which was a waste. But he was very pretty. Maybe too much so. She gazed at him with regret.

"Well, you don't have to," she said sullenly. She pulled out her other breeches from the side of the hidey, the over-size ones; and pulled out a sweater (she had three, all twice the size she needed); and flung them both at him. "Try those."

He blinked and let them lie there on the slats.

"You want 'em in the bilge, dammit?"

He gathered them up in one reach and never made another move. His face showed all white in the tentative dawn, his fair hair dried and curling. Another ship thumped to life, a fishing boat sending out a wake as it passed; and the water lapped and splashed against the pilings.

"You mute?"

He moved his head. No.

She squatted and rummaged the other little packet she had there by the hidey, unstopped a jug and took a bit of bread and cheese out of their wrapper. Offered it toward him. He shook his head.

Fool. Rushing at him like that. Man's been hit over the head, swallowed all that water. Offer him to be his lover, and him with a cracked skull. Damn silly, Jones. Try to use the brain you got. Probably thinks you're crazy. "You sick at your stomach, huh?"

A nod.

"Head hurt?"

A nod.

"You got a voice?"

"What am I doing here?"

Not *what'm'i'doin'ere*. Clear and pure as a voice could speak it, a quiet, immaculate voice that brought her and her outheld hand to a frozen stop.

She heard that kind of accent at distance, at the distance of lordly voices drifting from the heights of bridges and the insides of buildings and the other side of grilled doorways.

"I fished you out of the canal, that's what. You got a lump on your skull and you got that water in you. It'll rot your gut out." She came closer and squatted down again and offered the bottle at arm's-length, bare toes tensing on the slats against the heave of the boat. "Drink. Whiskey's best cure I know. *Take it.*"

He took it and downed a sip with a grimace. He drank carefully. Grimaced and swallowed, once, twice, and handed it back, wiping tears from his eyes. He began to shiver then, as she stopped the bottle. "Get some clothes on," she said. "Want people to stare? I got a reputation to think of."

Another blink. Maybe, she thought, the blow to the head had addled his wits. She waved a hand at him, move, move, and in a rush of remorse for the mistakes she had made: "Hey, I'll boil you up some tea. Sugar'n all. Go get warm."

Sugar cost dear. She could have bit her tongue for that impulse she threw atop it all. A lover was one thing; sugar cost money. Sugar, she had a tiny lump of and had hoarded it for some special need, months and months. But he was it, she decided, he was that special need, plain and simple, and maybe it would be what he needed, ease his poor stomach and put a little life in him.

So she got out a match and the oil stove, an old metal oil can, with the bottom of an old lamp; set it up on the slats of the well and carefully boiled up water in one of two metal bowls she had. She dusted tea into it; then (with a wince) the precious sugar. Took a sip herself out of self-indulgence, then edged over to her passenger. "Here. Don't you spill it."

He had worked the loose breeches on, with a perilous wobble when he essayed a rise to his knees; and lastly the baggy blue sweater—his wide shoulders and long arms were almost too much for it. He sat down again of a sudden on the bare slats of the well and for a moment swayed to the motion of the boat. But he took the bowl and drank in gingerly sips, there in the full dawn. All pale and scratched up and with a morning stubble on his beautiful face, and a swollen cut on his lip where they must have hit him. He drank; and she sat there on her haunches with her hands tucked up against her warm skin under her own sweater and thought and thought.

He *was* a rich man's son.

And there were those who wanted him dead, who might not take kindly to her interference. They might be bullyboys and no great trouble; a chance meeting and a mugging and a quick toss of a body into the canals. That was no great novelty hereabouts, and bully boys of their ilk were secure in their very numbers and facelessness—until they crossed a canaler.

On the other hand—there were other possibilities to consider. Like him having personal enemies. Like uptown trouble. Like trouble that could wash down on Altair Jones and her little boat like the Det in flood, and her bones

would settle down amongst the collection at the bottom of
the bay. Rich man's trouble.

Lover, indeed. *That* was why he was repulsed by her.
He was too high for her, that was all. Probably he had
never thought of sharing a canalrat's bed. Might get bugs.
She scowled over that thought and reckoned she need not
be *personally* offended at the turn-down. So she was sev-
enteen and he was the first man she ever asked. So she
started a shade high, that was all. Woman could always
try. And he was merchandise. This was money she was
looking at, by the Ancestors, she had in her hands the
most valuable bit of flotsam she had ever gathered out of
the Det. And perhaps—she looked curiously at that fine,
lost figure that sipped its tea and looked so out of place
against the bare old boards of her boat—perhaps *he* would
just as soon see her sunk to the depths the minute he was
safe with his own kind. Handsome did not mean fair-
minded. Or generous. That pretty face and that worried
look of his might mask a thorough-going villain.

Damn. He probably never even knew what that sugar
was worth, probably had it every day, heaped and piled on
his food.

There had to be a way to figure out what he was worth
and where. He was wobbly, but not weak enough to
handle carelessly. He showed signs of increasing steadi-
ness, in fact, which made her think of her knife and hook
under the rag-pile, and the boathook and the pole, which
she could wield a lot more deftly than a landsman would
think. And there was a paper of blueangel, which was for
the fever; but the whole paper in a man's tea and he would
be in no shape to protest being rolled overboard and in
even less shape to swim.

Not that she wanted to do these things. If he was worth
something, that might well mean collecting from his enemies, and Lord, she did not want to do that.

Not that, and not any deal with the damn Megarys
either, who dealt in disappear-able live bodies and sold
them to outbound ships and upriver slavers. The trade
went on. The law knew. Every canaler knew. But not a
sick cat would she trade to the Megarys.

Not to say he might not be a scoundrel after all and deserving of all he got.

Lord, he was so pretty. He was so damn pretty. He looked up from his tea-sipping while she was looking at him and thinking that, so she was caught with her guard down.

"You got a name?" she asked, sitting on the edge of the halfdeck and finger-combing her damp hair.

"Tom," he said.

It was certainly more than Tom. It was Tom-something. Something-Thomas-something, him being a high towner; so he was not willing to hand out his whole name to her. He was not all trusting, then. Not by a far ways.

"Tom. That all of it?" She reached for the empty tea-bowl. "You got a home?"

He did not answer that either. Not right away. "No."

"Live with the fishes, do you? Just follow the tides and dine on minnows and seaweed. Well, I don't doubt you'll be falling back in, then, having drunk up my tea and all."

She had not meant it for a threat. But he had a wary look when she said *back in*, and she saw he took it that way.

"Look, six bullylads threw you into the canal last night and I fished you out, having no better sense. Now if you've got any particular place you'd like to go, I c'n maybe get you there."

"I—" Long silence then. He sat and stared and a passing boat rocked the skip against the pilings.

"Who's after you?"

A blink. No more. Then: "My name's Mondragon. Thomas Mondragon."

She ran that through her memory. There was no Mondragon she knew of. That meant a lie or that meant up-river, Soghon. Remote, hostile Nev Hettek, even. Farmer he certainly was not. She felt cold despite the sweater and the thick trousers. Money seemed a little farther away than it had been; and not just to Nev Hettek and back. She put her hands on her knees and drew a deep breath.

"You got a place to go?"

Silence.

"Well, I'll tell you this, Mondragon. Whatever your name is. You better wrap up real good. You better get yourself back in that hidey and stay low, because it's getting light and I don't want folk seeing you; and you better think real hard what I'm going to do with you, because you got one day, and if you ain't got it by morning I'm going to come back up here to the harbor and let you off and you can just find your own way uptown."

"Where are we going?"

"Well. Someone's awake. You got a place in mind? You got a place up there on the Rock? Rimmon Isle?" Rimmon was a haven for foreigners among the rich. "Got friends?"

Blink. A long moment he sat there, passed a hand over the back of his head. Stared at her.

"Well?"

Wits addled for sure, she reckoned. He looked dazed. Lost. It was too good to be an act.

"Crack on the head'll do that for you," she muttered. "Damn. Damn mess. Look, Tom-whoever. Get yourself down under that hidey there and tuck yourself up and sleep it off, huh?" She got up on the deck, tugged on the mooring rope and slipped it, then walked back aft to throw up the engine cover. She gave it a crank. Gave it another while they drifted free beneath the pier.

"Where are we going?"

"No matter to you. Lord! don't you fall in—"

He was on his feet and the boat bumped a piling. He went down on one knee, caught himself and sat down hard on his backside.

"Brain's kind of shook," she said, and adjusted the choke. She gave the engine yet another crank. It gave a hollow cough. A fourth try and holding the choke against the suction did it. The engine tunked away, churning up a white surge on the dark water. She loosed the hook on the long tiller and put the holding pin in to get it in action before they hit another piling. Dropped the rudder and set its pin. "Go on, get under cover. If we meet anybody, hear, if you hear me talk, whatever, you don't put that blond head of yours out of that hidey.''

The boat tunked along, moving slowly in the chop beneath the deserted piers. Not wasting fuel. She put the tiller farther over and kept her course under the pilings, which was the quietest way to move. Mondragon got down on his knees and slid backward into the hidey under her feet, disappearing from her vantage.

"Thanks is fine," she said above the engine-noise, as the boat labored its way along under the pilings, eating up fuel that cost nearly as dear as the sugar. "I'm glad you're so grateful. That's real nice."

After a moment a hand caught hold of the deck-edge; an arm followed, and he put his head up. "Thanks," he said.

"Doing what I say is best." It was her mother's line. She delivered it sternly and with all the righteousness her mother had ever used. "What if them bullyboys get sight of you, huh, and come after me? Maybe you don't remember. Maybe you need time to get your brain unscrambled, huh? All right. I'll hide you out that long. You eat my food. You sleep in the hidey. You damn well do what I say. Hear? Now get back in there.''

He let go all at once and vanished.

She held onto the tiller and drew a great amazed breath.

So. She said and this rich man, this handsome uptowner, ducked and did as he was told. She drew yet another breath, with the timbers passing in insane perspective toward dawnlit brown water. She was in control of things on this her deck, this morning. She swung the tiller as the boat passed from under the New Wharves and headed under the Rimmon Isle bridges, a dark, dark passage toward the dawn-lit water of the Old Harbor.

It was open running after that—shallow water in places, so a body could go aground and maybe hurt a boat doing it, if a body did not look sharp and know the currents that swept the Dead Harbor, at least in principle. Knowing them thoroughly was a matter of sailing the harbor every day; which some did—the harbor-dwellers were out here, looking like tiny floating islands on their rag-canopied rafts. Some were pathetic, a lot old, riverfolk just gone beyond their prime and down on their luck, surviving till the end. Some were not old; some were downright dangerous. A lot of crazy had come down from the Ancestors, curse them; and the really lunatic haunted the marshes and ventured out on the Rim in numbers. Of those, the pathetic ones died and the dangerous ones flourished, having no more scruples than a razorfin and about as much hesitation when it came to prey. It was evolution at work. The *canny* crazy ones survived best, and occasionally the Governor declared a cleanup, and the law and the sporting uptowners came down and scoured the Rim until they had routed out the current crop.

Naturally the canny-crazies took to rafts and most got away, and laid low for a few days, to return again.

So it was wise to go wary crossing the water out here, steer well clear of others, and when it came to a harborage on the Rim in this season, a body just coasted along looking for an unoccupied niche, something with good visibility and a bit of beach.

Mondragon put his head out again, up over the edge of the hidey.

"You can come out," Altair said over the low mutter of the engine and the slap of the water. "Just as well someone does see you out here." He looked doubtfully leftward, where the bleak rocky shore of the Rim showed nothing but shallow anchorages and floating garbage that even the fish disdained. "Rough place," she said. "Just as soon have folks see I got a man with me. Understand?"

He gripped the edge of the halfdeck and slid out, kneeling there after with his arms on the deck surface. He still looked a little dazed.

"Look lively. I bring her in and you get up for'ard and step off with that bow rope and just give her a pull. You strong enough to do that?"

"Where are we?"

"You ain't local for sure."

No answer.

"This is the Rim. Old seawall, most natural, some the Ancestors built. Back there—" She waved an arm off toward the open water."That dark spot in the water is the Ghost Fleet. And further back, on that shore, that's the Dead Wharf; and over from it's the marsh; and that great hazy flat out there's the old port."

He twisted about to see, then got to his knees and got up, wobbling this way and that.

He sat down, thump! on the slats, with a wild wave of his arms and a quick catch of one hand against the deck.

"Damn, you're a lot of help."

He twisted round with a scowl—*not* her gentle bewildered fool; it was for a moment a hard-planed face that looked at her, looking somehow older and more dangerous. Then the planes relaxed. The fool was back.

"Dizzy?" she asked. She preferred to talk to the fool. What she had seen in his face the moment before was not something to rouse. What she had seen flicker there told her she was a fool herself not to swing that tiller about and head back for the canals where there were witnesses and a way to get this fellow taken up by the law, if nothing else.

He nodded, looking drowned and dazed and compliant.

So he didn't want to run ashore with that rope and maybe be stranded if she took it in her head to do it. Standoff. Neither did she. She had a spot in view, let the boat chug up as close as put them in shore-shallows and killed the engine. She let down the tiller and dropped the stern-anchor, then skipped blithely off the halfdeck and down the well to pick up the bow anchor and heave that overboard.

Off-shore tieup. So they floated. That idea had its merits, considering the area.

She turned and looked at him where he sat on the deck, his feet in the well, on the slats. "Been managing this boat a long time with no help to hand," she said cheerfully. "Safer to tie up here anyway. Crazies run the shore. With you all dizzy like that, I'd worry. Hate to think of you

wobbling around like that if we had to put out real fast
with shore under our bottom.''

"Crazies.''

She waved a hand off toward the rocks, the long ridge
of the west Rim. ''Rim there connects right onto the
marsh. All sorts of crazies can walk here as well as float.
Some won't hurt you. A lot will. You just sit there. I'll
just set up work here, do a little fishing. If I sing out Pull
the anchor, you get up to the bow and haul up on this rope
here—'' She put her bare foot on it. ''That easy enough
for you? I'll be aft hauling up the other, and there'll be
some real good reason for it. Not likely to happen. But just
so's we don't cross paths on the deck. Knock each other in
the wash, we would. Rules of the deck: poleman has right
of way. I move with that pole and you're in my way, you
just fall down and be walked on. You foul me, we could
hole this boat or I could hit you in the head and you don't
need another lump, do you? Second rule: you don't touch
my gear. It's right where I need it. I got two calls I use: I
yell Deck, hey! you just fall flat, like with the pole: this
here's a small boat, and it's real easy to get your skull
cracked. If I yell Scup! that means something's loose and
you grab it. Got no time on a boat to explain things.'' She
drew breath. It hardly mattered. Getting rid of him was the
idea. Not attracting undue attention with him was the
principal problem. ''Got to do something about that head
of yours. Never saw hair that blond. Anybody looking for
you, you shine like a beacon.'' She walked on up to the
halfdeck and rummaged in the first drop-bin along the
side. There was a scrap of a black shibba shawl she used
for a towel. It was clean. Mostly. She sniffed it and threw
it at him. ''Wrap that round your head. Look like a proper
rafter, you will.''

He looked nonplussed. ''Damn. Dumb.'' She came and
snatched it out of his hands and wrapped it for him,
turbanlike, herself up close against him.

She had not thought about it when she started; she did
before she was done, and she backed off when she had
given the cloth its final tuck, with the same embarrassed
unease she had had in the night—that he was not a boy,

not just anyone, and the only company in her whole life
had been female. He was just—different. Touching him
felt different; and it reminded her that when she had
offered him what she thought was the most profoundly
generous thing she had ever offered, he had flinched.
Nothing so calculated as a No. Just a gut reaction from a
dazed man, honest as it came. She had herself up in his
face and he just sat there. Never did what a man ought to
do, just tried not to notice.

I never thought I was pretty. I never thought I was that
bad. She touched her nose where she and the pole had
met, hard, when she was a girl struggling to learn the boat.
When she was slow getting to safe mooring in a storm,
and old Det got his knock in, back when she was first
alone and not so strong as she was now: first time she had
ever poled alone in bad storm, and got her nose broken.
She had gotten to mooring choking on blood and half-blind
with pain; but got to mooring. The nose was always a little
flat, a little broad. Maybe it was that. It was sure the pole
hadn't helped.

"Why are you helping me?"

She looked back. Hunted a quick answer and discovered
it made no sense. "Huh. I dunno."

He thought a moment. He had that look, that there was
thinking going on. "How did I get aboard?"

"I pulled you."

"Yourself?"

"Who else?" she asked. "You tried to climb aboard. I
grabbed you and I pulled."

He shook his head. "I don't remember. That's gone. I
remember the water. I remember a bridge."

"Half a dozen friendly fellows threw you off, nakeder
'n a newborn. Don't remember, huh?"

He said nothing. That saying nothing was a lie. She saw
it in the little flicker of his eyes. He looked around. "What
are we waiting for?"

"You got a place to go?"

He looked at her.

"You can rest," she said. "Sun's coming up warm,

you just lie there and bake those scratches till you feel better. No hurry.'' She walked over to starboard and got the lines and poles from their ties, skipped up onto the halfdeck and drew the stern anchor tighter. She heard him move and looked around to find him clambering up onto the halfdeck, swaying perilously rimward. He staggered again. ''Deck!'' she yelled, gut instinct; and he wobbled there widelegged till she grabbed him. ''Sit down! Damn, you near went in!''

He caught at her arm and sat down on the halfdeck, all wobbles. She squatted on secure bare feet and the facts slowly dawned on her. She became aware of the little scrunches her toes made, the constant shift of her leg muscles. She reached and shoved at his knees. ''Hey, you keep your feet down in the well, huh? Don't you stand up on the halfdeck, and you be damn careful standing up in the well. You got landlegs, not to mention a cracked skull, which don't help. Little boat does pitch a bit. You'll get used to it. You're wearing all the dry clothes I got.''

He swung his feet down onto the slats. Looked back at her. ''What are the sanitary arrangements?''

''Sanitary?''

''Toilet.'' And when she blinked in dull amazement: *''Piss,''* he shouted at her.

''There's that pot there for'ard and there's over the side, you takes your pick. Either you got to do.'' An image occurred to her. ''Piss over the side; you got to do something else, you use that bucket; *I* can do't; you'll fall in sure if you try the other.''

He looked at her and looked forward and aft and back again as if he hoped for something else. And sat where he was.

She felt genuinely sorry for him; and irritated. And personally insulted. Like the flinching-away from her. It was one and the same. She reached out and patted his hand much the same as she had touched the ingrate cat—quickly and carefully. ''Hey, I'll be fishing off the stern, all right? I won't look.''

He stared at her as if he thought there was surely some better answer.

"You some kind of religious?" she asked, as the thought leaped into her head. Some Revenantists were extreme in their modesty.

"No," he said.

"You like men?"

"No." More emphatic than the last. He looked desperate.

"Just not me, huh? Fine. I won't jump you. You don't have to look so worried." She patted his hand again and got up and went over and squatted down on the half-deck at the drop-bin where the rest of the tackle was stowed, meticulously untied it and tied lines and uncapped the bait-jar, wrinkling up her nose at the stench. She wadded a bit of it on one hook and cast.

She sat down then crosslegged on the stern by the engine housing and watched the float and the water and the dancing sunlight, same as a thousand days and a thousand more. Until finally she felt the little difference in the boat his moving about made; felt it in the way the balance and character of the boat went right up her spine and into every nerve. She let him be. Eventually he came back toward the halfdeck; and got up on it. She turned around, but he was being careful, walking bent over with his hand ready to the deck.

He wanted the company, she guessed as he settled near her. It was all right. It was pleasant. "You ever fish?" she asked. It was not a hightowner kind of business, but it was a thing she liked to do when business was slow. Best thing in the world, to watch the water dance and hope for a bobble in the float; it was all hope. At any moment luck could turn. A fisher had to be an optimist. A pessimist could never stand it.

"I—" He edged closer and started to sit down and drop his feet off the side.

"Hey, you'll scare the fish. Keep your shadow off the water, huh?"

"I'm sorry." He got back and tucked his feet up in his long arms. She turned and gave him a look to say it was not unfriendliness. "I—" He tried again. "I'm really grateful," he said. "For everything."

She shrugged, suddenly dragged back to business and feeling a little chill in the world. Bridges at midnight and black-cloaked no-goods. She looked at him.

"It's not that I don't—like you," he said. "I just—don't know what's going on."

"You mean you don't know who threw you in."

That *wasn't* what he didn't know. She read the eyes, the quick unfocusing and dart elsewhere and back.

"How did you happen to be there?"

"I was making a pickup at the tavern. You went in right near my boat. You come up looking for anything to grab. I was it. Lucky, I s'pose."

He digested that for a moment. The eyes flickered. They were green like the sea. No, murkier. Like the sea on a bad day. Then the cloud in them went away and he reached toward her face. She flinched in startlement.

He drew back quickly and looked uncomfortable.

"Hey," she said. It scared her. Her heart was pounding. Ancestors knew, he could be crazy as half the rafters out here. She took up on the pole. "I think I got a bite." It was a lie. It got her out of an uncomfortable situation. She wound the line in and examined the dangling float and hook. The bait was gone. "Damn sneak." She got up and went after more bait.

She cast again and fished standing up until he stretched out on the warm halfdeck boards and just went to sleep. Then she sat down, and fished, and reminded herself all she had to do was give him one good shove: that landsman wobble of his was no pretense, whatever the rest of it was.

He lay there, sprawled like an innocent in the sun, and she caught a little fish. She chopped it up for bait and fished the morning away with the heavy tackle.

He waked when she brought the first good one in. He scrambled in a hurry when it landed on the half-deck flapping and flopping and spattered water all over him.

"Lively," she snapped at him, because he was within

reach of it. He grabbed and got finned and grabbed it again. "Line!" she said, and he grabbed that and got it under control.

She got the hook out and put the fish on the stringer and dropped it over the side. "How's the hand?"

He showed a wound he had been sucking on, a good few punctures.

"You really are a son of the Ancestors, ain't you? That'll be sore."

He looked at her in offense and never said a word.

"I know," she said, "they don't teach you about fish uptown, you just eat 'em. My fault. Never thought you'd grab it on the back. Behind the fin and by the line. Least it didn't have teeth. Redfin, now, I wouldn't have had you grab that. Bad fins and they got teeth besides. You use a glove with that, that's all. Same with yellowbellies. Take a nice nip out of you. And deathangels, they're just what they say, they got poison'll kill you dead quicker'n you can turn around. Nice eating, but one of them spines can kill you three days after that fish was supper."

"I know that," he said somberly; and she remembered about assassins and deathangels; and the high bridges; and got another chill in the daylight. She rebaited her hook and turned and cast again. A flight of seabirds landed out by the Ghost Fleet, and raft-dwellers began a slow, drifting stalk. She watched them till the flock took flight.

By noon it was fish cooking on her little stove; and full stomachs and a nap afterward, herself on one side of the halfdeck, himself sleeping sitting up, where he had fallen asleep after lunch, down in the well. On a good slug of Hafiz's cheap whiskey and a bellyful of Dead Harbor fish.

She woke from time to time, looked over her pillowing arm to have a look at the shore, which was bare brown rock and yellow shingle; and at the passenger, whose only move had been to lie down on his side on the slats with his head on his arm. There he stayed, tucked up like a baby, one bare foot engagingly tucked behind the other knee. The sun was warm, the night had been hard, and she blinked out and let her head down to her arm again, too sleepy to do otherwise.

By late afternoon she fried some pan-bread to have with cold fish; and Mondragon-whatever came up and looked at the proceedings. "Have you got a razor?" he asked.

"Got a good knife," she said, thinking about it. "She's razor-sharp." She had the boathook in reach, and it was an honest question: he had a good stubble by now. She ducked aside and handed him up her ribbon-thin sheath knife, *not* the one she beheaded fish with. He looked doubtful till he tried his thumb on the edge and then he looked respectful of it.

"What do you use, whetstone?"

"Bluestone and you be damn careful." She drew the stone from her left pocket and handed it up.

"Soap."

" 'S in the can. There first as you go in the hidey. Little black can. You wait. We got supper coming."

"I reckoned to be clean for dinner."

"Lord, you *got* a bath last night."

He looked at her with such dumbfounded offense that she shut her mouth outright while he bent down and got the soap out of the can. A bath. After near drowning. With soap.

He went off to the rail and pulled off his sweater.

"I bet you hope I got clean clothes, too!" she yelled in derision.

He turned around. "I wish you had," he said fervently. And turned again and stripped off the too-large breeches, gathered up the knife and soap-cake in one hand, and launched himself in a shallow dive off the side.

"Damn!" It was not particularly deep at that side of the boat. She sprang up and ran to see if he had broken his neck, but there he was, swimming quite nicely. "You ever look where you are?"

"I'm all right."

"Damn, you lose my knife I'll make you find it before you get aboard."

He stood up, water at mid-chest, and held it up. Along

with the soap. He wrinkled his nose. "Is something burning?"

"Damn!" she yelled, and ran back.

It was burned. She turned out the black-bottomed bread onto the cold fish, put out the fire and sat there staring at the mess.

Then she pulled her sweater off, unfastened her breeches and went off the other side of the boat.

Second bath in a day. If he could be clean, she could be cleaner. She came up and kept the boat between them.

"You all right?" he asked from his side.

"I'm fine. Dinner's already burned. Might as well be cold too." She ducked again. The bottom was silty sand and felt awful. She tucked her feet up, swam a few strokes out and flipped and started to swim back.

He came round the edge of the boat. "You want the soap?"

She trod water, not standing up; and swam to his outstretched hand and got it. He went back around to his side. She scrubbed and spat and swore, and when she had scrubbed enough for ten women she laid the soap up on the half-deck and swam round to the side, came up over the rim on her belly and slid over into the well.

Back in possession of the boat. He had a good view out where he was. She refused to notice that or to look his way. She walked up on the halfdeck and put her breeches and her sweater on, stowed the soap, and sat there and ate her dinner with her hair dripping onto her shoulders.

So *he* had to come back aboard. She stared mercilessly, while he turned his back to dress and pretended quite as well that she was not there. He had come back with the knife. She saw that. And when he came her way with it she had the barrelhook down by her foot just in case. She looked up as he sat down with the bluestone from his pocket and caught a little grease up from the skillet; he proceeded to care for the blade (she had to admit) right properly.

"You can eat," she said.

"I'm taking care of your property."

"I can do it fine. Eat."

He kept working at it. A long while. She finished and went to the side and swept the bones of her portion off; wiped the plate off to stow it.

Then he ate his own and took the skillet to the side. Dunked it.

"Damn, what are you *doing?*"

He looked back at her. "Washing. Does *wash* ever—?" He cut that off before it went too far, but she caught it well enough.

"You don't wash an iron skillet, Mondragon. You wipe it. Just gets better. And you go washing your plates in the harbor, you get sick. You go wash too damn much you get sick. I don't like being dirty. But there ain't no damn place to wash, Mondragon, till it rains, and then it's too damn cold!"

She screamed it at him. Realized she was screaming, and shut it down with an exasperated heave of breath.

"I'm sorry," he said.

"Hey, you do all right for a landsman. You didn't even lose the soap."

"What do I do with the skillet?"

"Here." She took it and wiped it with a rag and stowed it. "First heat-up'll kill the germs. Skillet's the safest thing you could dunk."

"Bread wasn't bad."

"Thanks." She put the number two droplid down on the dishes and sat down on the halfdeck rim, bent down and got the whiskey bottle. She *wanted* a drink. Lord and Ancestors, he made a body want a drink.

She held it out to him then, figuring she might make him want one too. "Trade you for my knife."

He passed it and the bluestone, and took the whiskey and drank.

The bottle went back and forth several times; and she sighed then and looked at the bottle. An inch of amber fluid remained. "Oh, hell," she said, and passed it to him. He drank. She finished it.

Then she went back and fished some more, finding tranquility in the business. Across the water lights showed from Merovingen, a scatter of gold above the darkening waters. The water lapped and slapped and glittered, broken reflection of the fading sky. The float bobbed away, untroubled.

He moved up beside her on the deck, sat crosslegged. Silent. Water-watching. Thinking mist-thoughts, maybe, how old Det had tried for him and lost.

"You're real lucky," she said finally, out of her own. "Drink that old canal water, you get fever. You must've drunk a liter of it. Kept waiting all night for you to fever up. Maybe the whiskey killed the germs."

"Pills," he said. "I took a lot of pills against the water."

She turned her head. Pills. "You mean you knew somebody was going to throw you in?"

"No. The water all over Merovingen. Bad pipes. They say you have to be born here to drink it."

"You weren't."

"No."

"Where from?"

Silence.

She shrugged. A lot of river-rats and canalers had the same habit. Keeping to their own business. She got a nibble and missed the set when she jerked it. "Damn." She reeled the line in peered at the hook in the gathering night and had to take it in her hand to discover the hook had been cleaned. "Fish was supposed to be our breakfast. Didn't go to give him his."

"You live alone?"

That question made her nervous. "Sometimes. Got a lot of friends." She looked at the onsetting dark and sighed. "Well, no luck." She secured the tackle and put it away, lashed it neatly to the side near the rim-rail of the halfdeck.

And turned where she sat and looked at him where he sat, none so far on the narrow deck, in the last visible light. Her heart was beating hard again, for no sensible reason. Is that reasonable? What'm I scared of?

Oh, nothing. Six black skulkers who murder people and a man sitting in my boat in the dark, that's nothing.

They're probably looking all over for him. What if they found us?

He knows who they were.

She slid off the halfdeck and stood up in the well. He slid to the edge and set his feet over, got them out of the way as she bent and pulled a blanket from the hidey. "I'll sleep on the deck," she said, and did not add: you'd fall off. But she thought it. She stepped up on the deck and felt his hand on her ankle, not holding, just—there, and on her calf when she did stop.

"I don't want to put you out of your bed."

"That's fine. You want it, *I* won't roll over the side." She shook free and sat down, flinging the blanket around her. "I'll be just fine."

He reached out and put his hand on her knee this time. "Jones. Listen—I never meant to put you off. I just—hell, I'm shaken up, Jones, I don't know what I said. I think I insulted you. Come on. Come on inside."

"Cleaner up here." Of a sudden it was going the way she wanted *last* night; but it was not last night, she was not half that crazy, and she was scared.

"Come on," he said, rocked at her knee. "Come on, Jones."

Coward, she told herself. She sat there a good long while, and he sat still, showing no sign of going away.

"All right," she said, and edged toward the rim of the deck. He reached out a hand and steadied her—as if *he* could keep his feet. She got down on her knees and dragged the blanket into the hidey, and he came in after. Then came a great muddle of blanket-arranging, so that she banged her head in her nervousness. "Damn." Nothing went quite right. She lay down and he just lay there. "You going to do anything?" she asked finally.

"You want me to?"

"Damn! You son of the Ancestors, you—" She flung herself up on her elbows and began wriggling out as if the boat were afire.

He grabbed at her and she elbowed him hard enough to

get a sound out of him. He grabbed her hard then and got a knee over her midriff, holding onto her hands. "Jones. Jones—" And then he worked that far down the hidey too, and it was clear he had made up his mind.

In a little while she made up hers at least for the time being; clothes got shoved to this side and that and the blankets got tangled; she hit her head again in the throes of what he was doing and nearly knocked herself dim-witted. She fell right back down on him and lay there swearing while he gently probed the egg on the back of her skull. "Oh, damn, Jones, I'm sorry."

"Got a matching set," she said. He had a good one on his. She knew. She lay there warm and comfortable on a breathing human body, with someone's arms around her for the first time in years. And it was somewhere far and above the way she expected. He was clean and tried not to hurt her: ("Damn, girl, this your first?"—"Shut up! Don't you call me girl!" He shut up. And was worried about her; and when it got beyond hurting he made her forget it hurt.) He told her things and taught her things in his polite way, so she didn't say them hers: somehow it belonged with fine words, what he did; and what she expected belonged with hers.

Somehow it fit that she banged her head twice on her own overhead. She felt awkward; and kept quiet the way she took two baths in one day, not to have him look down on her. But karma took a hand and she made a fool of herself twice in the same night. And landed dazed on his chest and had his fine hands to take the hurt away.

She was in love. For at least the night.

You got no sense, Jones. You're a real daughter of the Ancestors. You know this Mondragon? You got any idea why six people want to throw him in the Grand? Maybe they had reason.

He *couldn't* be on the wrong side of it. If he was a murderer or a thief or a crazy I'd know it by now.

He's got to go back where he belongs. I got to get him there. He don't belong in a place like this.

Her heart hurt. It knotted up and hurt as if her whole self was trying to shrink up in that small space. His fingers worked at her shoulders.

"Jones, something wrong?"

"Nothing's wrong." Her shoulders were tight. She realized he was working at over-tense muscles and tried to relax.

"You sorry?"

"No. *No.*" She sucked in her breath. Spilling tomorrow on today, her mother called it. Damn nonsense. Today was fine. Tomorrow—well, tomorrow could maybe be *two* days away. Then it was time to use her wits and get him back where he belonged. She drew a breath and let it go. And snuggled up against his shoulder and tried to shut her eyes.

She opened them again at once. Sometimes she heard things at the edge of sleep, time doing tricks, things that might or might not be there.

But the waves had a rhythm. It was always there. The boat had a way of moving. The world rocked and moved forever in certain ways and with certain sounds; and right now, for no reason she had heard clearly, a cold bit of fear gathered in her gut. She tensed and started to get up; his hand pressed against her back. She put a quick hand over his mouth. "I think I heard something. I'm going to back out real easy. Stay put."

She eased back and felt him start to follow. She pushed him back. "No. Stay out of it." She had a vision of him stumbling about in the dark. "I got ways." She went on sliding, the wind cold on bare skin; came out into the starlight on her belly and came up on her hands ever so carefully to peer over the deck-rim.

A raft was out there, dark, amorphous island in the starlit water. She got the knife at the hidey entrance and slithered on her elbows down the well, cut the anchor rope with one quick slice, backed up and around and *he* was out in the starlight, keeping low as she was. She slithered back in a hurry. "Keep your head down," she whis-

pered under the water-noise. "We got a raft out there.
Thing can't move for spit, but they're crazies for sure."
They were in the deepest part of the well; she grabbed
a towel off the slats, rolled to get it on and knotted
it around her waist while he grabbed his pants. Then she
rose up and put her hand on the deckrim; he grabbed her
arm.

"Where are you going?"

"I'm going to start the engine. You want to crawl back
there with me and cut that anchor rope?"

"Does that thing always start?"

"Fifty-fifty," she said. She did not like to think about
that. She slapped the knife into his hand. "Get that rope
cut. I know my engine."

She eeled up over the deck, slithered across quick as she
could and got up on her knees behind the engine housing
to lift the wooden cover, while Mondragon was at the
rope.

Careful now, step by step and precise with the start-up.
The old engine was fussy; it preferred the warm sun to
damp nights.

The crazies saw her. There was an outright splash from
the polers on the raft. A rising mutter of whispers in the
dark that became voices—

Pump some fuel up, set the switch, wish to God she'd
cleaned the contact and checked the gap today—Ancestors,
save a fool! Her eyes picked up another bobbing darkness,
second raft beyond the first, and real terror went through
her. Mondragon was on his knees beside her, the boat was
slewing free and the traitor backsurge was carrying them
toward the rafts—She heaved the crank round once, twice,
steadied the choke against its tendency to suck in too far,
heard howls break out across the water and heaved on the
crank again, O God, not a sound from the engine. Adjust
the throttle again; crank. A little hiccup. Back the choke
out, just on the worn spot in the shaft; crank. Hiccup-
hiccup.

"Jones—"

"Get the damn boathook! In the rack! Move!" Open the

stop, drain the line down, she'll flood otherwise; the smell of fuel hit the air, and Mondragon was scrambling after the pole-rack, on his feet, the boat pitching as it slewed and bobbed to wave action and the rafts—God, God, *three* of them, one on the other angle, moving in with howls and hoots and splashes of water—Steady that choke, remember the throttle, back her down, crank again—hiccup. *Damn* it, engine! Crank. The nearer raft bristled with boathooks, a spiny thing like a sea-star, all of them waving and the night filled with howls and hoots. Men leaped into the water and splashed toward them.

Crank, hiccup, cough. She let go the choke, feathered the throttle and lost it. The rafts were a wall of spines. Mondragon had the boathook in his hands. Reset the throttle. Back the choke. Crank. Double-cough. The engine started, solid. Feather the throttle back; engage the screw—Tiller bar *up*, fool! Rudder's still down. She snatched the bar up and set the pin, and scanned the shoreside water ahead, frantically searching the dark for rocks and sand as the boat gained a little way. No room, no damn room but a thread of water along the shore where rock or sand might set them aground and helpless.

She slowed the bow around, heading that way. Water splashed. Mondragon swung at something in the water—Don't hook 'em!'' she yelled, ''hit 'em! You can lose the pole—Yi'' A swimmer was coming right up over the side. ''Ware port, ware port, God, *ware port!''*

He finally saw it and swung the pole into the boarder's skull just as the man hit their deck. Altair swung the tiller over and gritted her teeth as the surge and the boat's own sluggish way took them closer to the rafts than she wanted; or the rafts were closer to shore, poling more effectively in the shallows, and God knew where the bottom was under them right now—''Ware, ware, *Mondragon look out!''*

He was going to lose it, they were going to snag his hook and jerk him off, or get a hook into him—

''They'll try to snag the side! Mondragon, switch ends, switch *ends,* don't let 'em hook ye! *Ware afore—''*

Because they were going to skim close to the third raft, too close. She caught the dropbox handle at her foot with her toe and flipped it open, held the tiller with one hand and dived down and grabbed the pistol out— aimed it dead into the living wall that loomed up at an angle and squeezed the trigger: the recoil jolted her arm, the report jolted her ears, and the crazies screeched in one great shriek as something hit the water and one voice screamed above the rest. Pole cracked against pole: she looked left where Mondragon was in the finish of a swing, and aimed past him at the waving arms and hooks. A howl and a shriek; and she kept the tiller under her arm and put her third shot into the raft coming up closer, with similar result. Her right arm ached; she had the tiller under the left one and leaned on it, trying to keep the boat as far from the raft as she could, trying to judge it tight between the reach of those poles and the hazard of that near beach.

A hand came up over their rim, the boat felt it— "*Mondragon!* Boarder!"

He saw it, handled the boathook with a right smart reverse and the boarder went back where he came from; but they were too near, they were coming far too close, men were pouring off the second raft to come at them through the shallows—She fired; and the surge of bodies went every which way. Screams.

An arm and a head came up over the deckrim near her. "*Aft*, Mondragon! *Ware aft!*" She saved her bullet for the raft they were passing. Let it off to save them from the hooks. The man was climbing up the portside by her, one fast surge and he was rising—"*Mondragon!*"

The pole appeared out of nowhere and the man went under. The screw hit something: she felt the slight resistance; but the boat tunked on, the third raft beside them now, hooks reaching, bodies pouring off the raft. She fired. Mondragon yelled and poles cracked together.

A hook snagged the wood. "*Ware hook!*" she screamed, slewed the tiller; and the boat kept moving; the whack-whack-whack of poles was sharp and keen over the screaming and the engine noise. She saw open water, drove for it, as her own position came too near the hooks. She could see feral men, their spiky hair, their eyes agleam and their mouths howling in the starlight, the whole mass moving and reaching like some bad dream. One shot left. One shot. She clung to the tiller and kept judging that distance.

The bottom scraped sand on starboard. Her heart jumped. The scrape stopped; the boat went on, scraped again, silent in the deafening yells to portside, the reach of hooks Mondragon fended as he could. Blood ran on him. He staggered to a crack against the pole, caught his balance and swung a hard, sweeping blow that took a crazy off. More blows came back; and then they were passing the corner, *he* was in the clear, and the hooks reached for her, men jumped after the boat; but they were late. The boat chugged on, the water between them widened, and Altair heaved the tiller over to take them out into the harbor.

God, they could have had bows. One of them could have had a gun. She was shaking.

I killed five people. Maybe a dozen. Her whole arm ached. She remembered the man the screw had chopped and tried not to remember. Mondragon was looking at her, sitting on the deckrim, agleam with sweat in the starlight. The boathook lay aslant over side and deckrim, under his hand.

Altair set the tiller and squatted down and opened the ammunition box. She broke the old gun, rammed five new cartridges in and clicked the cylinder into place again. Her mother always told her not to fire the last round—"You never empty your gun, hear, you reload on five; you finish a fight, you damn well better have one bullet left." Why was not a question you asked Retribution Jones. You just said Yes, mama, and you did it. And she had. Her hands shook when she put the gun away, but Retribution's slim tanned fingers had handled that old gun like it was a metal part of them. Her whole body shook. She felt her mother crack her one for that, could *feel* the sting on her ear; and she sucked a breath and sobered up and remembered she was sitting half naked on her deck and the engine was running, drinking up precious fuel.

Damn. Damn. It was no time to cruise the harbor; if they spent fuel, they spent it getting *across* the harbor, which spent it the way she had planned. She had no money to buy more. She had about enough for Moghi's barrels without taking a loan. And she had two bottles of whiskey and a handful of flour and a paper of tea and two mouths to feed. Damn, damn, damn. She throttled back to a fuel-saving speed; they were crossing on the backflow of the tide and they would feel it about the time they crossed the Rimwash current: it would eat fuel like a drunk takes whiskey. They would make it on what was in the tank. And then she would be about flat.

She looked at Mondragon, who looked at her. Not awkward. No. She remembered him in motion, not well-skilled with that pole, but he took to it fast, he found his balance, he hadn't gotten snagged or let them get past his guard.

"Didn't know you had a gun," he said finally. His breath still came hard.

"Don't like to use it." As if she did it now and again. Better he believe that, and not get ideas. She stood up with a hand on the tiller for balance. The wind was cold on her sweat. She gave her head a shake and drew the wind into her nostrils as she scanned the water ahead. City lights were mostly out now, only a couple of sparks showing; and the way was clean—give or take the passage under the pillars of the Rimmon Isle bridges. *That* could be a sticky spot at night.

She thought about it more and shut the engine down all the way.

"Where are we going?" he asked.

"Dunno." And then because she wanted to appear to have the answers: "Had enough trouble tonight. I'm too tired to pole her through the bridges and I sure as hell don't want to tie up there; we had enough crazies tonight."

"Is that what they were?"

"Crazies or rafters, small difference with some." She drew in another large breath, blotted the killing from her mind and drank in a certain pride. *Her* boat. *Her* say, how it ran. She knew what she was doing and he knew she knew. She saw her mother, saw Retribution Jones handling that tiller in her earliest memories, sunlight on her face and those fine hands of hers so sure of what they did, the way she walked in those bright years, like the world had better move out of her way.

She hitched up her slipping towel and hopped off her halfdeck into the well, turned to Mondragon where he sat on the deck rim. "They got you a couple of times."

"Broke the skin." He stood up and caught her arms. "Damn, girl—"

She shook his hands off right quick. "*Jones*. Call me Jones."

"Jones." He stood there in the starlight and found nothing else to say.

Neither did she. The boat had lost most of its way, drifting with the chop.

"I got some salve," she said. And because she wanted to be clean again, sweat-slick and feeling the touch of the crazies still lingering: "I'm going to take a bath."

He said nothing. She dropped the towel, turned and stepped off the side, a straight drop.

Water shocked beside her, a gentle drift of bubbles against her skin as another body arrived. He found her, wrapped his arms around her. Damn fool, she thought, and in a moment of panic—Is he trying to drown me, a murderer after all, he wants the boat—?

Evidently not. She surfaced with him, rolled over in a sidestroke and felt him swimming at her back, stroke for stroke. She blinked back to sanity then, broke stroke and trod water. "Damn, we trying to lose the boat?" She saw it farther away and launched out for it with strong driving strokes.

He reached it first, none so far—held to the side and waited for her.

They almost lost it again when she caught up.

"Jones," he said in a way no one had ever said that word before. "Oh, Jones." And then they had to catch the boat a second time.

Chapter 3

MORNING was for slow waking; a little more of what they had done before under the stars on the halfdeck. And finally another swim: that was four baths in two days and Altair was amazed at herself. She washed her clothes too, soaped them up good and left them on the tiller to dry a bit in the wind, and he washed his, and they sat having breakfast in the afternoon wrapped in towels and letting the wind dry their hair. Hers went straight. His went curly and fine as pale silk. He was beautiful, every move he made was beautiful, the way the muscles stood when he reached for a bit of bread, the way the sun hit his face and turned his hair to light. She ate and stared at him every chance she got. And sighed.

"Where do we go now?" he asked finally, and she shrugged, not wanting to talk about it. He took that for his answer, it seemed.

But when she had put the breakfast dishes away, when she stood up and saw the rafters out floating like little islands on the Dead Harbor rim—she remembered the night and remembered what it might be like to try to find their way around the rim of the Dead Harbor, poling because they would be out of fuel. And that decided her. She sighed again and bent and took her pants from their hanging-spot over the tiller, and pulled them on. And the sweater.

"They're still wet, aren't they?" Mondragon asked, still wearing his towel, standing down in the well.

"We got to get moving is what. You want to tell me where?"

"Do we have some hurry?"

"Mondragon." She came and sat down where there was no need to yell it over the water-sound, on the deckrim in front of him. "We go out there to the Rim again, that takes all the fuel I got. And poling back from there's a bitch. Through the rafters and the crazies." She hooked a thumb back toward the town, toward the low hazy hump of Rimmon Isle. "We got enough to get to the shallows under the Rimmon bridges. And I can pole her where you want to go after that, unless it's out in the bay. But I'm about out of everything except whiskey, I got a living to make, and the current here's going to generally drift us further and further toward the Ghost Fleet, which ain't a good place: crazies hang out there, 'gainst the sandbar; and it's opposite to Rimmon and I got only so much fuel to get us back; I been watching the drift. So all in all, I think you better tell me where you want to go, because where I'm going is back in the canals and I think you got reason not to want to do that. I reckon you've got a riverboat you'd like to get to, or maybe that Falkenaer ship. I can't pole you to the Det-landing, she's too deep, but I can set you out right at the dike, there's stairs at Harbormouth; and you just go up and over and right down the dike to the Det-pier and down again, easy walk. Best I can do."

He was quiet a moment. He looked down at the slats and up again, arms folded. "Let me out in the town," he said.

Her heart did a skip-beat and tightened up again. "You going to go hunt up trouble? Once in the canal not enough for you. Tell me where they'll throw you next, I'll keep my boat waiting."

He looked down at her with a tightening of the mouth. It turned into a wry smile. "Stay out of my business."

"Right. Sure. Get your clothes on."

"Jones—" He took her face between his hands and made her look up at him. "I like you a lot, Jones."

That hurt. She drew a great breath and it felt like something would break. "Hey, you get me a kid, man, I'll kill you." Had her mother been that stupid? Was that how *she* had happened into the world? One time her mother let her guard down and liked a man like Mondragon? Or was it just some ugly accident or a rape somewhere her mother had lost a fight? She could not imagine her mother losing.

He brushed her hair back, kept looking at her. And let her go finally and skipped up onto the halfdeck to get his own clothes. When had he found his legs? When had he learned to move on the boat? Last night when he had to, when he stood there wielding that boathook with skill that grew by the minute—

—blade fighter, she thought. Fencer. Hightowner. They came in all types. Street rowdies. Duelists. The hightown had those too—some of them very rich. Some of them who would talk in that silk-soft kind of voice and not know spit about not dipping a iron skillet in the water or grabbing a prickleback round the fins.

He knew about deathangel spines all right. He knew how to take care of a good knife.

He had had no bad scars till the boathook caught him in the shoulder last night and he would carry that for the rest of his life—not a deep one, but wide as that blunt hook could make it. *(He'll remember me, won't he? Rest of his life. Everytime some soft uptown woman asks about that scar.)*

He knew how to fight. Which meant he was no easy prey for those black-cloaked devils on the bridge. How had they got him, anyway?

The knot was on the back of his head, that was what.

He pulled his pants on, wet around the seams as they would be. Sun would go on drying them: no worry of taking fever.

Altair sighed again, then bent down beside the hidey and swept up her well-worn cap, pulled it on hard against the wind, and winced and suffered a jolt of the heart: there was a knot on the back of her skull too, right where the band touched. She settled the cap a little back of that, tilted on her head, jammed it down and skipped up onto the halfdeck.

The traitor engine started on the third crank, regular as could be.

*   *   *

She shut the engine down finally with maybe enough fuel left for a startup, maybe a little more—"Never you run nothing down to empty." Her mother had dinned that into her. "You plan so's you don't. You lay yourself open and Murfy'll get you, sure he will." Even Adventists believed in Murfy. He was a saint in the Janist pantheon. "You gave old Murfy a chance," her mother would say when she slipped up. "I tell you, you can't give chances away. You need all you got."

She hauled the rudder up, pulled the tiller-pin and let the bar fall to be hooked stationary to the engine-box. So the boat coasted toward the tall pilings between the dike and Rimmon Isle on the way they had left; and she gauged it right. The bow skimmed over shallow water, the line that was dark and not green, without a pole to push it; and while it was crossing that line she unshipped the pole and walked to the front of the halfdeck to put it in, walking it along on starboard; then crossed over and walked it on port, while Mondragon stood out of her way in the well.

"Can I help with that?"

"Hell, no! You'd be clinging to that pole and the boat off on her own. I seen many a beginner go right off the deck."

Back to starboard. She was flatly showing off, keeping the boat moving at a reckless clip, making it look easy as it headed for the pilings. Moving cheered her. His bright face in the sunlight did, for what time she still had his company. Not raining on tomorrow, Retribution Jones would say. Or the afternoon. Her bare feet were sure on the deck. Not hard shoves. Deft ones. At the right time. "This kind of boat's called a skip, dunno why. Skip's got a halfdeck and an engine and she's bigger'n any poleboat. Moves real sweet in the water if you know her tricks; any boat's got 'em. She's engine-heavy and she slews bad, but you can use that on the turns, if you know what to do with the pole. She starts slow and she stops the same way when she's loaded; then you use the currents much as you can—canals have 'em, same as the harbor or old Det himself, and some of 'em's fierce. You plan way ahead. You don't feel that load right, she can ram a wall or another boat and tip everybody right over if her load shifts.''

They were coming up on the pilings. Mondragon turned as the shadow fell on them, and staggered when he faced that perspective, the black maze of pillars that was coming fast. ''Jones—''

''I know my way.'' She worked it fast, this side and that. ''Better be right, hey?''

They shot in amongst the pilings, into the dark of the bridges that linked the city to Rimmon Isle and its fortified mansions. Light gleamed hurting-bright at the end, which was the harbor, and the pilings rushed by them. Mondragon stood in silhouette against that light.

Trip through hell. Or purgatory.

She had her line planned. No way the boat was going to skew from it, except at the end when they hit the inflow from the harbor. They kited out into the dazzling light, the water throwing it back off its surface and swirling brown into the lucent jade of the deep bay.

''Ware!'' she sang out, meaning she was about to turn, and bottomed the pole and swung the bow over so smartly and shoved her off so deftly there was never a jolt. Mondragon kept his footing with a little stagger, turned and looked up at her as if he thought that was a trick designed to unsettle him.

''Hey, you got your legs, Mondragon.'' She grinned at him. ''You'll roll like a proper canaler when you walk ashore.''

''I don't drown easy, Jones.''

She grinned wider. A light sweat stood on her and the breeze cooled her skin. The wind smelled of waterfront and old wood, which was the smell of Merovingen and its harbor alike. They went into the dark again, under another pier. An idle boat was tied up there down the way, likely a fisher cursing the luck that kept him in for repair. The sound of hammering came to her, and echoed off the docks and the dikes. They slowed: they had lost a little way in the turn and she did not pick it up again. She just headed for the series of bright-dark water stripes ahead, between the series of water-blackened pilings.

"Where you going in town, Mondragon?" she asked. "You didn't tell me that."

He turned again and looked up at her. Sun hit his face as they skimmed into the light again, and he grimaced and shaded his eyes. "Jones, forget my name. Don't talk it around, just say you had a passenger, say my name was— whatever's common here."

"You won't pass for a Hafiz or a Gossen, not with that complexion. You got a burn, you know that?"

He took a reflexive look at his arm, which was reddened, raised it to shade his eyes again. "Believe me. Forget that name."

"Why'd you tell me?"

A moment's silence. He stood there with the hand up and let it fall again as they headed under another pier and into deep shadow. "Must have been the rap on the head," he said, quieter.

"You got real troubles. You sure you don't want me to take you to the Det-landing?"

"I'm sure."

Mondragon—She stopped herself short of the name, wiped it out of her reflexes. "You want my help?" *Fool!* "You want me to keep you under cover awhile?" She hoped suddenly. She took the chance the way she took the chance with the pilings, because she knew the maze, she knew the ways, she was adept at surviving and took some chances because it was style. It was—whatever made life worth having. He was one. "I could do that. Do it easy."

He stood there with a look on his face that said it tempted him. With a look in his eyes that said he was thinking. "No," he said. "No, you better not."

"You being a fool?"

"No."

"You already got a cracked skull. You going to go back where they can get another swing at it? Second time they'll split it. Second time I might not be there to pull you out."

"Hey, you going to take me for another night out there with the crazies?"

Her accent on his tongue; it was deft, too. She grinned in spite of herself. "Not bad. Not bad hit."

"Jones—" The light came back and he squinted. "Jones—thanks."

They had reached the Mouth, where the dike towered up before them and the warehouses of Ramseyhead were at their left. Her bare feet hit the deck in short, quick strides as she positioned for the turn, touched the pole on that side and drove them hard for the Mouth; a little hard work now: the Mouth was always a hard crossing, where some of the sewer effluent created a wash. She heard that *thanks* and there was no time to handle it, just the boat, just that quick, hard rhythm of her life, which went on before him and would go on after him. And maybe there was nothing worth saying.

Something stupid like Come back?

He was going to end up in the canal again; or he was going to take off those canaler's rags and dress himself in hightowners' velvet and silk and walk the high bridges with no more interest in the boats that plied the shadows than he had in the vermin and the feral cats that conducted their war in Merovingen's sinks and bowels. Velvet and silk. Not his back on bare boards and a dirty blanket. Whether he was one of the shady sort of hightowner or something else—he had no business with her.

Unless he maybe wanted a bit of freight moved.

Or a cheap night.

He had turned his back again, the ridiculous too-large breeches having slipped a bit—Lord and Ancestors, he'll be a fine sight where he's bound. They jump him, the damn pants will trip him. Maybe old Kilim's got a pair he'd trade for.

What am I thinking of? Like I got time? Like he's staying? He'll throw those damn things in the canal when he's uptown and back with his own. No, he'll have some servant do it.

Can't be out of the gangs. He can't. Not with that way he talks. Not the way he talks when he's got his hands on me, not then—couldn't talk fine words then except they come natural as breathing. I can't open my mouth, I can't think pretty, I wish I could. Wish I could.

She smiled and shoved the pole this side and that as the

towering black wall of the dike glided past. As they went under Harbor Bridge and headed onto the Grand. Mondragon turned round and hitched the pants up on reflex. "You cover that hair of yours," she said. "And you put that sweater on. You're too white."

He climbed up onto the deck to retrieve the sweater; she snagged it one-handed off the engine housing as she switched sides, tossed it at him. He worked it on, tugged it down and hitched the pants again before he sat down on the halfdeck edge to pick up the black scarf where it lay. He wrapped it round with several deft turns and tucked the end. "You can take me to the Hanging Bridge."

"Easy done, but this boat can do the little canals too if you need 'em."

"Hanging Bridge is fine."

She kept the boat moving, push and switch and push. Her feet were warm on the deck. Her breath came hard. Traffic ahead. She kept her side, starboard of a slow-moving pole-barge. She let the boat slow more, city-pace.

"You always work this boat alone?"

Uhnn. Now it comes. Spends a night or so and now the man gets to meddling. So much for love, Jones. Mama said.

"Jones?"

"Sure." She was breathing hard. Sweat rolled down her face and she wished she had a man's option to take the sweater off in the town. She lifted the cap and resettled it on the knot on the back of her head before she thought, set it again and made the next stroke in time. Her feet burned on the deck. Damn showoff. "Do right well for myself." Liar. She sucked a breath and gave him a half-grin and a tilt of the head while she was on the crosspace. "Little different than your hightown sorts, bet they're all soft."

"*I'm* not."

She grinned wide. "Hightowner." Gasp. "Be you?"

"What would you have done out there—last night—when the crazies came at you?"

Damn, here he goes. Damn fool question. His damn fault, too. "Hey, man, I wouldn't have been sleeping deaf and blind in the hidey, then, would I? You can bless your

Ancestors I got good ears, that's the truth. Never came so close. I tie up to the Rim, I sleep on the deck, I sleep like a cat, and they don't get up on me like that.''

"What if that engine had failed?"

The thought chilled her. She weighed things like that before she did them; she was not prone to mull them over after. "Well, it didn't.''

"It might someday.''

"Look, usually I go to the Rim in bad seasons; then there's more canalers and fewer crazies. If my engine goes down I get a tow and it costs me a hell of a lot—did it once." That was a lie. It was what she had done for another canaler, her fuel and theirs together in her struggling engine, and she had taken pay in bits and pieces for a month. "Any more of my business you want to know?"

He kept his mouth shut.

"Takes a damn fool man," she said, "to throw me off my regular ways. Take 'im out where his enemies can't get at him, risk my damn neck, I mean, you want a fool—*that's* a fool. How'd I know you wasn't a murderer? How'd I know but what that wasn't some uptown woman's kinfolk throwing you in because you up and jumped her, huh? *That's* a fool, being out there alone with you in my boat.''

"Why did you do it?"

"Damnfool, that's why. Need a better reason?"

He was quiet a moment. Then: "Jones, what's wrong?"

"Nothing.''

"Jones, slow down.''

Current hit the bow. She gasped for breath and shifted hard, staggered a bit and lost her balance in the shift of current. Tired. Her sides ached. Her arms were leaden. Sweat ran in her eyes.

"Jones, dammit. Are you trying to kill yourself? We're not in a race.''

She ignored him for another barge, maneuvered across the influx from the Snake's harborside loop across the Grand, and avoided the slew the current wanted to give her. It was no place to stop, folk would swear her deaf if she parked at the Jut and had herself in the traffic. Some barge would crack into her and just deserts for a fool. If she was alone she would pull off to the Snake's nearest tie-up and rest. She had shown him a fancy bit of moving; now the damn landsman had that worry-look on his face and that damn insistence in his voice—*Fool woman. Quit. Pull off. Let me, let me, let me*—pushing right in to have the boat, his way, tell her what to do, when to breathe and when to spit, and then walk out again with things a damn mess, because he had more important things in life than a damn woman. Walking through the damn world messing folk up and so damn smug-sure it was help. Man with that tone didn't deserve to be listened to. Her mother never would. Spit in their eye, she would. Man catcalled from other barges—*Hey, sweet, that boat's too big for you!* And worse things. *Hey, you want some help?* Followed by just what help the bastard thought she needed.

Stay out of my business, she wanted to say. But it was not the kind of parting she wanted; Mondragon wasn't to blame for the world. He just did what others did. Slept with a woman and thought he could get his hands into her life and fix it all before he went back to his hightown ways. Never even thought he'd just seen the fanciest bit of boatmanship he was like to see on the canals. A skip-freighter never got to show off to passengers like the flashy poleboaters; she had just showed him a dozen tricks of the sort canalers showed when they wanted to impress each other, the kind that made a difference in the trade, how a boat could move and handle the tight places. She showed a landsman that kind of thing. And he just saw a woman sweat and got all bothered.

Dammit.

Damned if she'd rest. Take him to the damn bridge and dump him in, she would. Put him back where she found him. Ask for the clothes back. *That'd* fix him good.

She sucked a quieter breath, easier now the strokes were fewer, up past the Jog, under Parley Bridge, and her breath rasped in her throat. She was resting. That was a canaler trick too, getting wind back while she worked. But he was blind to it, same as what it took to shoot the piers and all their currents.

"Jones—" he insisted, looking up at her from the well.
She managed a grin. "You got a problem?"

He evidently thought better of it. She grinned wider.
And took it slower still, breathing easier. "I tell you, man,
there's places you don't stop. Park at the Jog back there,
some barge'll run right over you. Current takes 'em real
close to that wall and they don't see you. Don't care
either. Bargemen got no regard for a boat."

That seemed to put some respect into him. He kept his
mouth shut, maybe having realized he knew less than he
thought.

Fine for you, Mondragon. Got a brain even if they did
rattle it. I wouldn't do so good in your hightown. Be a real
embarrassment, I would. Leave my boat to me, all right,
Mondragon? You don't own everything.

I'll have me a dozen lovers.

Take precautions too, I will.

O God, if he's got me pregnant.

I'd work this boat same's mama did, that's what I'd do;
have my kid; wouldn't be alone then. Have a daughter
with hair like that—

Lord, I'd have to fight off the bridge-boys with the
boathook; have to teach her to use a knife same as mama
did me . . . .

Give her to her damn father, that's what. I'd march right
up to hightown wherever he's got to and hand him the brat
and wish him luck.

Take precautions next time. Going to cost you a week's
work, old Mag's drugshop's supposed to be good. Should
of had the stuff aboard before now.

Have to walk in that shop in front of God and everybody
and ask for that stuff, old Mag'll grin; she'll tell that sister
of hers, Lord, it'll be all up and down the river by sunset
and *I'll* be fending off boarders.

Hey the icewoman's done thawed!

Hey, Jones-pretty. You wanta see what I got?

Damn, nothing's simple.

The bridge-shadows came over them, the air went cold
with that deep dankness of Merovingen's depths. The
shadows went darker still, a moment of blindness that

swept past to daylight. There was a copper taste in her mouth, the loom of a black boat passing beside her—she fended and evaded it, and evaded the gray rough-hewn stone of Mantovan's Jut on starboard. Another skip was ahead, dead-stopped at a mooring ring. "Damnfool." She maneuvered around it, slow drives of aching muscles. "Park in the Grand in daylight—" She reached out and rammed the pole end against the boat. "*Damn fool*, you!"

"*Damn bitch!*"

"Old man Muggin." She sucked wind as they passed. Looked at Mondragon standing just off the deckrim, gazing back at the boat and its ragged occupant. "Old man thinks he owns the water. He don't handle that boat so good nowadays, long stretches get him, and he won't stay off the Grand." She recovered her breath and poled along with steady strokes again. "You got rules here. You obey 'em, you get along."

"You want to rest, Jones?"

"Hey, I got no need. She's light today. You want to see work, push her when her well's full of cargo, *then's* work." She coughed from the bottom of her lungs, missed a stroke. "Just a little—" A second cough seized her, payment for the long push. "Damn." She coughed again, swallowed and got the spasm under control. "Cold. Change always does that to me. Going from sunlight in under the bridges." They passed a poleboat, out fareless. Hunting. It was true, they were well under Merovingen's bridges now, and the water was dark and the walls on either side untended and cheerless, their windows and doors barred with iron. No canal-level entry here, except to the lowest sorts of places, that served canalmen. The big isles took their canalside deliveries down guarded bays, within iron gates that guaranteed they got only what they ordered. "What's at Hanging Bridge?"

There was no answer. But it stopped the questions. She worked quietly, wiped the sweat. So much for clean clothes. Hardly dry yet and the sweat soaked them.

"You looking for Them?" she asked him.

He turned and looked at her. The easy manner was

gone, the humor fled. Yes. He was looking for them. For something. Plain as an answer.

"Yeah," she said. He said nothing. "Who were they?" she asked.

"I'll take care of it."

"Real fine. Maybe they'll be looking for me, you ever think of that?" She drew a breath, two. It was the Hanging Bridge ahead, and the current of the Snake's other exit. She fought it the moment it took.

"I thought of it."

"That's real nice."

"It wouldn't do you any good, Jones. It might do worse. Just stay clear of it. Far clear."

The sun was on them now, one of the only places on the Grand that had a view; which was what made the Hanging Bridge. It hove up, conspicuous with its fretworks and its angel and its ominous wooden arches.

"That's there's the Angel, shining there," Altair said, between pushes. "Revenantists say Merovingen'll stand long as the Angel stands on the bridge. Janes say he draws that sword a bit more every time the earth shakes. Adventists say he'll stand till Retribution."

"I've heard of him," Mondragon said. He turned his face to her again, looked ahead as they came closer to the bridge, looked back again.

She looked too, scanning the traffic. Her back prickled with the feeling she got skimming through some backwater. Running near crazies and rafters. Back to the starting-point. Fishmarket Bridge loomed beyond. There was Moghi's, dim and distant under Fishmarket shadow, Moghi's porch beyond Ventani Pier. There were skips and poleboats and the usual huddle of barges, the vegetable-sellers and the fish-sellers and the fish-freighters tied up to rings there by Fishmarket and spilling all the way along the edge. The wooden towers of Merovingen-above shone silver-gray in the sun above the dark, above the web of bridges beyond. And the Hanging Bridge Angel presided over it all, sword half-drawn. World half-ended.

Putting it away or taking it out again since the Great Quake?

Halfway between dooms.

She spied a place on the east bank and eased the bow over that way, there amongst the fish-sellers. Mondragon sat on the deck-edge, turned again to look up at her as they glided in.

Wondering what she wanted, maybe. Wondering how to make parting fast and clean. She was too busy; shipped the pole and took up the boathook. "Hey, Del," she hailed the old man of the neighboring skip, and snagged the ring, hauling them close. She bent and took up the mooring rope one-handed, ran in through the ring and made them fast. Hopped down and walked up forward where her bow touched the other skip. "Hey, Del, you want to give me a bow tie-up there?"

"What you selling?"

"Not a thing. Not trading. Just a little stop."

No competition. Del Suleiman's old mouth snaggled into a grin. "I take 'er. Tie on."

"Well, you got to lend me the rope, I lost my anchor stern and bow."

White brows went up and lowered again. A scragglebearded chin worked. A gap-toothed woman sat aft on the half-deck, female mountain behind the baskets of eels. "How'd ye lose 'er?"

"Hey, got a lander." She reset her cap and in the move brushed knuckle to right eyebrow: *got business going with this landsman; settle ours later*. The old man grinned and the woman grinned and the old man got his boathook to do the tie-up.

She walked back to Mondragon, who stood in the well within a stride of the stone walk. Waiting on her.

He stood there a moment longer, looking into her eyes. And for a moment she remembered the sun on him in the morning.

Then he turned and skipped up onto the landing, barefoot as a canaler, in her misfit breeches, a blue sweater out at the elbows and a black turban that did nothing to hide that white, sun-burned skin of his. He looked back from that vantage. Once.

She stood with her hands in her waistband and her bare

feet solid on her deck. "Luck," she said. "Mind your
back next time."

It got a flicker from him, as if that had shot true.
"Luck," he said, and turned and headed for the stairs.

Not another look back. Not one.

Not an offer to bring the clothes back. Too rich to think
it was all she had but what she was wearing.

Or just not going to promise what he couldn't do.

She turned and walked down to the bow where old Del
was tying up. She squatted down there. "Del, what I got
to give you so's you watch my boat?"

The old man's wits were sharp. His face never looked
it. He chewed the cud he had, spat a little green juice
overside between her bow and his side. "Hey, watcher
into, Jones? You clean?"

"Swear." She lifted a solemn hand. "What I got to
give you?"

"I think on 'er."

"Well, think, ye damn sherk!" Altair sprang up in
despair. Old Del knew how to wring advantage out of a
bargain, and retreating quarry was a mighty lever. "I'll
pay you, I'll pay you, my heart's blood I'll pay you; and
heaven help you if I got a scratch on my boat!" She pelted
up the slats, grabbed up the knife and the barrelhook and
hit the stones running. *Hooo—oo!* The appreciation of
other canalers followed that bit of theater. *Hooo—Run for
'er, Jones! Hooo—Del!*

Damn. He could get away, go either direction. She
thumped up the age-smooth wood of the Hanging Stair, up
and up the four turns to the wide bridge and its gallows-
arches.

There, blue sweater and black turban heading over the
bridge to Ventani.

Headed right for the neighborhood that dumped him
into old man Det's jaws in the first place.

Man with his mind set on trouble, that was what. Crazy
man. Crazy as the rafters.

She headed after him, bare feet soft-silent on the boards,
belting on her knife and hanging the barrelhook from that
belt too.

Chapter 4

NOW it was a real fool went racing across that bridge.
And one following after him, barefoot on the sun-
warmed planks, a canaler among the hightowners—the
folk in plain chambrys and leather, the tradesfolk and the
hightown shopfolk; and Signeury guards and sober Colle-
gians and the highest of the hightowners, uptown folk all
decked in lace and fine fabrics and dainty heeled shoes that
rat-tat-tatted on the boards like a holiday drummer. A
sweet-seller bawled her wares at bridgehead, beneath the
ominous, thoughtful face of the Angel, whose gilt hand
was on his sword. Altair strode past and imagined the
sword regretfully shoved an immeasurable fraction back
into its sheath: a fool's act put off the Retribution. Daughter, the Angel would say, his grave beautiful face very like
Mondragon's, just *why* are you doing this?

And she would stand and stammer and say: Retribution
(the Angel had her mother's name), I dunno, but excuse
me now (hasty mental curtsy), there's the other fool and
he's off down the walk, I daren't run—Let me keep up
with him, Angel, I'll mind my business tomorrow, I will—

She pattered off the bridge and along the side of Ventani
Isle, on its balconies, with its higher-level bridges in still
more layers above, that shadowed Margrave Canal and
Coffin Bridge and sent a few bright stripes on sunlight
right down onto the walk. A merchant had set a potted
plant in one broad stripe, possessor of a bit of sun, precious commodity on this level. An old man dozed in
another patch of light.

Ahead in the crowd, Mondragon walked more slowly

now; so she did, keeping that black scarf and blue sweater in sight. A canaler moved quite freely on this level, nothing at all remarkable. Someone on an errand. Someone taking an order. Moghi's Tavern was on the waterfront down below, at the Ventani's opposite corner, that which supported Fishmarket Bridge; but Mondragon, if he was going to Fishmarket, was certainly taking a roundabout route.

No. He took the short span over to Princeton, where it was much harder to track him without being seen. She reached Princeton Bridge and lounged there against the post for a moment until she saw her quarry take out to the right, down Princeton Walk.

She hurried then, walked along with a canaler's habitually rolling gait.

See the fool up there. Dressed like a canalrat, he is, and walks like a landsman for all to see. Landsman might not notice. But a canaler would notice something wrong, and look twice at him, and that twice might be trouble for him, might for sure—

Right across to Calliste Isle. Headed uptown. She strolled along with ease, took her time and faded back against the shopfronts and the posts among the passers-by when he would stop and take a look around him.

—So he's worried. He thinks about who might see him. He's trying to act natural and he daren't take to the high bridges, no, got to keep to the low, got to creep about down here with us canalers and the rats, he does.

Thank ye, Angel. He's being real easy. And if he goes back for Fishmarket round the Calliste I'll know he's a proper fool.

No. It was on north again, over the bridge to Yan Isle and never a hint of stopping. A canaler passed him and stopped against Yan Bridge rail and stared at his back; it was halfblind Ness. And Ness was still doing that when Altair walked past trying her best to look nonchalant.

"Hey," Ness said. " 'lo."

"Hey," Altair said, not to make a scene; and Mondragon was plainly in sight and had to be as long as he was on that bridge. A man hailed you politely, you hailed back. "I got a 'pointment, Ness. How you doing?"

"Oh, fair. Hey, you *do* be in some hurry—"

Altair simply left him, for Mondragon took an unexpected turn south. She hurried across the bridge, and took out on the same tack.

Round the band of Yan then, round and on round, and onto the short bridge and across to Williams and the Salazar, which fronted on Port Canal.

I could have ferried him here easy as not. Not that much further. What's he into? Why's he afraid of me letting him out at Port? Afraid of who could see him? Not wanting me to see?

Why?

Her heart thumped. Mondragon had slipped aside into a galleria that pierced Salazar's second level. She headed after him at greater speed, closing the gap in this darker place, this wooden cavern teeming with marketers and crowded with leather goods and shoemakers. Merchants bawled after shoppers. Merchants shouted at leather-dealers. The whole place smelled of leathers and oils above the prevalent canal-smell. And sunlight pierced it all by portsoleils and at the end, throwing figures into silhouette where the galleria turned out onto Port Canal, making everyone alike and without detail. She kept going, having lost her quarry for a moment, blinked when she came out into the sunlight and then caught sight of him on the bridge that led over north, to Mars.

Lord, the man's trying to kill me. No. He had rested the entire trip up from the harbor, that was how he moved so quick. Her side hurt again. Her feet felt stripped of calluses. He kept going round the side of Mars and over the bridge to Gallandry and around the corner.

And he vanished, before she could round the side of Gallandry. She took a running step, plastered herself to the stone side of Gallandry and took a quick look down the cut that led most of the way through Gallandry Isle, roofed with a solid next floor overhead, but not below, where an iron-railed balcony overlooked the water: narrow dark little nook of Gallandry business, the Gallandrys being shippers, factors, importers who sent their big motor-barges up and down the Port and the Grand.

Down that brick-floored balcony Mondragon knocked at a door. And talked with someone and got in.

So. Altair slumped against the wall, disheartened.

Gallandry. Gallandry was hardly interesting. Importers. Freighters. Traders. Certainly not among the uptown families.

Well, how could anything that came to her be more wonderful than that? How could he be more than that, some upriver merchant's son in difficulty in a canalside dive. Offend one of the Families, insult someone like the Mantovans or even some canalside riffraff, and get dumped in to feed the fishes. Easy as that.

So he went to his Merovingian factor to get money and clothes on his papa's name, and maybe to hire revenge. Simple. Simple done. *Then* to the Det and the boat before it left, probably on one of the Gallandry barges, probably hiding till they could spirit him out of town, safe and proper.

She gave a great sigh. It ached all the way to the bottom of her heart and she nursed an aching side and sore feet. It was nothing she could pursue further. It was nothing she had any more claim on—unless she walked up and rapped on the door and said Mondragon, give me my clothes back.

He might talk the Gallandrys into giving her a reward. And wish to his Ancestors she was not there in front of his business partners.

If she was not a fool she would embarrass him right proper, get all the money she could. Maybe hold out for doing light freight for the Gallandrys. That favor was worth a damnsight more than any coin. Canalers would respect her then, by the Ancestors.

She slid down to squat on her heels, pushed her cap back and ran a hand through her hair.

Fool. Triple fool. I'm sorry, Angel. I'll be sane tomorrow; but hanged if I'll beg, damn him. Could have said right out: Jones, take me to Port Canal, take me to Gallandry. *I* could have done 'er, easy as spit.

Come up with me, he could have said, come on, Jones, want you to meet these folk.

He could have given me my damn clothes back.

Could have said goodbye proper at the Gallandry landing, he could. 'Bye, Jones. Been nice. Don't 'spect I'll see you again, but good luck to ye.

She gnawed a hangnail, spat, cast a look back down the stone wall to the door, invisible from her angle.

Why didn't he have me take him here?

What's he up to?

The pain stopped. There began to be prickling up her back.

What's the fool up to? What's he doing in there?

Is he all right in there?

Damn, no, it ain't all on the table. Skulk over here, dive in a door in this damn gallery, disappear like that—Whoever he's meeting here is somebody he knows, somebody maybe a friend, but he ain't wanting to be seen, ain't wanting me to know—

—*Stay out of my business, Jones.*

Damnfool. Trust the Gallandrys. Maybe. Maybe about as far as you can trust any of the breed. *They'll cut your throat, Mondragon, fool.*

Or maybe you're a meaner fellow than they want to take on.

Not if they didn't push you so's you knew it, maybe. Not if you didn't see it coming, and, Lord and Ancestors, you didn't see that coming that near cracked your skull for you, now, did you? And you don't damn well know Merovingen, had to ask me things a man ought to know if he knew Merovingen, didn't you, Mondragon?

She reset her cap on her head, jammed it down and finally got up—walked quietly down the deserted dark gallery and stopped at the door. She took a further chance and set her ear against it.

There were voices. None of them were raised. The words were all a mumble.

She padded back where she had come from. Over the iron rail beside her, the gallery ended in a black wall and a watery bottom, a cut where a big barge could moor safely for loading. Green-black water, beyond all direct touch of sun. She went back into the sunlight on her end, where she could pretend to be about some honest business—but traffic was sparse here. A few passers-by. She sat herself down on the brick balcony with her feet adangle under the iron rail that overlooked wide Port Canal, just sat, elbows on the bottom rail, feet swinging, like any idle canaler waiting on a bit of business in a Gallandry office. And meanwhile she had that door under the tail of her eye and not a way in the world he could get out on this level without her knowing.

On this level. That was what gnawed at her. There were inside stairs in such buildings. There were ways to come and go. He could go in here and come out up above, on some upper level, clear across the building. Bridges laced back and forth to Gallandry on still another level, going back across the Port, over the West Canal to Mars or diNero and places north. Near a dozen bridges, most of them blind from where she sat. It was hopeless, if that was what he did. Unless—

She suddenly realized another fixture of the area, a man sitting the same as she was, over on the balcony of Arden Isle, next level up.

She did not look quick, but after a moment she glanced up again and scanned the area as if she were surveying the bridges.

Watcher on the West Arden bridge, too, on her level, just sitting.

Her heart beat faster. Gallandry folk? They might be. There were a lot of things they might be. She got up slowly, dusted herself off and leaned her elbows on the rail, looking down Port Canal, watching the traffic go, watching a slow barge and a flotilla of skips and poleboats. Shifted her eye back to Arden again. The watcher up there had moved, sat with one leg over the balcony rim; his hands made motions like whittling.

Damn. Damn. Real nervous sorts.

They got him under their eye.

They got *me*, too.

Fool, Jones, you got no protection.

Hope he walks right out that door with a dozen Gallandrys.

No, damn, I hope he *don't*. Him and all the Gallandrys'd walk right into it. Lord knows—they could be law watching the place. What if they're the law. What's Mondragon *into?*

If they're blacklegs, they can sweep me up right with the Gallandrys and all. Sweep me up to talk to even if they can't get him, if they're close enough to see me clear.

They might not *be* law either.

Oh, Jones, what have you got yourself into?

How'd they pick him up? Waiting all up and down the Grand? On the Ventani? No, dammit, there're too many, they'd have to get word out—They were watching Gallandry already. Either they're Gallandry or blacklegs or maybe some gang, and what's *my* chances of walking out of here by any bridge, huh, Jones?

Mondragon goes his way and some damn Gallandry knifes me on a bridge, he does, just precautionary. What's a dead water-rat, come floating down the Port tomorrow morning with the garbage?

She drew in a slow breath, shifted her eye toward the barge-gallery and worked her fingers together.

Law could have been watching Gallandry all this time. *Anybody* could. Mondragon, you walked into a trap, you're in it up to your ears, Mondragon.

She rose and dusted off her breeches again, shoved her cap back and scratched her head. Put her hands in her hip pockets and strolled a dozen paces down the balcony toward Mars. Then back again. Stop. Take the pose of a canaler tired of waiting. She stood on one foot, brought the other up to her knee and examined the calluses, pretended to pick a splinter. Then she took a stroll down the shadowed gallery again, hands in pockets, the very image of a boatman gone impatient over a wait.

She knocked at the door. Knocked again.

It opened. A man in work-clothes towered in the doorway. "Hey," she said, "is my partner through in here yet?"

The man had a heavy face; big gut. He filled the door-

way but around the edges of him there was sight of
windows on the canalside that let in light; there was the
expected lot of desks and clutter; another man, the same
sort, standing back alongside a lot of boxes. The heavy-
faced man looked disturbed and confused. Then: "Come
on in." He moved his bulk aside and Altair stepped up on
the sill and got through that little space he left into the
room.

Boxes and desk and papers and more boxes. Two windows. A door that made this room only half the space
available on this floor. No Mondragon. And Man Two was
moving up like a fish on bait, while Man One shoved the
door shut at her side and set his bulk ominously in front of
it.

"What's this about a partner?" Man Two asked.

Altair swallowed hard. Her heart was trying to come up
her windpipe. She hooked a thumb toward Port Canal in
general. "What you got out there, ser, is eyes all over this
place. I got two watchers in sight meself, and they don't
look friendly. I figure they got all the bridges off Gallandry
blocked. So if you'd kindly tell my partner, I think I'd like
to talk to him."

"What partner?" Man Two asked.

Oh, here it is. Body sinks real good, Jones, with a
couple of rocks. Right to the bottom of Gallandry-dock
and nobody the wiser.

She set hands on hips. "Him as I delivered to your
door."

"Did you now?" Man One hitched up his belt and a
good weight of belly. "You got a good imagination, girl."

Jones, that's Jones, damn great fool. Altair bristled and
choked it down. *Mondragon said forget his name in town;
won't be a bigger fool and give them mine.* "What I got,"
she said equably, "is a partner I brought here. You don't
want to talk to me you can talk to the law that's all round
this place."

Uh-uh. The eyes went opaque in a way that said wrong
guess.

"So it *ain't* the law out there, then. That means Gallandry
folk. Or it means Gallandry's got troubles." She folded

her arms and planted her bare feet on their floor. "You got a damnsight more if you don't fetch up my partner."

"I think," said Man Two, "you'd better go upstairs with us."

"I ain't going nowhere. You bring 'im here—*hey!*" The man reached and she moved, one jerk at her belt and the barrelhook was in her hand, meaning business. *"Don't* you try it, man. You get him down here or I'll carve up *your* partner here—hook him good, I will. You get up those stairs and you get my partner down here."

It was standoff. Man One, by the door, showed no enthusiasm to be the one hooked. Man Two backed out of range.

"Get him." Altair said. "Get him down here."

"What's it matter?" Man One said. His voice was high with panic.

"This is ridiculous," Man Two said, made an advance and snatched his hand out of range in a hurry.

"I ain't particular which, really," Altair said, and backed and kept her eye on both of them. "Now, you Gallandrys—I'm guessing you're Gallandrys—you ain't of the Trade, but you ain't hightown either; maybe you seen up close what one of these things can do. I can hook up a barrel full to the brim and put 'er where I want—just where you hook it and how you sling. Want to see? One of you might weigh about the same."

Man Two walked over the desk, walked further still, taking himself out of her line of sight. She drew her knife left-handed, right hand to jerk a man into range and left hand to slice or stab.

"On the other hand," she said, "you go and split up like that, I'm going to have to stick him so's I can watch you."

"Hale," Man One said earnestly, against the door. "Hale, get up those damn stairs and get him down here. We don't want to get somebody hurt. He *might* have hired some boatman. Let him answer it."

There was a profound silence. Altair kept both of them in sight; but Man Two, the one he called Hale, had stopped his stalking.

"Let's be sensible," Hale said. "You put that sticker and that hook away and you can come upstairs."

"Let's be better than that. Let's you get him down here. He'll come, right ready. *Friend* of mine. If he won't I'll know you done him some harm, won't I?"

"Get him," Man One said. "Dammit, Hale, get up there."

Hale thought about it. "All right, " he said. "All right. Jon, you stay in front of that door."

Jon thought about that one too. And there was a fine sweat on his face.

"That's all right," Altair said as Hale opened the door and headed up a stairwell, "Jonny-lad, I got no hurry. You just don't move and I'll wait on my partner."

And how much else, Jones? That Hale, he'll either get Mondragon or he'll get a great lot of men and them with swords, and what do you do then, Jones? You're going to die here, Mondragon's going to be real sorry, but this is business, and a tumble and a night out on Dead Harbor don't mean a thing in the world's scales. Way the world runs, Jones. Sorry, Jones. You're about to die here, make part of Gallandry's foundations, you will, or you'll just wash right on down to the boneheap in the bottom of the harbor. Feed the fishes. Real stupid, Jones. What are you doing here? Why ain't you back at your boat?

Mama, I'm sorry. You got any suggestions?

Don't be here.

I wish I wasn't.

Her heart hammered against her ribs now that the imminent threat was abated. Steps creaked across the floor above. Her knees felt like water. She could maybe scare this man out of the way and get that door open before he came at her back—

But there were the bridges to pass. There were either Gallandrys or some other kind of watchers out there and it was the devil's own choice.

She grinned at Jonny-lad, her most engaging let's-be-friends kind of grin. The man looked nervous. "Hey," she said, "you think your partner's got any ideas about bring-. ing back a whole mess of people? I sure hope not."

"Who are you?"

"Ask my partner. Really, I ain't the sort that goes breaking into places. But those fellows out there on the bridges don't look real inviting. You want me to fall into their hands with all *I* know?"

Jonny looked worried at that thought.

"Uhhh. They ain't Gallandry, are they? Who? Who would they be?"

Jonny kept his mouth shut.

"Well, I'll bet you could guess," Altair said. She held the knife up and studied it, and carefully put it away into its sheath, at which Jonny-lad looked at first worried and then a great deal easier. The sweat stood in beads on his brow. And someone was walking upstairs again, a heavier squeaking of beams. The walking reached the landing and headed down at speed. More than one set of footsteps, like half a dozen, down the last steps to the door and the light.

Hale came out that door and something russet came behind him down the steps, ahead of others—Lord, *Mondragon,* all in velvet breeches and a red cost and his pale hair all damp—

—Another of his damned baths.

Beside her, Jonny moved, abandoning defense of the door to the men with drawn swords that poured out of the stairwell behind Mondragon and into the room and around the edges of it. Altair stared, not at them, but at Mondragon, at that lordly creature he had become; at the sight she had imagined suddenly standing there in front of her. Men poured all about her, swords to deal with one canaler and her hook and her knife—it was altogether too much. She stood still, not wanting to be skewered, and one of the long swords came up and batted her hook-hand aside— stand still, that meant plainly. She stood, while Jonny in a fit of bravery came up, grabbed the hook and took it away from her. Fool. If she had decided to die right then Jonny-lad would have gone on his own men's blades and with her foot where it hurt. She stared straight at Mondragon, never quit staring, though one of the Gallandrys came up and grabbed her by the arm, and a second did, hard, so it cut off the blood.

"I want my clothes back," she said. "Hear me, partner?"

His eyes met hers. He stood there staring.

"They going to break my arm?" she asked. And never used his name. "I tell you you got a lot of—" —people outside this place—she started to say; and then went cold inside.

Lord, maybe they're his! Maybe I just spilled something that puts him in a lot of trouble.

"Let her go," Mondragon said sternly. "Jones, you keep your hands from that knife. Hear me?"

He held out his hand, expecting to be obeyed. The men holding her arms let go and the swords angled away.

"Damn nonsense," she said, and advanced on Jonny-lad. "Give me that. Give me that here."

"Give it to her," Mondragon said, and she put out a hand for her barrelhook. To her humiliation that hand was shaking. Badly.

"Give it here, damn you." She held the hand steady as she could. "Or some night I'll hang your guts over the—"

"Jones!" Mondragon said. "Gallandry, give it to her. She's not going to use it."

The big man held it out. She took it and stuck it in her belt, point down in the split place made for it; and dusted herself off and walked over toward Mondragon, who turned his back and walked off through the door and up the stairs.

She trod after him. Behind her Hale was saying something about bolting the door; and armed men followed them up.

Canal-bottom, Altair thought glumly, climbing the old board stairs at Mondragon's back. Bone-pile down at Detmouth. Ancestor-fools, I've done it, I've done it good, old Del and his wife're going to have my boat and the Det's going to have me before all's said and done.

O Lord, Mondragon, what *are* you?

There was a door at the top of the stairs. The Gallandry man in the lead, one of the swordsmen, opened it ahead of Mondragon, walked in and put himself by it as Mondragon and the rest of them came in.

Altair walked out into the room—it was a large room

with too little furniture to fill it, a few tables, most small,
one huge one, a handful of spindly chairs, a yellowed map
hung on the wall. And windows, window after window,
each tall as three men, panes clouded with neglect. Sparse.
Rich men could afford to waste so much room. She had
never imagined it. She turned and put her hands in her
waist and looked at Mondragon, who stood there with the
Gallandry men at his back.

She walked as far as the window and looked out the
cloudy glass. The Port Canal was outside. The balcony
over on third-level Arden was empty except for a casual
stroller. She could not see the second-level bridge. Blue
sky showed over Arden's wooden spires. She glanced back
at Mondragon. "Cozy. You can see everything from up
here."

Give me a cue, Mondragon.

"What are you doing here?"

"Hey, I told you. You owe me."

He stood very still. Finally he walked over to one of the
side tables, unstopped a fine crystal holder and tipped a bit
of amber liquid into one glass and another. He brought
them back and gave her one.

"This poison?" she asked, with him up close and able
to pass her hints with his eyes. Dammit, I'm scared,
Mondragon. Where are the sides in this?

"I thought your taste was whiskey."

She sipped. It went down like water and hit like fire.
The pleasantry went down even better, a little warmth after
the coldness downstairs. He walked away from her as
footsteps sounded on the board stairs and Hale came puffing into the room. "My transportation," Mondragon said
to them. He took a sip of his own glass, held it outward in
a warding-gesture to the others. "I owe her money."

Damn you, Mondragon.

"And a few other things," Mondragon said. He took
another sip, came back and handed the glass to her. "Here,
finish it, Jones. Hale, I want to talk with you."

He walked out behind Hale and three of the others.
Closed the door. Altair stood there with two half-glasses of
whiskey in her hands and a slow fit of rage heating up her

face. Three of the man had stayed. One propped himself,
arms folded, by the door. Two stood grim as death and the
governor's tax.

She slowly poured one glass into the other, held the
result up to the light of the tall window, and walked over
to the nearest chair with a sidetable. She sat down, curling
her bare toes under, and set the empty glass on the frail
little table; leaned back and pushed her cap back to a
precarious tilt and sipped at the whiskey in full sight of the
Gallandrys, keeping them under a heavy-lidded scrutiny.

Owe her *money*. Damn your black heart, Mondragon.

She smiled at the guards. Her right arm had fingermarks,
she knew that it did; it ached up and down.

Rip your guts out, Gallandry. I'll remember your face.
You'll never see mine, some dark night.

Mama said.

I killed a dozen people, mama. Even if they were
crazies. Did it right, I did, one bullet left.

What'd you do now—besides not be here?

The doorlatch moved. Mondragon came back in, with
Hale and the others.

"Jones. Where's that boat of yours?"

She held the whiskey glass and regarded him with a
suspicious eye. "Real nice of you to use my name."

"Jones, it's all right." He walked closer, him in his fine
clothes. "Who was watching the bridges? Anyone you
know?"

She shook her head. "No. I just saw 'em. They saw me
hanging about. Right then I had it figured it wasn't going
to be real smart to walk past 'em. So I walked up and
knocked."

"Where did you leave the boat?"

"That's my business, ain't it?"

"Jones." He beckoned with a finger. Get up. Come on.
She sat there and stared at him. "Come on, Jones." This
time it was the outheld hand.

She tossed off the whiskey, got up and coldly put the
glass in his hand.

His face was as cold. Then slowly his mouth curved into
a smile. He took the glass aside with a flourish of a

lace-cuffed wrist and set it down. "This way, Jones—"
With a gesture toward the far end of the room, and another
door.

She was out of choices. She walked where he told her to
walk, and only Hale went with them. Hale opened the
door onto a place with windows like the other room, but
with real furniture: overstuffed chairs; wall-hangings, car-
pets, papers. There was a stair there, wood polished as sin
with red carpet going up it. Mondragon put his hand on the
newel and motioned her up those steps.

So. She was taking orders for the moment. She climbed
the stairs and Mondragon went closely behind her.

At the top, beyond the first landing, was a second flight
of steps, and an open door beside. She hesitated. Mondragon's hand caught her elbow and propelled her through
the door into an oiled-wood splendor of stuffed flowered
chairs, a flounced poster-bed, and fancy carpet.

She turned about when he let her go. He shut the door
and set his back against it, just the two of them.

"Dammit, Jones. What are you up to?"

"*Up* to? Lord, I thought a poor fool was going to get
hisself thrown into the canal again. I walked along behind,
nice-like, just in case, see—and those skulkers out there—"
She waved a hand at the windows and the rooftops and
towers of Arden beyond. "They cut me off."

He leaned there against the door, and there was still the
flush of sunburn on his face. Or of anger. "You didn't
need to get involved in this."

That was heartening. It was a better tone than she had
heard out of him since setting eyes on him in Gallandry.
Relief turned her joints shivery. "So what do you want? I
got my boat. I know the canals. I spotted them out there—"
She jerked a thumb toward the windows. "—when you let
'em get at your back."

"Not saying what else you did, hanging around outside
and attracting attention."

"Well, you weren't doing a real fine job of watching
yourself! Else how'd *I* track you, huh?"

He said nothing to that.

"They—ain't yours, are they?"

"No." He drew a great breath and walked over to a
nearby chair. He unbuckled his sword and hung it over the
chair finial, reached up and unbuttoned his lace-front collar. "They're not. I think I know whose they are. But now
a quiet pact's been broken. Maybe to the better." He
turned and looked at her again. "Jones. Jones. You didn't
need this kind of trouble."

"Well, I got 'er, don't I?" She walked over and flung
herself down in one of the spindly chairs, caught the cap
before it fell off her head backward, and reset it. "Damn
fool near broke my arm. Try to help a man. Try to see he
gets through the town all right—"

"—try to see where he's going."

"Well, how'm I to see he gets there if I don't see where
he's going?"

"Are you being a fool, Jones?" with that soft gentle
voice. "Jones, you *are* a fool."

"Lot of trouble, huh?"

He walked away to the window and stared out toward
the canal.

"They out there again?"

"I think they'll be quieter about it."

"Who were they?"

He turned back again. "Jones." In a sad tone. "There's
no going anywhere till dark. You want something to eat?"

"I'm not starving."

"Call it favor for favor. I owe you a meal or so. I
ordered something, it ought to be here soon." He gestured
to a side door. "There's a bath in there, the water's not
cold yet, you didn't give it time. Take the aches out."

Heat leaped to her face. She sat there very still, then got
up and took off her cap and dusted it across her leg.
"Sure. Fine. Take the aches out." She walked across the
room and flung her cap into a chair. Unfastened her trousers. "Mondragon, you're going to wash yourself away to
nothing. No wonder you're so damn white."

She walked onto white tiles and stood in front of a great
brass tub—Brass! Lord and my Ancestors. The whole
damn tub. Shining brass.

Smells like a drugshop.

She pulled the sweater off, dropped the pants and stuck a hand into the water. Warm as sunshine. She suddenly remembered the view Mondragon probably had and looked back to kick the door shut.

That for his intentions.

Damn well know what he's up to.

She climbed gingerly over the rim, let herself down into warm water, up to the chin in the perfumed bath.

She had dreamed of things like this, without knowing what to dream of. She had caught the smell of perfume from uptowners and wondered what it was made them smell so clean underneath it.

It was bathing four or five times a day, that was what; it was brass tubs and perfume and soap and water full of oil.

She turned up her right foot and took a brush that floated in the tub and scrubbed the black off the sole, did the same for the other. She took the soap from the tray at the foot and scrubbed her hair and ducked and came up again with perfume in her nose and eyes and sweet-bitter oil in her mouth.

O Lord and Ancestors, the stuff tasted like it smelled.

The light was an oil-light, all gold, with a brass plate to reflect it. There was a water closet across the room and it of brass, with all the accouterments she had seen in a shop window in hightown.

What's that? she had asked her mother. And Retribution Jones had explained how rich people were. How she had learned this, she did not say. But it was true, and there it was, with its outlet right down to the canals, where it gave old Det what everyone did, rich and poor alike.

She tried the taps on the tub. They were like the public water taps from the fill-up tanks, that cost you a penny a can, only this was private, people *owned* these tanks. She sat a heartbeat or two watching it run, then turned it off and got out of the tub to go inspect the watercloset, this supreme elegance. There was paper, *perfumed* paper, to use and throw away, by the Ancestors; rich people wasted *everything*. She used the thing and it worked. She pulled the chain a second time in pure fascination to see the water go down and the bowl fill.

Lord and my Ancestors. And this not even *hightown*.

She went back to her bath and sank down again over her head and came up for the sheer pleasure of it. Soaped and ducked again, and lay there a lazy while with her chin underwater.

The door opened. Mondragon came in coatless, and had a wineglass in his lace-cuffed hand. "Dinner's come," he said, and handed it to her as she slid up as far as her armpits.

"Man, you're trying to get me drunk."

"Of course I am." He settled on the curved rim of the brass tub heedless of water on his fine trousers. "I hope you'll oblige. We've got the whole evening."

She sipped the wine. It was not at all sour like Moghi's. It found whole new flavors after a mouthful went down. She took a second sip and looked up at him. "You figure it's easier to drop me in the canal if I'm drunk."

"Jones." He managed to sound offended.

And a bit of panic took her.

Whole evening—till what?

Del Suleiman was out there with her boat tied up to his; and adding up what she owed by the hour. That rate would go up considerably when he wanted to move on and had a boat in tow. Old Mira could pole her boat on her own behind Del, puffing and swearing all the way: they would move right on up to Hightown Bridge where they always tied up. And begin thinking thoughts like—

—like Jones might not come back. Like something could happen to Jones and they would be rich. Honest as they were, it was a thing to think of.

She drank another sip of the wine. "You going to drop me in the canal or hire me?"

"Here's a robe." He held up the glittery garment. "Want me to help you into it?"

"You're real clever, ain't you?"

He stood up and held it up for her. She stood up and climbed out and slipped one arm through, traded hands on the wineglass and stuck the other through. He wrapped it about her from behind, his touch light and at no time anywhere but her waist. She looked down, outright stared in shock at the shining stuff, all black and gold on her body and dragging about her feet, and her brown hand holding it, callused from the pole and the ropes and barrels. It was crazy. Crazy as all the rest of it. She clutched it up in a careful left fist and followed him out the door, trying not to trip and spill the wine on it. Her hair dripped, soaking her shoulders.

Lord, ain't rich folk careful o' nothing? Don't he care?

There was a heaping tray of food on the little table by the door—Lord, there was *fruit* and there was upriver cheese and there was bread and two pitchers of wine, red and white, and things she could not even identify, like Nev Hettek sausages, only fancy, with dark and light checks and stripes; there was red meat, by the Ancestors, red meat the like of which canalers saw in shop windows uptown and she had never had a taste of in her life.

"Sit down," Mondragon said.

She gathered the silky-stiff fabric around her and settled reverently into one of the fragile-looking chairs in front of this monument. He motioned at her and she let go the robe and snagged a thin slice of meat. It was peppery on the outside and strange on the inside and made as many flavors as the wine she washed it down with.

She tried the sausages each, and the cheeses, and had a real bit of fruit that squished in her mouth with impossible green-stuff flavors—Mondragon composed himself a sandwich, seated opposite, and took his time about it; but she settled on the red meat and the fruit and used her fingers, one slice and a berry, one thin slice and a berry, because other things were rare, but nothing so rare as that.

She hiccupped. And blinked in mortification.

"Have another glass," Mondragon said with calculation.

She took it gravely and stopped the hiccups. There was at the far side of the room that broad real bed, all draped in lacy frills, which was another thing she had never known in her whole life. She drank the wine and looked at that and smelled perfume everywhere. A sudden warm and panicked feeling ran from her head to her toes and down again.

She held the stem of the wineglass in her fingers and looked Mondragon right in the eyes. "I got a boat to get to," she said. "Am I going to get back to it?"

He reached for the wineglass and took it out of her hand, held on to the hand as he set it aside. He looked very close into her eyes. "Jones. They know your face. They know you're with me. I don't know what to do with you, but I'm trying to keep you out of the canal, you understand me? I don't want you hurt. Tonight there's a barge going out of here. You and I are going to be on it. A Gallandry barge, the same as barges come and go all the time—"

"To get past them?"

"If we're lucky."

"Lucky? I got my boat, I got to get back, they'll be watching every boat and barge comes in and out of Gallandry, won't they? Mondragon, that's the damn dumbest thing you could do—*call the law in*, f'Lord's sake—"

"I don't want to do that."

She looked at him. Maybe she was too many drinks along. She found herself staring.

Other side of the law, huh? Gallandrys *too?*

"Where's this barge going?"

"Out to the Grand. Let you off at your boat." He lifted her hand and held it. "Anywhere you like."

"Tell you what, you come with me, I'll make a proper canaler out of you."

He said nothing to that. Only thoughts went on behind his eyes, in that pretty face. "Jones. How drunk do I have to get you?"

"To do what? That bed? Or get in that damn barge with you?"

He took up the glass and put it back in her hand. "Finish that."

She gulped the remaining third down in two swallows. Set the glass down. "I finished."

"Dammit, Jones." He stood up and took her face be-

tween his hands, tilted it painfully up and looked at her so
closely her eyes wanted to cross. "How old are you?"

She flinched back and failed to escape. "What difference does that make?"

"A lot." His hands held hard. "A damnable lot of
difference. Jones, Jones, I know—I know. I come into
your life, first man ever. I shouldn't have done it, I knew
you'd set more on it than I would—than I *can,* Jones,
you're not young but once; and here you toss all that good
sense of yours away and go following after me for no good
reason, no good reason at all. You don't even know what
you want, except you aren't ready to turn loose of that first
time and be like the rest of the world. If you want me to
make love to you, I will. Or you can sleep it off in that
bed over there. In either case I'm going to get you back
where you belong."

She listened; and her face went unbearably hot and then
cold. Her eyes were going to water right there in front of
him, and then she shoved the pain away and laid down the
lid on it and sat on it the way she had learned to do.
Snuffling don't win a thing, Jones. Real world don't *give* a
thing; who said it did? He's being nice, damn him anyhow.

She reached up and laid her hands on his arms ever so
tenderly and soberly. "Mondragon, you sure got an opinion of yourself, don't you?"

He backed up a bit. He dropped his hands. Maybe there
was a bit of flush in *his* face.

"Now," she said, seizing on that little shred of power,
"what you got, Mondragon, is me in a terrible mess, with
those skulkers out there knowing my face and all. And you
having handed my name out so nice to the Gallandrys.
Thanks a lot."

"They won't hurt you."

"If you think *that* you're younger'n I am."

"They're not interested in you."

"Well, they are now. I embarrassed Jonny-boy and
Hale real bad."

"Then why did you walk into it, dammit?"

"I told you. No, you could've introduced me nice.
Could've said, hey, this is Jones, she's a good'un, you

want a job done, call Jones. You wouldn't do that. Now I got trouble with them.''

"Well, *you* bought it. I told you stay out of my business."

"Well, what would you do? Let a fellow walk off with his head all cracked and him in a strange town and his belly full of my breakfast, I might add!''

He took her by both arms and pulled her right off her chair, right up to her feet and shook her.

"Jones, this isn't a game."

"I been trying to tell you that."

"Jones, for God's sake."

She was shivering. She did not know why but a tremor got started in her muscles. Maybe it was his hand hurting the bruise on her arm which went all the way to the bone.

"What am I going to do with you?"

"I dunno. You could start by not breaking my arm."

He let go and pushed up her sleeve and looked at it. The bruise showed already, distinct fingermarks. "Lord. I'm sorry."

"Hey, that's fine." She reached up and patted his face. "That's fine." The wine and the double whiskey hit all at once, a slight fuzziness about everything. She wobbled and blinked at him. Her eyes might be crossing for sure this time. "I don't mind."

He gathered her up and picked her up. She let out a yell, not convinced anyone could pick her up without dropping her, and grabbed his neck so that he did go off his balance: it was a panic passage across the floor until she did fall; and landed on the bed; and he came down with his hands on either side of her.

"Dammit, Jones!"

She lay there with the alcohol spinning round and round and blinked at him. He recovered himself and pulled the robe off her and threw the covers back. "Under."

She got under. He threw the covers over her and walked off.

"Where you going?" She was honestly confused.

"I'm going," he said, "to get similarly drunk."

"Oh," she said. *Oh.* While it was sinking in. Then it lay at her gut and hurt so that she turned over on her side

and hugged the overstuffed pillow. She watched him for-
lornly, while he poured himself another glass of wine,
took the bottle with him, and sat down in the overstuffed
chair. When the one glass was gone he poured another.

His face had no more sunny lightness. With the fancy
clothes, with this place, it had gone all somber, full of
thoughts. He was not the man she had known out there,
the man who laughed and whose eyes danced. He was
someone the Gallandrys were afraid of, that was what. He
was someone a lot of people might be afraid of. He had
that way about him.

He came to bed finally. She felt the mattress give and
woke up, for one dizzy moment trying to remember where
she was and why she was lying on something soft and
steady with dim daylight coming through tall windows.
Then her mind caught up and she looked over at Mondragon;
but he lay there on his back with his eyes shut and she
sensed he wanted to be let alone.

She lay there with hers open for a while, and looked
back across the room where a pitcher of wine stood all but
empty on the table.

He trusts the Gallandrys, she thought, adding it up: parts
of her mind went on even when it was hazed. He's trying
to rest. Maybe he hurts. He's talking about a barge and
tonight and he's trying to rest up while he can.

Make love. He ain't any kid. He's got his mind full of
something, that's what, he'd do that to keep me quiet, but
he don't want to, he don't want me, he don't need any kid
tagging after him, don't need anybody crazy to come in
and do God knows what at the wrong time—You got him
shouting, Jones; this ain't a man who yells, and here he is
drinking hisself numb and blind.

You got him worried, Jones.

What've you got, huh? Man scared of the law. Man
with nasty friends and nastier enemies.

She shut her eyes and drifted again in a vague, heart-
aching nowhere.

Woke in the dark in a tangle of his limbs and hers, with
someone banging at the door. "I hear you, I hear you,"
Mondragon bellowed back coming up on his arms and

leaning over her. "Give me time, dammit!" And put a hand in the middle of her by accident. He felt his way to her face and patted it. "Sorry. Sorry."

She groped dazedly at his arm. "'S all right. I'm all right."

His hand wandered to her shoulder, than patted her cheek again. Like love. Distractedly. "Damn. Got to get up. Get moving. Come on."

He got out of bed, leaving a draft. It was hard to move. Every muscle she had protested, not major aches, but little ones; and her back and her bruised arm felt afire. She put her feet out and walked a few paces, feeling her way past unfamiliar furniture. There was a dim wick burning in the bath, there was starlight from the tall windows, and Mondragon cracked the hall door open, sending another dim light into the room as he snagged something off the floor outside. He closed it and came to her where she clung dazedly to the back of an armchair. "We've got to dress in the dark," he said, "we don't want to show any more lights in the house than normal. Here. Sweater and pants. Ought to fit. I'm not sure about the shoes. They guessed."

Shoes. Lord! Socks. And clothes clean as never-worn. She held them to her nose and smelled them, and it was new-smell. She had never had new. She smelled the leather-smell of the shoes that was heady as a cobbler's shop. The whole business set her heart to pounding and sent prickles up her back: new clothes, the dark, the stealth that was no game at all; no. She imagined blackrobed skulkers down on the bridges, lurking down by the barge-dock of Gallandry—we're after getting killed and he's worried about new clothes, him and his baths and baths and baths, probably thinks I smell bad as old Muggin. Her mouth tasted awful. She saw him head for the bath, a shadow against the nightlight, and went over to the table to wash her mouth out with the wine while he took care of business there. Water rushed and gurgled. She pulled on the pants and they fit; pulled on her sweater and the socks, and shoved her feet into the shoes. They were snug and they pinched, but they did all right. She stood up and stamped one foot and the other, then went after Mondragon, to that glimmer of light that came out the bathroom door: her shoes showed, when she looked down, shiny-new with a fancy buckle on each, and fine black socks under blue cord knee-britches. Lord, fine as a kept poleboatman's, the whole outfit was.

"Uhhn." Mondragon splashed water, got his eyes clear and offered her his toothbrush.

Toothbrushes, shoes with buckles, and them trying to kill us! It all took on a dreamlike unreality, her face lamplit in the hanging mirror as Mondragon made room for her. She dipped a toothbrush in soda, scrubbed and spat—"Water drinkable?" she asked prudently, same as one had to know which public tap was which. "Safe," he said; and she turned the tap and washed out her mouth. Mondragon lent her his towel and went off and out the door.

Am I clean? Did I do everything he'd do? Does he think I'm dirty?

She scrubbed a second time with soap, and started to dose herself with a perfumy lotion she found in the bottle on the lavatory, but a prudent thought came to her: Damn, those bullyboys'll get wind of us that way sure.

She scrubbed her hand off, shivering suddenly as if it had become deep winter. Her teeth wanted to chatter. She used the watercloset and hurried out again, fearful of being left. Mondragon had put on a dark shirt: his face stood out pale in the starlight, disappeared and reappeared as he pulled a sweater on. The light winked coldly off the hilt of the rapier as he picked it up and belted it on. The trousers were dark as the rest.

"If you want not to be seen," she said through chattering teeth, "get something over that head of yours."

"I've got it." A shadow fluttered across his hands, became a scarf; he tied it at his nape and it was only his face that stood out. "Your knife and your hook are on that table with your belt."

She gathered her knife-belt up and buckled it on. Looked back and saw him like a stranger in the starlight.

"Lord, you're grim as death." And then wished she

hadn't said that. She tugged her sweater down in back and
snatched a lump of cheese off last night's plate as Mondragon
headed for the door.

Leaving this place. This luxury. This safe haven. This
last place she might ever see him if things went wrong
down there on that loading dock. The dim light of the hall
shafted through the opened door. "Come on," Mondragon
said. She came, hurrying, and pocketed the cheese.

And made one dive back in the dark, to the chair where
she had thrown her cap and the bathroom floor where she
had left her old clothes. She wound them into a bundle
under her arm, pulled her cap on and set it firm even while
she rushed for the door; and out then into the light with
Mondragon beside her. He caught her arm and headed
down the steps.

Chapter 5

IT was down the stairs once, and through to the plain room with the map—a group of shadows waited there in the starlight from the tall windows, and Altair hung back against Mondragon's grip on her arm. But he was going forward among them, and she went, his hand on her left arm, her other clenched tight on her bundle of clothes. Her heart beat hard against her ribs and her new shoes hurt her feet.

It was Hale and some of the others. She was not glad of the company. The great tall windows gave her the shivers; she imagined faces peering in the starlit glass (but no one could climb those walls on Port Canal; the balcony on this side of Gallandry was a level below) and she imagined black figures flowing along the bridges, along the balconies, down by the water where they had to go next—

Are you thinking of that Mondragon? These ain't good men, these Gallandrys. Can you trust them? Do you know how they are, do you know they got to push and push and beat a body down if she talks back, do you know they're cowards and maybe none too honest, 'cause thief goes with coward like salt with fish, mama said. Coward's only another word for cheat, take the easiest way, most comfortable way. Mama said.

(Retribution Jones with the pistol in her fine brown hands, oiling it down. And young Altair sitting there with the shivers in the sunlight, because her mother was talking quietly about a landsman who reneged on a deal. They found that man floating in the Snake come Monday, and her mother pursed her lips and said: ''Well,'' when Muggin told the news, a cleaner Muggin in those days. But her mother never said more than that.)

Altair caught her breath and kept the new shoes quiet as she could as Mondragon pulled her along in the wake of the Gallandrys. Through a dark door—

"Mind your step," Hale said; and Mondragon held her arm tightly as she groped for the banister of a stairs.

Down and down, in total dark. She freed her arm, shifted her clothes-bundle and clung carefully to the bannister as she went down the steps on new slick soles, blind in the dark with a cluster of Gallandry men about her and them all smelling of foreign stuff and waterfront and something her nose could not identify past the soft familiar canal-smell of the old clothes in her arm and the bath-smells on her skin. There was too much rush. They jostled her. Mondragon crowded her behind, down and down until they picked up a little light two levels down. A nightlight was in its niche; it flared and leapt and set their shadows to jumping in huge perspective on the walls and on the stairs as they came around this last turn. Her knees shook: a half dozen grown men slinking about like this and all of them clinking and rattling with swords and knives—What are you doing here? she heard her mother ask in her mind. She saw Retribution shake her dark head and look at her with stern disapproval. Altair, what in this sorry world are you doing?

I wish I knew, mama.

Forgive me, Angel.

It's this man—

She came down off the last step with her knees like to collapse to shivers under her and her feet all but numb in the pinch of the shoes and the socks—Damn, if I've got to skip fast I can't do 'er. She flexed her toes with a resolute effort, and watched solemnly as the men around her while Hale unbolted another door: the gold light flared in the draft as it opened and cast sinister lights on somber faces. Mondragon in his black scarf and his dark clothes was all hollow-cheeked and hawk-nosed and grim as any hangman. He turned that face her way as the men started through the dark beyond; he caught her arm and pulled her along with him—

—He don't trust 'em. Stay with me, he's saying. Lord, I *hope* that's what he's saying.

She drew a long breath as she went into the black closeness of a tunnel that smelled of old brick and damp and mold. Someone closed the door at their backs and it was utterly black then.

"Not far," someone said; Mondragon's hand squeezed her arm.

Lord, they could murder us both, they could take us here, this is Gallandry territory, they know this dark, we've come down near the water and it's an easy thing to dump us in and no one the wiser.

Someone up ahead opened a door before any of them could have gotten to it. It just opened, with less dark there than elsewhere, a trick of the eyes and the lap of water louder than the noise they made walking. It was the kind of sound water would make under a building vault, an echoey noise. Gallandry Main Cut, that was where they had come out: she had poled past it all her life.

They came out into that dark watery vault, that got only the ghostly starlight bounced from outside and not much of that. A black huge shape loomed up in front of them in the Cut, an impression of something blacker than the rest of the place and moving to the waves, and this was the barge. Black human figures moved along the narrow stone dock, silhouetted against starlight-on-water outside, going about their business of tending this monster in a deathly hush.

There was movement at their side; a scuff of a leather sole. Mondragon tugged at her arm and she went where he led. Someone led him, someone else crouched down waiting for them at dock-edge where a shadow-plank went up to that barge—no, two someones, one on a side, who knelt there and reached out to keep them steady as Mondragon headed up that plank—Damn. Unexpected cross-boards and the shoes made her feet slip with their unaccustomed heels: she felt Mondragon falter and recover on the tilted, moving surface; felt a hand reach up the inside of her knee and close hard, nothing familiar, a man trying to keep her

upright. A second shove steadied her on the other side,
and she caught her balance, clutched her bundle and made
a quicker, steadier step as the plank rose and fell with the
surge, sure of the cross-board interval now. Two more
Gallandrys waited at the deckside end of the plank to
steady them as they came off it; and as they hit the narrow
wooden sideboard that ran around the huge cargo well.
She knew these craft. She walked that narrow rim carefully, shook her arm to free it of Mondragon's assisting
hand as she walked after the shadow-figure to the deck-
edge and the ladder. The guide waited there, stopped her
and gripped her sore arm. "Step," the man whispered,
and gave her unwanted help, hauling her along down the
short railless ladder to the well. Then he pushed her head
and shoulders down and shoved her onto her knees toward
the barge's version of a hidey, which was a cavern com-
pared to a skip's.

She went in pushing her bundle of spare clothes in front
of her on the slats, and crouched there facing the dark
inside with the panic fear someone in that black hole might
be waiting to grab her and do God knew what, and her not
knowing whether to defend herself or not. Her teeth started
to chatter and she clenched them. She heard faint footsteps
thump overhead and on the boards outside and turned
around as someone else came in after her.

A hand groped out, brushing her leg. "That you?" she
whispered, hoping it was Mondragon, stifling a reaction if
it was not.

"It's me," the whisper came back; and it had better be.
The owner of it crouched down and felt his way up her leg
and put his arm around her, hugging her close against him.
She had not been shivering since upstairs. She began to
then, and tried to stop. It was the hour, it was being roused
out of bed and bundled out without breakfast, a body
always shivered when she was waked prematurely and had
to work in chill. His arm tightened as if he thought it was
terror, damn him. He trusted this lot of pirates and knew
where he was going on their barge.

"Yo," someone called out, meaning they were starting
to make natural noise now, just a barge going out of

Gallandry the way big barges had to, by night. A lantern flared, bright after all that dark: the deep empty well of the barge showed bare slats and a clutter of folded tarps and coils of rope. Shadows moved crazily across the narrow view of vaulted ceiling and disappeared into the dark of the canal. Steps thumped on the deck overhead, bargemen cursed and made ordinary conversation.

"They'll *know*," she objected to Mondragon.

"They'll know, I don't doubt. But they'd have to do something about it."

The engine coughed and coughed under its crank. Caught and tunked away till the helm engaged the screw and the resistance brought the engine down to a steady low thump and echo in the confined Cut. Water surged and washed aft. "Ware cable," someone yelled, which meant they were casting off. Altair felt the motion and put her arm about Mondragon's waist, her head against his shoulder. Cold. Lord, this place was cold. The engine beat and beat its power into her bones.

Big barge could ride a small boat under. Engine noise lumping through the night was no strange thing: biggest barges always moved by night, avoiding traffic. Their lonely sounds haunted the dark—rare, thank the Ancestors; from time to time a bell tolled on darkest nights: Ware, ye little folk, give way, give way, the giant'll roll ye down, grind ye to splinters, send your bones to old Det. Moor a skip too wide beneath the bridges when such as this wanted through and it was ruin; she had seen the like once. Man, woman, and a boy ridden down one rainy night that canalers tied up too numerous beneath the Midtown Bridge; voices screaming, canalers trying in chorus to make themselves heard—Fools, her mother had said after, couldn't have stopped that barge nohow, they knew it. But a body yells anyhow. Makes the gut feel better. —A horrid scrape of wood on iron. Splintering sounds. Cries of rage; and that great black shadow chugging on through the rain, wreckage bobbing near Midtown pilings.

That great black shadow held them in its gut now, and eased out of its berth in the bowels of Gallandry, engine disengaged for the moment as they slewed round up Port Canal.

The engine took hold again, lump, lump, lump. She shivered again. Mondragon's arm tightened around her.

"Where's this thing going?" she asked.

"Right now, to the Grand. It slows and you step off—"

"The hell I will."

"—at the turn. It'll bring up a few seconds on the far bank. You can do it. I know you can."

"You with me?"

"I've got other business. I told you. You go back to your boat."

"The hell I *can*. You trying to kill me?"

"You go somewhere and lie low then. The noise won't last. I swear to you. Look." Mondragon shifted and fished after something about his middle, took her hand and put two round, flat metal objects into it. "That's gold, Jones. That's two sols, it's the best I can do: hide yourself and hide that boat awhile—buy some supplies and go anchor out in the bay. Buy yourself an anchor while you're at it. They can't come at you out there: this is city trouble."

She thought she had run out of shivers finally. One sharp tremor ran through her. The gold pieces lay in her hand, huge and heavy and unfamiliar. She had never so much as touched a gold piece like that. Not one. It was a fortune in her palm. "I can't use these damn things, I show these round, they'll call the law on me, I can't walk *in* a place they'll change these pieces. Dammit, Mondragon, you got no sense! Hide me, hide my boat—man gives me what I can't use and gives me advice how to keep away from trouble—how good's your advice, from a man who'd dump my best and only skillet in harbor water?"

"Hush." He touched her face, laid a finger on her lips. Tipped her chin up and followed it with a kiss, the night all giddy with the thumping of the engine, this crazy business of hiding in a barge's gut. She caught her breath.

"Jones," he said. "You'll do all right. I have confidence in you."

"I ain't going."

"You're going," he said softly.

"Maybe I'll just find the law, maybe I'll tell the black-legs just what—"

He stopped her mouth with a hard grip. "You could die. You could *die*, Jones. You hear me?"

She bobbed her head. He took his hand away. It had bruised her jaw.

"So you get off this barge," he said. "You take what I gave you, go take care of yourself. I haven't got time to."

"Where was *my* time? Where was *my* 'haven't got time to' when I fished you out of the harbor, where was me shivering my teeth loose keeping you warm all night and maybe losing the only damn customers I got while I'm keeping you away from them damn killers, huh?"

The engine chugged on. Water whispered under the hull.

"I can't ever pay you," he said. "That's all. I can't ever pay you. Do what I told you."

"In a—"

Water showered and thundered down into the well, over the deck, pouring down from above; Lord, *no*, not water: there were fumes. "Damn!" Altair cried, wiping her eyes from the splash and scrambling to her haunches. And: *"Ware, hey!"* from a bargeman above. Fire meteored down into the well, a lantern that shattered, glared, and licked out fire, fire running in instant tongues, serpents of fire flaring up in the bilge, through the wooden slats toward them. "My God, my God," Altair cried, and shoved at Mondragon in panic fear: *out, out* of this hole!

He was dragging at her in the same moment, and the fire leaping up in their faces, running under the slats that floored the hidey the same as the well. It was inferno, instant and complete: searing heat and glare in their faces, men screaming and herself with a fistful of Mondragon's sweater as she scrambled for the stairs, him grabbing at hers, and it was both of them on the stairs at once, trying to climb to the deck with a sheet of flame at left and hellish glare off brick and doorways at right.

She grabbed her cap and dived, still with a fistful of sweater; and he came with her all in one wild wobble for balance, all legs and change of center. She fell sideways,

water solid as a floor when she hit, and the breath near left
her. She kicked, clothing weighted with water, hunting the
surface with Mondragon's sweater still in one fist. She felt
him kick and let him go as of a sudden something huge
and rough brushed her shoulder—God, the barge, the
propeller—O *God*—She heard the thumping getting nearer
and kicked in cold panic, ran into Mondragon or someone
and broke the surface with the glare of fire everywhere,
with fire running and burning on the water, and the giant
black shape of the barge a moving wall as it slewed about
and ground against a brick wall. She saw other splashes of
hell-lit water, other dark heads bobbing, fighting for their
lives. Doors opened. Alarm bells pealed and boomed.

Fire! Fire on the canal!

She trod water and cast about wildly, saw Mondragon's
pale face close at hand. He shouted something against the
roar of the fire, waved toward the bank, and waved again.

She discovered herself clutching the damned cap, thought
of letting go and then in profoundest bewilderment simply
slapped it on her head, water and all, and struck out
swimming. Clothing dragged at her, had her breathing in
great gasps, scissor kicking and dogpaddling and any other
stroke that gave her room to breathe. It was Mars over
there. It was Mars' narrow rim, and crowds appeared
suddenly everywhere, black figures pouring out onto bridges, onto walkways, desperate cries and shrieks drowning
in the roar of the fire.

The bank loomed up, closer and closer, a blank wall
there, where Mars had sunk: window-arches and former
doors were bricked, the old ground-floor filled, the merest
rim of the old walk left as a tilted slab a boat had to
remember the breadth of when it skirted that isle. Mondragon
pulled ahead of her with hard strokes, hit that sloping shelf
and floundered ashore with a firelit splash of water as he
staggered to his feet, turned and caught his balance. He
had lost the black scarf: his pale hair was plastered down
around his face. Somehow he had kept the rapier; it swung
at his side, its guard winking as he got down on one knee
on the submerged and tilted edge and leaned out with his
hand outheld to her.

She mustered a last few hard kicks, calm and sane, and reached up to his grasp, reached up a second hand when he grabbed after it, and he rose up and backstepped, pulled her out with her scrambling after footing and near taking them both in before he caught his balance and held on to her—"God," she said, and choked and just leaned on him breathing and with her clothes weighing half as much as herself.

"Come on." He faced her about, got her into motion, his hand on her elbow. She went, splashing along with him, trying to flail her arms for balance, but his grip tightened about her left arm and he pulled her faster: she gasped and spat water that ran down from her hair and her cap, and nigh tore her knees keeping her balance on the outside of the ledge where his hold put her. Her feet went: the ledge just quit; and she went in up to her waist before he hauled her up again and she scrabbled to solid stone, gasping and feeling a stitch in a rib.

Then they reached clear ground, staggered round the corner and full into a crowd of locals trying to get a floating-boom across the side canal, to stop the fire that might come drifting that way on the water. The crowd yelled, vague angry shouts, curses at two wet fugitives who might have some responsibility in the calamity—"That your boat?" one yelled, dropping his part of the makeshift boom to grab at Mondragon. "That your boat out there?"

"No!" Mondragon yelled back, his voice deep and furious. "We were on a poleboat, the damned barge nearly killed us!"

It was quick, it was credible, Mondragon's hightown accent, the outraged uptown passenger who would have nothing conceivable to do with a barge—it confused the man, who let Mondragon tear past, dragging her with him; and now Altair tried to run in earnest, past other arriving crowds. Two wet people now were far enough away from the immediate calamity they might be soaked firefighters, and they had the advantage of moving fast, before questions could get organized. Altair gasped for air and squished along in sodden, weak-kneed jolts.

A vaster pealing added itself to the night—the great bell

of the Signeury ringing in alarm: *Help, fire, catastrophe, turn out, turn out!*

Mondragon reached Mars' north stair at the landing, laid his hand to the rail and headed up, hauling her along. She gasped like a fish and stumbled on the steps, caught herself with her left hand as Mondragon hauled on her sore right arm.

Then it was a gentle jog, thumping across the boards of Mars' north bridge over to Wex, and onto that balcony, on which a scattered few shopkeepers ran toward the fire with hand-pumps and fending-poles. On the higher bridges crowds gathered, peering out toward the site of the fire which glowed like an unnatural sun in the city. The great Signeury bell tolled its alarm. People passed them on the balcony, distraught: "What is it?" one cried, catching at Altair's arm.

"Barge," she gasped over her shoulder, and Mondragon pulled her on and on, around the corner of Wex to the Splice, where a bridge led over to Porfirio.

Sedate walk then. Two drenched fugitives walking, one holding the other, down the boards, ignoring stares. Mondragon turned off at Porfirio Stair, where it led down to the landing; and it was down and down the steps till they were on canalside again, black water lapping at the stone walk. It was a quiet place, a warehouse on this side of Porfirio, its iron gates shut. Mondragon stopped and let her go and leaned against the corner of the door-inset, and she leaned her back against the iron door itself and held her aching side and just breathed for a moment. Mondragon's face shone pale in the starlight, fair hair starting to dry and curl.

"Where we going?" Altair asked.

"I don't know," he said.

"Don't know!" She yanked her sodden cap off and slapped it against her leg. "Damn, then why you been pulling *me*?"

He looked all blank for a moment, even offended, then gestured wildly at the bridges above them. "What do you want?" he asked, voice cracking. "Stand gawking in the crowd, dripping wet? Go back to Gallandry? They'll have ambush laid at every bridge.''

"Then ask someone who knows the town, dammit! Come on.''

He stood fast. "Where do you have in mind?''

She jerked her head in general toward her own territory, toward the Grand. The heavy bell of the Signeury dinned calamity into the night and jarred along her nerves. She sorted and discarded a dozen possible refugees in an eyeblink. "We got to walk there. Damn, we go up to a boat wet as we are, we got questions, and questions we don't need. Got to be somewheres we can walk. Moghi's. Moghi or Liberty'd do 'er for—Lord!'' She plunged her hand into her right pocket. Against all expectation her fingers met two metal rounds she had not remembered putting there. Instinct had done it, unthought. Her knees went to water. She took her hand out carefully without bringing the coins to light. "I got 'em, I got 'em, oh, Lord, I got 'em.'' she began to shake all over. "Come on.'' She grabbed at his arm. "Come on, dammit! We waiting on your friends?''

· He brushed off her hand and took her by both arms. "Jones—''

"Listen, you going to be a damnfool? Damnfools go cheap in this town. Ain't just your friends in the hoods can cut your throat. You go walking along canalside at night looking like you got two coppers, they'll find you when you float. You hear me?''

His fingers relaxed. He was listening.

"I know this place,'' she said on her next breath. "You going to trust me? We been going the wrong damn direction. Now come on, before sun comes up on us and you and me are too public.''

"Jones, they'll kill you.''

"I kind of figured that.'' Damn, folk pouring tanks of fuel off bridges onto barges, folk setting fires on the canals. The heavy bell of the Signeury still tolled, dinning calamity into the air. The noise rattled her brains, the enormity of it sank into her bones like the enormity of what she had in her pocket. She locked her arm into

Mondragon's and faced about; and when she turned the sky was orange above the dark, jagged hulk of Wex and Mars. "Lord! Look at that! If that fire gets beyond those booms, it could take the whole damn city—"

"Where are we going? Back there?" His voice said no. She shook at him, pointed off southwest.

"Gallandry's that way, and not far. So they got it watched. We're on the Grand, almost, we go up a level, we got Oldmarket Bridge, and we go over east and we go down canalside."

He hesitated. Took her arms then. "Jones. Jones, Boregy. That's where I'm going."

"The Ten." *Old* money. Next the Signeury. She stood still. Smoke wafted on the wind and the windward side of her wet body began to chill. "Friends of yours, huh?"

"You think if we got to your boat you could get me that far?"

"To do what?"

"I'm asking about the boat. Can you do it?"

"To do what, dammit?"

No answer. None but that stare of his. Her teeth started chattering; she hugged her arms about herself.

"Jones, it's all right."

"Damned if it is." She clenched her teeth and hugged herself with one arm and hooked a gesture off eastward. "We got to go across the Grand no matter what. I'm freezing. Come on."

He came, gave her his arm and pulled her close, so at least it was warmer on that side as they walked along the side of Porfirio, along the Splice.

Damn, tell me to go find my boat, will you? That's what you're about—Go off and find your boat, Jones, go get your throat cut, never mind the questions, Jones, never mind who it is that don't mind a bit pouring oil into Port Canal and trying to burn the city down—no, no, you don't need to know that, do you? Damn him.

She sneezed. "Damn."

"I'm sorry."

"You got an attraction to water, you know that?" Her feet hurt when she walked, heavy wet socks, new shoes that pinched, and all waterlogged. It was all one with the rest of the misery, wind chilled her right side; and numbness promised relief soon for her feet. The air stank of burning, even here, and the bell went on and on.

Around the north of Porfirio, over to sight of Oldmarket Bridge. He slowed to a stop here, against the brick wall of Porfirio. The Grand spread itself wide and dark under the pilings of the bridge. Boats ought to ride here at mooring, five or six at least huddled together out of the current—they had night-rights there; she knew their names, knew who belonged and who did not. There was only one boat tied there at present, a ramshackle little skip tucked up under the shadow of the Oldmarket Stair.

"Stay put." Altair went out around the broad shelf of the landing, peered down the dark length of the canal, toward Midtown Bridge. and the outflow of Port Canal. No light of fire. *That* was good news. It had not escaped Port. Yet. She glanced back, to be sure Mondragon stayed put.

She caught his worried look. She signaled quiet and walked quietly along the landing, quietly as she could in this eerie desertion. There were only a few boats in sight even farther down the Grand's dark waters, and those were steadily retreating. Canalers had moved when that alarm bell rang, any fool would. They had headed fast as they could either down the Grand to help stem the fire, or they outright ran in panic, having visions of the whole of wooden Merovingen going up like so much tinder—ran down the canal or up toward the Rock and the sullen flow of the Greve, where they might be out of danger if the whole town caught fire.

Only this one has stayed. And Lord and the Ancestors only knew where Del Suleiman might have taken her boat. He *would* have taken it. Powered up and towed it behind if he got worried enough to want speed.

She walked carefully round the stairs. She saw the ragged tarp shielding part of the well of the skip that sheltered there at tie. Its sides were weathered, silvery-wooden in the starlight in what patches showed in the shadow. Old boat; boat going the way of its owner, one of the sort that huddled along in traffic with other boats, trying not to leave safe company. "Hey," she said, to let the occupant know she was no land-dweller. "Hey the boat."

The shadowy tarp curtain drew back on an edge. An eye looked out, a wisp of white hair in the starlight and deep shadow.

"Jones," Altair identified herself. She hooked a thumb toward the canal. "They got a barge afire down there. Got cut off from my boat, I did. Trying to find where old Del Suleiman took 'er."

"He ain't been here." The old voice was a little stronger. "Retribution? Is it Retribution?"

Altair came a little closer. "Mintaka?"

The curtain widened. All of a frizzy white head came out. "What's going on down there? What be it?"

"They got a fire, that's what. A bad 'un." Altair sank down on her heels, winced at sore feet and caught her balance on her hand. "Left you here, huh?"

"Them damn fools. I ain't going off down there." The voice quavered. It was not age, not petulance. It was outright terror. "Retribution's dead."

"My mama. She died five years ago. You want me to move your boat for you?"

Coward, Jones. Callous.

But, damn, she's in worse danger here. Damn them all that left her. What's the Grand coming to? Where's Muggin tonight? Where's all the old 'uns?

"You do that?"

"My boat's somewheres that way." She pointed off toward the south, toward trouble. Mintaka never looked. "I tell you what, you give me a ride and I pole your boat for you, huh? Get you back where there's people."

Mintaka's chin wobbled. "It's my arthritis. Sometimes I can push 'er, sometimes I can't. I think I'd rather die than push 'er down there. What could I do? Push and shove with all them boats? Get caught in the fire, that's what."

"Well, I'll get you through. You wait a minute. I got a man here—uptowner; he got soaked down there, you won't mind if I bring him along."

"I dunno, I didn't say no other—"

Afraid. It was a habit with the old loners. "Hey," Altair said, "he's a nice 'un." She looked over her shoulder where Mondragon waited in Porfirio's shadow. "Ser. You want to come over here, let Gran have a look at you, tell her you ain't any trouble?"

Mondragon came, not cheerfully. He came close and sank down on his heels beside her and the little skip. "M'sera," he said gravely.

Mintaka gave a strange little laugh. It was the *m'sera*, for sure. Then she went wary and sober again. "My boat ain't no poleboat."

"M'sera, she's a very welcome boat, and I'd be glad to pay you."

Mintaka's eyes went round. It was the *pay* that did that. "He all right, huh?"

"He's fine, gran Mintaka." Altair stood up and untied the single mooring rope with a jerk of a slipknot. Held the skip hard against the landing. "You want to step aboard, ser, sort of duck down under that tarp—He got soaked, like I said, gran. Hair's all wet—you got a scarf? Got something to keep him warm? I'll buy 'er off you next week."

"Oh, I got 'er," Mintaka said, "I do got her."

Mondragon stepped to the rim and dropped down into the well; the skip rocked, rocked again as Altair snubbed the rope about the post and offered the end to Mintaka. "Hey, you want to hold that snub, gran?"

Mintaka got herself up, limped her bent way forward and took the rope, while Altair ran alongside and made a jump for the halfdeck before it swayed out too far. Her feet shot pain to her nerves. She winced and recovered herself and took the pole from the rack.

"Let 'er free, gran."

The old canalrat pulled the snub and Altair put the pole in and shoved off, letting the skip take the gentle current to get the bow clear—hard to manage a skip when there was no option to run forward, the tarp-shelter being in the way: it was necessarily slower. But the skip was the lightest she had ever handled, no motor behind, not much freeboard either, just a light shell that rode the water like a poleboat, with a commendable trim. "Hey, she's good," Altair sang out, to please the old woman, "handles real sweet, she does."

"She does, she does," Mintaka said, and came along the slats with a canaler's rolling gait, hunched as she was. Mondragon crouched down and headed under the tarp, and Mintaka lifted the tarp edge and peered under. "Ser, you make yourself liberal there, don't mind my mess."

"You go on in with him, gran," Altair said. "He won't mind."

"I got a cap for 'im," Mintaka said, and bent down. "Son, c'n you feel about a bit and find a sack, she'll be right over to the starb'd—"

There was a bit of to-do. There were several sacks. Altair poled them out into starlight and sent the little skip scudding along at a fair rate; and Mintaka kept on at her chatter, hunting the proper sack.

"Gran," Mondragon said from inside, "come on in, I truly wish you would."

"Well," Mintaka said, and finally dithered her way inside. A nervous chuckle then, over the gentle whisper of the water. "Been a long time since I had a handsome fellow to myself in the hidey, you're such a nice boy. You got a wife?"

"No," Mondragon said in a small, definite voice. Altair gave the boat a cheerful shove.

That for you, Mondragon. Serves you right, got yourself cornered, have you? Old woman's not so old as that, is she, Mondragon?

"Here she be," came the old voice, "here she be—got all my yarns. Ogh, you do be wet, don't you? Here, here, here we be. Folk give me yarn scrap, sometime give me yarn to do up for 'em—I knit real fancy, me hands being stiff all the same—here, here, I wish I had a light, can't afford a light, 'cept my little cookstove. I do up sweaters, real fine sweaters, ain't no man wearing one of my sweaters going to catch sick, I make the stitches fine, I tell you, you ever want a good sweater, you give me the yarn, I do you a sweater better'n you get in hightown. Do you a scarf, do you nice warm socks. . . ."

The skip glided under the starlight and Altair watched the canalside at every weaving step, this side and that. Barred windows and iron shutters showed on canal level; old brick and old board and old stone, and here and there one of Merovingen's feral cats, stopping to stare with fixed curiosity at the unusual sight of a solitary skip on a wide black canal.

Must be a good one, cat, that set-to down there. You can still see the glow. Lord, I bet a bridge caught. Probably cut 'er down quick, Lord, salvage to be had, even to the charcoal. If it don't spread.

". . . I had me twenty, thirty lovers," Mintaka was saying to her prisoner. "Oh, I moved light in them days, I used ter wear a feather in me cap an' I used to work that skip with me ma and me pa—Min, pa used ter say—"

Altair looked back. It was black, empty water, dancing to city lights; a web of bridges above. Eerie solitude all about. Ahead, Midtown Bridge spanned the Grand, pilings abundant at either end and clear water to the middle where barge traffic came, a sheen of deep water there.

And beyond, down by Port outlet, a scattering of boats like shadows, reflecting nothing, on water-shine that reflected fire.

Lord. Is it on the Grand now? Those'll be boats after the city penny, them as got strong backs, keeping those fire-booms where they belong.

She kept up the pace, long since warmed, the feet long since numb.

Better to go barefoot, got no time to tend to it, don't hurt much now, anyhow.

She spared a hand to lift her cap and rake her hair with her fingers, settled it again. Took a sharp look to starboard where a small huddle of boats remained.

Old folk. Same as gran Mintaka. Same as Muggin.

The bow came into the open again, and Altair kept a steady pace, her hands sweating on the pole now as Port Canal outflow and the boats and the fire glare came closer and closer.

Questions, dammit, we don't need.

". . . you buy that sweater uptown?" Mintaka was

saying inside the tarp-shelter, with doubtless professional interest. "Lord, now they done used too big a needle, stuff stretches, them stitches got too much give. Now I could make ye one—"

Altair scanned the floating gathering ahead for the easiest course through, and suddenly thought wistful thoughts of taking the long way round, up the Foundry canal and up and around. It was a chancy backwater, old warehouses, an area where old Det was winning and buildings would have to be filled and torn down and built again. It had not happened yet.

Evade the questions, that was all. And oh, Lord, now there was Mintaka to reckon with.

Closer and closer, watching that fire-sheen and the drift of boats. She managed a steady pace, sweating now despite the chill of her clothing, breathing in great raw gasps.

It's all right, you're just Altair Jones, coming back with old gran Mintaka, doing a kindly act, just mind your own business—

She glided in amongst the first boats that anchored there, *anchored*, no less, right in the Grand channel. Families huddled on skip halfdecks, all wrapped in blankets, watching the commotion like it was holiday or a hanging. Intent on the fire and not on her, thank the Ancestors. Intent on the commotion of distant shouting round the bend where Port met Grand, where fire still showed, but dimmer now. Boats clustered there too, black and busy against the glare.

Mind your business, Jones, knock into someone and you'll have more than one question to answer, that you will.

There was a great deal of commotion now, noise from other boats as she worked and glided her way through. And the tarp stirred. "Lord, look at this," Mintaka's high voice said, and Altair cringed and kept poling.

"Ain't nothing, gran," she said. "You found that cap for him yet?"

"Oh, that I do." Mintaka hauled herself up and staggered perilously in the well, hunched, irregular silhouette against the fire-reflections and the passing shadows of boats. "Look at this, look at this—I tell you I ain't seen such a to-do since them two barges jammed up in the Grand. I tell you, they ought ter have a law, governor ought to do something, them damn bargefolk got no respect for nothing."

"They don't," Altair agreed.

Damn, the lonely old soul was a tale-teller. Chatter your brains away.

And come dawn gran Mintaka would have a good one, how Jones and a fair-haired uptowner showed up all wet and draggled and poled her back to safety. O Lord, Jones, now what do you do?

Scatter stories wide, that's all.

"I heard this barge run down a poleboater," she said. "There she was all blazing fire and come grinding up the bank there by Mars Bridge; and this poler, he jumped and his passenger did; and here was this uptown man swimming down the Port—did you know who that was, ser?"

"No," Mondragon said from beneath the tarp. "Myself —I had to jump when I ran afoul of a crew bringing a boom up. I hardly knew what hit me."

"I saw him go," Altair said cheerfully. "Right off the Mars walk, he went, damn fools rushing off to get to the fire. I got down and gave him a hand and this damn fool trod on me, never a care in the wide world. Stepped right on me leg. I tell you I'd like to've got up right then and settled with him, but it was bad enough this m'ser got shoved in, I couldn't leave off pulling him out. I asked him did he swallow any of that water, he said no. I just get my boat off old Del Suleiman and get to moving—"

The sight off the starboard distracted her: a welter of boats; watchers clustered there: and beyond that, fire-glare, a huge black hulk run up against a wall, something else ablaze in the river. One of the bridges was missing, *that* was what was burning in the river, and that black, dead hulk listing down onto the bottom—that was the barge they had been in.

A cold feeling hit her, belated shock. She glided a moment, recovered her wits and moved quickly to turn the bow from a potential scrape along another boat's anchor-cable. She rocked them. Heads turned her way, silhouettes. The light was at their backs and on her.

"Oh, she were close," Mintaka said.

"Sorry, gran." She sweated and made a close turn amid the still boats and anchor-ropes.

We were *on* that black thing. We were under that deck. Lord, if we'd been a second slower to get out of that hidey we'd have been trapped in there, that fuel running back in the slats under us—cinders and bits of bone. They never would've told us from the rest of the charcoal. Did everybody get *off* that thing?

What kind of folk'd do a thing like that?

"Ain't no place t' anchor," Mintaka said. And shouted at the next boat: *"Ain't no place t' anchor, hear?"*

"Shut it down!" a voice yelled back, and voices yelled other things. *"Who's that?"*

"I'm Mintaka Fahd," the old woman yelled back, *"and this here's Retribution working my boat, no thanks to you that left me!"*

"She's crazy," someone else sang out. *"Who is that?"*

Altair gave a shove on the pole. *"It's Altair Jones,"* she yelled to the night at large, *"taking this boat to dock, no thanks to them that ran off and left her! Who's seen Del Suleiman?"*

A moment of relative silence and no answer. "You tell 'em," Mintaka said, and waddled forward. *"You hear?"*

"I think they did," Altair muttered. "Gran, your arthritis is going to do you bad, you better sit."

"I'm doing fine," Mintaka said, standing wide-legged in the bow. Probably she was not doing fine. Too cussed to agree.

And Del had not answered the hail.

The crowd of boats went right under Foundry Bridge, in the center as well as on the sides by the pilings. Altair went gingerly, fearing collision in that dark place; while Mintaka waddled back closer to the tarp.

"Almost there, gran," Altair said. "You want to sit a while?"

"Hey," Mintaka said; and Altair heard the silence too.

The great bell had stopped, proclaiming the emergency done.

"They got 'er," Altair said. Of course they had. Merovingen could not burn, her people were too canny and moved too quick, whatever the hood-wearing crazies did. Whatever she had gotten herself involved in.

She gave a shrug to rid herself of the chill it gave her, and shoved the boat on, past other moored boats, these with sense to clear the channel, boats tied up thick as birds at roost. Safer territory. The skip moved faster now, easy in the water on the outflow. Southtown Bridge loomed up, and the tall triple span of Fishmarket Bridge was the imagination of a shadow behind that.

"Oh," Mintaka said, standing by the tarp, "she do move, she do move. I used ter push her like this."

"She's a good boat," Altair said.

Mintaka said nothing then. Folded her arms up till she made a roundish lump in the dark.

Southtown bridge shadow went over them, narrowest span in the city. A body listened sharp for a barge bell here at night or early morning and got over right smartly if one sounded.

"Where you got in mind?" Mintaka asked. "Love, I ain't got no strength to fight Snake current."

"Well, I wouldn't leave you at the Southtown narrows, gran. I tell you, how's Ventani corner do you?"

"Oh, Ventani's fine, love. I tell you I don't know what I'd of done."

"Good thing I come along, that's what." Altair put her over to the side, where dozens of boats were moored, some few to each other thinning down as they came down to shallows where Ventani's rock stood firm, one of four upthrusts of stone in all of sinking Merovingen. "Hey," she said, spotting a vacancy. "There's one. Uptown canalers probably scared of the bottom, you got no problem light as she rides. Tide's already run." She gasped after breath, walking the skip in. "You want to tie her in, gran?"

They slid in next a number of skips—"How's she doing down there?" one man asked as they tied in. "They got that out?"

"They got 'er out," Mintaka said, walking to the side. And started filling in the details.

Lord. At it already.

Altair ran in the pole and got down on her knees on the halfdeck. Likely Mintaka collapsed and raised the tarp to get about, what times she moved at all. But there was no tie to the halfdeck and Altair slid down into the shelter, got head and shoulders under, into that closeness. It stank of old blankets and wet wool and mildew. "You awake?" she asked Mondragon.

"I assure you," he said in a voice all frosty cold. "*Now* where?"

"Forward." She found him in the dark and gave him a push, reaching then to keep her cap on as she crawled out the curtain after him into the dark.

"—Jones here got me in," Mintaka was saying to the folk next over, and: "Lord, here's the nice uptown lad, ain't he fine? And Jones here pulled him from the water—I got to tell ye that—"

"Gran," Altair said, and took her by one thick sweatered arm and drew her across the well to the other side. "Gran, I got to go, I got to get my boat and take this nice m'ser uptown. And I'll pay you next week."

"You sure you want to go? You want to take me around while you find Suleiman—why, I'd even ride along when you go take the m'ser home."

"Gran, she's right across the way, right over Fishmarket, not a bit of trouble, and I don't want that arthritis to bother you."

"Gran Mintaka," Mondragon said, and fished in his pocket and came up with coin two of which were silver-pale among the copper-dark. "I want you to have this. For the loan of your boat."

Mintaka's face was a cipher in the shadow.

"Will you take it?"

She cupped her hands beneath his, and took the coins. "That be fine," she said, and there was a quaver in her voice. "That be right fine."

"I'd like to come back and get that sweater sometime."

"Oh, I be by Miller's Bridge a lot." It was reverence in her voice. It was adoration.

Damn you, Mondragon, you got no heart, lead an old woman on like that. She believes you, you know it?

"Come on," Altair said.

"M'sera," he said to Mintaka, "but say I was small and dark, because if my father knew I was down on Port he'd take his stick to me. There's this girl down there, and our families—It's trouble for her too, do you see?"

"Oh," said Mintaka, "oh, I do."

"Come on, ser," Altair said, and swept off her cap and beckoned sternly shoreward.

Chapter 6

THE shore was a brick rim that held the tie-rings and made a walk all uneven and shadowy around Ventani's great bulk and the towering triple structure of Fishmarket Bridge. Altair walked along rapidly, dodged her way along the storefront on the corner and headed for the bridgehead and a gleam of light from Moghi's.

Till Mondragon caught her by the arm.

"That's Fishmarket," he hissed.

"That she is."

"Dammit!" It was a whisper, but his voice cracked doing it. "I told you uptown!"

"You want to get there alive?" she hissed back.

"We've come in a circle! We're back behind where we started, dammitall! You think it's some damn joke?"

"Shut it down, you want gran to hear? Come on."

"Where are we going?"

"We're going to get you under cover whiles I get my boat. You got any more coin?"

"Some." It was a reasonable voice. Scantly. "For what?"

"How much?"

"I don't damn well know. Maybe a dem in change. I gave you—"

"I just wanted to know." She hooked his arm and slid her fingers down to his hand. "Come on."

"Where are we going?"

"Round here." One of Merovingen-below's rare walk-ways opened behind the stonework that supported the stair timbers, a dark cut between two buildings that became one building up above. "Leads over to Moghi's. Back way.

You know this place. You ought to. This is where they dumped you off the bridge. Now we can go in here or we can go over the bridge; or we can sort of slip round the Ventani on the other side and I can find you a hole that ain't occupied while I go hunt my boat. But Moghi's is dry and I can deal with him. Which d'you want?''

He had stopped. He had her hand or she had his and he was gentle about it, but she remembered that strength of his.

Lord, Mondragon, you got a twisty mind and I wish I knew which way it was turning.

"Sun's coming up," she said, " 'bout now. See that sky over there? *That* ain't fire. Now we can just walk after my boat together if you want. But I got the feeling you'd like to stay out of sight. And you ain't particularly scared of this place, for all it done to you—not when you told me to tie up over there at Hanging Bridge, you didn't.''

"I didn't tell you to tie up there. Let me off, I said.''

"Well, it's lucky for you I followed you, ain't it?''

He jerked his hand loose and motioned her ahead.

" 'S truth,'' she said; and walked on into the alley. She slipped her hook loose and carried it, the wood crosspiece firm in her fist. In case. She heard Mondragon's steps behind her, grit on stone in this maze that crooked round to Moghi's backside.

The door to the shed there was always unlocked. And strangely nothing got stolen, not so much as a stray bit of wood when the rains washed the boards loose. She pulled the rickety door open and walked in, heard Mondragon still behind her. "Close that.''

"It's dark enough as it is.''

"You show a light here Moghi'll slit our throats. Close the damn door.''

It closed. She found a rope along the wall and pulled it, so that elsewhere in Moghi's rambling little den a bell rang.

"Is this it?''

"Will be. I just rang. They'll come. Don't get so nervous.''

"Dammit, I don't take to being kidnapped from one end of town to the other."

"Just go coasting up to Boregy, huh?"

"That's what I thought you'd do, I kept thinking you had some back way in mind; the old woman's boat was the best thing we could have used—no one would look twice at it. Jones is smart, I told myself, I go along with it. Then, no, we weren't going uptown; but you were going to find that boat of yours and we'd get uptown on our own. Dammit, you didn't have to get into that jam-up on the canal if it was going to take all night. Now we've got an old woman telling the tale up and down the city, we've got one more of your damn ideas here, and no boat; and if you think you're playing some damn petty childish trick to hang yourself round my neck, you're playing a damn dangerous game."

There was a hook in her hand. She held that hand still; and drew in a breath and another one and a third before she had her throat under control. "I'd damn well hit you," she said. "I wish I could. Sure, I did it to get back at you. *I been doing the work*, ye damned layaround, I been waked out of sleep and scorched and flung in the canal and run half dead, and I poled you up and down this damned city till my gut hurts—" Her throat closed up. She tried for air and shoved hard with the heel of her hand when he tried to lay hands on her. "I'll find my boat, dammit, I'll take you to hell, but don't you go telling me how to do it!"

"Jones—"

"You keep your damn hands off me!"

She hit his arm. Hard. The door rattled and opened, and lantern-light glared into their faces. She turned and held up a hand to shade her eyes. "It's Jones," she said.

"Who you got? *Who you got?*"

"Name's Carlesson."

"Falkenaer?"

"Not him. Hey, I know him, Jep. You c'n let us in. I need that upstairs room. Private stuff."

There was silence. Then a chuckle. "Well. The ice done thawed."

"Shut it down, Jep, and let me talk to Moghi."

"You come right on in." The lantern shifted, held higher. "Ser, you come along and don't mistake us, we're a quiet house."

"They'll kill you," Altair translated. There were men outside by now, blocking the alley; the door beyond Jep was locked. If it had been trouble, the trouble would have gone into a little boat and out to harbor, slip-splash. End of it. But there was no rough talk in Moghi's house. Moghi insisted. And Moghi never tried to take a weapon away from anyone: another rule. Man wants ter carry an arsenal, Moghi would say, that's his business; we don't never argue with a customer.

Slip-splash.

She stepped up to the sill and passed Jep, walked through the cluttered storeroom to the inside door and waited for Jep and Mondragon. Jep bolted up. And the watcher through the peephole inside (Altair always suspected) came and unlocked the inside door.

" 'Morning, Ali."

"Morning." Curly-headed Ali blinked in the lanternlight and looked to be in pain, his broad brown face all screwed up. "House just going to sleep with all this ruckus. You got no decency?"

"I want the quiet room, Ali."

"You got the cash?"

"I got it. Now you tell Moghi when he wakes up I'm going to be in and out the front way. And I want my friend here left alone. I'll talk to Moghi about it."

Ali's dark eyes shifted and shifted again in the lanternlight. "Room, huh? Come on. We got one."

Slip-splash. Moghi had another saying about debts.

Or business associates who caused trouble.

The Room Upstairs (there might in fact, Altair thought, be more than one Room) was a tidy place with a lamp—Jep lit it with a certain elegant flair of wrist, from a match in his calloused fingers. And a wide bed and a hard chair and a table with a little vase of Chattalen jade flowers (the vase was cheap). No window. One wall was brick, the other three were lathing and plaster.

"Bath's across the hall," Ali said. "Heater's got fuel, water's fine for washing, come from a tank atop: boy empties it, and the can. Drinking water in the jug there. You're paying for a first class room here, we don't stint on nothing." Ali walked over to a tall cabinet. "We got bathrobes, got towels, got genuine brandy here, clean glasses, extra blankets. Boy'll set a breakfast by the door in about an hour. We don't disturb our clients. They don't got to leave the room if they don't want to."

"That's real fine," Altair said.

"You got a little scorch on your face, Jones."

She almost reached; stopped herself. "Sunburn. Been out fishing."

"You want them clothes cleaned up?"

"He will. I got to go out again."

"You can wait," Mondragon said. "Get some food in you."

She did not look at him. "I tell you what," she said to Ali, "you tell Moghi when he wakes up I want to talk to him."

"You going to be having breakfast?"

"I'll have breakfast. I'll be back."

"Jones," Mondragon said.

She left by the open door and never looked back at him.

Down the double turn of stairs, quickly through another door and through a curtain and into Moghi's front room, where the tables were all vacant and the chairs stacked on them for sweeping. A night-lamp burned, and the front door was shut.

She opened that door carefully, and went out into the gray hint of morning, onto Moghi's canalside porch and off those boards again, down the gravelly canalside and up again onto the bricked-up rim. Fishmarket Stair loomed up, triple-tiered; she scanned the shadowy boats tied up beyond the Stair, by Lewyt's second-hand store. Their owners slept mostly down in the hideys, a couple on their halfdeck. There was no sign of Del Suleiman and her boat; and she felt the whole weight of Fishmarket Stair over her head, with constantly the feeling someone might be watching her.

A pale body hurtling off over the rail into the dark. Splash into dark water.

Why no clothes? Why not be sure of him? They damn near burned the town down—what's a knifing more or less?

She walked along—(walk, Jones, don't run, don't draw attention, stroll casual-like, canaler on a shore-jaunt)—the other way, up over Moghi's porch again and along the canalside toward Hanging Bridge.

The usual clutter of canalside homeless huddled asleep against the Ventani's brick wall, where the law would take a stick to them if the law happened by, along the bridge sides. But the law was too few and folk got hit and did it again, till the law got to a bad mood and took them on a boatride to Dead Harbor, to live with the crazies and the rafters. There had never seemed anything threatening about this pathetic sort, until now, until that she walked, helpless and afoot. Now and again a raggedy shape stirred and a pair of eyes fixed on someone who had more than they did.

Boats were tied up along the way. More sleepers, late stirring in this morning after calamity. She came to Hanging Stair and climbed up and up, padded past the Angel with his sword—'Morning, Angel, seen my boat? I know. I'm real sorry. I'm sorry I near burned the city down.

Perhaps the hand clenched tighter on the sword; in this light the Angel's face was grim and remote.

Sleepers lay here too—each one to a nook. She walked along hating the sound of her shod footsteps. She stopped finally in a sleeper-free spot and looked over the rail, scanning the east bank and the boats moored there.

Del was not where he had tied up yesterday. She pushed away from the rail and kept walking.

"Hey." She knocked at the door, stood back so that Mondragon could see her through the peephole. The bolt rattled back. The door opened wide. She limped in without a look at him holding the door.

"Find it?"

"No." Breakfast was on the table, two of the house's big breakfasts, and her stomach turned over in nauseated exhaustion. Mondragon shut the door and shot the bolt. Mondragon had had his bath. Of course he had had his bath. he stood there in a nice borrowed robe and with the lamplight shining on curling pale hair and the ruddiness of burn about his face. She plumped down on the bed and contemplated her feet. Tears were in her eyes, not pain yet, just the suspicion that behind the numbness there was going to be a great deal of pain. Her feet had dried a bit. Now the right one went squish again, and she suspected why.

"Where would it be?" Mondragon asked.

"Well, if I knew that I'd go there, wouldn't I?"

"I don't know that. You want some breakfast?"

"No." She crossed an ankle over her knee and pulled off the shoe. She peeled down the black sock next, bit by careful bit.

"O Lord, Jones."

She looked curiously at the red stain between her toes and over most of her sole and heel. At missing skin and skin in bloody blistered strips. She changed feet and pulled off the left shoe and sock. It was only rubbed raw. She dropped the shoe and sock and sat there working her toes.

"I heated water for you," Mondragon said. "You want me to help you over there?"

"I just come back from across the bridge, I can walk." She got up and winced her way across the floor to the door, her right foot all sticky on the carpet. She shoved the doorlatch down and hobbled out.

Put her head back in. "You don't come in there," she said.

And slammed the door.

She glumly dressed again in the bathroom, having further business to take care of—new clothes and they looked like old, dusty and stained and the sweater still damp. So was her cap. She carried it in her hand when she went out of the warm little room and limped and winced down the stairs to the tavern-proper.

The help had been putting the chairs to rights when she came in; unshuttered windows and the open front door let sunlight in. Ali was behind the bar, serving a straggle of blear-eyed customers; Ali hooked a thumb toward Moghi's office.

So Ali had indicated when she came back to the front door that Moghi was stirring about. So now Moghi was up to talking. In the office.

She went to that door beside the bar. She had ventured only rarely into that cubbyhole full of papers and bits of this and that, once when she had started work, once when Moghi had told a gangling kid she had a couple of special barrels to handle, because someone who worked for him had taken sick. Fatally. Case of greed. Moghi towered in her memory of that night, bulked larger than reality. And she never could get rid of that shivery feeling when she stood at Moghi's door.

She knocked. "Moghi. It's Jones."

A grunt came back. "Yeah," that was. She shoved the latch down and walked into the cluttered office.

Dusty light streamed through two unshuttered windows— inside shutters folded back against the shelves inside; and *those* could be drop-barred top and bottom, backup to the iron gratings outside the dirty glass. Papers and crates were everywhere, a tide that rose around the littered surface of Moghi's desk. Moghi sat amid it all, a balding, jowled man with massive arms that said even that vast gut was not all fat.

"How you doin', Jones?"

"Good and bad."

He motioned to the well-worn chair by his desk-side. She dragged it over where she could look at him, and sat. Not a sound from Moghi. Her heart was beating hard of a sudden. —Lord, I got to be careful. I got to be real careful.

"Need your help," she said. "I got a boat missing."

"Where'd you leave it?"

"Del Suleiman, by Hanging Bridge."

"That all you need?"

"Quiet. Lot of quiet. It'd be real nice if that boat just showed up to the porch tonight."

Moghi's seam of a mouth went straight; his jaw clamped and calculation went on in his murky eyes. "Well, now, you come up in life, Jones, up there in the Room. Real pretty fellow, so I hear. And you a canaler. Now I know somehow you c'n afford all this. I got standing orders, anybody asks for that room, they gets it. And we don't talk about money. You get fancy stuff. You want a bottle of something special, you just tell the boys; you want a little favor, you just tell me. If there's expenses above and beyond I add 'em to the tab. You know me. I never ask into private business. It's *character* I ask about. You I got no doubts of. But what's this pretty boy you took up with?"

"He's real quiet."

"Now that's nice to hear. But you know there's lots of trouble in town. Lots. And here comes Jones with money—I know you got money, Jones, you wouldn't run a tab you couldn't pay—and you got this pretty feller and you mislaid your boat. Now, I don't ask into your business. But look at things from my side. Would you want to take in a fellow you don't know right about now? I don't like noise. I sure don't want the blacklegs chasing nobody in here."

"Moghi." She lifted her right hand. "I swear. No blacklegs."

"What's his trouble?"

"Six guys trying to kill him."

"Ali says he talks real nice."

"He's no canaler."

"Now, Jones, you know there's a lot of difference there. Man has a set-to with the gangs, that's a little problem. Gang goes after an uptowner—big money's hired 'em. You c'n figure that all by yourself. You want to tell me, Jones; this nice-talking feller done talked nice to you? Maybe got you twisted all round? Maybe got hisself where nobody ever got with you, huh?"

Her face burned. "I ain't stupid, Moghi."

"Now you and me ain't talked since you was a kid.

Lord, first time I saw you, you went round in them baggy pants with that cap down round your ears—your ma lately dead; and I set you up with old Hafiz, didn't I? He didn't want to deal with no kid, had this feller all set up to do that job—some fellow going to do things a bit on old Hafiz' side, huh? And I told you then—what'd I tell you, Jones?''

"Said if I wasn't smarter that man'd send me to the bottom.''

Moghi chuckled, a heave of massive shoulders. "I tell you, Jones, long as I had you or your ma running my barrels, ain't never worried 'bout the count on 'em. You got good sense. You still got it?''

"I hope I do.''

"Pays your debts?''

"You know I do.''

"Anything comes under this roof is business, Jones. I got a rule. You know what I say about my men and manners under this roof? If Ali out there ever laid a hand to you I'd kill him. Flat. I'd kill him. He knows that. Now I got to tell you: if you laid one to him, I'd kill you. You know why? 'Cause you work for me. You ain't on salary, but it's all the same. I don't want no team-ups with my employees unless they come to me and ask proper. Mad lovers get spiteful. And a man in my business don't need nobody spiteful going talking outside. You understand me? I ain't talking to no kid anymore.''

"I understand you.''

"When I want a woman, I go over to eastside. I never bring no woman here. I never make no move at a woman who works for me. So I'm talking to you like you was my daughter. I tell you if you been stupid and brought somebody here because he's got you thinking all skewed, what you got to do is tell me, and I forget anything you owe me, so don't think about the money. You just let me have him. You got to think, Jones, you got to go on living here, and by living I mean if we get trouble I'll find you.''

Her hands wanted to tremble. She shoved her right into her pocket and came up with one of the gold sols. Laid it on the desk in front of him.

Moghi picked it up, rubbed it in his fingers. Looked at her with no expression at all.

"He's business," Altair said. "Man upstairs is business."

"What kind of business?"

"Not the kind you're thinking, dammit, Moghi! You know me." She tossed off a gesture toward his hands and the sol. "You tell me what the rate is, eastside. You hand out that kind of money for a night?"

Moghi's heavy brows lifted. "For what, then?"

"Gratitude. Keeping the gangs off him. Getting him here alive. This is *money*, Moghi. This is more damn money than I ever saw, and maybe connections."

"Maybe a throat cut." Moghi hammered the coin edge into the desktop. "You think on that, girl?"

"Jones. *Jones*, Moghi; and I'm damn tired of scraping by. You think I'd risk my boat for some man wanted to *pay* me for a night? Damn, I'd gut him. I got this to spend. I got better prospects 'n I ever had. So I come to a man I trust like kin, a man who might as well have good of this money I got to spend—"

"—and uptown trouble."

"Uptown trouble and uptown *friends*, Moghi, one goes with the other."

Moghi's eyes half-lidded in their fleshy pits. "You think you're up to that?"

"First time you saw me, you give me two silvers and told me you were betting I'd get back alive with those barrels off Hafiz' dock. That's a sol come out of my pocket to yours this morning. You tell me, Moghi."

Moghi sat and turned that big gold coin round and round and round against the desktop; and Altair's heart thumped away with every turn and every blink of his dark eyes.

"I tell you," said Moghi finally, "that two silvers I lent? I was betting another way. I was getting that man Hafiz hired'd kill you; and I was going to put the word out he'd robbed a courier of mine and he'd turn up dead. Be rid of old Hafiz' hire-on, I would. I was surprised as hell when you turned up with them barrels at the porch."

She grinned Moghi's grin back at him. Never you back

up with that bastard, her mother used to say about Moghi. And added: Never you cross 'im either.

"Now, Moghi, you bet on sure things, don't you? One way he'd kill me; or I'd kill him or I'd dodge him and you'd put old Hafiz one down. One or the other. Now you got that sol there says here's an old employee come into money, and if the thing goes right there's all kinds of money to be had; and if it goes wrong, there ain't any stink on you or this place."

"Sure I don't smell smoke?"

Her heart near stopped. Lie to Moghi? Same as drinking Det water. She was quiet a long moment and then leaned forward, arms folded on his desk edge.

"*They* got the smoke-stink," she said. "Him and me—we didn't come anywhere near there."

"Word's out someone's asking after a blond man."

"Who?"

"Dunno. They got money. They ain't the regular gangs. Strangers. I might find out. Who saw you here?"

"Nobody saw us go to your door."

"How'd he get to the Ventani?"

"Mintaka Fahd. In the hidey."

Moghi's brows went up. Dangerously.

"Wasn't what I'd like either," Altair said. "But who'd get a straight story out of her? I told her a dozen. Told her we was going eastside."

"If there's rumors," Moghi said.

"Moghi, I got to tell you something. You know what they did, those enemies of his, they flung him right off Fishmarket Stair, slunk right along the Grand and up that stair and off they flung him, right by your porch out there. Now you didn't do that. I knew that right off. You'd have 'im to the harbor . . . if you was ever to do such a thing. So here's somebody who don't know you so well, to be flinging bodies off the Ventani, right under your windows. I'd think you'd take real bad to that kind of thing."

"My porch."

"I was right out there—" She pointed canalward. "Missed that barrel pickup. Well, that was the night. You c'n ask your potboy. Tommy never opened that door. And

I haul this poor wet soul out of the river. Mind, I don't
bring him here, no. Not then. I'd save a drowning man
and set him on the bank. But I wouldn't bring just anybody in here. Wouldn't have 'im to that room. He's got
friends.''

"Like who?''

"Gallandrys.''

Another lifting of the eyebrows and a settling of the
face. "Gallandrys've been arrested.''

Her stomach wrenched over.

"Little matter of a fire," Moghi said. "Little matter of
a barge done took out Mars Bridge and sunk in the Port,
that's all. *Was you there?''*

"You know we were. I want my boat, Moghi. I want
everything you know might be stirring uptown.''

"Dammit, they arrested the Gallandrys and somebody
broke into Boregy and Malvino while the fire was going
on. Killed three people in Boregy and one in Malvino. *My
porch*. My porch. Now this can get expensive, Jones.''

"Took me a while to think what to do. Man can take
care of himself, Moghi, man ain't no fool. Neither am I.''

"Going to be expensive.''

"I figured.''

"You got a down-payment here.'' The sol made another
turn in his thick fingers. "And, Jones, I'm a sentimental
man. I'd really hate for you to make a mistake.''

"Hey, if I'm wrong you tell me and we'll talk about
it.''

"If you're wrong," Moghi said, "just one way you'll
find it out. You ain't running brandy barrels now, Jones.
You ain't my employee anymore, you're talking a whole
different kind of business. You're talking big fees. Gang
business. You're in it, now, Jones. Me, I just sell beer and
rent rooms. People make me trouble they don't come back
here.'' He leaned back and slipped the coin into his pocket.
"I hear a lot of things. I might find that boat of yours.''

"Let gran Fahd be. Something happens to her, somebody'd remember I was on her boat. Somebody might pay
attention to things she said.''

"That was real sloppy, that.''

"Best of bad choices. I told you, didn't I?"

"Jones, if you hadn't I'd have been real upset."

"I knew that too."

Moghi nodded slowly, chins doubling. "Like I said, a down payment. You go enjoy that room."

"In private."

Moghi grinned, a showing of teeth. "Private. Seeing it's you."

It was up the stairs again, tired, Lord, and with a limp in her step and an ache in her ribs and her shoulders and her arm and between her eyes.

Fool. Damnfool.

What else could I do? Moghi'd kill him.

Don't want him anymore. But Moghi'd kill him. One damn more enemy he doesn't need.

Boregy being hit—somebody *knew*. And Moghi—he always knows more than he says, maybe he already knew I picked up somebody out there t'other night, he's already been asking round, knows about strangers after him, O Lord and my ancestors, what am I going to do?

Where's my boat? Dammit, where's my boat? Nobody's seen Del, nobody seen him *or* my boat—

The door to the Room opened as she came up into the hall. Mondragon stood at the top of the steps, all worried-looking.

Just stood there in his bathrobe, not saying a word.

Knows better, he does.

Her heart hurt. She avoided his eyes as she topped the steps and walked past him into the door he held open, went and sat down at the table where the cold breakfast waited.

He closed the door and pulled it till the latch clicked. She ate cold toast and never looked up as he walked over and sat down on the side of the bed, arms on knees.

Damn, it's *friends* of his got arrested and killed. I got to tell him about the Gallandrys and Boregy and all. Me. I made another damn mess down there and how do I tell somebody that kind of news, and him mad at me?

The toast made a cold lump in her throat. She washed it

down with lukewarm tea. "I heard," she said, and looked
his way, "the law took a bunch of people at Gallandry.
Somebody else broke into Boregy and killed some people.
Malvino too. Heard it from Moghi."

The muscles knotted up in his jaw. He breathed a little
faster. That was all. "Moghi owns this place."

"Moghi owns this place." She took another sip of cold
tea and slopped it; her hands shook. "I hunted that whole
damn canalside trying to find my boat. Moghi's people are
going to look. He knows about the barge. About us and
Gallandry. About folk throwing you off the bridge. Knows
you're uptowner and somebody with money wants you
bad. Says there's been questions asked about a blond man.
Strangers asking. I got Moghi to say he'd let us have this
room; Moghi's—got lots of people. Lot of others are
afraid of him."

"Trust him?"

"We got no choice." Her voice was all hoarse. She
took up the toast again and dropped it in listless disgust.
"I got you here. Dammit, I knew it was going crazy last
night, knew I had to get to somewhere, damn lucky it
wasn't Boregy."

He stood up, leaned next her ear. "Who's listening?"
he asked, faintest of whispers against her hair.

"Nobody. Moghi said. "That's truth."

He straightened and leaned his hands on the table. Worried. Lord, not a shout, not a word of blame. He laid a
gentle hand on her shoulder, then walked a few steps off,
stood with his back to her and his arms folded.

She ate at the cold toast, bite after bite. Finally he came
back and sat down on the side of the bed, one knee tucked
up into his arms.

"I wanted you out of this," he said, all quiet. "Jones,
you were right, all the way."

She swallowed hard and a bite forced its way down past
a knot in her throat. Her eyes stung. She drank the tea,
then got up and went and opened the cabinet where the
brandy was, and the glasses. She unstopped the decanter
and poured a bit.

She stood there with her back to him to drink a sip. That took the knot out.

Damn him. Damn it all.

Manners, Jones. Man's trying.

She poured the other glass and walked back and gave it to him. He took it and she never looked him quite in the eyes. She just walked away with a pain in her chest that hurt like a knife.

Memory of a pale body hurtling through the dark.

Through the sun into the harbor water, splash scattering like glass beads in the light.

Him standing there all elegant in Gallandry lamplight, russet velvet and lace, sword at his side.

She turned around finally when she heard the bedsprings give. He had put the glass down on the table. Had gotten up to turn down his side of the bed.

He slipped the robe off and got in and drew the covers up over his shoulder and his head, leaving her the light.

She took a mouthful of brandy and swallowed it down till her eyes stung. Not a stir out of him, not a word.

She drank another half glass, then stripped off her sweater and took the remaining sol and put it in her shoe, there by the bed. She unbuttoned the trousers and kicked them elsewhere.

She lit the nightwick at the side of the lamp, then blew out the top light and got into bed on her side.

She edged over after a moment. Edged over again until she came up against him. His muscles stayed tense when she put an arm over him.

She let go a sigh and lay there and hurt, inside and out, till sleep came closer, till maybe at the edge of his own sleep he turned over and put an arm about her. Better, better. She gave a great sigh and shifted. There was a moment of moving about and fitting limbs and limbs and wincing, her with sore arms and him with a sore back, until finally she found herself comfortable and her skull throbbing away in a dull dark daze that went down and down toward nothing at all.

"You went to sleep on me," he said into her ear when she came to, and she mumbled and shifted sore muscles and almost went to sleep again until his hands got her attention.

"Damn," she said, remembering she was not speaking to him. And then remembering she was, confused in the middle of the night. Moghi's. A gold piece in the toe of her shoe and her boat missing and herself with a lover in the second shore-bound unmoving room in a day. "Damn."

"What's wrong?"

"Wrong?" She thought about it and laughed. The laugh got crazier, at an indelicate time. "What's wrong?" She gasped after breath. Laughed again till it hurt and she ran out of breath with the tears dampening her eyes. "Damn, they're going to kill us."

"Jones?"

"Wrong," was all she could manage, with another hysterical wheeze. Till he got her stopped, and she lay with her ribs and her gut hurting. "Oh, Lord, Lord."

They held onto each other. Like two drowners headed for the bottom. Down into the dark, dark nowhere. "Jones," he murmured. "Jones, are you all right?"

"Don't—don't make me laugh again."

"I'm not. I'm not." His hands traveled over her, absent-like.

Her own moved. A while. She ran out of momentum, and lay still against his arm. "Jones," he said, waking her up. "You awake?"

"Uuuhhn," she said. And thought back to the harbor. To waking on the deck. The room seemed to move a moment. To the lamplit room, the brass tub. Mondragon with the glass in his hand. Wine red as blood. Mondragon with his face in lampshadow, drinking and brooding, full of thoughts. Older. Deeper and darker. Old as sins and lies. She felt a fall at the edge of sleep and blinked into a stranger's face, at Mondragon with the nightlamp turning his hair to lamp-fire. For a moment her heart sped, a rush of panic and waking.

Damn, who is he? *What* is he? What'm I doing in bed with him?

What do I know about him?

"What are you looking at?" he asked.

"Dunno." Her heart still beat, nightmare panic. What're you looking at?"

He brushed the hair back from her ear. Did it twice and it fell back. He gave her no answer. The silence pounded in her chest, painful as grief and fear.

"You're shivering. Jones, are you all right?"

"I'm all right."

He pulled her close, burrowed his head next her ear.

She shivered the worse.

Damn. I never get him and me in the same mood at once.

Image of Mondragon edging across the deck in the morning light. Backward.

He just wants me to get him to his friends. Thinks he has to make love to me. Thinks that's what it costs.

Man with the cat for sale. *Come be nice, I give 'er to ye.*

What's a man pay for his life?

"You don't have to."

"What?"

"Be nice to me. You don't have to do it if you don't want."

Things stopped in full career. "Did I ever say I didn't?"

"I dunno. Sometimes I think not."

"Jones,—I—"

"On the boat. In the harbor. You backed across the deck like I was poison."

"I didn't."

"You damn well did!" She jerked her head back and stared at him near cross-eyed at close range. "You trying to get me to do things, trying to get me to take you here and there, you don't have to do that."

"Lord, Jones, I *tried* to get rid of you! What more can I do?" The words fell out and died. He lay there with a kind of confused, distressed look. "I didn't mean that."

A warm feeling spread through her. The knots unknotted in a kind of benign satisfaction.

Got 'im muddled, I do. Lord, he's nicer'n any man I ever knew. Lots nicer'n those foul-mouthed bridge-boys.

Fight for this 'un, I would.

She smiled, lazy-like. Took a curl of his hair and wound it round her finger. Shifted closer and closer again where she could whisper her lowest. "Damn right you tried to shake me. Ain't no good. 'Bout time you started listening, ain't it? Lost my boat for your sake. Soon's I get it back we got some thinking to do."

"I've tried to think." His voice sank down to the faintest whisper. "Jones, I've got to get to uptown. I've got contacts there. Don't ask me what or why."

"I'm asking. You want me to find a way up there I got to know the choices. What are you into? Who are those crazies?"

Silence for a long while.

"Sword of God."

She heard that and her heart thumped once and lurched into a heavier beat. She rolled onto her elbow and leaned over his ear where she could talk in absolute quiet. "Damn, what are you?"

"Let it be."

"Let it be?"

He stared up at her, a long thinking look. He blinked once, twice. "You have an Adventist name. Altair."

"So'd my mother, it never meant we was Sword of God. Dammit, there ain't no such thing in Merovingen."

"There is now."

"You're crazy!"

"It's the truth."

She rolled onto her back and stared at the ceiling, at the nightlamp casting shadow-play off the timbers and the dust.

Sword of God. Militant crazies bent on exterminating impurities, bent on exterminating the sharrh themselves if they could get their hands on any. They helped the Retribution along with assassination, Lord knew what else.

Angel out on the bridge, you standing there so long, you got nothing to do with those lunatics. Your sword ain't that sword.

"I told you," Mondragon whispered into her ear, "you didn't want to know."

She turned her head, stared at him at closest range in the lamplight. ''Where'd you get messed up with them,?''

He gave no answer.

''Well, they ain't so much,'' she said then, to get the chill out of her throat, ''they ain't so much. If I was going to murder someone I'd be sure of 'im before I threw 'im off any bridge.''

''If they were Sword.'' He moved his hand distractingly onto her stomach. ''Say I walked down the wrong alley.''

''Well, why—why for Lord's sake did they take your clothes?''

''Because if I lived it'd teach me a lesson, and if I didn't I couldn't be traced. Except by those that would know.''

''*Why?*''

There was long silence. ''Say I ignored a warning.''

''They weren't Sword of God, then what were they?''

''The warning came behind a mask. Say the Sword's not the only trouble in town.''

''Who?''

''I've said enough.''

''You haven't. You haven't started. What've you got to do with them, that they want you that bad?''

He traced the side of her face with the back of his finger. ''Don't ask any more, Jones.''

She froze, outright froze.

''No.'' He gripped her shoulder hard. ''No, Jones. Don't look at me like that.''

''What are you, f'God's sake? A Jane? *Sharrist?*''

He was quiet a moment. His fingers relaxed belatedly, tightened again, not as hard. ''I was Sword. Once.'' His mouth made a hard line and his eyes glittered, darted. ''I quit.''

''Are you from Nev Hettek?''

''Do I talk like it?''

''I dunno. I never knew a Nev Hettekker. But you ain't no Falkenaer and you ain't Chat and you ain't Merovingian.''

''You don't need to know. You understand why I don't want you around me. The Sword just might take you up, take you to some quiet nook—you understand me? They don't like publicity. Not even in the north. They *are* here, there's money behind them. The law knows it.''

"And don't stop 'em?"

"They won't stop them. I ignored a warning. I stayed. That was a friendly group that threw me off that bridge.''

"Friendly.''

"Not like it was murder. Just a second warning. Because I'm here. Now Gallandry's been arrested. Do you follow me?''

"No.'' She shook her head desperately. "You mean— the law? The *law's*—''

"—got pressure on it. The Signeury's trying to put a fear into Gallandry. The Sword hit Boregy; Malvino. They weren't sure I was on that barge. They were hunting. Now people are dead. Jones, it was the police that threw me off that bridge.''

"Lord.''

"The governor doesn't want any noise. Doesn't want me *here*, in Merovingen. The governor's afraid of the Sword; afraid of the College; afraid of his own police and who's been bought, and he's afraid of the money that can hire assassins. Most of all he's afraid of what Nev Hettek might do and he's afraid of riots. A sick man with heirs at each other's throats—He can't afford to have foreign trouble.''

She drew a great breath and lay there staring at the ceiling, at the shadows the lamp made. The Sword of God: Adventist crazies. Militants. Assassins.

Mondragon wielding the boathook with skill that became greater and greater—

Mondragon with the rapier at his side, there on Gallandry's stairs—

He settled slowly beside her, wound his fingers into her fingers. Lay there quiet too.

Fool, she heard her mother saying. Dammit, now, Altair, this is too far. Sword of God. Murders. So a lot of muck floats down old Det. Never surprised at anything that turns up in this town. But you don't need to go poking your hand into it, do you?''

She turned and put her lips against Mondragon's ear.

"Mondragon. What are you doing here? What are you after?"

Silence for a long time. He shifted up then and put his arm on the other side of her so that he cut off the light. His breath stirred her hair. "Don't use that name. I never should have told you. I was crazy out there."

"I was too." She turned her head and mouth brushed mouth, sleepily, far from the kind of craziness that had been out there. Old warmth. Sun on skin, on water. He let his head down on her shoulder, his hand straying down her side.

"Too damn tired, Jones, too damn tired."

"What'll I do?" she murmured. Her own mind fuzzed round the edges, half-gone. "What'll I do?" It was part nightmare, part dream. A sheet of fire washed across her mind, the canalsides and the blank faces of buildings jolted and moved, firelit and casting back orange from old brick and dusty windows; Merovingen-above towered overhead, bridge-webbed, wooden and vulnerable.

The golden Angel stood on his bridge and his firelit hair turned to gold wire, to sunlight, to Mondragon's pale blond. The hand that gripped the hilt was alive, was Mondragon's hand, down to the fine bones and the way the veins stood out, despite that it was gold. It clenched and the sword moved outward by fractions.

Sword of God.

She could not see the face. If she had seen the face it would have blasted her sense.

Don't do it yet, she asked the Angel; and fought back against the dream. She set Mondragon there beside her on that bridge so that she could know that face was not his face. She made it night again, and the river quiet. The Angel stood there shining and not-shining, because no one else in the city could have seen him that way: he was always alive, only he lived slower, and it was taking him all of a human lifetime to take a single breath. Only his thoughts ran quick, quick as lightning strokes; and if they saw the sword move the city would have lived a hundred years around them

Don't do it yet. It was a wicked thought for an Adven-

tist. It was her business to wish the Retribution closer:
Sword of God wanted it with fanatic zeal—but ordinary,
common little Adventists hoped for it someday, secretly
wanted it in someone else's lifetime, close, maybe, because the world was not that good; but not too close,
because she had plans, and if Merovingen changed, where
would she be and where would she go and what would
become of her?

I thought so too, her mother said, sitting on the bridge,
there in the dark—cap atilt, arms clasped about her knees.
And with a look at Mondragon: *Who's he? He's right
pretty. I like the look of him. But you got to know, Altair,
he don't belong.*

The bridge-rail was empty then. Just the river and the
dark. The dark grew worse, and things moved in it.

Something was hammering.

"Jones," it said.

"Jones."

The world shifted. She felt cold air, flailed with her
hand and caught herself on a sore shoulder. Someone was
knocking at the door, a gentle tapping, and Mondragon
was getting out of bed.

She followed—winced as her feet hit the floor, waved a
cautioning hand at Mondragon as he grabbed his robe off
the floor with one hand and came up with the rapier in the
other. "Minute," she said aloud. She grabbed her sweater
off the floor and pulled that on, located her pants, a puddle
of shadow over by the cabinet, and pulled those on, grabbed
the boathook out of her belt where it lay on the floor.
Mondragon had gotten the robe on by the time she padded
over to the door. "Who is it?"

"Ali. They found your boat. They got it down to the
tie-up near the Stair."

Her heart did a turnover and a restart. "Thank God."
She shot the bolt back and cracked the door open, took it
wider when she saw it was Ali alone, Ali with a bundle in
his hands. "What time it it?"

" 'Bout mid of the first." Ali shoved the bundle into
her hands, hook and all. "His clothes. All cleaned. Moghi

wants you should move that boat. Boy's watching it. He ain't much.''

"Lord, where'd you find it? How'd you get it here?"

"Del Suleiman brought 'er, found 'im off by the Sanke, he's wanting you should ferry him back. Moghi wants that boat moved—''

"I'm going, I'm going." She rubbed her eyes with her free hand and shouldered the door shut, headed over for the bed to toss the clothes. Mondragon arrived and disengaged them from her arm and from the hook. She caught up her belt, put the hook where it belonged, rubbed her eyes into focus again and saw Mondragon busy buttoning his pants as she buckled her knife belt on.

"You c'n go back," she said, "get some sleep. I don't know what time it is, but I got Del to get back." Her wits woke up. "Give me some change. Couple pennies. I got to pay Del.''

"I'm going with you."

"I told you. You keep that blond head of yours in this room. I paid damn well enough for it." She discovered her cap on the iron bedpost and slapped it on her head. "Don't you budge from here. I got to explain you to Del? You want gossip all over?''

"We've got it." His face flushed ruddy in the light. "What can he say that that Mintaka woman won't, tell me that?''

"You stay put! I don't need more trouble than I got! Stay put! Hear?''

"Dammit, Jones—"

"Just give me the money."

He went and got his boot by the bedside, came up with pennies. Gave her four. And scowled when he handed them over.

"Thanks."

"Jones. Be careful."

"Hey, I been running these canals all my life, I got friends out there and Del's one of 'em. You keep inside. Keep that door locked!''

She escaped out it, closed it tight.

"Bolt it," she yelled back through the door.

The bolt shot.

Damn. A man that listens.

She turned to Ali and the lantern, in time to follow him down the stairs, quick on bare feet in the wildly swinging light—no shoes and no socks for canal work, by the Ancestors. Her own boards under her feet again, silky-smooth and all her own, better than town floors, than Moghi's carpet. She went after Ali at speed, caught him up at the bottom.

Moghi himself was waiting at the bottom of the stairs, lanternlight gleaming on his stout face and perspiring head; Moghi with his sleeves rolled up and the sounds of customers coming from the front room, noisy talk, the string-sounds of a gitar half-drowned, all filtered through a closed door.

"Your friend ain't going."

From Moghi it was query, meaning You planning to stay around; and Where's the fee?

"He ain't going," she said. "You keep an eye to him."

"Cost you," Moghi said.

Her stomach tightened. So. Rich an hour or two and poor again. "Hey, it ain't like he's all that much trouble. I *paid* you—"

"Got your boat back, didn't you? Got it delivered right here. *Service* comes expensive. You plan to have that fellow stay on another day—"

"Till I get back for him. I'll get him out of here."

Moghi's fat-rimmed eyes looked somewhat pained. "You got a destination in mind."

"That's his business, he'd skin me."

"I was offering, Jones."

"I'll think on it."

"We got some charges still."

"We'll talk about it when I get back." Lord, he might give Mondragon trouble, hunting money. "You let him be, Moghi! You let my partner be! We'll talk, all right?"

Moghi waved a hand. "Get, get, that damn boat's sitting out there, I got customers."

She went out the back way into the storeroom, and headed for the shed.

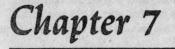

Chapter 7

THE boat was there, out to the front of the second-hand store, beyond Fishmarket Stair—sleepy-looking scene, boat on black water, boatman drowsing on the halfdeck, nearest of four boats night-tied at that corner. But that one boatman was watching: he lifted his head as Altair padded barefoot down the stone bank. Ali was back there— watching. Tommy the potboy was installed somewhere, probably high up on the bridge, sitting there with feet adangle and young eyes alert. She resisted the impulse to look and see: Tommy was Moghi's; and if Ali said he was there, he was there or Moghi would kill him.

Tommy was there the same way that Del Suleiman would haul himself out of a sound sleep and pole a boat across town just because Moghi's men suggested it. Not unpaid, of course. Moghi paid. *She* had paid Moghi. Value for value.

She came up to the edge and the halfdeck, her own precious deck, her little bit of planking and everything she owned in the world. "Hey," she said by way of greeting, set her cap firm against the light breeze—a little wind kicking up, clean air, a clean night: she landed on her own deck and a wealth of things were better.

"Hey." Del Suleiman, pole in both hands, tucked both bare feet up on the deck rim and stood up on the deck with his toes curled over—canaler's sense of balance. "Hey, damn lousy hour, Jones."

"Sorry. I got worried."

"Moghi's men. Moghi's men. Come rousting the canalside—"

149

"Hey, I never set 'em at that."

"Where'd you get to shift Moghi's crew yey and haw, huh? Damn, next you be out collecting."

"Give me that pole. I get you back."

"Ne, ne, not to get aslant, ye. C'm on. You want starb'd?"

Lord. Generosity. Del was going to pole double with her into the bargain. The old man was in a hurry. "Ne. You c'n call it." Altair dropped onto her haunches and pulled the side-tie, waiting-tie. Del would have bow-tied for any longer wait, stern-anchored (if there was one) and never chosen this stone-bottomed shelf in the first place, where the bottom was like to scrape on the ebb if some big barge came by. (If there was one. If there was any *likely* to move, if they had gotten the hulk and the bridge out of Port—) Not Del's way, this skulking around shallow ties and back doors. The old man was nervous. It was in the way he moved.

I don't blame him none. Mira off to herself and him off with them bullylads. She's got to be wondering, Lord, Lord, Del come with them and her left off in the dark somewheres.

The boat drifted free and bumped bottom. She snatched up the boathook from the rack and crossed over to the left side while Del shoved off. She put the boathook's pole-end down on stony bottom and leaned on it when Del's push ebbed down. "Bow a-port," Del said, and she kept her pole grounded while Del shoved, bringing the bow around to the bridge. "Hup." Signal to lift. She took her time from Del, from starboard-side poler, hit the stroke again as the boat slipped along. "Hin," Del said, which was warning he was grounding on his side and the final turning shove was hers.

She shoved. The bow came round with the skip nosed neatly toward a gap in the bridge pilings. "Hup," she said. Del shoved and lifted.

"Yoss," she said cheerfully, meaning straight on; and "yoss," Del echoed, as the skip slid into shadow.

Poling double with her mother. Her young arms hardly

strong enough to handle the pole if it got off its center of balance.

Miss it, I do. Lord, how she flies. Got me a man and he don't know hin from hey on a skip.

He could learn, couldn't he? If he wasn't uptowner.

Sword of God. O Lord and my Ancestors, if he could shake all of that and stay on the canals, if he could learn—

If he wouldn't leave—

If he wouldn't ever leave—

The skip shot out from the shadow of Fishmarket Bridge. Lantern light gleamed brightly out unshuttered windows and open door, onto the porch and a huddle of boats tied up around Moghi's porch. The wan notes of the gitar and the voices of canalers flowed out onto the water and lost themselves in the dark.

"This lander you went off after," Del said. "That deal still going?"

Her heart sped beyond what the poling needed. "Hey, I lost m'skip, I got enough business tracking you, don't I?"

"Where you got the stuff to get Moghi out, huh?"

"I work for 'im. He's doing me a favor, ain't nothing to him to send a few fellows around, is it?" Ventani Pier passed on the right. Hanging Bridge loomed up ahead. Stroke and stroke, and the skip flew along. Damn, *think*. Man's curious. Man's been brought here on Moghi's money, going to hit me for the why of it surer'n hell. What'd I tell 'im already? What's he heard? O Lord. *Mintaka*. Altair drew breath and shoved. The depth was increasing, chancy poling with the boathook. "Damn, she's a wash. Let her ride."

"Yoss," Del agreed, and the skip glided in the center of the barge-channel, between the two sets of piers. He turned his gaunt, unshaven face her way in the starlight. " 'Bout Moghi now—"

"Hey, I don't gossip Moghi's business."

"That blond fellow Moghi's?"

"Dammit, Del—"

They were slewing. Del trailed his pole and the drag brought them true again. "Heard a lot of gossip today. Lot of stories. How long I known you, huh? Knowed you

since you was a babe in your mama's arms. Damn, you
listen to me, girl. Your mama'd knock you to next week,
you taking up with some damn landsman.''

Heat mounted in her face. She probed for the bottom
with the boathook and it was still too deep. "My mama
had a word 'bout gossip too. Who said I took up with
anybody? I run Moghi's freight."

That shut the old man up a moment. He gave a brief
shove at the pole as they slipped under Hanging Bridge
shadow. "You better watch that kind, young'un, and I
don't mean Moghi. He'll talk real fine, but that ain't how
he'll do ye."

"Who said? Who said I been with anybody?" She
fended off a piling. "Ware, there, dammit, Del."

"Hin, you got bottom, use the damn piling, hain't your
mama taught you?"

"All right, all right, you want to take port, let *me* call
it, I'll give you hurry."

"*I'll* give you hurry. That I will. Hin, there. Damn
nonsense. Damn nonsense you got mixed up in, just like
your mama."

Her heart skipped. She missed another stroke. Her blistered feet burned on the boards. "What about my mama?"
Her whole life was hint and innuendo. Retribution Jones
did this. Retribution did that. *"What* was she into?"

"Every damn thing in town. Moghi. Hafiz. You come
along, and she never slowed down. Mira and I, we told
her, we told her, 'Jones,' we said—'You go taking that
baby up them dark ways, that's asking for grief. Tried to
talk her into giving you over to us, we did, you might've
been ours—hell of a surprise we'd of got, you being a
girl—Yoss, there. —But hain't no difference t'me or Mira.
We'd of taken ye. I offered when your mama died. 'Member? I told ye I'd treat ye fair. I guess you was scared. I
guess I know why. You was still a boy then. Still playing
your mama's game, doing Moghi's work, running them
dark ways, getting in darker and deeper."

Her heart beat for something other than that work. It
was the old business. Give a man a word and two and he
moved in and tried to run things. Anger rose up in her,

blinded her. "Hin," Del said. She shoved and the bow slewed off to the Snake current, headed for the corner, high end of the Snake.

"*This* end o' town, was you! Damn, Del, I searched up and down this morning. Where was you?"

"Snake tail. Down by Mantovan. Moghi's men found us. By then I was hunting you. *Heard* you been in and out of Moghi's. Hell, with all's been going on, you got that tank near empty, I ain't spending mine on you, and Moghi's boys hunting your boat and shoving folk around—yoss, there, yoss."

"I'm sorry."

"You say."

"I say; it's the truth. You want to say I been lying?"

"I'm saying you're a kid. I'm saying all your mama's life she was on the edge 'tween here and the law; *she* knew where the holes were, *she* come over that line one side and t'other, I knowed it, ain't no one don't know she done it; but your mama, she never took her one foot off that safe side. Maybe she's born again off this sorry old world; maybe she's born somewheres better'n us, but she sure weren't through with here yet, neither, leaving a kid and all, and you taught 'bout half she knowed, you going to that Moghi and freighting them barrels in and out of the Tidewater—"

There were tie-ups alongside the Snake, on this stretch between Bogar and huge Mantovan, skips and poleboats tucked up one after the other, sleepers on their decks and in their wells. "Hush," Altair hissed, with a foul look Del's way. "You got a free way with others' business. I asked you watch my boat. That's all."

"I watch it all right. And here come these rumors—I'm towing your skip, young'un, you don't expect talk come with it?"

"I said I was sorry!"

Del looked at her, stared with the pole trailing in his hands. Then: "Damn—hin, there, hin, slow. Fourth-on. We're on 'er."

Come in, Del meant. He swung the pole up and in again to brake, slowing along the side of Bogar. Fourth boat was a skip, was his: of a sudden the human hulk on the halfdeck made itself into Mira's seated self, the boat revised itself into familiar lines. Altair shoved the hook-pole down hard and slewed the bow, while Del timed his approach and slowed them on his side.

Slower and slower. Mira stood up in the well, deep in Bogar's shadow. "Ain't taking no tie-on," Altair muttered to Del. "Ain't got time to talk. I swear, I pay you what I owe, I get myself back to where I got business, and I'll tell you and Mira the whole story next week." She held the boathook to one hand and skipped down to the well to toss the portside tie over for Mira to hold while Del boarded— courtesy, not to scar Del's boat up with the hook. Mira bent her large shadowy self, grabbed the rope and drew them close in, with a whisper of the rope on the pin. "Hey," Altair said, "don't tie 'er, Mira."

Del racked the pole. Altair walked across the well to drop the boathook into the rack with it, eased her cap back on her head and walked back again with her hand in her pocket, seeking after the pennies there.

And stopped cold, with a reach to the barrelhook instead, Mira bending over, Mira a shade hard of hearing anyway and doggedly going on to make the tie-up, her big bulk oblivious to shadows on the Bogar bank, shadows creeping up and dropping suddenly into the skip at Mira's back. "*Ware!* Mira!"

There was a rattle of a pole behind her, Del running out a weapon. But Mira never turned. Mira straightened as if she had never felt a half-dozen feet hit her well. Del came behind with the pole, with the shadow-figures at Mira's back rocking the boat and Mira paying no attention—wrong, wrong, from the gut, wrong. Altair snatched her knife out left-handed in panic and lunged for the mooring rope.

The pole whacked down onto the rim, rope and all, shy of her knife and her fingers. *Del*'s pole. As the shadow-figures surged up about Mira and vaulted over into her own well, all in a rush.

"Damn you!" she yelled at Del, and vaulted the side to Del's deck, barreled straight up against Mira with that knife in her fist. Mira yelled and staggered backward.

"No!" Del howled. *"No!"*

About the time men hit her back and she grabbed a handful of Mira's shirt in the same fist as the knife; gave a wrench, as the hands on her shoulders hauled her off the deck to the well.

"Dammit!"

Fool!

Hard arms immobilized either elbow, knife-hand and hook-hand together. "Don't you hurt her," Mira was saying, "don't you hurt her, damn your hides!"

Someone was on her side. Her victim was. She quit kicking and fighting; the men who held her let up so that some feeling came back to her hands. She drew a breath, sense getting back to her brain as she saw Del and Mira and boaters standing up solemn as judges in every boat well and deck along the side of Bogar Isle.

Canalers. All of them. Canaler-law. Canalers with a grudge or questions or something in mind. There was no place to run, not in all Merovingen.

"She never hurt me," Mira was saying. "Let 'er go, let go. Altair, Altair, sweet—Let her go!"

"Let me go," Altair said. "Damn, you want to talk to me, you get your damn hands off me!"

Hands pried the hook and the knife from her numb fingers. They let her go then; and she hugged her arms back with a wince, holding them till it felt the joints had settled. She recognized a few of the men. And women. "Come on," a male voice said, and caught her arm and dragged her across the slats toward the shoreside.

She flailed out, braced her feet, trying to free herself. "I ain't—"

"You'll go with us." Another hand caught her left arm again, and bent it back till it was near to cracking. She yelled and winced to save it, and banged her knee on the boatside as they dragged her bodily over it.

"Let me go, dammit!" The arm strained at the socket. There was no fighting it. She stumbled on the uneven brickwork of Bogar Cut ledge, *knew* where they were taking her. "I'll *walk*, dammit, you're breaking my arm!"

Pressure eased up. Her vision came and went in flares of

pain, and she stumbled again as a man shoved her toward
a break in the wall. *"Ow!"* she yelled. And bashed her
head on a brick as the man pushed her in through a rubbled
split in Bogar's foundations. She was blind for a moment,
free and reeling and staggering until some other man grabbed
her and held her arm.

Body after body came into the place. She heard them in
the dark, heard the shuffling and heard someone else bash
his head on the same brick and swear. She jerked at the
hands that held her. "Dammit, you can let go, I ain't
running."

A match flared. A single candle took light, picked out a
tumbled cavern of water-dripping brick and rubble-piles of
fill, and a score of canalers, all in the same gold. It was
the old Bogar warehouse, gone rotten at the foundations,
halfway to its use as a new stone base for the isle, to shore
it up from ruin.

Canalers knew such places. Like the vermin and the cats
knew them.

There was a flat rock, a large slab of rock. A big man
with an open shirt and a neck-scarf brought the candle
there, sat down and fixed the candle on its own wax in
front of him. Sweat glistened on his unshaven face. It
showed like a devil's in the flicker of breeze from outside.
Rufio Jobe was his name. He was not official. Nothing
was, in the canals. But Jobe was a man who did things.
Who got things done. Direct and final. And no one
backtalked him.

"Give me my stuff back," she said.

Rufio Jobe settled his largish bulk square, set his hands
on his knees. "Maybe you give us some answers, Little
Jones."

"Answers. What answers?"

"Like what you been doing."

"I ain't doing nothing!"

"Del," Jobe said, and looked aside. She looked, and
spotted Del Suleiman and his wife at her left, silent, his
white hair and white stubble gone all neutral gold in the
candlelight, her face gone all to tear-streaked jowls.

"Where you been?" Del asked.

"Where've I been?" Altair sucked air and shook her arms loose again, the left one fit to bring tears to her eyes. "I been trusting a damn liar, that's what I been doing! Ye might've knifed me while you was at it, mightn't you, Del? All that talk was a *lie*, Del Suleiman! *Damn liar!* You want my boat, that's what you want, that's what you wanted for years—"

"You set your hand to Mira again, I'll show you, you—"

"She never did!" Mira yelled; and: "*Shut it down!*" —from Jobe.

There was quiet then, the yell reverberating off the brick. A bit of stone fell. Water dripped. Brick shifted under someone's foot. Altair shook off hands that threatened to grip her arms again. She was shaking. Her gut felt like water. The faces ringed her round and round. "Damn liar," she muttered and looked up and glared at Jobe. "I got *private* business. I left my boat with somebody I thought I trusted. That's what I done."

"You being a kid," Jobe said, "we ain't got no desire to be rough with you. Just want to talk. It was you took the knife out."

"How'd *I* know what you was? First I thought you was going for Mira's back. Then I still didn't know what you was. Old friends've sold out friends before. Like now. Am I going to wait round to see? Hell, I'm going to cut my boat loose an' when someone I know goes at my back and stops me I'm getting clear of 'im. World's gone crazy. World's gone clear crazy. Never would've knifed Mira; she didn't knife me neither. I knew that. But I figured if Del'd gone crazy she wouldn't be too."

"Now that may be and that may not be. Fact is, we got a lot of craziness going on. Like that fire the other night. Like killings in the uptown and them that did it is moving round the city somehow. I tell you, Little Jones, it ain't any real pleasure for me to be asking you: I was a friend of your mother's. But we got a real serious question for you. You know anything about that fire?"

"I was down there. Doesn't mean I did it. I was just there."

"You got this passenger. You want to tell us about 'im?"

"What's that got to do with it?"

"They got you to leave your boat. Suleiman can swear to that. You was following after some tall fellow dressed all like a canaler and walking like an uptowner. Later you was heading away from that fire with this tall fellow looked like a Falkenaer. You rode Mintaka Fahd's boat down from Oldmarket and told her he was running after some hightown girl."

"So I found him when I went off across the city, so we happened to be cut off by the fire and couldn't get back to Moghi's till we ran into gran Fahd. Who's this been so interested in my business?" Her heart was pounding in her chest. Lying to these was a fatal thing to do. A little lie was one thing; a big lie and something going wrong, that was a way to die, just to turn up dead some morning and no one caring at all. Even suspicion was enough to starve on, harassed and pranked till a body had nowhere to go but the Harbor. If she ever got out of this basement alive. "Who said I was up to no good? Who said? Was it you, Del Suleiman? Was it you?"

"Girl," Jobe said, "there's just been a lot of gossip. *Lot* of gossip. Now you knows the rule: trouble ain't good for canalers. Ain't good at all. We got canalers ain't moving, we got a canal blocked, we got the law out poking round the canals, we got a whole lot less freight 'cause of this trouble in the town, and that means hungry kids and hungry old 'uns. Now d'you agree we got a legitimate concern here?"

"Same's me. Same as me, dammit!"

"Not same as you if ye're running a different kind of freight."

"What? *What* d'you say I'm doing? I ain't doing nothing illegal, and I don't owe you nor nobody my private business! Where's things got to, huh? Ever'body got to tell their business to ever'body? Tell ever'body what's in their barrels? Where we go? That ain't what it is!" She drew breath. Never you back up, mama said. Go to 'em, Altair. "Think you can shove Jones around, think you all can bully Jones 'cause she runs solo. Well, I'll remember, I'll damn well remember who shoved, and don't you ever try to nose your damn boat in front of me and don't you try no tricks, 'cause I know all of 'em! Ain't no way you'd've tried this on my mama and you'll learn you don't try it on her daughter, that you will, Jobe!''

"Being as you're a kid," Jobe said when she left a gap.

"I ain't no kid!"

"You ain't grown neither. You better tell it plain, Little Jones. You better tell it plain whiles we got the patience. What kind of business is going on and why's Jones' kid all of a sudden going here and there round all the trouble in town?''

Who said I was?''

"*Half the town said!* You want us to discuss this the hard way? Now we ain't liking to do it. But we c'n just start to talk real serious here, you and me and some of your neighbors, we c'n just talk all night here; and we c'n do things you won't like. So you want to talk, or you want to find out what we'll do?''

Two dozen and more of them, mostly men and mostly huge. She refused to look, to give them the satisfaction. Her gut went queasier still and her muscles went to water.

Don't give way. Don't you back up none, don't back up or they got you once and all.

Think, Jones! You got to tell 'em most of it; busted up, ye can't do nobody any good; and lying to this bunch, that's dead inside a year.

"Altair." Mira's voice came soft. The big woman's jowls wobbled, stangely shadowed in the light. "Altair, sweet, you ain't done nothing wrong, I know you haven't. And these is your own, they ain't going to do nothing t' you, whatever you done, all you got to do's tell 'em what you got into—''

"That's right," said Jobe. "You tell us what you know, ain't no one going to lay a hand on you. It ain't personal, Little Jones, ain't no way we want to hurt no kid—ye're just all we got.''

"I ain't Little Jones no more! I'm the only, I run my boat. And I ain't done nothing against the Trade!''

"Well, now, you're going to make us believe that, then, right now, or 'fore morning. Or 'fore next day. You know what we do to them that hurts the trade? We starts with fingers and toes, Jones. You don't need all of 'em. But they make work pure hell. Grown men cry about the time we gets from just breaking 'em to taking 'em off. And there's ears. You don't need 'em both. And if ye don't talk—well, Bogar Isle's not going to mind a canaler's bones down here. You want to start losing fingers, Little Jones. We c'n break the littlest. Won't damage you too much."

She spun around as the man by her grabbed her arm, and Mira screamed: "No, no, no—" The scream went right into her nerves; and the man—it was one of the Mergesers, short on wits and long on muscle—Mergeser got her hand and flexed the little finger back and back, despite her wincing and kicking. She pounded his shoulder; as soon hit the Rock itself. She flung a wild look at Jobe. "All right, all right—*ow!* Damn you, stop! dammit—"

"Stop," Jobe said, and Mergeser stopped and let her go. She clutched her sprained hand and gasped for air. "So?" said Jobe. "Tell it, Little Jones."

She gasped another breath, jerked free as Mergeser laid .a hand on her arm. "It's this rich man, this rich man—"

"Who?"

"I dunno his name. Tom, Tom, he calls himself. He got crosswise of a gang. They been trying to kill him."

"Rich men got ways to stop that kind o' thing."

"Well, they been trying. The governor ain't doing damn nothing, what'd'ye expect? This is some damn uptowner mess, and this client o' mine ain't in the wrong of it."

"Who set the fire?"

"How'd *I* know?" She flinched again as Jobe made a move. More truth. Faster truth. Much as she had to tell. Pain ran up her arm like fire. "Dammit, *he* ain't the one burned that barge. Them that's after him is pure crazies, pure damn crazies. The governor's hauled Gallandry in 'cause that's his way o' keeping peace, can't damn well find the crazies that burned Mars Bridge and set a fire in the town, so he goes and hauls in Gallandry that was the victim! Ain't that sense? Ain't that the way things work in this town?''

"Where's you in this?" Jobe asked, cold and calm. "What business you got? What freight you running?"

"I ain't running nothing but a passenger and I ain't on the side of nobody that goes setting fires, I been damn *trying* to get this fellow uptown wheres he's got friends, which is what's going to stop this bunch before they do some other damn crazy thing—They broke in uptown, they *killed* four people, you want to lay a silver to it that there ain't uptown folk going to sit on these crazies? Damn right they will! Damn right that's *alls'* got the way to settle with 'em, ain't no canaler got that kind of resources—I ain't done no damn thing against the Trade, I ain't got no damn deal with no damn fools going to burn a bridge, and if I see 'em at Hanging Bridge I'll cheer for it!"

"Maybe you ought to have thought of that early, huh, Jones? Maybe you ought to have thought about your friends."

"Listen, I never knew they was crazies when I left my boat with Del and Mira here; I never brought no trouble on them knowing it, I just left my boat to make sure my passenger got where he was going, I caught up to him and he got worried, 'cause he knew then they might kill me and I didn't; he hid me out over to Gallandry a few hours and when these crazies burned the bridge I took *him* and I run for it, 'cause by then I knew sure they was going to kill him and get clean away with it—Is that against the Trade? Is that wrong, what I done?"

"You're a damnfool, Jones."

"*What's* a damnfool? Is a damnfool someone that'll reach out a hand to a man that tried to do 'er good? Then I'm a damnfool, but I ain't no slink, Jobe, I ain't going to be, if I got to be one or the other!"

There was a muttering. It hit, hit solid. Jobe stuck his hands in his belt and stood up in the wind-fluttered candle-light like a towering monument of shadow.

"She told ye," a different voice said, a woman's voice; and a small, wispy woman pushed her way through the shadows. "She told ye true, now ye let her go, hear?"

Mary Gentry. And the big man who came through
behind her was her man Rahman. Altair looked their way
with her pulse thumping away in her throat—Mary Gentry
from that boat all those years gone, Mary's the baby boy
she had tried to save, and near drowned doing it. And
there was never a time that Mary Gentry could look on her
after that boy took fever and died.

Till now.

Till now, when it counted.

Lord take you to something better, Mary Gentry.

"What do you know?" somebody asked Gentry and:
"Shut it down," her husband yelled; and her son, her
living son, dark as Rahman and growing fast and big:
"You don't downtalk my mama, Stinner, I'll have your
guts on a hook!"

Altair drew a breath and let it go. The whole business
went to shoving and threat of hooks till someone got the
Gentry-Diazes and the Stinners apart, the candle-light all
crazy with shadows and the hollow echoing and racketing
with shouted argument.

"Shut it down!" Jobe roared; and it shut down, slowly.
Altair stood there with her knees quaking and Jobe clenched
his fists. "Jones, this account you give better be straight.
It damn sure better be straight!"

"You go accusing somebody of setting fires, Rufio
Jobe, you damn well make sure you're right!" She clenched
a fist of her own and made a gesture at him, ancient and
evident. "I make my living on the water same's ever'one,
I haul barrels and I never got crosswise of no one, not me
nor my boat, dammit! I do my tie-ups proper, I watch your
boats, I pays my debts—which being, Del Suleiman—"
She found Del in range and swung that hand his way,
flat-out and contemptuous. "You tell me what I owe you,
you name me what it is for watching my boat, and you
name it here in front of ever'body. I'll pay ye. I'll pay ye
ever' penny."

"Penny'll do 'er," Del muttered, shifting his feet.
"Jones—I was trying to help—"

She stared at him. "Ye called council on me trying to
help?"

"Ye damnfool kid, ye're in with scoundrels!"

"*So you want to break my fingers?*"

"It was Jobe said it about the fingers," Del cried. "Lord and my Ancestors, Jones, Jobe never would've done it—Jones, f'rget the penny, I don't want no pay."

Her breath came and went in a series of dizzy gulps.

Kill him, I'll kill 'im.

Damn, this sad old fool. Him an' Mira. Like Gran Mintaka. No kid. All these years, no kid.

Look at 'em. Crazy. Crazy with wanting to push me around.

Crazy with wanting.

"Man wanted to 'dopt me," Altair said, looking around at Jobe. "Him and Mira. —I don't hold no grudge. Not you either, Jobe. But you better get it in your heads good—" She swung round and shouted at the lot of them, looking one and the other in the eye, Mergeser in particular. "If I was guilty I'd've gutted half of ye! Take advantage of a body 'cause they ain't looking for no wrong from ye, shove 'er around and call 'er a liar, huh? Del, I'll pay you that penny next week. I don't want no debts, but I ain't going to argue it here."

"Jones," Jobe said, "you'd do real well to get out of that business of yours. You ain't all that clean. I'm telling you, you got yourself in fast water. Real fast. A kid's balance just ain't that good."

"Thanks," she said sourly. And rubbed a sore arm. "Give me my stuff back. Where's my knife?"

There was silence. "Give it to her," Jobe said, and Alim Settey moved up and gave the knife over. One of the Casey brothers gave the hook into her other hand, and she sheathed both of them. Her hands were shaking, bad as her knees, but it was her hands they could see in the light, her hands shamed her so her face went hot and rage wound tight down in her gut. "Thanks," she said. Be polite, Altair. Her mother's voice in her head. Retribution's ghost sat over on a pile of brick, feet a-dangle, cap tilted back. They ain't so bad, Retribution said. They're your neighbors, they're all you got, you got to be civil 'cept when they're fools.

They're fools, mama.

They didn't believe you, half, Retribution's voice said inside her skull. And they let you go, didn't they? Is that a fool? Or is that neighbors?

The Mergeser's youngest offered her cap, all solemn-faced and polite. Altair knotted her fist up and unknotted it and took the cap without snatching it. Set it on again, and walked to the exit through the others, her legs shaking so she could hardly negotiate the rubbled passage. She came out into windy Bogar Cut, and drank down a cold lungful of air.

A bell was ringing somewhere far away, whisper of sound in the night. The wind and the bridges and the twisting waterways played games with such sounds, making it near and far by turns.

She started to move, jogging down the narrow strip of stone on knees that wanted to go out from under her all the way. Others came behind her, multiple footfalls on the rugged bricks.

"Somebody's got trouble," someone said. And then the ringing stopped.

She jumped Del's side to his halfdeck and jumped on over to her own skip, got down on her haunches and started untying as the rest of the crowd reached the canalside. Some delayed to talk. Others stood and stared. Her knees wobbled and her hands shook, the knot resisting.

Bells happened many times a night in Merovingen. A shop got broken into, a shopkeeper hailed the blacklegs and his neighbors. Nothing unusual.

But she cursed and got the knot loose, stood up and rattled and fumbled with the pole as she ran it out, gritting her teeth against the pain of her arms. She nearly had her legs go out from under her as she skipped down into the well and hurried up forward to put the pole in and turn the skip about.

"Jones." It was Del. Del had made it back to his boat, Mira panting a distance behind. "Jones, I got to talk to you. Mira—"

"I ain't got time." She fended a bit from Del's boat, shoved the bow out against the Snake's current and let the current slew her hard as she ran back to stern again, getting underway.

"Jones," Del called out. And: "Altair!" from Mira.

"Where's she going?" someone asked.

Water lapped noisily at the sides of Bogar and Mantovan, and voices dimmed as she came out and got moving.

Damn fool panic, ain't no cause of it, folk'll see you.

Slow down, Retribution said in her mind. You want those fools back there to see you run like this? What you thinking of, Altair?

I dunno, I dunno, mama. I don't care, damn them all. I got to get back again to Moghi's. I got to find Mondragon, something's wrong, something's wrong somewhere.

And wrong's got this way of finding him.

Breath came hard, came on an edge of grinding pain as the pilings of Hanging Bridge closed all about her, with the skip riding the Snake current. No boats, her eye picked up not a single skip or poleboat moored under Hanging Bridge, nowhere about the point—there had been a single skip making its slow way down the Margrave, under Coffin Bridge. No one else. The desertion was ominous, but the boats that belonged hereabouts were mostly down at Bogar—Council called was a good enough draw to account for scarce boats: she had seen it scarcer on a rumor or a wedding or a wake—A hundred reasons.

Past Hanging Bridge shadow. Ventani Pier loomed blackly into the sheen of water and bright light glittered on the water in front of Moghi's open door, showed a half-dozen or so boats moored to Moghi's porch. *That* was normal. The windows were unshuttered, the door wide.

Fool. See? Kill yourself for nothing. Mondragon's abed, sleeping all nice and warm and never knowing a thing.

Got to get him up and moving. Got to get him up to Boregy fast as we can. Lord, my arms, my hand. Oh, damn, *damn*, my finger hurts.

But where's the music?

Where's the noise?

I ain't hearing music, not a voice. O Lord! Lord—why ain't there any noise yonder?

She poled another stroke, let the skip glide, wind cooling her skin through the sweater.

Tie up to the porch, slip round back, by the shed?

Walk that dark cut, back into who knows what kind of trap?

O Lord, O Lord! It *was* here, it *was* Moghi's bell—Where's the watch? Ain't the damn blacklegs going to come?

What'm I going into?

She veered off toward Ventani Pier, so sharply the skip crabbed along sideways and made way slowly toward that dark set of pilings and the sloping freight-dock.

Her mouth tasted of blood. Her ribs ached. She drove in hard toward the pilings, scraped the skip side against them so hard it staggered her in her footing.

No watchers along the stone rim. No homeless and no mendicants waiting there to pilfer a boat's goods. Nothing. The poor and the cats—they knew when to move. They had more sense than a fool canaler, than a meddler in others' business. They were gone. Safe. They saw nothing. And everything.

She turned the bow again and poled along the dark, shallow edge up to the south side of Moghi's porch, snagged a piling rope with the barrel hook, wrapped the portside tie around it and scrambled up the ladder in the light and the unnatural quiet from inside.

She stopped dead in her tracks then, numb at the sight of bodies all over the well-lit floor, slumped at tables, in chairs, as if catastrophe had been sudden and violent.

"Moghi!" She wavered there in the impulse to run, to bolt back to the safety of her own boat and take herself where a canaler belonged.

But Mondragon—but *him*, asleep upstairs—

She took her knife and her hook in either hand and walked in, looking this way and that, finding nothing astir. She walked the length of the room, through puddles of spilled drinks. There was a lingering acrid smell, a haziness in the air. The smell made her head ache.

Through the back curtain, into the hall, and through that

narrow doorway where the stairs were. Another body. More bodies. One moved.

"Ali!" She got to one unsteady knee and shook at him. "Ali! What happened? Where's Moghi? What's—"

"Uhhnn," Ali said, and raised a hand to point upstairs. It fell again. He made another effort. There was blood on his mouth. "Moghi—out back—" He was trying to get up. Altair left him and scrambled up the stairs.

The door of the Room was open. She ran to it, ran inside, where the nightlight still burned and the bedclothes lay ripped half from the bed. She ran to the other side of the bed, and there was nothing lying there but Mondragon's sword.

She flung the bedclothes this way and that. Not a trace of blood, nowhere any blood. Or of Mondragon's clothes, except the knit cap. *That* hung there. No boots. So he had been dressed when the trouble came. He had not been taken asleep. But he had been dragged across that bed—*someone* had.

She grabbed up the sword in her hook-hand and went back around the end of the bed to discover her own shoes still lying where she had left them. She squatted there and shook out the one with her knife hand.

The gold piece thudded out onto the floor, lay there shining in the lamplight.

So they—They—had not bothered to rob, either. Had not searched the place at all. It was nothing in the world they cared about but Mondragon himself—so they were not ordinary thieves, not hired help; and him gone without a trace of a struggle but the bedclothes ripped and the sword lying and the air filled with that acrid stench.

She pocketed the goldpiece, sheathed the useless knife and hook and pelted barefoot across the hall to check the bath, in one last vain thought of finding him.

Nothing. Her head pounded, her eyes watered and her nose ran—she swiped her sweater-sleeve across the latter, hearing a commotion below, men's voices and muffled oaths.

They were alive down there. Whatever noxious stuff

had gotten loose in the building, someone was alive, and someone was down there walking around.

If it was not the Sword of God themselves, come back to kill them all.

O Lord, ain't nobody heard that bell? Don't even Ventani care, upstairs of us? Governor's police won't come, they won't about come down here, 'cepting they might want their hands on Mondragon—

—and now there's me, up here in the upstairs with no way down but them stairs—

There were clear voices and muzzy ones, all male; then: *"Jones!"*

Moghi's distinct bellow, however strained and cracked. She clenched her fist on Mondragon's sword and headed stairward.

Moghi was down in the hall, propped on a bench against the hanging clutter of clothes and towels on the wall. Ali was there, with a half dozen of the bullylads and a single youth whose lavender-and-black silk shirt and outraged manner said Ventani all over him. Upstairs had come to call—the Ventani landlords sent to know what was amiss down in their basement and why the bell had rung. From the room beyond came thumps and weak oaths. A chair scraped and crashed. The pretty boy from Upstairs Ventani looked anxiously up at her and said something to Moghi: then he hurried out, avoiding witnesses, even if it was no more than a canaler headed downstairs with an uptowner's sword in her hand. Ventani got itself clear. It *would* be clear, if and when the law came calling. Ventani would see to that.

"He there?" Moghi asked, a ghost of his ordinary voice. The handful of men hovered around him, all of them with dour, ugly looks *"He there, Jones?"*

She clutched the sword in her left fist and stopped on the bottom steps, outnumbered and outweighed and with no more place to run than canaler justice gave her. Not raise a sword against Moghi, nor take a hook to him. That was a way to die, right off or in a few days, slow and painfully.

"No," she said. "He ain't there." And stamped the last

two steps down to stand square in Moghi's little court. "Dammit, Moghi—how'd they get him?"

"Smoke," Moghi said, "this damn smoke—" He waved a pasty-hued hand. Sweat stood on his face. He looked like a man about to be sick. "They came in, all hoods and masks—Wesh got to the bell and they flung one of them Chat stars—Wesh's 'bout dead out there—" Moghi coughed, the spasm rocking his whole body. "Ain't seen Tommy or Jep. Damn them. Damn 'em anyhow!"

"I got to get help—"

"Ain't no help going to come—Ain't no blacklegs going to mix in this."

"We'll see about that." She started past, for the door, but that door got blocked. Two men moved into it. She turned around and looked Moghi's way. "I got to find 'im!"

"Wait," Moghi said. "Jones. Come back here."

She came. With that tone of voice, with Moghi's men in the way, she had no choice. She stood in front of Moghi and Moghi's mouth made a thin pale line in his sweating face.

"You going after him," Moghi said. "You know what you're after?"

"I got names. Boregy. Malvino. They c'n get help somewheres." She squatted down on her heels, the sword across her knees, so that Moghi did not have to look up. "They got gold to buy trouble for them bastards, they can get him back."

"They ain't no gang," Moghi said, his voice all hoarse. "I seen 'em walk in—bold as boils, them and them black masks—never spoke a word, just this smoking pot rolled through the door and these black devils came through, just walked through, with customers dropping to the floor and that damn smoke—They flung a star at Wesh. Old Lewy cussed 'em and I thought he was gone, but they walked on through like they knew where they was going—They damn well *knew*, Jones."

"Well, I never told 'em!"

"They walk in here like they own it all, like they know

where they's going—They ain't no gang, Jones, they ain't nothing like that."

"I got t'other half of what I give you." She fished desperately in her pocket and came up with the gold piece. "Moghi, I pay ye, I make it good as I can, I go away."

Moghi hesitated, staring at the gold round—just staring at it and not taking it, as if Moghi had ever hesitated at money in his life. Then he clamped his jaw tight, reached out a waxy hand and took it between two fingers to carry it back and hold it up. "You 'member what I said, the time you come in here looking to haul barrels, Jones? You 'member what I told you about that, how I give you them two silvers and put you up against that bullyboy of Hafiz's? You 'member what I said? If you got the load back you was hired and if you got to harbor-bottom I had me an excuse."

"I come back, Moghi."

"I want these black fellows' guts on a hook, Jones. I ain't expecting to see you again. But I'm turning you loose. Ain't no lot of hooded bullies come into *my* place and take none of *my* guests. I'll have their guts for breakfast, ain't no way they get away with that. Now you tell me, Jones—" He reached out and carefully gathered the neck of her sweater in his fist and pulled her close, up in his whiskey-laden breath. The sword was still in her lap; she dared not touch it, more than to keep it from falling. "Jones, you tell me true—ever'thing. Or I gut ye. And you tell me ever'thing and I give you the same bet I give you five years ago—I give you anything you need. This ain't a money-thing. This is killing. You understand me, Jones? Who is he? What's these black fellers? Why'd they bust up my bar and poison my customers?"

"Sword of God." The breath came out strangled, choked on its way; Moghi meant it: meant it about the killing and meant it about sending her out. It was in his eyes that stared into hers, it was in the fist that held her sweater and shook with rage. "Sword of God—He run afoul of 'em, he run from somewheres north, I think—he's a rich man, Moghi, I never lied. He's got rich friends, he's got money— You'll get it back—"

"It ain't money." The fist tightened more, twisted at the sweater and cut off her wind. "You going to go to them friends, are you?"

"Yes."

"Sword of God." He shook her. Her eyes rattled in their sockets. She went to her knees and the sword hit the floor between them. "Sword of God! Why d'they want him? Huh?"

"I think—" Another shake. Her brain reeled. "I think they want to shut him up. He—knows too much."

"They ain't killed him! They took him right out the front door! Right in front of ever'one, they took him away!"

"Then—I dunno, Moghi, I dunno. I think they want him back."

"Back!"

"I dunno, Moghi!"

The fist relaxed, slowly. Moghi's face stayed all white and hectic-flushed and beaded with sweat.

"You said—" Altair sucked a mouthful of whiskey-tainted air. "You said you'd give me what I need. Give me a can of fuel. Give me one of your boys to go with me—Moghi, my arms is like to break, I poled from one end of this damn town to the other—I got to get uptown, Moghi, I got to be able to run."

"Folk'll think I'm getting old. Folk'll think they can walk in here anytime and cause trouble. Folk'll think they can do any damn thing they like to my boys in the town— Damn them, damn them anyhow! You get your fuel, you get any damn thing you want, Jones. And you get back here with what you find out, you let me know it, hear?"

"I hear you, I hear you, Moghi."

"Get two of them cans," Moghi said, motioning back at the storeroom. "Mako, Killy, all o' you, you get that stuff out to her boat. Jones, you go out there, you get that boat round to the landing, you get yourself uptown and you get them rich folks moving. *And you be careful, Jones, or I'll sink ye!*"

She grabbed Mondragon's sword, scrambled up and pushed her way through the men around Moghi, past Ali,

who delayed bewildered in the doorway. She jogged out
through the common-room, where dazed customers showed
life, where several were busy heaving up their stomachs
where they lay. Canalers. She saw familiar faces, saw one
in the doorway, young and pimply-faced and spiky-haired,
staring at the scene as if his wits had left him.

"Tommy!" She grabbed his skinny arm and shook him
till his eyes showed he knew her. "Tommy! There's a lot
of canalers off by Bogar Cut! You run, hear me, you run
and tell 'em what happened here, run say I said there's a
blond man been carried off by them as poisoned folks
here—*hear me*, Tommy?"

"Yeah," Tommy said through the chattering of his
teeth.

"Moghi's alive. He'll skin you if you don't, hear that?
Tell 'em report to Moghi, tell 'em to come here with what
they know. Hear?"

"Huuuh," Tommy said when she shook him.

"Then git!"

He got. He turned and ran, was halfway to Hanging
Bridge by the time she got down the porch ladder to her
deck and looked to see. She shoved Mondragon's sword
into the hidey, jerked the tie loose, ran out the pole and
backed—

Easy, Jones, use the wits, Jones. Hurry don't never
move a boat from dead-stop.

She got it maneuvered around, used a shove from the
bow and ran back to the halfdeck, fending from this and
that piling, while a to-do down by the darker, deeper maze
under the main bridgehead told her where Moghi's men
were. She eased in there, and a hook out of the dark
snagged her bow and helped her bring the bow in to the
dark landing-slip.

Men brought two cans aboard, walked down to the slats,
setting the skip to rocking—"You set one here," she said,
tapping the spot with the pole-end. "You there—get 'er up
here, tip 'er into the intake, she'll hold it." She racked the
pole and hurried to fling up the engine cover to get at the
fuel intake. A flip of the cap and Moghi's man unstopped

the can and heaved the whole can nozzle-down into the intake, a fumy flood that gurgled into the empty tank.

If I'd've had time to work on the engine, if I could count on 'er starting, Lord and glory, I can't trust that thing less she's running and I known her to die outright when she goes cranky.

The last of the fuel spilled in. The man took the can and headed off the halfdeck in haste. "Who's staying?" she asked, seeing one and another man quit the deck. "Who's going with me?"

"It's me," a voice said, all hoarse and wobbly, and a smallish curly-headed man staggered his way up to his feet. "Moghi said."

"Ali?"

"I don't like boats," Ali said. "Jones, my belly hurts. My head's killing me."

"Damn, damn—" *That* was Moghi's help. The refuse. A man too sick to crawl. She ran out the pole again, feeling the boat let loose from its grapple up forward. "Get the boat hook," she said to Ali."

"We *poling!*"

"We ain't going to run the motor and get them black bandits on our trail out of here, are we? *Get that damn hook!*"

Ali staggered to the rack and got the hook. "I dunno how," he said. "Jones, I ain't no—"

"Ye stroke opposite me up to bow and ye don't fall in, ye useless baggage! Ye just don't fall in, or I swear I'll leave ye to drown!" She shoved with the pole. "We got upcurrent to fight, damn ye, *shove!*"

Ali got to point and got the blunt end of the hook in. It was not much of a push, but it helped; breeze at their backs helped. She counted for him—"hin, Ali, hin, dammit, ain't you got no feeling what I'm doing?" —and drove with all the strength left in her shoulders and her back. "Get back to here, get back here aft and move 'er, man."

Then there was just breath enough to push with, and none left for talk. There were her gasps and Ali's, and the slap of the water as the skip moved along at all the speed one poler and unskilled help could manage.

Damn 'em. Damn 'em all.

No boots. Mondragon had lain down to sleep but he had never undressed again—he *must've* been asleep and not heard the fracas below, til the smoke got to his door, til he was trapped in that room and the smoke got inside it.

She built a picture in her mind—Mondragon lying fully-clothed abed after she had gone. Falling back to sleep lying atop the covers til the smoke got to him and he knew something was wrong, til his kidnappers broke the door in and he put up a last failing defense, the sword falling to the floor on the far side of the bed as they overpowered him, a struggle that tore the sheets free and strewed them outward toward the door—

But the boots. The boots were gone. And the door—she did not remember any splintering about the doorframe.

A knock at the door? Mondragon being called to the door by a voice he knew—surprised and borne backward in a struggle that ended in a wild dive for the sword—

Mondragon handing her the money he had left. Holding the boot in his hand and complaining about her intentions.

Had he gone on to finish dressing?

She gasped for air and looked over to Ali—to the one who came and went in Moghi's Upstairs Room. "They get Jep?"

Ali turned a sickly, widemouthed grimace her way. "Dunno." Between breaths.

"You see 'em?"

"I saw 'em—Yow!" Ali wobbled, hanging his pole, and flailed wildly for balance on the edge of the deck. She crossed over and grabbed him by the back of the shirt.

"Who? How'd they get up there?"

"I dunno!" He swung about and his elbow grazed her ribs as she sucked air and skipped back. "I dunno!"

"I'll give that report to Moghi." She gripped the pole crosswise as she faced him. He had the boathook, but no landsman could use it right. "You want to try me with that thing?"

"You gone crazy?"

"How'd they get in? Why'd my partner have his boots on?"

"I dunno, I never saw—"

"Was it Moghi himself?"

"Front door." Ali's teeth chattered. "D-d-amn door was open, they walked in—"

"Smoke went off in the upstairs hall too. *Didn't it?*"

"Jep—Jep—done it."

"You did, ye damn sneak!"

He swung the boathook at her. She swung. Down. Ali slumped on the deck like a sack of meal, and she hit him with the pole-end when he showed signs of getting to his knees. The boathook rolled aft. She stamped on the pole and stopped it. No further sign of movement from Ali.

She gathered up the boathook and shoved Ali with her foot, thump, down into the well. He landed on his shoulders and twisted up.

Damn! *Moghi?"*

No. Moghi weren't lying, that weren't no lie, I *know* him, I ought to take this traitor back to Moghi and let Moghi get truth out of him.

Lord, Lord, they got Mondragon somewheres, they want him alive—

What'll they be doing to him?

The timbers of Southtown Bridge hove up ahead. Canalers were night-tied there, along by Calliste. She put the pole in and shoved off in that direction, driving on pain in her ribs and pain in her arms. She came gliding in and fended off a poleboat with a clumsy scrape of hull against hull.

"Damn fool!" a male voice yelled, a sleeper startled out of slumber with collision and damage to his boat.

"Name's Jones," she gasped, and squatted down there in the dark and tried to keep the skip immobile. "'I got to have help."

"Help—*Jones.* Jones, is it? There's a word out on you. You set that fire."

"Damned if I set it! I got that straight with Jobe an hour ago!"

"I ain't having no part of your business!"

"Go on!" someone else cried from another boat. "That's Jones, a'right. That's her what burned Mars Bridge!"

"You keep your distance!" She shoved with the pole and put water between her and the poleboatman. "This lander tried to kill me. There's been a fight down to Moghi's. This baggage of mine poisoned a dozen canalers, he's took a bribe from someone—Oh, damn!" There was life from the well. She sprang up and swung the pole, a sweeping crack across Ali's ribs—"Yow!" Ali screamed, and cartwheeled right out of the boat with a great splash of water.

"There," she said, "you better fish him out, I don't know if he swims!" She put the pole in and shoved off, and shoved again, with Ali flailing the water and choking in great shouts and gulps. "I don't think he does swim!" she amended that. "You tell Moghi ask him how come my partner didn't put up no fight and why that door weren't broke in! That fellow's worth money, there!"

More and more water between them. She faced about and kicked the engine cover up, primed it and pulled the choke and made the first try while shouts rose behind her. Thump, into a piling. The skip slewed around, dizzily following the current.

"Get after her!" someone yelled. "She's trying to start that engine."

Second try. Cough, tunk.

Come on, engine.

She heard the splashes, heard Ali screaming, heard boats moving. She never looked. She reset the choke. Tried again. Cough-cough-chug-tunktunk.

She feathered it down, engaged the propeller and it faltered. Held. The skip lumbered forward, aimed at open water. Screams diminished over the noise of the engine.

She pulled the pin and got the rudder down; pulled the second pin and got the tiller up and home. She leaned on the bar and swung round as two canalers moved their boats out to stop her, stringing out from moorings.

Not fast enough. She put the throttle down and the engine lumbered away with more and more way on the skip. She let the pole lie abandoned on the deck, slanted into the well, put the tiller over hard to choose a clear way through the pilings of Southtown Bridge, and powered through. She looked back, where an unaccustomed white wake showed in the moonlight, and ahead where Foundry Bridge was.

All about her, boats were moored along the bridgehead, wherever the projection of pilings gave them shelter out of the Grand channel. All about her, eyes would peer into the dark and the commotion would spread. She thought of dodging round into Foundry Canal, getting at Boregy the quiet way—but there *was* no quiet way, canalers could cut her off, block any canal but the wide, free-flowing Grand.

She put the throttle in full and spent fuel recklessly, took time to rack the poles when there was a moment's straightway between Foundry and Hightown bridges, and got back to the tiller before it slewed in the current.

Boregy had already been hit once. Opposite the Signeury. So much for town authorities and the governor and all his militia. Damnfool and his clockmaker son and his whole damn pet police.

The night kept its false quiet, with only the sound of one boat engine running hard through the town heart, alerting every enemy that might be watching and listening.

Chapter 8

THE engine-sound echoed off the walls of the Signeury, those big blank walls that showed nothing but rifle-slits to the outside, and had precious few bridges for all its great bulk. Stone was under its foundations; it was all of stone itself, and while Merovingen-above glittered with its night-lights, while the high houses had their windows shining into the night and casting their reflections down into Merovingen-below, the Signeury crouched like a baneful giant in the dark water of the Grand, turning engine-sound into hollow thunder. No boats sheltered under Signeury Cross: it was prohibited. *Nothing* lurked about those bridges but the law themselves. Altair hugged the tiller under her arm, kneeling on the deck, and took the throttle down, letting the skip glide for Golden Bridge and Boregy. There was plenty of way on her, no need of the pole, here where the Grand itself went treacherous with Greve-current and none so far upcanal they had to sink great slabs of upriver stone to keep the bottom from washing. It was strange territory, uptown; it was all blank walls and high, suspicious Isles without the under-the-bridges conglomeration of shops and manufactures that was canalside life belowtown.

Boregy hove up beyond the dark web of the Golden, dark as the Signeury, merest shadow excepting a light or two in its uppermost levels. Its sides were deserted. It *had* no tie-rings, being the Signeury's neighbor. It had one of the Signeury's bridges going to it alone; and by its balconies was the walk eastern hightowners had to take to council and to the Signeury: *that* was influence. That was the kind of place Boregy was.

But it got attacked, and people got killed; and the governor just arrested Gallandry, who was one of the victims.

O Lord and my Ancestors, I got to go inside this place, I got to make 'em help—

She wobbled to her feet, cut the motor and used the pole the last few feet, fending off a drift into Boregy's wall with a jolt that near took her off the deck. The pole shed a splinter into her palm with a faint far pain somewhere lost in the buzzing of her brain, the throbbing of a headache. She saw the gardeporte, a grim little pierced tile with a devil-face that was Boregy's canalside window. A bell-pole dangled a cord there in the reach of a skip deck. She maneuvered up to it and pulled.

A bell tinkled inside, a tiny sound against the water slap in the wide Grand.

She pulled the cord again, and the gardeporte rattled. The devil's mouth and eyes flared and shadowed as a human face looked out behind it.

"Who?" a gruff voice asked through the devil-mouth, a voice like thunder itself—Boregy's gate-warder, called from whatever occupied him. "Who are you?"

"Name's Jones. I got to talk with the Boregy."

"You say. Go to hell. Honest business can wait till morning." The face withdrew, the devil's eyes flared gold lamplight and went out as the port thunked shut.

"Dammit!" She grabbed the cord again and jangled it over and over. The devil-face fleered light and the man reappeared behind its grimace.

"You want I call the law?"

"Mondragon," she said. *"Mondragon!"* And her knees shook when she had said it. She felt sick inside. Forget my name, he had said. I was crazy out there.

"What's your name?"

"It's Jones."

"You alone on that boat?"

"I'm alone."

"Pull into the Cut, up to the door."

Thunk. The tile shut again. The devil-face returned to dark. She drifted a moment away from the wall, then moved her aching arms and put the pole in again, pushing toward the solid iron gate,

Now's done it. Now you got yourself uptowner trouble, Jones. They know your name and his together. Was that smart at all?

But, Mama, Angel, I got to go there. I ain't got nowhere else.

Have I?

She turned the skip. The pole grated on stone below the water, the bow slewed about and bumped the iron gates. Chain took up suddenly, hand-cranked gears rattled and clanked as the big valves grated, groaning their way apart enough to admit a skip. She drove on the pole. Nothing but black lay beyond those jaws.

Retribution's ghost perched on the bow, mending a bit of rope. Looked up at her, all dimly sunlit in the dark.

The ghost said not a thing. It was just company.

You was always into things, mama. You never let nobody near me. Never let none of your dealings touch me. Never knew how that was. Never knew why we didn't have no friends and I had to be a boy.

Dammit, mama, you could've said why that was. Now you come back. *Now* you got no advice either.

You were a kid, the ghost said finally. What could you tell a kid?

Tears stung her eyes. She poled blind in the dark. The chains rattled behind her and the doors slowly clanked shut, cutting off the wholesome breeze. For a breath or two there was total dark and she glided.

Damn place, Altair, damnfool stunt, you're going to smack into a wall or a step—slow 'er down.

The ghost was gone. The dark was complete. Then light burst in a rectangle of an opening door, and scattered on the black water and the buff stone of the Cut walls.

She poled over to the porch-landing and blinked into the lamplight. The open door was invitation—from a place that had lately suffered murder and invasion.

Fool to go in there. Fool to come this far, Altair.

She bumped into the landing and caught a tie-ring with her bare hands, letting the pole-end fall in the well and the rest lie aslant across the deck-rim. Muscles strained, the way of the boat fighting back; sore joints protested. She braced bare feet, snatched the rope through and made fast.

Then she stepped across to that stone porch, climbed the single step and walked into the lighted stone hall.

The door swung to, kicked from behind it. She spun and staggered to a quick freeze, facing a man with a knife, as another door crashed open and poured armed men into the hall at her other side.

It was a climb up back stairs and into dim places, with men in front of her and behind. They had not taken her hook and her knife; and they had kept their hands off her; but they had their own weapons, and those were out, bare steel.

Up two turns of that inside stairs, with an electric here and there—she did not gawk; she had no mind for anything but the man in front of her and the men behind her and the haste in which they moved her along.

Then they opened a door onto a red stone hall that left her standing numb, mouth open until she realized it and shut it on a gulp of air.

Lord and my Ancestors.

Polished stone, white-veined red; columns, statues out of white and black stone. Light agleam as bright as day— the white light of electric, in a gold-and-glass lamp that broke up light and threw it everywhere. They had to shove her to get her moving again; and the cold red stone of the floor was like silk under her wounded feet.

More climbing, up a staircase wide as Moghi's whole front room. It dwarfed all her imaginations.

Money—O Lord, money enough to buy lives and souls. Money enough to drink down all the troubles in the world. Gallandry was *nothing* to this! O Mondragon, I see why ye backed up from me on that boat, belonging here. O Lord and Glory!

A great gilt table crowned the summit; a man in a blue and gilt bathrobe stood by it, a black-haired man with a fierce down-turning mustache and black eyes that burned her to ash even before she had climbed the last steps.

Get this man out of his bed, make 'em light all these electrics—This is a man don't talk to no canalrats, this man looks at me like something dead and floating—O Lord, I got to watch my mouth with this one, I got to talk uptown talk, make this m'ser believe I know Mondragon for sure or they'll take me downstairs and beat me. Is that The Boregy hisself, and him that young? No. *Can't* be. Boregy's old, ain't he? Got to be some son of his. I got to argue with *him* first and then Boregy.

O Lord, I'm all sweated, and them with all them baths.

She stopped and jerked her hat off and clutched it in both hands, there in front of this m'ser who was probably straight from his bed, whatever he was doing there, this m'ser with all these armed men standing around him.

"You mentioned a name," the Boregy said.

"Yessir," she murmured. If he was not going to say that name outright here, she reckoned she ought not to. She looked straight in those black eyes and felt like she was going underwater. Down in the dark of old Det.

"Well?"

"He's got trouble. I got to say its name?"

"You know its name?"

"They got 'im. they broke in where he was sleeping and they took 'im—I don't know where. You got to help. He said you was friends. He said—he had to get here. Now he can't. They got him."

"Who *are* you?"

"Jones, ser, Altair Jones. You c'n ask anyone" No, fool. This man don't *talk* to the likes of us, this man don't ask his own questions.

'Cept now.

"It must be the girl from Gallandry," a man muttered.

"So he did get off that barge," the Boregy said.

"He got off," Altair said. "We jumped, him and me."

"Did you take him to your friends?"

"Only thing I could do—" O Lord, no, that ain't what he means, *O* Lord, see his eyes, he's thinking about his basement right now. "Damn, I ain't turned him over to *them,* no, I didn't!"

The Boregy went on staring. Her knees went to jelly.

It's the basement, it's the basement sure. O Lord, save a fool! What do I say, do I tell him we was lovers, do I say anything at all until he wants to talk to me?

"Where is he now?" the Boregy asked.

"I dunno, I dunno where he is, I come to you to ask where they'd go."

"To me?"

"He give me your name. You got to go to the governor, get the law, get the hightown go find him—They didn't kill him, there wasn't any blood, it ain't killing him they want—not yet. You got to do something."

The Boregy stared and stared. Finally he moved his hand. "Chair," he said; and one of the men ran to the side of the hall where a chair was. Boregy turned the one already there, a great wooden chair at the table-end; and sat down, staring up at her. "Sit down," he said when the chair arrived, a spindly gilt thing with white and brown cloth. The man set it down across the angle of the table-corner. "Sit," Boregy said.

"My pants is dirty." It came out all strangled. Heat rushed to her face.

"Sit down anyway."

She sat.

"Wine." He made another gesture aside. "Where was this? What happened?"

"I put him up to Moghi's. This tavern, down on Ventani-bottom. 'Neath Fishmarket Stair. I went for my boat, friend had 'er. I come back and some damn—Somebody broke in there—" Her teeth started to chatter and her eyes to water, and she drew a great breath and fought both tendencies down. She spread her hands to cover the interval. Her palms were blistered, calluses and all. "They flung this smoke stuff. Knocked out the whole d—whole tavern. They got him that way."

"Pathati."

She blinked stupidly.

"Pathati. Gas. It's a sharrist weapon."

"Sharrist." The whole world tumbled in and reason fell after it. "O Lord, what's sharrh to do with it?"

Boregy did not answer. A man brought the wine up, red wine in a bottle all of cut glass; and stem-glasses the same. The man set it down and poured, gave Boregy one glass and set the other beside her on the big table. She picked it up and her hand shook. She used both to get it steady, and drank a sip.

"The law," Boregy said, "is not an option in this matter."

She blinked at him, helpless.

"The police will not be interested," Boregy said.

"They flung him off the bridge."

"What?"

"The law flung him off Fishmarket Bridge. I pulled him out." Her teeth wanted to chatter again. There was an ache in her gut, in her bones, in her skull behind the eyes. "I figured maybe—maybe you got friends could put the shove on the law on the other side, that's why I come here, I mean, someone's bribed 'em against him, a bribe from the other side'll work *for* him. Won't it?"

"You don't appreciate the difficulty.

"I don't." The words muddled up, made no sense. It sounded like *no*. She held the glass in both hands to keep it from shaking. She made a shift of her eyes about the room, where a half dozen men stood waiting on a Boregy and a canalrat to drink their wine. She made that look a gesture. "You got *them*, don't you?" Landsmen that they were, they looked dangerous. They looked more dangerous than the law ever looked. "If you know where they went—Lord, we got to do something, they *got* him, they could be doing anything—"

"They might well." Boregy turned his glass on the tabletop, fingers long and white and slender. He shot a glance up at her. "You have to understand the inconvenience. Your coming here is an embarrassment, one we can ill afford. You weren't in a position to understand that, perhaps. But if the police did, as you say, throw him off the bridge, that does indicate the governor's official position, doesn't it? Or someone's opinion—very high and influential. It's virtually the same."

"Lord, them blacklegs'll sell for a penny!"

"Not in this case. No. Nor for coin. It takes a different currency. Neither of us has it. Your coming here is inconvenient, to say the least."

"You're his friends!"

"We were his family's friends." The glass made another revolution and Boregy never looked down to see what his hands did. "That family no longer exists. Presently he's a hazard. Consider Gallandry's fortunes, if you doubt it. Mondragon's a contagion."

She set the wine down, shoved the chair back and started to get up, hat in hand. A man stepped up and shoved her down and shoved the chair forward.

"Damn you!" Her yell echoed round the hall. A heavy hand descended onto her shoulder and men moved uneasily where they stood. Her knife occurred to her. Draw and she was dead. She understood that. She glared at Boregy, and Boregy waved his man off. The weight left her shoulder.

"Your loyalty does you credit," he said. "You've done as much for him as a girl could. I don't say I don't appreciate that quality—you don't have to be afraid of us. I could use a resourceful employee. What are you—a poleboater? You'd be in Boregy service, have a place for the rest of your life, a very well-paid place."

"I'm a skip freighter," she muttered. "And I'll come back later if ye want me, and I won't say I was here if you want, but I got to go, I got to find him if you won't say where they'd've took him—You could tell me that! You could give me that much!"

Boregy stared at her with that black gaze of his and never blinked. "Why are you so interested?"

" 'Cause he ain't got no damn help from you!"

"Drink your wine."

"I ain't drinking any wine. Let me out of here!"

"Jones, your name is. Do you have a first name?"

"Altair." Lord, now her mouth was going to go weak, her chin was going to tremble like a baby's. O Lord, I could kill this man. I could kill him, and then they'd kill me, if they ain't going to do it already—

"I'm Vega Borey." He folded his white hands in front of him on the table. "So we have something in common. You'll understand when I say our influence is limited in this. I have a cousin and two of my men dead yesterday. The Sword has reached into this hall: *that's* why Gallandry was arrested and we were not—the governor has that for evidence that we are victims and not perpetrators. We dare not speak for Gallandry. Are you understanding me? As Adventists, we cannot afford a tie to the Mondragons, except a historical one. Your friend is an irritance, a dangerous inconvenience."

"He trusted you!"

"That he might have, had he come quietly. But someone betrayed him. Someone he trusted, surely. Fear, you understand. They set the law on his track and that led his enemies to him—by extension, to all his possible allies. Don't imagine that the Sword doesn't extend even into the militia. Or that *sharrist* influence might not extend to Merovingen. Do you see what you've involved yourself in?"

"I don't see. I don't understand. I don't want to see. Let me out of here and I won't say a thing."

"Do you intend to go searching for him?"

"I ain't saying what I'll do."

"What *can* you do?"

"I got my knife."

"Your knife! Do you know what the Sword of God *is*?"

"I know as much as any honest canaler knows, which is that I don't want nothing to do with 'em. But I ain't going to quit. You sleep good, m'ser, you sleep real good, and just let me go do what I got to do and I ain't going to repeat to no other soul what you told me."

"Girl, you're a fool."

"I am. I been one for days. But I ain't going to leave him to 'em."

"You know he's from Nev Hettek."

"I never knew that proper, but that was high on my guesses."

"The governor of Nev Hettek is a man named Karl Fon. Do you know Fon is in the Sword?"

Her heart lurched a few painful thumps harder than it had been. "I heard that rumor."

"The Mondragons were ordinary Adventists, like most of Nev Hettek. An old, well-placed household. Thomas— the youngest son—was drawn into the Sword. Does that shock you?"

"He told me he was, once. He said he quit them."

"What more did he say?"

She shook her head.

"That's important, you see. *Why* he quit them. And how far he was in on their councils. He was Fon's close friend: he was in very high councils in Nev Hettek, above even his father's access to those levels. Perhaps Mondragon learned more than he wanted to know. But whatever involvement he had with them—terminated. The whole family was killed. Except Thomas Mondragon. He was put up on trial as a sharrist saboteur."

"He ain't!"

"That was the standard accusation—for any enemy of the governor. He was sentenced to death. His execution was set three times and three times postponed. Then he escaped, escaped the governor's own residence, so the rumor came down the river. With everything he knows. Do you see why our own governor might urge him to get out of Merovingen? He's trouble. He's truth on two feet. He knows things our governor doesn't—officially—ever want to know about Nev Hettek's internal workings. The word is *war*, girl. War against wicked Nev Hettek and its apostate governor—if certain forces in the Signeury can get public confirmation of the things Thomas Mondragon knows. *They'd* want him too. The sharrists assuredly want him: he knows intimate details about Sword of God operations and tactics against them. The police here would question him if they dared know the answers officially. The Sword absolutely wants him back: *they're* agents of Karl Fon. And if the Priest of the College finds out what they've got within their reach, and they get their hands on him, the Revenantists will want to extract a public confes-

sion from him before they hang him. While our governor—
the governor just wants him out of town before Nev Hettek
becomes convinced Merovingen has the wherewithal to stir
up a war. He's old and he has the succession to worry
about and this is the kind of thing that could create—great
difficulty with the heirs. Shifts in power. The Sword has
been here for years; and that fact is known in very high
places. So are the sharrists active here—but that's not a
thing you'd better breathe even to yourself, young woman.''

"Was it *sharrists* that got him? This pathat—patha—"

"*All* the terrorists borrow from each other. Sword uses
pathati. So do the sharrists and the Janes. That tells you
nothing. It was likeliest the Sword. But I don't rule the
other out. I don't rule it out even if they declared what
they were. The factions lie. It's their great weapon. They
blame their actions on each other. And Mondragon knows
what all those lies are. He's been inside their most intimate
councils.''

"But—But you got these men—" She passed a gesture
round them, at the armed guards. "Man, they killed your
cousin, they broke into your house, ain't you anxious to do
nothing—"

"Don't you see past the moment? Boregy *can't* act. We
could start that war. We could touch it all off—and your
friend Mondragon will still end up with his head in a
noose—at best. No matter which faction gets hold of him.
And some are worse. I'd rather not have any of my house
standing with him in the Justiciary.''

"Well, I ain't *got* nobody, I ain't got nothing in my
way. You damn well let me out of here, you let me go, I'll
find them sons of damnation, I'll have their damn guts
out—" It was yell or cry. She shoved the chair back but
the man behind her stopped it with a grip on the back of it.
"Damn you all.''

"Girl. What's your name again?''

"Jones. It's *Jones*, damn your heart to hell. You ain't no
use, you ain't nothing, you can damn well let me go, it
don't cost you nothing.''

"But it could cost me a great deal, sera. It could cost us
everything.'' He stood up, stood looking down at her

trapped there against the table, reached down and lifted her chin with his hand.

Spit at him. Lord, they'd gut me. Here and now.

"But you don't think in those terms, do you? You don't understand a thing I'm saying."

"What's it to me?"

"What's a war more or less? Maybe nothing to you. Maybe it makes no difference to you. I assure you it does to me. How much time have they had?"

"Maybe—maybe an hour, hour and a half—" Her chin trembled in his hand. He let her go. She clenched her fists and ground her cap to shapelessness in her hands. "Why?"

"I can't tell you where he is. I can make two guesses. One is the riverboat out there in the harbor: it brought him here and it might well take him out again. They might have taken him straight aboard. It's also possible they didn't—since that ship is the first place any opposition might look, and opposition is more than a possibility, once this news spreads. I'd place my bet they haven't gone at once and they won't use so conspicuous a boat. Something less evident, a fishing-boat, a coaster. There are sea-gates all along the Old Dike. *That*'s the quarter I'd bet on. They'll have to find their boat, get their prisoner to it—"

"Then they can't've moved 'im out yet! Ye don't move nothing by them gates at ebb. Ye got four deces difference in them Tidewater canals, high tide to low—"

"There's another reason, however unpleasant to contemplate. They'll have questions to ask. We're not talking about the gangs, understand. We're talking about an organization that penetrates into the Signeury, one that knows he's been here long enough to expose certain of them if he chose to do it. Certain people might be very interested in discovering all his contacts here. Their safety is at stake and Karl Fon's orders may well take second place to their own concerns. They'll want a place and a time to question him on their own behalf, a place close to the harbor, a place where neighbors don't call the police."

"That's the whole damn Tidewater!"

"So I understand." Boregy made a motion to his men. "She'll be leaving."

Altair shoved the chair back, and this time it moved. She levered herself up and got her knees locked.

"I'm sending you, you understand. That's the help I can provide. I personally advise you take what you know and what I've told you and say nothing and do nothing. But I doubt you'll regard that. Do you want food? Money?"

She shook her head. "I got to go, is all." Lord, he's got me tagged, he's told me too much, I'll drop into a canal some night real soon, by his intention. I got to make the door, is all, that's all I can do, I can't think about food, can't stomach nothing, can't sleep while they got their hands on him—

Prison. O God. And what else?

"M'sera." She heard Boregy. Distantly. Talking to some woman. "Jones." *That* was her. She turned around at the dizzy edge of the stairs, caught her balance and stared at him staring at her.

So what's he want? He going to stop me after all?

"Who have you mentioned our name to?"

"Nobody." She shook her head violently. "I ain't—"

Lord, is that the thing he needs to know, 'fore they make some accident? Who's to care? Who's to care here?

"No one?"

"That's for me to know," she said, and turned and negotiated the stairs. Balance faltered. The whole world came closer and farther by turns, went fuzzy and came clear again, the hall with its veined red stone, its glare of electrics.

A hand caught her elbow. She shook it off and it came back. So she walked to the door and down the steps, the rough stone steps that led down and down to the hall, to the porch-landing, to her boat that rode there in the rectangle of lamplight from the open door. She drew a breath to clear her aching head. The air was cold with the water, dank with the stone of the Cut vault. Iron and stone and rot. She started down the step. An elbow nudged her.

"Here," a man said, one of the three who had brought here downstairs. Coins shone in his outstretched hand, a scatter of silver and bronze in the lamplight. She stared down at it and up at him.

"That ain't no help," she said, not even bitter. A choking lump rose in her throat. "Damn, that ain't no help at all."

She stepped across to the deck, jerked the tie loose. "You mind if I start the motor in here?"

"The family would appreciate it if you'd—"

"Sure, sure." Tears dried and strength roared through her veins like a blast of heat. " 'Preciate yourself to hell." She ran out the pole, with the water widening between herself and the Boregys. "Ye damn cowards!"

It was work turning the skip. Part of it was in the dark, when the men went back in and shut the door. Then wheels squealed, chain rattled, and the big watergate began to admit the ghostly starlight-on-water of the canal outside. The breeze came back, skirled free into Boregy Cut, raced out again.

She drove with the pole, sent the skip scudding out the narrow opening, and made the turn that took it on in the dark, with the Signeury walls high and blank and grim, and Golden Bridge hung across the Grand like a dark webby strand across the Signeury's face.

She pushed it as far as the first bridge-pilings of the Golden, till her gut hurt and her sore feet burned on the deck. Then she lifted one hand in a rude gesture up at Boregy Isle and shipped the pole, went back to start the engine.

One try at the crank. Second. She fussed with the choke and her hands shook. A third jerk at the crank. Cough. A fourth. Cough and start. The breeze skipped and skirled round the corner of Boregy. She jammed her cap down, set the tiller and sat down to steer, the tiller tucked under her arm. The strength had gone, leaving cold behind, leaving shivers that drew her legs up and made her teeth chatter.

Prison. Him in prison.

A worse image occurred. She shut her eyes and opened them wide, trying to banish it, picture of a dark place and lamplight, like Bogar's basement, but no friends in sight, none, no hope and no help and no fair-minded council in judgment, only enemies.

O God. Tidewater. Tidewater and sea-gates. It's got to
be. I come up the Snake onto the Grand just after that bell
was ringing and they was there when that bell rung—they
got Wesh for it—I wasn't that far behind, I almost saw
'em, I was that close, and I never saw any boat going
down-Grand. Just that boat away on Margrave—on Margrave going west—Damn, I *did* see 'em, they was going
away, they had him in that boat, and me not knowing—

Of Tidewater gates there's Pogy and there's Wharf, and
there's Marsh, over by Hafiz's. If it was flood they could
go by the Port Gap, but they can't do that, they got to use
the Gates, that prig Boregy's right in that. And tide don't
crest till the top of the sixth. They got to—

She blinked, jerked her head up with the point of the
Signeury wall coming up at her, veered wildly and veered
again for the center of the channel as she headed for the
massive pilings of Signeury Cross. She kept going into
bridge-shadow, a place so dark there was no hint of obsta-
cles and a body had to run it blind. The breeze gusted in
sudden violence, turned colder. The motor echoed, a lonely
throb that carried into her sore hand and aching elbow
through the tiller, and she had not even the enthusiasm left
to shift the bone off contact with the wood. Hurts, something distant told her. And: Good, her conscious mind
answered back, because it kept her mind focused.

Damn stupid fool, where you going?

Mama, you got an answer for this one?

Hell, you got yourself a good one this time. Crazies.
You ain't thinking, Altair. You checked that gun? You
sure it's still there?

She reached in panic and opened the dropbox nearest the
engine compartment. Her fingers found rags, burrowed to
touch the smooth metal of the gun. Shells were there too,
in their small box. She tested the weight. Intact. The blood
sought its former course and her heart settled down to its
exhausted throb, thumping along with the motor sound.
She blinked, focused again. The headache was fiercest at
the back and behind the eyes.

Damn smoke. Had that headache since the smoke. That
pathat-stuff. All them that breathed it must be worse.

He's got to be sicker'n hell.

Mondragon—I'm trying. What'm I going to do, you knowing more'n I do—Sword of God and all, and what'm I? All them fellows and Moghi couldn't stop 'em, and they got canaler help, had to have been them on that canal, folk'd see 'em if they went to carrying a body very far over the bridges—

—Canalers. Canalers who'd do anything.

That's a longish list. That's the whole damn Tidewater and all the vermin in it.

Borg Isle passed, and Bucher.

Could turn off toward Malvino. Could go to them, maybe they got more guts than Boregy.

No. Uptowners. I was lucky once. I got out of there. I got all I can get. Next 'un might just cut my throat.

Where do I go? Which way? Cut off down by the Splice and go down West? Damn, where *is* ever'body?

Under bridge shadow and on toward Porphyrio. Oldmarket Bridge was next. The tie-rings and the pilings had no boats, nothing, not even the shabby-canopied skip that ought to be there. The engine throbbed on, drinking up the fuel.

I c'n turn off by Wex Bend—no. That damn bridge might be blocking it. Go off by Portmouth, pick up the Sanchez Branch and go by the West—

There *was* a boat, a dark lump making rapid headway up the Grand from under Miller's Bridge, dead-center of the channel and spreading a starlit wake in a great V to either side.

Damn, it's under power, what is it, *who* is it up there?

The beat of that engine came off the walls, in and out of phase with hers. It was a skip. That could mean anybody. And the canal was deserted. That meant trouble.

They looking for *me?* Lord.

She strained her eyes, arm clenched on the tiller, ready to swim about and try for the Splice, her other hand on the throttle, ready to throw it open wide and go roaring past the boat that kept the center-channel, between the two groups of pilings.

But someone was standing in that skip, an upright silhouette in the bow, a double glimmering of white in the starlight, one moving frantically. That was a flag-down. Someone waving.

Making a target of hisself, whoever.

That wake faltered, the engine cut back. She cut back her own, gathered her aching self up on her feet and strained her eyes into the dark as the gap narrowed. One skip was like most skips in the dark, in the bridge-shadow.

But that figure in the bow was gran Mintaka, one bit of white was her hair and the other a white rag that fluttered in her waving hand.

She waved back, tentatively. Her heart pounded against her ribs. What is this? What news?

They found 'im? Somebody found 'im? Is he alive?

"Jones," Mintaka's cracked voice hailed her.

She stopped the propeller, swung the bow to lose way, slewed till she had come to a crazed drift, and slowed the engine down to a low pop and thump. The other skip slowed and someone had a boathook out.

She got her own from the rack, leaving the steering to the other skip, let them meet her, them with several aboard. And it was not for the skip she had that hook.

"Jones," Mintaka said across the narrowing gap, her high voice cracking. "Jones—that young man—that young man o' yours—Moghi send word—"

She used the hook to grapple with after all, got to the side and hooked on as the hook took from the other side. It was Del wielding that hook, Del's skip; and the other with a hook was Mira. Beyond them was a stick-limbed shadow that came up to the side, and that was Tommy, Tommy from Moghi's.

"What word?" Altair shouted as Mintaka ran out of breath or good sense. "Where is he?"

"You got to talk to Moghi," Tommy blurted out. "Jones, he beat Ali—Ali was still talking when we left—"

"Figured we could stop you," Del said.

"Sword o' god," Mintaka said, her voice all a-wobble, her white hair wild in the wind. "Jones, that there was Sword o' God grabbed that nice boy—He wasn't running

from no papa, that wasn't what he come running from, he
told us a story, Jones—he's some kind o' foreigner—"

"*Where* is he?" Sanity tottered. She appealed to Del.
"Del, for the love o' God, where is he?"

"We dunno. We got a dozen boats gone down to harbor
in the case they got that way, we got the word out east and
west—"

"Thank God for that." She banged Del's pole with
hers. "Hof, there. I got to get down there."

"Them crazies is who burned that bridge!" Mintaka
cried. "Them damn fools trying to burn the town down,
poisoning folks, cutting folks—"

Del got his pole clear. The boats began to drift. Altair
flung the boathook end-down into the well and scrambled
back to get the tiller.

Over by her, Del's engine came up quickly, the whole
racket echoing off the walls of Wex and Spellman, shivering off the water.

Why? What's it to them what comes to me and mine?

It's what the Sword's done, that's what, it's burning that
barge, it's gassing all them canalers, it's cutting old Wesh.
Ain't nothing pushes the Trade, ain't nothing and no one
pushes canalers without them pushing back.

Boats to the harbor! They got 'em stymied, they got 'em
running.

But if the Sword was to know they was caught—

—What'd they do to *him*?

She shoved the throttle down hard, full-out.

There was a crowd of boats gathered at Moghi's, a
jam-up of epic proportions. Altair cut the engine under the
Fishmarket, steered up to the mass in front of Moghi's
porch, there in Moghi's light, and bumped against the
skips there. "Watch my boat!" Altair yelled at the nearest. " 'Scuse me!" She bounded off her bow into another
well, handed her bow-rope to a man and kept going, onto
the half-deck of another and down its length.

"Hoooo! Jones!" someone yelled. "That's Jones!" And:
"'Here come Del and them!"

She traversed another skip and a poleboat at a run and

clambered up Moghi's short ladder ahead of half a dozen curious.

"Moghi?" She hung in the doorway, in a gust of cold wind, facing a gathering of canalers in the main room; but their attention was all turned to inside. A scream came suddenly from the back, not a full-voiced scream but something uglier and hurt. *"Moghi?"*

Folk turned and stared her way, stared the other as Moghi showed up from inside, a grim, draggled Moghi in a blue shirt that had more than grime on it. He wiped his hands on a towel and it came away red. "Jones." With a nod back to the hallway behind.

"Moghi, I got no—"

A second nod. She went, and Moghi grabbed her arm, bringing her through and into the back willy nilly, back into lanternlight and stink and blood and something Ali-like tied to a chair. Five of Moghi's other men were there. One was Jep, with a cut on his temple and an ugly look on his whole face. "This damn traitor," Moghi said, and grabbed a handful of Ali's curly hair. Ali yelped and bubbled blood out the nose and over his mouth. "You tell 'er, you tell 'er, damn you, what you just told."

"It's Megarys," Ali blubbered, "Megarys—ow!"

"Why?"

"Moghi, don't, don't, Moghi—*ow!*"

"Had a feller or two to dispose of now and again—This damnfool done sold 'em, sold 'em off to Megary. Ain't throwed 'em in the harbor proper, no, this thief's been selling 'em, live and dead, right down the canal. Been taking them poor bridgefolk. Crazies. Been getting along right prosperous, ain't ye, Ali?"

"Ow!"

"That wasn't any Megarys broke in here!" Altair objected. "Who'd he let in here? Where from?"

"He dunno. He was just to wait for a heller to start up front and set this poison off to the upstairs, to get that man o' yours. *That* was what. Only it didn't work that way. They come on through the front. It weren't nothing quiet. That smoke knocked *him* cold. And they come through and got your man. Ain't that so, Ali?"

"That's so, that's so—Moghi, I ain't never meant harm to the place, I was going to carry 'im out quiet-like. They was going to tell, Moghi! They was going to tell you what I done—"

"You damn dumb fool! I'd've broke your arm for what you done. Now I'm going to see you take a trip to harbor!"

"No, Moghi, no, Moghi!"

"Then you better talk, you better talk good."

"I told you, I told you it, they give me all this money, they told me they got to get this blond fellow, I figured it was some gang—I was supposed to carry 'im out back, just like he'd gone out—just let 'im disappear natural-like. They didn't tell me they was going to do the other, they didn't tell me the damn gas was going to smell up the place, they didn't tell me they was coming in after 'im and all—"

"Damn you," Altair yelled, "where'd they go? Where d'you meet these people?"

"Megary, Megary, Megary—"

"And the Sword of God," Moghi said, wiping his hand on his shirt. "The minute this fool heard you put that name to what got your man, he ain't had good sense. He was up to kill you. Out on that canal. Good job you tossed him out, damn good job."

"I never was!" Ali cried, "I never would've—"

"Would've what?" Jep grabbed himself a fistful of Ali's shirt. "Sell 'er? Sell 'er too? You damn sneak!"

"I ain't never, I ain't never! Jones, I never laid hand to you, I was going to help, I swear I was! I was going to make amends! Tell 'im, Jones!"

"Go for me with my own boathook, ye sherk! Ye deserve what ye got!"

"Don't let 'em kill me, Jones!"

She stepped back, gave a shiver.

"Jones! Jones, I go get 'im, I go find 'im, I buy 'im back!"

"You damnfool! They're Sword of God, you don't buy 'em!—Moghi, Moghi, Jobe's got some canalers gone to the harbor, and if things get too hot the Sword'll kill 'im. You know they will. They won't let him go. Without him to talk, they'll slide into this town like fish to water. We got to get 'im out before somebody gets to them.''

"Your money ain't worth my men, Jones.''

"They broke up your place, Moghi! What's the matter, you getting *old*, Moghi? You going to be an *old man*, let them crazies get a man out of here, let them bribe your help—!''

"Damn your mouth, girl!"

"It ain't girl, Moghi!"

"It ain't old man, either! You're a damn fool, meddling with them cults! What you want? What you want me to do?"

They were shouting. The room was full outside. She clenched her fists and brought her voice down. "What I need is about six, seven fellows to go with me, go break into Megary, that's what we got to do, we got to get him *out* of there before they got time to panic.''

There was a muttering in the room, a general melting-away of bystanders.

"What with?'' Moghi said. "Have we got that smoke, huh? that's a damnfool move.''

"Where's your guts?'' She looked around the room, at men edging farther and farther back.

"Not me,'' one said. "I ain't half that fool.''

"Moghi—''

"They ain't too enthusiastic,'' Moghi said. "They ain't fools. I ain't. We'll get 'em, we'll get 'em, but I ain't ordering no man of mine to go breaking into Megary. Jep?''

"I ain't too enthused either.'' Jep shifted his feet and scratched his neck. *"Blacklegs* don't go in there.''

"I'll go,'' Ali cried. And: *"Ow!"* when Moghi hit him.

"We can block the harbor out,'' Moghi said. "Do this the smart way. Carlos, Pavel, you're going round to the harbor, maybe help them canalers. Maybe talk to old Chance on that riverboat. Done him a few favors, he'll talk to me.''

"Dammit, that won't help him!''

"I'm telling you, Jones, you leave the thinking to them that has to do the bleeding! You want to go out there, they'll get them damn Megarys a nice pretty piece of merchandise if they don't blow your head right off. And then they'll sell you all the same, to them doctors. You'll end up on a slab up to the College, that you will! Or in some whorehouse up to Nex. You want that?''

''I'll take care of myself, dammit! I'll find *someone* that's got the—''

''Me!'' Ali yelled, ''Jones! Jones! I swear I never do it again, I made a mistake, Jones, I'll go, I'll go, I swear I will, I'll make it good, Jones, I'll make it, swear on my mother, Jones, I swear, I swear, I swear!''

''I give ye Ali,'' Moghi said, with that sweet-nasty look in his deepset eyes. ''Go with you right to Nex, he would.''

''Dammit, Moghi, I'll take him, you give 'im to me, I'll take him!''

''You're crazy.''

''I ain't crazy. I'm looking for a *man* in this damn hole! If he's all I got, he's what I'll take!''

''Damn you, Jones!''

''You said it, give him to me! If he can walk I'll take him.''

''I c'n walk,'' Ali said, hoarse and bubbly. ''Jones, I c'n walk, I c'n—''

''You want this trash,'' Moghi said, ''you got 'im.'' Moghi drew his belt-knife and cut the cords, one, two, three.

''Ow!'' Ali yelled: Moghi grabbed him by the hair and flung him out of the chair and face around again.

''If she don't get back,'' Moghi said, looking close into Ali's eyes, ''you'll die for it. But you die slower. And I'll find ye, ye know I will.''

''With my life,'' Ali said, a faint, bubbly voice, ''with my life, I swear, Moghi, I swear on my—''

''Get!'' Moghi flung him. Altair turned her back and stalked out of the hall and through again to the main room, with Ali shuffling and limping along at her back, all bubbly and snuffling. Canalers stared.

''Ye eavesdroppers,'' Altair called out around her, ''ears in a body's business, any of ye want a piece of the Megarys?''

Eyes shifted the other way, shoulders turned. Del was there. He stared at her, his white-stubbled chin working. "I'll go," Del said.

"You got responsibilities," Altair said, and evaded the look in the old man's eyes. "C'mon, Ali."

She went out the door onto the porch—looked back at Ali shambling along after her holding his gut, saw a ring of staring faces around them both, canalers on the porch, out in the boats. "Megarys!" she yelled out. "It was Megarys helped them that done this! Anybody want to go over there in my boat? We got a man to get out of there!"

No one stood up and volunteered.

"Well, damn," she said. "Then some of you might at least get out there round West and here and there and clutter up them canals so they don't get a boat through."

"I'll do 'er," Mintaka Fahd cried out, waving her scarf. "Lord and Glory, I'll do 'er!"

"Who's this fellow?" That was old Jess Gray calling up from the middle of the boats. "Who's this they got?"

"Name's Mondragon!" *That* for you, Boregy, and all your secrets. "He come to town to get away from them devils up in Nev Hettek. Megary's been trading with Nev Hettek and they got foreign help, it was Nev Hettek gold bought that poison, it was Nev Hettek and Megarys carried him off. You got no stake in him, but you damn well got one in what the Megarys done tonight!"

"You want them canals blocked, Jones, they get blocked!"

"Good!" She swung off the porch onto the ladder. Ali came down after, faltering on the rungs. She stepped down to the well of the Newell skip and Ali made it behind her, a grunt of pain and a stagger that rocked the boat. Newell kids squatted with mouths agape and eyes wide as she took her bloody shadow through the well.

Across that skip and onto Lewis's and the Delacroix. To her own, and Ali struggling and gasping to keep up with her. She heard another thumping across boat-wells, and a second, lighter, behind that. A man besides Ali landed in her well, all shadow against the light, a big man with a ragged coat.

"You got my help," he said, a voice half-familiar. She remembered the coat then, the cant of the battered hat.

Mary Gentry's man. Rahman Diaz. Mary who had lost the baby. Mary still had a son left, and her man came volunteering. Rahman scared her, scared her with the whole karma of it.

"Damn," she said. And another scrambling figure reached her deck, skinny-limbed shadow, spiky hair blowing in the wind. "who's that? Who's that? Tommy? Damn, get off of here."

"I come along," Tommy said in that high adolescent voice of his. "I ain't scared."

"Ain't scared!" She headed past her troop to the halfdeck. "Ain't scared! Damn! Rahman, get that rope free!"

Rahman moved for the bow-rope. Ali hunched his bent way up to the deck-edge and sank down there, arm on the deck, the other holding his gut. "Jones. Jones, I swear I never, Jones, I never had no heart for killing."

"Sure you didn't." She ran out the pole while Rahman got the boathook from his position in the well and Tommy dithered this way and that. "You going or staying?" she yelled at Tommy. "Get yourself back here off that bow, dammit, make ballast out of yourself, you c'n at least do that much—"

"Jones," Ali said, "Jones, that place is a maze, they got doors and doors—"

"You going to tell me that now?" She put the pole in, shoved past Del's skip. "Watch 'im, Mira—"

Mira lifted a forlorn hand and waved, that was all. And Mintaka Fahd waved her scarf. "Hooo," Mintaka hooted after her. "Hooo, there."

Hooo-oo, from a dozen mouths.

Mary Gentry's face she never tried to see.

"You got to go south," Ali stammered: it came out all liquid. "Jones, they don't use no big boat, it's Wharf Gate, they take their cargo out Wharf Gate—"

"Rahman, yey." She left the stroke to Rahman, swung the pole inboard and squatted down where she stood, toes tense on the deck. Her shadow fell on Ali's face, Moghi's lights falling behind them. "You want to talk truth, you damn flesh-peddler? *Where?*"

"It's truth, it's truth, Wharf Gate. They take 'em all that way."

"You damn sneak. How d'I believe ye?"

"I ain't lying. I ain't, Jones, I swear to you. Wharf Gate. They got these riverrunners, they come right up by the Dead Wharf, I heard 'em talk. Jones, Moghi give me this poor old sod to throw in harbor—he come to, he begged me, he begged me, Jones, he didn't want to go in that water. I ain't no killer. I sold 'im. That was the first. Ain't they better off? Ain't they? They *wanted* it, Jones, they wanted it—I ain't never thrown nobody in harbor. Megarys don't kill 'em. They just—"

"—sell 'em. You got the morals of a sherk, Ali! How much you get for a body, huh?"

"They was going to tell! They was going to tell if I didn't do it this time—Jones, it wasn't supposed to go this way—"

"I'll bet it wasn't." She stood up, caught sight of Tommy's pale, round-eyed face.

Accomplice? Or innocent?

She ran the pole in, took up the stroke. "We're going over to Megary. First. Look it over. Know what we're dealing with."

"Jones!" Ali protested.

"You shut it down."

Rahman just made his stroke and never said a word.

Chapter 9

IT was easy work, moving the skip with Rahman on the other pole. No panic now, just the rhythmic move of water, the same as any night-time trip through Merovingen-below. Altair took her strokes sure and quiet, letting Rahman do most of the real push.

Man ain't been t' one end of town and the other tonight. Lord, how much time have we got? Just after dark when I was with Jobe; past midnight getting back from Boregy, damn his guts.

We got, what, three, four hours to dawn. Shy side of two hours before the tide clears boat-draft at those gates.

If they're going to leave town tonight.

They got to. Too damn many people looking for Mondragon— Sword'll get wind of that gathering over by Moghi's—they'll sure know when them canals get blocked and they try to get anywhere. And what's Megary doing with all of this? Megarys has got to be *scared*, is what. Megarys bought themselves trouble, got their arm twisted right good with their foreign friends—

Sword's running this. Nobody else. I got to get him loose, I got to be ready when the Trade gets those canals blocked. Got to be ready to do something, got to have it figured.

Got to get him out of there before they know they're trapped.

—Got to get 'im out of Merovingen.

Find him some ship, out to sea.

Get him out of here. For good.

Never see 'im again.

What else can I do?

She shoved hard, til her arms hurt more and her gut hurt less.

Damnfool, Jones. Tomorrow ain't in reach, is it? Ain't nothing good there, is there?

So stop thinking on it.

Mama, mama, you gone away tonight? I don't blame you. This is a proper mess I made. No wonder you ain't too proud of me.

The way bent to Old Grand, and shadow closed darker still beneath the maze of bridges that roofed the Old Harbor's onetime thoroughfare.

Boats were moving, somewhere at their backs. Those skips and poleboats tied up here were few and far between, mere shadows along the edges of buildings. Old folk. The disinterested. The isolate.

Those so far into the dark ways that they had no part or traffic with honest canalers.

Those same honest canalers back at Moghi's were making haste as fast as canalers were apt to, and trying to sort out just where what boat was going: she could figure how long that would take. And the canals and those sea-gates would get blocked. In about an hour or so, when enough of them got organized and got into position. When they had talked enough hardheaded water-rats never *at* Moghi's into going along with a jam-up around Megary, and settled who was going to block those places where there was likely to be shooting.

More talk and more delay.

"Cut over to Factory," she said to Rahman, and swung the bow over for that turn. The eddy of the Old Grand jog was shoving at the skip; wind hit in a gust. It slewed, but practice borrowed the slew into the turn, her pole down for the moment it took. Rahman picked up the push again with never a word, not a piece of advice since he had come aboard.

Rahman never did talk. He never did talk all those years ago when I brought his and Mary's baby up from Detbottom, when he come up from hunting that bottom empty-handed.

He knew, that's what, he knew that baby was gone, even when it was still alive. Mama knew and he knew, him standing there and never saying thank-you. He don't talk now. What's he know that I don't?

Lord, he's Revenantist. I put karma on 'im, didn't I, bringing that baby up alive. I laid karma on that dead baby's soul, on all of 'em, Rahman and Mary and Javi, and Rahman ain't having me get killed without he clears that debt, he's got to save all their souls from what I done saving that baby, or they can't never get free of this world till they and me all get born together again and they pay me off. He's thinking on his next life, that's what he's doing, Lord and my Ancestors, I got a suicide on my hands.

Tommy—he's just plain fool, coming out here, whatever brought him. And I *know* why I got Ali.

A suicide, a fool, and a damn traitor.

They passed Mendez Isle and Fife, where vermin scampered along the narrow ledges and squeaked and squealed at a passing skip. A cat eeled round a starlit corner of Mendez, shadow as much as its intended victims.

"Hey, we got a marker up there," she breathed, spotting the standing pole at Ulger's crumbling corner. "Hin."

"Yey," Rahman agreed. "Ware hook." The bow swung under his strong push.

"Ware afore." She swung the pole into the well past Ali's head and squatted where she stood, let her hookman cross past her to grapple the tie-up nearest that marker. She read that aged pole where she squatted, peering through the dark at the rope-banding on the pole while she made the jury tie to hold them at the ring. "Damn place," she said, seeing how the topmost rope was rotted and salt-crusted. "Level's changed here and they ain't fixed this thing in a ten-year."

"Running in fast," Rahman said. "Tide'll go high, we got that seawind."

"Smugglers is bound to be wise to that too," she said, and sat there and gnawed her knuckle. The wind gusted. then something boomed, boomed and rumbled with authority. Explosion? It seemed a trick of the wind for the moment. Then she took that instinctive look skyward all the same, and it rumbled out again. "O God, that's *thunder.*"

"Sounds like *something*'s blowing in," Rahman said, crouched by her.

Nothing showed yet. The stars were still clear above the black hulks of Tidewater isles. Her mind built sea-storm, black wall rolling in, pregnant with lightnings, the way such storms came. Calm before it, and the winds—the winds—

Thunder rumbled again, distant and not distant enough.

"They'll hear that. Lord, that boat coming in—they'll have their eye to that, they'll move in early—"

"Or pull out."

"I ain't betting on it. O Lord, it's *us* got the trouble, we got that sea coming in and they ain't organized back at Moghi's yet—I *know* they ain't—"

"They hear the thunder," Tommy said, "they hear it, Jones."

"So do the damn slavers! They'll go early, go while it's still dark. Lord knows who else is moving—We got to go, we got no time to wait around."

Rahman grunted, shrugged his big shoulders and spat off the deck. "Yey."

Karma.

Suicide. Thunder rumbled again.

"Dammit—" Her focus shortened to the dark, curly-headed lump huddled there in front of her. She shifted the pole in her hands and nudged him so that he looked up at her. "Ali. How d'they go out? Megary Cut?"

"I don't know."

She nudged him hard. "Ali, I thought you was going to be more helpful than that."

"I ain't lying!"

"Well, you ain't helping, either."

"There's this landing south. By the Cut."

"I know it."

"An old freight door, little slip there." Ali's breath hissed and faltered. Wind rattled a board somewhere. "I run Moghi's boat right up there on the slip. I knock at that door. They come out and they take—take the delivery.''

"*That* how it works.''

"Jones.'' He shifted up, leaned on the deck-rim. "My God, Jones, you ain't getting in that way, you *can't* get in, they'll kill us.''

"They won't kill us. They'll sell us right up the river, won't they? Rahman, I got some things to ask our friend here. You want to top off that tank? I got a full can down in the well.''

"I'll help,'' Tommy said, a whisper too close to voice.

"Keep it down,'' Altair said. "You got to learn to keep that voice down—'' Retribution had said it to her in these same tidewater canals, taught her to pitch down, snapped her on the ear when she forgot—

—Taught me the dark ways, mama. I thought ever'one knew 'em.

"Now, Ali,'' she said in her softest, lowest voice. Wind sighed down the canal, stirred her hair at the front of her cap. "I killed folk before this, Ali. That's truth. It don't scare me. Just in case you think of shouting out.'' Quiet movement in the well to their left, where Rahman found the fuel can. He set it on the deck and came up after it, cat-footed, big as he was. "Ali,'' she said. "You hear me? You hear me good?''

"I hear you,'' Ali said. He leaned his forehead on the deck, one arm tucked across his gut. "Jones, Wharf gate, I swear on my mother it's Wharf Gate, I ain't lying, we can't go into that place, they got doors and bars—''

"You been in there, huh?''

The whites of Ali's eyes shone as he looked up. "I never.''

"Lie, Ali. You wasn't going to lie to me. Your mama's gathering a lot of karma, ain't she?''

"Once. Once, I was inside.''

"Deeper and deeper, ain't ye? Selling bridge-folk—''

"In the winter, in the winter—Jones, they lie there freezing, Megarys give 'em food, they got a warm bed—''

"Just like my partner.''

"That was different!''

"I tell you, Ali, you remember that little scene back to Moghi's porch. Now, it takes a lot to get the Trade stirred up, but they're stirred. And there you stood up in public with me when I said it, about the Megarys. You know what that makes you?"

"A dead man."

"About three different ways. Me or Moghi or them Megarys. Or 'bout any canaler in town. Lot of folks ain't too fond of you right now."

"I ain't never lied to you!"

"You got a way to buy out with me. *Maybe* I could put it right with Moghi. You understand me? You know what those Megarys'd give ye? Ye know that, Ali?"

"I know." His breath came through chattering teeth. "But I don't know the rest. I swear I don't know, I never done that end."

"You know what I want you to do for me, Ali?"

"O God, Jones. I can't. I won't."

"You c'n lie real good, Ali. I know ye can." Fuel-smell wafted to her. She heard Rahman and Tommy quiet at their work, liquid gurgling and thumping its way into the tank. "Rahman. Save some of that back. I got this bottle down in the number-five. You want to fill that thing for me? Stick an old rag in it."

"You got matches?" Rahman asked, matter of fact.

"Plenty."

"Jones," Ali said, half a whisper. "What'ye think you're doing?"

"Just something my mama taught me."

"What's she mean?" Tommy asked. "What's she mean?" But no one answered him. Rahman went down on one knee, got the bottle and the rag.

More fuel-smell, carried away on the fickle wind.

"Got two bottles," Rahman said.

"That ain't too many." She sat there and chewed thoughtfully at a callus-shred.

You sure he's in there, Jones? No, you ain't. You ain't dealing with the Megarys, you know it. Sword of God—

Sword is rich folk.

City's Revenantist. And what else could get foreigners in and out of the city as well as them Megary boats?

Lord, they got the law bought, they trade corpses to the doctors up at the College, nobody ever questions 'em, ain't no way them boats get searched.

Lord, *questions*, Boregy said. They want to ask him questions. What are they doing to him?

"Where do they keep 'em?" she asked Ali. "Top floor or bottom?"

"Bottom. I think it's bottom."

Damn, all barred. Ain't no way to break in there; they'll have took real good care so's no one could break out.

Lord and Glory. So no one could break *out*. Who else in town don't ever have to worry about burglars breaking in?

"How's that bottom floor? How's it set?"

"They got—" Ali traced a design on the deck at the side of her foot, trembling finger moving on worn paint. "Got the hall I seen. South door. You go in. You got these hallways left and right and these stairs—"

"Where do they go?"

"I don't know, up—up. They got some kind of warehouse, I think they got this big place over here they put the regular stuff, the legal stuff; that's here. All above, I dunno, Megarys live up there. Maybe they got other things, I don't know. They just got two stories."

"You going to do me that favor?"

"Jones—" Ali's teeth fairly chattered. "I hurt, dammit. I can't—"

"Hey, you're still alive, ain't ye? You ain't at harbor-bottom. It don't hurt a bit down in Old Det's gut. You want I tell Moghi you went back on me?"

"No." They did chatter. "No."

"You going to do it for me?"

"I—All right, all right—"

"Rahman. Let's move 'er up a bit, you ready?"

"Yey," he agreed. The fuel was capped up. Loose stuff was stowed. Rahman squatted resting on the deck and Tommy had gotten down to the well. Rahman got to his feet as she slipped the tie and stood up with the pole.

She pushed gently off the ledge. Rahman pushed from

his side and the skip moved along smoothly under way, off
Ulger's corner and back to Factory's narrow center.

Calder and Ulger's length inched past, dimly starlit.
Bridges were rarer in the Tidewater. Most of the isles were
two-storey now, their old first-floors filled and mostly
sunken. Calder had no ledge at all, just a balcony round
the upstairs, and the last bridge off Ulger showed as a
decrepit low span that hardly admitted a skip with the
poler standing.

Rahman grunted, having seen it too.

"Little port there," she said to Rahman as they headed
under. "Hin. Hin cinte."

"Yey." He nudged the boat to the high center of the
bridge and dodged a hanging board with small headroom
to spare. No pilings. It was a jury-bridge between two
second-storey doorways, abandoned as flood and rot took
Calder's canalside.

"Damn, city ought to take that thing." Her head was
clear, quite clear. She smelled fuel-stink, very faint over
the canal-smell. "Where you got them bottles?"

"Number five."

"Port, ya-hin."

Factory jogged, bent toward broad West; the boat edged
northerly with the push off West Canal. A solitary, rag-
canopied skip occupied the jog. A waft of bad air came
down the wind as they passed.

Muggin. O Lord, it's Old Man Muggin—Lord, Angel,
keep him sleeping.

What does he *do* to keep that damn skip running?

Megarys? He couldn't. Old fool don't have the wit left.
Couldn't catch them bridgefolk.

"Muggin, ne," Rahman breathed.

"Yey," she whispered. "Starb'd, hin."

The bow swung gently. Wind hit them as they entered
West Canal and she cast a look up, blinked in dismay at
the shadow in the black, a third of the way up the sky. No
stars, just that gold-through-smoke flicker of lightnings.
She shortened her glance down to Megary Isle, to a bar-
ren, scant-windowed face of aged brick and board. They
were exposed now, under those grim barred windows. But

they were just a skip on its business. A skip with no more aboard than might be family, ordinary traffic passing in this night—they might well be the only ordinary-looking thing on the canal, boats being scarce in the Tidewater tonight.

Trouble's got this sure stink about it. The homeless don't hang round here, honest boats don't stop, and nobody else is hereabouts. Usually six or seven ratty skips and nothing.

They smell it, smell it all over Tidewater.

Lord, are they watching out the windows?

No waterside ledge on Megary either. And above, it showed nothing but barred windows, closed shutters, top story to canalside. She could not, in the way of things looked at and looked past all her life, recall the look of that building's upper storey on the other sides.

She signaled turn at Megary's north corner, there off West Canal, familiar turn that she had taken many a night, shortcut on the return from Hafiz', down the way. But she had never looked *up* before.

Northside was the front landing. That door looked solid. Windows to either side were barred and shuttered. Not the least sliver of light showed inside. The windows above were barred and sealed with weathered shutters that ought to leak light if any existed.

Suppose they got the windows blacked from inside?

Lord. Suppose—suppose they already took 'im on from here, suppose they *saw* that storm from them upper windows, and took him somewheres else and I can't find 'im—

Suppose they never came here at all—

"Ya-hin." She took a deep breath, used it all in a push to slew the skip close to the Isle and around the turn, there where Hafiz' south point showed in the Tidewater canal. She looked up, strained to see the few windows at Megary's narrow end. They were dark as the rest.

Megary's corner bent on round by Southdike. Their bow aimed a moment at the short channel to Marsh Gate, and that was no more than a dark pit ahead with an ominous

flicker of lightning-lit dark beyond. Dead Harbor out there.
The Ghost Fleet.

Storm, stalking up virtually silent the way sea-storms
did, pushing the tide before them to flood those earthquake-
frozen sea-gates.

They kept swinging, brought the bow round to the
buttressed point of the dike, to the narrow bend between
Megary and Amparo.

And Megary had a balcony on this side second level,
Lord and Glory, a great beautiful balcony without a stairway. Not one damn bridge to anybody. Rostov had had
one to Megary from the north, and dismantled it in a feud.
The south to Amparo—that fell in a quake and nobody put
it back. Amparo went across to Calder. Rostov had its
back turned to the slavers.

But there was that hanging balcony, to left of the boat-
cut, and that cut had two boats tied up, one a dilapidated
skip, one a sleek pleasureboat.

Lord, that's *uptown*. That's a fancy. *Look* at that paint
shine.

"Ssst. Ho." She braced the pole to slow. Rahman set
his side and the skip's motion ebbed down as she looked
up and up that cut. "I got to get in there."

"Yey," Rahman said, and put out the hook, snagging
the old skip's bow. She shipped the pole without a rattle,
felt her belt for the hook and the knife, then got down
cat-footed into the well and pried the lid on the match-can
there by the edge of the hidey, put a few in her pocket and
glanced over at Ali, who huddled close by.

"You mind what I said."

"Jones, we're going to die."

"Likeliest be your fault, then. *Hear?*"

"I got ye. I got ye." Ali's teeth were chattering again.
He kept his arms clenched across his gut. She looked up at
Rahman's sullen face, at Tommy's wide eyes.

"Rahman," she whispered, "that engine, takes three
tries, light prime and ye got to hold the choke out by hand.
Here." She handed him up the matches, reached down and
picked a quiet handful of metal out of a second can. Nuts
and bolts and screws. She held one up and pocketed the

rest. "I toss one of these, you hear that splash, you put Ali here t' that door. You get that freight door open. Hear? You take one of them bottles. You toss 'er and you get the hell down this way and toss the other right into these boats."

"Yey." Rahman's sullen eyes flickered in the shadow, thinking-moving. Calculating as she got to her feet and the wind skirled in the cut.

Damn, *never* do a Revenantist a favor. He suspects it, he'll hate you for it. Man *wants* to die. Wants Mary and his kids clear. Damn, he hates me.

She got to the drop by the engine, took out the gun and pocketed a few extra shells. She held it in plain light to check the chambers, and when she looked up Rahman had a different kind of look.

The kid ain't planning anything small, man. This kid ain't the fool you thought. This kid's her mama's daughter. Figure *that*, Rahman Diaz.

She rose up off her knee and took off her cap, passed it to Tommy. "Hold that. Lose it and I'll skin ye."

"Yeah," Tommy said. Terrified.

She stuck the pry-bar in her belt, and looked up, up at the underside of the balcony, at the timber bracings that laced back and forth inside the cut.

A tumbledown boatshed finished off that cut at the back, there by the boatdock door. Windows around the cut were all barred, all shuttered, and no light showing.

She stepped aboard the old skip, a wary eye to the hidey; but nothing stirred there. She crossed onto the sleek deck of the fancy and walked it to the ledge of the cut.

The door there was locked. Of course it was locked. She looked up at the shed, looked at the old timber piled there.

She laid the gun down and took a plank, set it to the boatshed roof, tested it for angle and looked up again where the bracings kept Megary's upper story true. Right above the shed.

She's going to creak, she's going to squeal the moment I stand on that roof.

But, Lord, ain't that pretty, how they got that brace

going from that wall, that's good black upriver timber and the cut wall's all brick, solid as an uptown bridge.

If I don't break my fool neck getting up there.

She picked up the gun, gauged her angle and the traction of bare feet with the grain of the plank going up-wise. Drew a deep breath.

Ain't no different than a deck in weather, is it? Damn lot steadier.

Do I wonder whether that roof's rotten? Where would them roof-studs be?

She ran the plank, hit the roof and a shingle went loose. It fell. Her knee came down on the yielding roof, found a rotten spot and she sprawled, afraid to move while the awful noise of the broken board resounded in the cut. She shuddered convulsively, felt acute pain in her thigh and gasped for air as she dragged her weight up.

Didn't lose the gun, damn, I didn't lose the gun and I didn't drop nothing.

Am I cut? Is that a nail?

She dragged the leg farther and farther off the broken board, spread like a seastar across the rotten shingles as a wind-gust fluttered a loose board and thunder rumbled. the pain blacked her vision, eased slowly. She kept crawling, up and up to the rooftree.

If that gives way, I'm done, I'm dead or worse—

O Lord, Lord, if I can just stand up and reach that timber up there—

She cast a look back, at her skip riding quiet in the dark, like any skip at night-tie. Another hitch higher on the shingles. Another shingle slipped and slid and hit the water with a splash.

Lord, *no*, no, Rahman, that ain't no signal, don't go for that door.

Climb, you got to hurry, fool!

Breath came hard. She edged up and up and felt the whole building protest.

Don't leave your weight on that rooftree one second longer'n need be, and what you going to do with the damn *gun*, Altair?

Her mother's voice. Retribution perched up on the tim-

bers, in the big black fork of them where they held totter-
ing Megary's upper section apart.

Blow my damn gut out, mama.

She stuffed her sweater into her pants and tightened her
belt till it hurt, pulled her sweater collar wide and stuffed
the gun down her front. Then she rose up on her knees,
scrambling for that timber with both arms as the shed
trembled under her departing feet.

She swung up, hung upside down by arms and legs,
edged along and felt the gun slide slowly off her stomach
and plunk down into her sweater at the back. Damn. Oh,
damn. It swung there.

How'm I going to get rightside up?

You damn well *do* it, Altair.

Thanks, mama, thanks.

She edged higher with one heel and a knee. The gun
swung over farther against her back. The sprained finger
shot fire and she lost her vision for a moment, sucked
wind as she hung in the old position again.

Won't work. O Lord, I can't hold on, my arms are
going to go.

She crept closer to the balcony. Banged her head against
the boards where thinner supports were nailed in after-
thought.

She transferred one grip to a brace-board. It seemed
solid. She risked the lame hand, hooked that elbow around
the board, sucked more air and let go the timber with her
feet.

Strained arms wrenched under her whole weight. She
pulled and pulled and got the other elbow hooked around a
brace. Higher, then. She snatched another hold with the
right forearm and got a knee onto a board while the gun
dragged at the back of her sweater and the damn pry-bar
caught on a board.

Another push upward. A nail creaked. She got the
second foot on a brace, hooked her left foot up onto the
timber again and climbed and inched with her whole mid-
section arched up and trembling over nothing.

And a cascade of objects left her pocket and thunked
and splashed into water down below.

Oh, *damn,* damn, no, Rahman, that ain't it either, don't you move—

She hung there gasping. A last flurry of changed hand-holds and elbow-hooks, one small brace to the next, and she ended up with her head higher than her feet this time and one foot in agony, wedged in the vee of two brace-boards.

She stood on it, grabbed the corner-brace of the balcony and found the next footing. The whole rail wobbled when she touched it. She set her foot carefully sideways on the rim of the balcony outside the rail, used the rail for balance with her weight square-down on it, and snatched a hold with her good hand on the chain that anchored the balcony from the main building face.

O God.

Her knees wobbled worse than the rail. Her legs wanted to go out from under her. She swung a leg over the rail and onto solid planking, clung to the chain with arms gone almost limp and dragged the other leg over the shaky railing. A row of shutters showed light along the balcony, a door shed a little glow from the bottom out onto weathered boards. The whole balcony had a precarious, twisted look, tilted toward the canal, slung by chains from the roof overhang. Wind whistled round the corner. And the cloud-mass showed above Amparo roof, closer and ominous with lightnings.

She leaned out from the corner. The end of the skip was visible. Still there. She gulped air and fished the gun around under the sweater until she could pull the sweater loose by main force and get the gun out. Her hands trembled with fatigue; she needed both to support the weight of the pistol. Her brain reeled this way and that in blind panic.

Door, fool! Try the door.

She edged back on the rickety balcony to the brick of the face, clenched the gun in both hands and padded over to the door, put an ear to the paint-peeling wood and heard male voices. Heard a sound then that sounded like something else. It turned into a moan that sent ice through her nerves.

Damn 'em, damn 'em. Her heart spasmed. Her hands shook as she gripped the gun in the right and tried the latch ever so softly.

Locked.

But they're here. They're damn well in there, the Sword and all, with that fancy boat down to the dock. *That* ain't nothing Megary owns. You got a chance. *Think*, Jones, get your brain to work and shake the trembles out, who's going to save him else?

Careful steps, one and another down the balcony that girded Megary's topmost level.

Creak.

She recovered her pulsebeat and made the next step, walked closer to the brick, where the boards were firmer underfoot, as far as the first shuttered window and a crack that let light out.

Men inside. Moving figures in that little sliver of vision the crack afforded. A body passed right in front of the window and she ducked down a moment, holding her breath.

Then a voice shrilled out on the canal below the balcony: *"Who you be? Who you be?"*

God, it's Muggin!

Steps crossed the room inside. "Leave that alone," somebody said, somebody with a hightown voice. "Don't show a light."

"It's just some canaler ruckus—" Another. While her heart beat and beat against her ribs.

From below: *"What you doing sneaking round here? Ain't up to no good, I seen you, Ali! I seen you too, Tommy-boy! Where you get that there skip?"*

More steps. A door opened and shut somewhere to the right in the room.

O Lord, if they're coming out here—Where's that wall end? O if I'd holed them boats down there first, if I'd drained them tanks—

She looked frantically for a hiding-spot. There was none. Even the door itself opened inward. She clutched the gun and aimed toward the door, hands shaking.

Quiet from below then. The slap of water.

More quiet.

It's gone askew, it's all gone askew, Rahman ain't going to get that back door open now, I got no help coming, I should've done for them boats. O Lord, maybe Rahman c'n do something. Maybe *he'll* think of it.

What can he do? He's got Muggin.

Water splashed, the gentle sound of a pole at work through the thunder of wind and loose shingles.

"Well, I'm sorry!" Muggin's voice drifted up.

She put her ear to the shutter. The voices inside came fainter now.

"—find out. —Megary will see to it. —harbor. —aren't going to get anything—"

Thunder muttered from the clouds, nearer than it had been.

Where is he, dammit, is Mondragon even in there? I daren't look, man's probably looking out that crack, I'll go eyeball to eyeball with 'im if I go in front of that shutter.

"—forget it," someone said. "—storm moving in—out there—tide—"

"—through the harbor—"

Another voice.

"—damned—"

A sudden outcry, quickly muffled. A groan.

She clenched her hand on the gun.

"Yo!" came from far below. And there was hammering, fist on distant door. *"It's Ali, dammit, let me in! I got news—"*

"—What's that?" From inside.

"Damn. What are they doing out there?" From near the door.

"You'd better go down and see."

A door opened and slammed. The hammering kept up at the freight-door.

O Lord and Glory, Rahman's give me the best he can.

She ducked under the first window, headed for the next and straightened up slowly, drawing her knife left-handed. She spotted the latch, shadow across the slit, put her eye to the crack to be sure. Big vault of a room, plaster walls, a

door, scant furniture. Three men moving about. She shifted
her vantage, got sight of a brick wall, of—

—Mondragon slumped there on the floor, just lying.
One of the others kicked him in the gut and he curled
tighter to protect himself, blond head tucked in chained
arms.

She swallowed hard. Sucked several breaths like preparing for a deep dive. *Think. Think, Jones. Get the blood
moving.* Her hand sweated on the gunbutt and her eye
went on scanning, cold now, quick and all-inclusive, while
thunder muttered up in the clouds.

Man by those shutters. And a bright brass lock and bolt
on that shut door.

She slipped the thin knife into the shutter-slit, lifted,
caught the wood with the knife-tip and pulled it outward.

Damn 'em.

She flung the shutter open on dirty glass and a shut
window, opened fire right through it, and the first man
dropped on the second shot. The second man ran for the
door and the third, uptown-dressed, dived for cover behind
a couch.

She dropped him, shot at the second and leaned through
the shattered window for a shot at the fourth. Winged him.
He spun with the shot and she shot again. Man-two got the
door open and made it out as she raked glass from the
window and threw a leg in, winced at a cut and hopped to
both feet inside. She stumbled once, found her balance on
one foot and ran.

She hit the door bodily, snapped the lock shut and shot
the bolt.

"*Jones!*" Mondragon screamed.

She spun about, saw the man on his knees behind the
couch; and blasted him over backwards.

Five, is that five bullets? No, *six*, dammit! She snatched
at pockets, felt them desperately.

Nothing. Not a shell left. She flung herself to her knees
by Mondragon as he dragged himself up against the bricks.
His white face was all sweat-beaded and stained from a cut
on his forehead. His hair was plastered against his temples
and bloodstain spread through the sweat. "Jones," he

said—Steps came thundering up the stairs inside. He grabbed with manacled hands at the collar-chain, jerked at it frantically where it connected to the brickwork. "Jones—*shoot the damn chain!*"

"I'm out!" She dropped gun and knife, jerked at the pry-bar at her belt, working it loose as blows hit the door. "I got this."

"Oh, damn, damn—give it to me, get out that window—"

"*Shoot the lock!*" someone yelled outside.

"Jones, get out of here! You can't help me!"

"Damned if I can't." She got the pry-bar free of her belt and jammed the hook-end under the edge of the chain-bracket while shots splintered away at the solid door.

"God," Mondragon said and twisted round on his knees to get his own hands on the bar, threw all his strength into it till the veins stood out and his face turned dark.

Bolts squealed loose from the mortar, one and two. The other two loosened. Blows hit the door again. More shots outside, deafening. She put her weight with his and the bracket flew free, pins and all.

"Come on!" She grabbed up the gun and sheathed the knife. "F' God's sake, *get up!*—" She pulled at him. He staggered up, reeled and kept his feet. "*Come on!*"

He was behind her when she got to the door. She fumbled desperately with the latch and lock. Behind them the inside door was giving way, crack after crack of wood splintering under repeated battering.

The door stuck in the frame. She jerked and it came free. "Jump," she yelled on her way to the rail.

And tried to vault it. The whole rail cracked and gave way, spilling her outward.

She yelled in shock at the rush of dark air, tried to compose herself for the landing, and went into the water somewhere toward rump-first, water driven up her nose in the tumble, her wits nearly knocked from her as another large impact whumped into the water.

They'll be on us, they'll have us in the water, they got guns up there—

Is he swimming? That chain could've knocked him cold, broke his neck, o Lord! Mondragon—

She hit the canal bottom on her back, righted herself and kicked off the mucky bottom for the surface. Her head broke clear of the water—she sucked a foul breath, spat Det-water and stared wildly at the side of a skip, at a ragged-canopied skip bobbing there in front of her. Mondragon broke to surface, lost it again. A hook came out in the hands of a raggedy figure on the skip-deck and snagged him by the sweater, hauling him up to air.

"Dammit!" Jones choked, spitting water.

"Damn near hit my boat," old Muggin yelled in his cracked voice. "Ye damn fools!"

An engine coughed from off in the dark. Coughed again. A third time. Took. And fire flared up across the water, off the walls, off Muggin's ragged canopy, flinging his features into demonic highlights.

She kicked and turned as a skip bore down on them under power, and Tommy was there in the bow trying to find them.

Explosions. Shots kicked up little plumes in the firelit water.

"Jones!" Tommy was yelling, waving one hand wildly as the bow came up toward her head and she kicked desperately out of the way, clawed her way up Muggin's side and got a hold on that rim as her own skip rode close, throttled back. "Mondragon—Damn, let him *go*, Muggin!"

Muggin shoved hook and Mondragon down, and Mondragon flailed out desperately with chained hands, turned and caught her skip in one wild lunge. She flung the gun aboard in a sweep of water, hurled herelf for her skip rim. "Help *him!*" she screamed at Tommy, who abandoned Mondragon to sink. "Damn ye, help *him*, he'll go under the damn bow!" She bounced underwater, hurled herself up and got her arms over the side with the last of her strength as the skip started to move. A shot slammed into the well. Another kicked up water beyond. Tommy got Mondragon in and Rahman put the throttle in full.

"Tom-mm-my!" Altair yelled, holding by both arms over the rim. Water dragged harder and harder at her legs.

Her arms bruised themselves on the rim and muscle-strength faded. *"Tommy, dammit!"*

A shadow loomed up. Someone grabbed her sweater in the middle of the back, hauled, grabbed the seat of her pants and slipped her up and over the rim in a sprawl of his limbs and hers.

She clambered over the body, heard a grunt of pain, caught a firelit impression of Ali's sweating face as the skip sped around the corner of Amparo west. *"Boats!"* she screamed at Ali as they rounded the turn. "Boats, dammit—*go round again!"* And in the protected interval as they raced behind Amparo: "Mondragon," she gasped, scrambling over the well-slats, where he lay sprawled on his face. "Mondragon—"

He moved. He got up on his hands and she scrambled aft again to get to the firebomb. Behind Amparo, echoing off the dike, another engine roared to life; one, and a second.

"Rahman!" She looked up where Rahman crouched by the tiller,.hanging on for all he was worth. "They're going to cut us off!"

."Yey," Rahman yelled. The throttle was already in full.

"Get the damn chain off," Mondragon was saying. "Get the chain—"

"Ax." Wits came back. She abandoned the move for the bomb and dived instead for the ax at the edge of the well, laid hand on it and scrambled over the slats where Mondragon had positioned himself, manacled hands on either side of the boat-rim. Ali took the ax from her, brought it down with one great whack that parted the links and drove into the wood.

Amparo's brick-and-shutters gave way suddenly to West Canal, to a fancyboat roaring down on them broadside.

"Deck!" she yelped, and hit it in a tangle with Mondragon and Ali as shots whined over the side. Rahman gave a strangled sound, and the tiller swung over. "Rahman? *Rahman!"*

"Deck!" Rahman yelled hoarsely, and the high walls of

Southdike swung front of them, the sea-gate and the Old Harbor in the lightning-flicker.

"Damn, she'll bottom!"

"Seawind!" Rahman yelled, naming his bet, and Altair hit the deck on her face, clung to the slats waiting for the shock to take the skip apart.

The engine roared off the dike, and sound receded into clear space.

She put her head up and saw harbor around them, the Dead Wharf, the chop of shallow water ahead in a moment of lightning-flash.

Ghost Fleet shallows. She scrambled to her knees and saw Rahman slumped on the tiller, the skip skewing wild.

"Jones!" Mondragon yelled as she clawed her way up onto the deck. She looked, grabbed the tiller under Rahman's failing arm, wrenched the bar over as a black wall loomed up where none had a right to be. She slewed it, passed between high-prowed fisher-boat and its anchor-cable; and shots spanged and splintered off the stern, engine sound still behind them. Light flared. More shots. She got as low behind the engine box as she could, swung wild, over to the shallows, and veered off them—veered off where the wind-borne smell of dead weed and the drifting hulks of rafters warned her of shallower and shallower water.

A bigger engine thumped to life.

"It's that fisher!" Ali yelled. "That's the slaver! Get away from it, get out of here!"

"I'm trying! Tommy, get a rag in that damn leak, we got drag!" Beside her, Rahman moved, tried to help, slumped down again. A rafter loomed up, spiny with hooks. Wild cries hooted through the night.

Crazies, it's *crazies!*

Rahman moved again, got to the side of the deck, strobed in lightning. "Get back!" she yelled as shots popped behind them. Dead Wharf was off portside. She shoved the throttle for any last fraction she could get out of it, swung the tiller and saw what Rahman was after. Ali had seen and crawled up there. The last bottle. Fuel-smell came over the wind and the rot.

"Get down!" she yelled at them. "Get down in the well—"

As the engine gave a fuel-out cough and died.

"What happened?" Tommy yelled. "What happened?"

They kept gliding, wind-battered, tossed by the chop. She got to her knees and tried the prime, hurled the crank over. Dry cough. Again.

O God.

"Gimme my gun!" she yelled. "Tommy! *My gun! In the well!*"

Shells in the drop. She flung the lid up and groped for the heavy little box among the rags, cast a look at the boats coming up fast, at the crazies closing on them from one side and the big shadow of the fisher coming up from behind.

It was Mondragon came up with the gun, came clattering onto the halfdeck at a slithering crawl, chain trailing. "Sword's in the hidey," she said. "I brung it—"

He shoved the gun at her and scrambled down into the well again backward. She broke the chamber and began to load, precisely, hands a-tremble and way falling off the skip by the second. She kept the bow to the waves, kept gaining what she could. No more shots back there. They *knew* their prey was slowing, knew that engine had to be dead.

She snapped the chamber shut, saw the spiny hulk of a raft closing nearer and nearer to portside, lightning-lit. Ragged figures worked a score of poles, doggedly and slowly revolving the raft in that way that rafters moved. And the engines of the lighter boats behind them drowned in the heavier thump of the fisher-engine as the big boat gathered way and came on them.

Closer and closer, till it filled everything aft and throttled down for the overtake.

"Rahman!" she yelled.

"I got 'er," Ali yelled, and fire sparked in the wind, a rag caught, and that fire-spark went sailing up and over that high bow.

Fire broke on the slaver-deck. Men screamed and cursed. One appeared in sight and she fired. He fell back. More came, and the skip came round to the side, engine dying. Men stood ready with boathooks, and she picked another off as the skip crashed bow-on into their side and men leaped aboard. "Mondragon—*dammit!*"

The sword flashed in firelight, a dark-clothed, blond streak swung into the boarders and dumped them into their own boat. One swung a hook for him and she blew that man off the boat. Rahman yelled and she fired into the fancy-boat coming up on his side as boarders kept trying and Mondragon kept discouraging them on the one side with the sword and Ali on the other with the axe. Tommy got the boathook unracked and nearly took Ali in the back with it.

"Ware aft!" Rahman yelled. She looked up as he did and popped a fire-limned rifleman off the fisher-bow as a thunder grew in her ears, like engines, like one big engine, bigger even than the fisher.

A bow arrived out of the fire-glare and the lightning-shot dark and crunched the fancy-boat to splinters, rode it and the men down; and of a sudden their last boarders dived for the remaining boat and tried to start it. Shots from elsewhere toppled them into the water.

The big boat rode past like a moving wall, came to a powered slow that churned the sea to chop. Shots popped and whined overhead, aimed at the burning fisher and the crazies. Howls went up from the raft. And all along that towering side men appeared with rifles aimed down at them.

Ali froze. Tommy let the pole down. Only Mondragon kept the sword a moment. And slowly, slowly let it sink to his side and drop to the deck.

She slipped the gun back to the drop-box, covering what she did with her knee. She let the lid down, all little motions, while Rahman rested on an arm, staring bleakly up at the dark-clothed men who held the guns on them all. The fisher went on burning.

"Take a line!" a voice shouted down at them. "Canaler, take a line!"

"The hell!" Altair stood up and shouted up at the faces

and the guns. "The hell! You going to give us a tow, say where!"

A pale face appeared along the rim among the others. Firelight glittered off his collar, red as blood or rubies. "There are other choices," white-face called down. "And none of them favor you!"

"Trade'll have a say in it!"

"Take them," white-face said, pointing with a long, jewel-cuffed arm. And turned and vanished from the rail, leaving only the guns and the boarding crew.

"Dammit, I'll take the line," Altair cried. *"I'll take the line!"*

The deck was huge, smooth pale wood, brass fittings, a lofty quarterdeck aft. She gaped about her dazedly, standing at Mondragon's side, looked back left as they hauled Rahman aboard, all strapped to a board and wrapped up with blankets.

They going to save him or what?

Tommy and Ali came last, under their own power. They began to take Ali away, a man on a side. They took Tommy, who belatedly began to struggle in panic. It did no good. They were big men. And there was not much of Tommy.

Guns were on them. They carried Rahman off, never taking him loose from the board they had tied him to, and disappeared belowdecks.

She shivered, wanted to lean on Mondragon, wanted to hold onto him. But he kept apart from her. She guessed why. It was about the only favor he could do her.

A man searched him for weapons. Mondragon stood still, swaying on his feet. The same man laid hands on her and she saw Mondragon's face go hard. She looked past that man's shoulder, looked at him, shut her eyes and opened them again.

Don't do nothing stupid, Mondragon. Please.

"Whose boat is this?" she asked hoarsely. "Whose?"

But no one answered.

And the fisher kept burning, black skeleton sinking down to join the Ghost Fleet. With all hands.

Chapter 10

THE trip belowdecks was dizzy nightmare, a confusion of steps and a passage forward, to a dark cubby of a compartment that smelled of the huge coils of rope that half filled it, all neat, all big-ship orderly. There were electrics up and down the corridor and a man turned on electrics inside the rope-storage, throwing it all into light.

Altair went in first, Mondragon second, and the door slammed. And locked, leaving them the light as footsteps went away. Electrics. In a boat-belly. White-face and his jewels and his glitter above the rail, arm stabbing down at them with the order that swept them up.

That big iron-shod bow grinding a boat to splinters. Without much noticing, same as it might have ground them under, except white-face wanted Mondragon; and took up the rest of them as something extra.

She sank down on the nearest coil of rope, legs going out from under her, and dropped her head down between her knees so it would quit spinning. Her arms went all but limp. The hand hurt with a dull throb. The feet—they stung, that was all. Her gut hurt. She heard chain rattle and crash and lifted her head, saw Mondragon had sunk down in like attitude on another such coil, and the trailing collar-chain had hit the planking. He looked up at her.

She sneezed, a violent, helpless explosion. "Damn," she said in a squeak of a voice, "you and water. Did it again, didn't you?"

He just looked at her.

"Who are they?" she asked.

"I don't know," he said.

"Sword?"

"I don't know." His voice sank to a hoarse whisper. He tapped his ear, made a thumb-move at the walls, the ceiling.

Listening?

Someone listening?

Then a slow thunder began in the boat, different than what muttered on the horizon. The deck steadied from its heaving.

"Going to find out," she said, thinking of the little skips out there in the New Harbor, the skips and the neighbors that would have helped them if they could have gotten that far, if a shot had not hit that fuel-tank.

Skips this monster could ride under with no trouble at all.

Take them out to sea.

Upriver.

Maybe it wants my boat so's they can search it. Maybe it just wants to sink it.

Could've done it, easier'n spitting. It's something else. It's searching it wants. Lord, what're they doing with Rahman? And Tommy and Ali? Questioning them, and Rahman already half-dead?

Poor Mary. I'm sorry, Mary Gentry, ain't nothing I ever done but harm with you.

She looked bleakly at Mondragon. He stared bleakly back.

"Jones," he said in a creaky voice. "Why couldn't you let me alone?"

"I dunno." She gave a shrug and her throat hurt. "Stupid, I guess."

His face made a hurt kind of grimace. "Dammit," he said, and put his head down against his hands and slid his hands behind his neck. He rested that way, and she stared at him the while the boat thundered away in that peculiar boil of a big engine backing.

They began to move against that, then, and Mondragon lifted his face as if he could see where they were going. She had a good map of it in her head. They were coming round the end of the Dead Wharf, headed for Rimmon

Bridge, which was how this monster had gotten into the harbor anyhow. The center of it was about high enough to let a boat this big pass beneath, storm-tide and all.

"You all right?" she asked finally.

He blinked and shifted his eyes to her. "Sure," he said. He picked the chain up and hung it over his shoulder, half this side and half the other so the weight got off the collar. He fingered the gall-mark on his neck.

"It's bleeding," she said.

"Figured." He looked at his fingers, wiped them on his knee. His eyes looked bruised. His mouth was swollen on one side where they had hit him. His hair was drying with blood in it. "How the hell did you get there?"

She shrugged. "Up a shed."

"Up a shed."

"Outside." She made a gesture, vaguely up. "I tracked you all over the damn town."

"How'd you find me?"

"Man talked."

He blinked, looking lost.

"It was supposed to work better," she said.

"Hell, we nearly made it."

"Even with the tank gone." For a moment she felt better. Then she became aware of the engine-sound, thumping away with never a falter.

Not stopping for Rimmon, are we?

She got up, wobbled in the doing and saw him tense up and his hands move as if he would catch her. She came and sat down by him, leaned on him for a pillow, and he put an arm around her middle, bowed his head down next to hers. Chain clanked. The metal on his wrist shone in the light where it rested across her stomach, and blurred along with the rest of the glare.

She snuffled, wiped her nose. Leaned where it was warm and he wrapped his other arm around her.

Right under Rimmon bridges. She heard the engine-sound, heard the distant thunder, heard the backpitched sound off the bridges.

Then the engines slowed, and her own heart beat faster, faster.

"Turning to sea," Mondragon said eventually, when the motion made itself felt.

But the engines went slower, slower still, and the boat rolled to the wind. "Rimmon," she breathed, looked up at nothing but beams and rope and a glaring light and twisted over then to glance in panic at Mondragon. "Ain't going to sea, ain't towing no skip with a storm coming. There's Rimmon-slips. That's where this boat come from. This is a Rimmon-yacht."

"Belongs to some family."

"Belongs to white-face and whoever. You got any friends on Rimmon Isle?"

"No," he said.

Which said it plain enough.

The whole boat was busy with shouts and coming and going for a long while after the engines eased her into some Rimmon Isle mooring. Thunder muttered above. The boat made that quiet motion of a vessel at dock, and it was a while after that til steps came and went in the below-decks.

"Those Rimmon Isle bridges," Mondragon asked. "Guarded?"

"Doubt it." she caught a spark of interest. Her pulse picked up. "We be real nice. Maybe they'll get careless."

"Break if we can," Mondragon said. "You know this place?"

"Better'n you."

He looked her straight in the eyes. Someone came down the steps into the corridor. More than one heavy-booted someone. "All right. You cue it."

She felt the aches, felt every bruise and knock. She stood up on legs that ached. Knees wobbled painfully.

You can't run, Jones.

You can't run no more.

"I ain't the one that broke out of no governor's prison," she hissed. "*You* pick it."

"Who said?" He got to his feet and laid his hands on her arms. "Who told you that?"

"Up in Nev Hettek. Wasn't it?"

"*Who've you been talking to?*"

The steps came up to the door.

"Boregy—Vega Boregy," she hissed. "He threw me out when I went there."

"O God."

The lock rattled. Her heart sank at that look of his, like a last hope gone down to bottom. "I done wrong, huh?"

Desperately. Searching his eyes for any hope at all.

He just stared as if she had shot him in the heart.

The door opened. She looked that way, hoping for fewer guns than she saw there.

Four of 'em. Lord, they'd blow us to tatters.

"Word is," one said, a man in dark sweater and rain-spattered leather coat, identical with all the rest, "you've got all kinds of tricks, Hettekker. Sword of God, aren't you?"

"You've got the guns," Mondragon said, and lifted an empty hand.

"Word is," the man said, "you might just run and hope we'd shoot you. So we just blow her legs off. Minute you look like you're making a move. You're valuable. She isn't. So you go over against that wall and spread out."

"I hear you." Mondragon gave her a light touch on the arm, went over against the side and took the attitude they wanted. A man got in her way with a gun aimed at her gut.

Do something? Give 'im a chance? Oh, hell.

She gauged the gun and threw her shoulder into it.

A blow exploded against her skull. She was sprawled backward on the deck with a gunbarrel in her face, and a man was dragging Mondragon back to the wall without a fight. He stood with his head leaned against the wood and let them chain his hands behind him.

Damn.

Staring up at the gun and the man.

They're going to kill me anyhow. I ain't nothing to them. Ain't worth a copper, o Mondragon, they got you, now they're going to make a hole here where my head is.

"Up," the man with the gun said. Her legs and her arms moved, automatic to the chance. She was halfway up when the man grabbed her sweater at the shoulder and flung her at the door.

Another grabbed her arm and jerked her through it.

Down the corridor with its electrics. Up the stairs and out into gray dawn and wind and the spit of rain.

She looked back, blinking at a haze in her vision, flinching from the sting of hair in her eyes. They had Mondragon between two men. His white face and pale hair glowed unnaturally white in the storm-light, and it was a stranger's face, it was that face she had seen in Gallandry's downstairs hall, all dead grim in the lamplight.

It was the Angel's face from the bridge, it was Retribution come to life, all pale and terrible.

No. He ain't. Angel he ain't. Sword of God. He don't *have* no special karma, no more'n me. He's thinking on Retribution, on staying alive, he ain't about quit and they know it, they're *scared* o' him even yet.

The man jerked at her elbow. She blinked in the mist and went where they made her go, toward the side of the ship, the gangway and the ramp down to the wharf.

She walked it, the grip on her arm numbing. Looked up as buildings and locations made sense; Takazawa was in front of them, mostly wood, towers rising crazily. But the man turned her, faced her to the building to the south, grim brown stone, barred windows, a sprawl of wings and terraces and buttresses added here and there as earthquake cracked the walls.

Nikolaev. Richest on Rimmon Isle. *That* was what white-face came from. One of them. With fingers in the College and the Signeury both.

She cast a look back at Mondragon, lost sight of him at once as the man jerked her forward and kept her going.

Down the pier, with Mondragon and his guards behind. Up ranks and ranks of cracked stone steps laid in the rare bedrock of Merovingen. Up at last to a door nothing but earthquake could ever shake from its pins, solid wood, bound with iron and fitted with brass.

It opened for them—someone had seen them coming. It gaped and swallowed them out of rain-spit and wind and chill, into a place as echoing and polished as Borey. There were more guards, directions. *Her*, the orders said, *take her to the east room.*

"I ain't going!" she yelled, and: *going-going-going* the vault gave back in crazed repetition. She looked wildly back at Mondragon, who made a move with his eyes that just meant *go on.* Thunder cracked and rolled above the hall. Rain sheeted down outside and whipped in to spatter the polished floor and men heaved the door shut. The one holding her arm jerked her away.

"Damn you—" she yelled.

"Damn you," the hall gave back. The sound racketed like judgment as the man pulled her along down a side hall.

He going to get familiar? I'll kill him. I'll kill him dead before they kill me.

Up stairs, down another hallway to a room where other men caught up from the side. They opened a door and the man holding her arm spun her into it so that she staggered in the middle of fancy carpet, in the face of polished furniture and a solitary window with the rain sheeting down past diamond-panes.

And iron bars.

The door slammed at her back and a lock clicked.

She paced, paced because she was too tired and she hurt too much to fall down.

Kill 'em, she thought. If I ever get out o' here I'll come back some night and gut 'em. I'll burn this fancy place and take Rimmon with it.

They got to know that too. So I ain't getting out of here, am I?

Oh, mama, your daughter got herself down a way with no exit. I'm sorry about that.

But it was something, wasn't it, how we done that damn slaver and the whole Sword of God?

Retribution Jones turned up crosslegged on the bed. Shoved her cap back on dark hair and looked left and right.

Well, she's some place, Altair, ain't it?

Dammit, mama, what do I do?

She stopped in her pacing. The wraith went away from her mind's eye and left not even a wrinkle on the bed.

Altair dusted her good hand on her leg. The leg stung, and she saw the rip in her pants.

It *was* a nail.

Then it started hurting. Hurt in the way everything else did, dull and distant ache. She paced again, walked to the window and back. Nothing but gray sea out there and cloud and spats of rain against the glass. To the bath and back. A marble tub and a brass commode. Fancier still than Gallandry's. There were bottles on the marble rim. Perfume-stuff. That put her in mind of drawers and maybe somebody forgetting something useful in this polished prison. She tried them all, tried the clothes-press.

Nothing but towels, sheets, and a rack full of men's clothes. Silk stuff. Wool. A couple of sweaters.

She tottered back to the bed and hung onto the poster staring at that embroidered coverlet, those fine soft pillows. Her arm hooked round the poster as she swayed on her feet.

Damn, no. I'm *dirty*.

With a swipe of her sleeve across a running nose. the sleeve tasted of salt and harbor water.

He wouldn't, damned if I will.

Damn hightown prigs.

She staggered into the bath, set all the bottles on the wide rim of the marble tub and got into it dry. Turned the taps on full, plugged the drain, and ducked her head under the cold water, discovering the cold water going warm. Muscles braced for cold relaxed, went sick and shivery. She hung there a moment just getting warm, and ran hands through her hair. Winced, when her fingers found the lump on the side of her skull. Then she felt around the back of her head where the old one was fading, and remembering how she had gotten it, she gulped air and gulped it again and ducked her head under the water to wash the salt out of her eyes and the sting out of her throat.

Bottles. Damn. *Glass*.

She scrambled out of the tub with water still running,

poured perfume from a sizable bottle down the drain and wrapped the empty in a fat towel.

Brought it down on the tub rim.

It took two bottles to get a good one, one long sliver of stout glass. She folded the rest in the towel and pulled the drawer in the clothes-press and dropped the little bundle down behind the drawer.

Then she dressed, in her own salt-ridden trousers and a man's blue sweater. And she carefully tucked that sizable sliver of glass into her waistband, part above like a handle, the rest aslant in the front hollow of her hip. She adjusted the sweater down over it and sat down carefully on the bed. It moved, but with her body, easy and safe. She let out a sigh and lay back clothes and all and shut her eyes, tumbling back into dark.

—ain't going to have 'em breaking in here, by the Ancestors, hauling me off nowhere stark naked—

—ain't going to give 'em any ideas they ain't got. They want me, that's fine, I go along with 'em, I let 'em do what they want till I got a chance—

Where they got him? They treating him same as me? Lord, I hope, I hope—

Rich man's jail, that's what this is. Rich man gets on the outs with the Signeury, they send 'im to some family to keep.

And they take 'im by that long black boat into the Justiciary, and he don't ever see the light again.

No hanging on the bridge for a rich man. They got different ways. They don't want folks like me to see no rich man swing up on the gallows—

They cut their heads off, don't they?

After they got what they want.

A lock rattled. She came out of it in a panic realization that a man had walked in. She lifted her head, forgot about the glass till she felt the top slide on the skin above her waist and straighten again as she got up. Rain was washing at the window. Thunder muttered away. The man stood there. There were others behind him outside.

"Bring her," that one said.

Two men came in to do that. She held up her hands. "Hey, I'm coming, I'm coming."

Get me where there's doors. Find out where he is— Man, don't you lay hand to me!

"Wald. Let her."

The man nearest gave her room. She sidled past, walked out into the hall. "Where—?" she started to ask. But the man in charge just motioned down the hall and started walking. She fell in behind, barefoot amid their booted footfalls and thinking about that unprotected back in front of her.

And thinking about the three armed men behind her.

Another group was coming their way from up ahead, the other side of a big descending stairway. She saw the Nikolaev men, saw the blond head tall and conspicuous among them—closer and closer. His hands were free. They had got the chain off his neck. He had a white shirt on. He saw her. She just kept walking, meek and quiet, to that stairs where the two groups met; and fell in with him on that wide marble stair.

He looked her way once. That was all.

He don't want me talking. I won't. I won't say a thing.

She caught his eyes a second time, halfway down, made a slight tightening of her lids, a gesture with the eyes.

I ain't helpless, Mondragon.

His own eyes flickered. Maybe he picked it up. He looked away from her, looked where they were going, into an echoing stone hall lit from a skylight above. Rain spattered down on it like thunder, louder when they had gotten clear of the overhang. And faded away as their guides led them farther, steps echoing back as they passed by a side hall, hard-heeled steps loud and echoing in this huge place.

Cold sounds. Hard sounds. Water and stone.

I got me a knife, Mondragon. I dunno if we can get out, but if they put us in that black boat it's over the side and swim far as we can.

City's got as many holes as bridges. I know 'em all.

I'm scared, dammit. I don't like these polite folk. Them

and their ways of waving this way and waving that and poisoning the drink they hand you.

A corridor left the big hall near the front; they turned that way, and a man ahead knocked at a door, cracked it and then opened it wide for them to go through.

It was a middle-sized room by rich-folk standards, all finished in wood and lit with electrics that glowed warm-gold as fire. Altair stopped cold at Mondragon's side, seeing white-face there before a true fireplace, him in his black shirt and glitter of rubies about the high collar, sitting sideways in a chair and with one booted leg slung over the arm. He had a paper in his hand, cream and crisp and new. He laid that on the little table by him where a brandy glass sat.

Then he bothered to notice them.

"Ser Mondragon," he said then, leaned back without ever taking his leg from the chair arm, lacing his hands across his belly. "I'm glad to see you looking more fit."

Mondragon said not a thing.

"Sit down, ser." A wave of his hand. "Bring a chair for the young woman." He gathered up the brandy glass and offered it toward them with a lift of the brows while a man was moving a chair over. "Have some? No? I don't doubt m'sera has some acquaintance with brandy. In its traffic."

She stared at the man. Smuggling, he meant.

Lord, they need a charge against me?

"I hired her," Mondragon said. "She was just transport."

"A skip, ser, runs *freight*. What were you running?" He lifted the glass of amber liquid. "Brandy-barrels from Tidewater? I think that's m'sera's specialty. Are you sure you won't have a glass?"

Mondragon shrugged. White-face snapped his fingers, and glasses happened, a clink or two from a table at the side of the room and a man arrived with a tray and a pair of brandy glasses. Mondragon took his. Altair lifted hers off the lace doily and looked up into the serving-man's expressionless face—Lord, what *is* he, some kind of wind-up?

And she looked back to white-face, to that quiet, quiet

voice that was all Merovingen and all uptown. Not even
Rimmon Isle. Uptown as uptown got, and Revenantist
beyond a doubt, in this house.

"I have to congratulate you," white-face said. "In one
night you've quite well set the slavers *and* the Sword of
God in total disarray. The entire militia has hardly effected
that much in a year. What project do you propose for the
weekend?"

Mondragon lifted his glass, gestured aside with it to
Altair. "Let her go. You want to ask me questions. She
doesn't need to be privy to anything I know."

"Ah. You propose to answer, then."

"I'll tell you anything you want. Just give her her boat
back and let her out of here."

White-face pursed bearded lips. "Now how far would
you expect to get, m'sera?"

"I dunno. I'm willing to try."

"Try what? Another assault with firebombs, this time
on my hosts of Nikolaev?"

That landed on the mark. She sat still and tried to keep
her face quite dead. She set the glass down on the table
between her and Mondragon. No sip of that brandy, don't
need no alcohol, with my wits already mush. Damn you,
white-face.

I got a glass knife in my pocket, white-face. Before they
could stop me, he and I'd at least send you to your next
life.

Maybe get out of here. Get to Rimmon alleyways.
Bridges.

Past that damn great door out there. And half a hundred
bullyboys. Sure.

"Canaler," white-face said, "where *did* you get involved in this?"

"She picked me up on the Grand," Mondragon said.
"A fare. Just a fare."

"Is that so, m'sera?"

"He wouldn't lie."

White-face's lips curved in a sardonic smile. He lifted
his glass again, drank, and the smile was no better. "You

have a career in government, m'sera. What do you know about this man?''

"Just what he said."

A dead, long silence.

"I said I'd answer your questions," Mondragon said.

"You will. Yes." Another sip of brandy. White-face set the glass down and shifted round in his chair to set both feet on the floor. "Do you know who you're dealing with, Mondragon?"

"It doesn't matter. I know what you aren't."

"Eeling your way from point to point. You *have* no loyalties. A clever man without the least compunction in shifting sides as the wind shifts. Hourly. You're the kind of man everyone should be afraid of—with your abilities."

"I've told you I'll tell you all you want. Do you want me into the bargain? I'll agree. I've told you my price."

White-face set his elbows on the chair arms and touched his fingertips together. "The m'sera."

Thunder rumbled outside. Altair flinched, clenched her hands on the chair arm. "You want me quiet, you let *him* go."

"Shut up, Jones."

"No, no." White-face lifted an elegant hand, elbow on the chair arm. "M'sera Jones has an excellent grasp of the problem. She doesn't think she'll live to get to that boat—"

True, white-face. True.

"—and she wants you to know it. A small hand, but she plays it with devastating force. And takes the game from me and you. You were buying time in the hope I'd not shed too much information on m'sera. Your hand is altogether weakest. You have the ace but you have altogether too many liabilities."

Mondragon made a helpless move of his hand on the chair arm. "You have me in a bad position. I don't doubt you can apply persuasion now. But that doesn't guarantee you the truth—does it?"

"Ah, well, well-played. Do I threaten m'sera now?" His eyes shifted to Altair. "But he would lie in half he told me. Wouldn't he?"

"He ain't no fool."

"I tell you, m'sera, you do have a talent for the councilhall. Indeed, he's still turning this way and that. But the turns are narrower and narrower, aren't they? Your behavior would be relatively simple to guarantee—all I have to do is keep him in good health. Maybe let you visit him now and again."

O God, it's prison again, it's prison for him same as the other—

She cast a look Mondragon's way, caught one from him, caught that expression in the eye—fear, quiet, profound fear.

"Acceptable," Mondragon said, glancing back at white-face.

"But then—you'd dole out the things I want to know. To preserve both your lives. And the m'sera remains—an explosion on a slow fuse. Other factions would find her—very quickly. Uncomfortable and dangerous for you, m'sera."

"I stay with him." She looked at Mondragon and saw something come apart, some crack of something vital.

"He'll kill us both," Mondragon said plainly. "When he's done."

"He won't, you and I'll hire out to him. I'll bet these fancy bullylads ain't all that good. You want somebody knows the canalside, you want somebody knows ever' hole and nook on the Isles? *I* do. Ain't no damn cult going to get hands on him and me, ain't no way! I'll gut 'em!"

White-face regarded her with a lively flicker of the eyes. Then those eyes hooded in amusement. "Now there, *there*, Mondragon, beats the true dark heart of Merovingen, this sharp-eyed m'sera who doubtless provided us this fine brandy. You don't trifle with the under-city. It has a limited patience and it demonstrated that last night. I'm sure there are inquiries on her behalf right now. An honest woman. She would bargain. But how do I hold *you*, ser?"

Mondragon said nothing.

"So. You see, m'sera. He knows that I know his character. That he will never resist persuasion unless he cares to. If he swore and meant it today, tomorrow's circumstances would have him swear to my enemies with quite as complete a passion. Which is to say, none at all. I think he must once have been a great idealist. And out of those ashes, of course, a total amoralist. Nev Hettek put him behind bars—and see how *that* succeeded. He might be hired—mightn't you, Mondragon?''

Mondragon shrugged. "For sufficient.''

"He'll deal with you,'' Altair said. Her heart beat away, harder and harder and her hands sweated. "Mondragon, f' God's sake—''

"Let's talk about coin,'' white-face said. "Let's talk about my resources. You say you don't know me. Do you, m'sera? No? Well, I should be offended. But then I doubt you'd know my father's face either.''

Father. Uptown. Altair blinked and shook her head desperately. Boregy? Is this another Boregy?

In a Revenantist house?

"Kalugin,'' white-face said. "Pavel Anastasi Kalugin.''

My God. The governor's son. The governor. The Signeury. "Mondragon, he's—''

"Kalugin,'' Mondragon said in a faint, far voice. "Then this is official.''

"Hardly.'' Kalugin crossed one leg over the other, set his hand on that booted ankle. "Tell him, m'sera.''

"He—'' Lord, what do I say and not say? "He's number three son. Lives up on the Rock. His brother and his sister live in the Signeury.''

"You're too diplomatic, m'sera. What m'sera *means* to say is that my father and I don't get on well. Very old story, isn't it? Brother Mikhail is so amenable to papa's directions, brother Mikhail doesn't have a single interest except his clocks and his little inventions, couldn't find the lavatory if he didn't have a directive from papa and a councillor to guide him. Poor Mikhail won't last the week when he succeeds, and of course Council will vote him in. Tatiana's the next choice. Sister's so good with papa, so practical. Just like her mother, papa says. She certainly is. Tatiana knows where every body in the Signeury is buried and brother Mikhail will be one of them in very short order.'' Kalugin reached beside him, took the brandy and took a sip. "Not that I'm bereft of partisans. It's stalemate, you see. I see a certain danger in Nev Hettek. *I* favor the militia. That advice is not popular. And here are you. Do you see?''

Altair looked from one to the other—Kalugin smiled. Mondragon's face was quiet and cold as the Angel's.

''I begin to.''

Altair gnawed at her lip. Tasted blood. ''What's he want? Mondragon? Mondragon, it ain't good, is it?''

Mondragon set his brandy glass aside on the table at his elbow. ''He's talking about a public confession, a trial. Public vindication for him. He gets a cause, he gets public opinion slanted his way, he gets power for the militia and his own partisans. I get the ax, I suppose, is that what they do here? But that puts us right where we were before. You can't leave Jones alive to contradict you. I know that. We all know it. Now, I don't know how long I can hold out if you apply persuasion—but then, *you* don't know that either. You won't be able to trust a thing I tell you.''

Kalugin's eyes flickered. His mouth pursed in amusement, stretched into a lazy smile. ''The last card down, is it?''

''You don't really know how many I have.''

The smile grew colder.

O Lord, he's going to start on me, he is. What do I do? Killing him'd kill Mondragon sure.

But quicker.

''No,'' Kalugin said. ''In fact I don't. But you betray something very interesting. It took m'sera to find it, didn't she, found a little undefended spot and there you are, a splendid amoralist all in ruins. You *are* capable of loyalty. Profound loyalty. All I have to do is keep her alive. All you have to believe is that I'll do it as long as I have the power to do it.''

''Your word?'' Mondragon asked, all soft and all false.

Lord, Mondragon, you know and I know that's a snowball in hell, ain't it?

Kalugin pursed his lips. ''You doubt it, do you?''

''Of course not.''

''Of course not. But I wouldn't impose that far on your credulity.''

"You have a proposal?"

"God, you have no nerves."

"Not when I don't believe you, m'ser."

Kalugin lifted a hand, waved at the men about. "M'sera will need clothes. Something—for house. M'ser is in some better case, but hardly." He waved the hand a second time, lowered it to rest across his middle. "There, you see. Guests. An instant transformation. Easy as that."

What's he up to, Mondragon?

He's got tricks, I know he's got tricks, all over the city they tell stories on this Anastasi Kalugin.

"I got friends here," Altair said. "They alive? You going to let them go? Man's got a family. Got a wife and a kid—" Shut *up*, Jones, fool, this is the devil himself you're dealing with.

"The best of care," Kalugin said. "My own doctor travels with me. The one man was a bit chancy for a while this morning, wasn't he, Iosef? But he's doing quite nicely? Yes. You see? Nothing but the best. I daresay the boy can go as soon as the rain stops. The other two as soon as they're willing and able. No thanks, m'sera?"

"Thanks."

Kalugin laughed without a sound. His hand idly rotated the brandy glass by its stem as it sat on the table. A man came and filled it from the decanter by him, and Kalugin never looked to see. "M'sera came to Boregy last night. She made an appeal for your rescue. To Vega Boregy, of all people. His cousin lately murdered, his aging uncle in and out of coma—doubtless they haven't told the old man about poor Espoir. And Vega returns from his exile in Rajwade, quietly gathers the household into his hands in a matter of hours. Vega is *my* partisan, m'sera. A fact he's not at all made public, but one that has estranged him from his uncle. And your news so impressed him he sent straight to me here at Nikolaev. In the meantime the harbor was uncommonly busy with canalers—always a bad sign. I dispatched a message to the Signeury, of course: it never hurts to observe the forms. I hardly dreamed m'sera would succeed. But that slaver-craft comes and goes—pardon, *did* come and go with some regularity. The Signeury knows. It's just never been worth the bother.''

Go to hell, Kalugin.

"So you were waiting in the harbor," Mondragon said.

"I was waiting. You see that not much passes by me."

"You make the point successfully."

"I'm glad. I plan to survive both my sibs. I want you to appreciate that fact. The terms, Mondragon. I'm going to turn you loose. Both of you. There's your skip, m'sera, tied to the Nikolaev yacht, in full view of God and everyone. I'm a guest of the Nikolaevs, no secret. There will be the gossip of your three companions. And should imagination utterly fail this town, my agents will loose certain vague rumors concerning your attachment to me and the fate of opposition who might think to lay hands on you. Do you see? If you serve my interests you'll find my arm is very long to protect you. Betray those interests in any particular or give me one false piece of information in our interviews and you'll discover the same. Does that satisfy you, m'sera? Will you not firebomb Kalugin?''

She shivered. Clenched her hands and drew a deep breath. O God. Alive. *Out* of this place alive. Mondragon, what's truth? What's a lie, from the devil?

"I don't need to wait till the rain stops, m'ser."

"What, not stay and enjoy Mondragon's I'm sure very entertaining company for the while?"

"You said you were letting him go!"

"Oh, but *after* he's told me all I want to hear. After he's sat with me and gone over my maps and helped me make my lists, m'sera.''

"We're back to the beginning," Mondragon said. "You letting her go. Me here—not knowing what your word is worth.''

"Oh, but she could stay. And you'd still wonder whether you'd leave alive. You have to trust me. In that little thing.''

Mondragon reached for the brandy and drank it down to nothing. Set the empty glass down. "Compromise. She'll leave a message daily. At Moghi's, on Ventani. Your agents will deliver one from me.''

"Elaborate. Wasteful."

"It gets her out of here."

"It gives her a chance to go to hiding if you slip her a suspicion of bad faith. Of course it does. I don't doubt you'll think of other little nuisances. Like telling her everything."

"I'm glad it was you who said that. I don't want you to think I *have*."

Kalugin sat expressionless a moment, then once and sharply an eyebrow twitched. "Very reckless, Mondragon."

"I'm quite serious."

"I'm sure you are. I also doubt you could have told her everything. I'm sure m'sera's expertise in statecraft has its limits; and her ability with maps probably greater limits. No, m'sera. Is your boat in running order?"

"Tank's holed; got a hole in her bottom, too. It's how you damn well caught us."

"Jones."

"I believe m'sera. A hole in the tank and a hole in the bottom. I don't think that should present much of a problem. Some of my staff will go down with you. I'm sure Rimmon is adequate to a repair of that size. You did say you had no need to wait on the weather."

"I changed my mind. I c'n wait. I c'n wait here a whole week. Two weeks."

"You'd not want to complicate matters. No, m'sera. I'm very anxious to have our friend's undivided attention. Your engine running. Supplies as you need them. Money if you require it. You *are* in my employ."

The hell I am. The hell I am if you lay a hand to him. I'll have your guts on a hook, Kalugin.

"M'sera, do you understand the arrangement? Each morning without fail, you'll leave a note with the Ventani tavern. Each morning a man will take that away. You do write, m'sera?"

"I write. I ain't got nothing to write *on*."

"Supplies. It's very simple. All that sort of thing is very simple. My staff takes care of details. All you have to do is ask. But you have to go now, m'sera, I very much regret, without any private word between you. This man would do something devious, I'm well sure, and I don't want you to bear that burden. Just say a public goodbye and go gather your belongings."

She looked at Mondragon. He nodded, with a private motion of the eyes. Truth, then. Go. Get out. Her eyes suddenly stung and threatened to spill over. She shoved herself to her feet.

Can't damn well *walk*. I can't walk, my legs'll go.

Mondragon reached his hand out. Took hers and squeezed it. She found life for her fingers and squeezed back till he let go. Fingers trailed apart.

She walked a few steps, looked back at Mondragon's back and Kalugin's white face above that ruby collar and black shirt—set her left hand on her hip, brushing her sweater aside, and cast what she pulled up.

The glass blade hit the carpet well to the side of Kalugin's chair and broke in half as guns came out of holsters all around the edge of the room. Mondragon started from his chair, stopped motionless as everyone else.

"That," she said, with heat all over where the cold had been, "that was in case."

She turned and walked out. "Sit down," she heard Kalugin say behind her. She heard guns go back into holsters and several men walk after her.

Can't hurt me. Yet. They got to have them letters, don't they?"

Moghi had a down look this morning, Moghi behind the bar himself this breakfast-time, his sullen jowls all set in a tuck of his chin as he polished away at glasses. Ali stopped his sweeping—Ali with the last traces of his black eye; and started it up again when Altair looked his way.

She went up to the bar with tomorrow's letter, all done up with yarn-tie, and there seemed an uncommon quiet about the tavern's morning patrons too, poleboatmen and Ventani regulars, mostly, having their breakfasts. They knew her. Everyone in Merovingen-below knew Altair Jones and knew mysterious letters passed between her and an uptowner-man who came to Moghi's every morning.

"It ain't here," Moghi said, and polished away at a glass too scratched to be helped. "Ain't come yet."

"What time is it?"

"Dunno, 'bout time."

She stood there a moment. Put the letter on the counter. Her hand shook when she did it. "Well, put that with my other. Man can take 'em both. Just late, that's all."

"Right," Moghi said. "Have an egg. On the house."

Generosity. From Moghi. Moghi thought it was bad.

"Thanks. Thanks." She walked back through the rear door to the kitchen. "Tea and egg," she said, and Jep gave her a look. "No," she said, "it ain't come."

"Unh." Jep got a gray-speckled egg from the tray, looked it over and got a second one. Broke them both onto the grill and added a slice of bread.

She slouched over and got the plate when the food came off. Took that and a cup of tea back to the main room and sat down to eat it.

Late. That's all it is, just late, they got some kind of tangle-up, some damned hire-on taking his damn time.

Eat your breakfast, Jones, damnfool, it don't cost you nothing.

She pushed the egg around on the plate, ate it in too-large bites and got the bread and tea down.

She waited. The boy came and filled up her tea again and she drank that.

Damnfools, staring at me.

She shoved the chair back finally, a scrape on the wooden floor. Walked over by the bar and had Moghi's attention before she got there. "Going for a walk," she said. "I'll be back in a while."

"Huh," Moghi said, and went on arranging his glasses.

She walked out the door into the full daylight, pulled her cap tightly down and stared out over the morning-gray waters of the Grand, between Fishmarket's towering span and the plainer gray wood of Hanging Bridge. Skips were gathered there, gathered at Fishmarket's far side; a couple of poleboatmen came out of Moghi's at her back and headed down the laddeer to the boats moored at Moghi's porch, a gathering like so many black fish with her own bigger boat moored beyond.

"Hey," she yelled from the porch, "you back out all right, you want me back my skip?"

"Ney, we got room."

It was tight. The poleboats began to move out, one and the other. More boatmen came out from Moghi's, talking the day's business.

Damn. Never figured to be tied up that long.

"I move 'er," she muttered, and climbed down the ladder, walked across half a dozen tightly-packed poleboats and the length of one, stepped into her own bow and slipped the jury-tie. Boats backed, taking their own time about it. She kept the skip still with the pole, worked into a developing gap at the porch edge and racked the pole, moved fast to grab the bow-rope and tied on in the last ebb of poleboatmen outward bound and the retreating clogs-on-board thunder of shoresiders on their way to their shops.

She retreated to the stern and sat down on the halfdeck-rim, got the bluestone out of its storage by her foot, took out her thin-bladed knife and set to sharpening it since yesterday's use on a bit of line.

Damn hightowner sense of time.

I give 'im another hour.

Then I got to think of something. I got to get to Rimmon, that's what I got to do.

No. I find where Kalugin *is*. He's slippery. Could be in Nikolaev. Could be back to Kalugin. I don't do nothing stupid, just real slow and calm.

I give 'em a little present like I give that slaver-boat. they got to come running out. And me and this is waiting.

The blade blurred.

I give 'im an hour, then I got to go somewhere they don't find me so easy.

Water fell onto the steel. She wiped her eyes with the back of the knife-hand and kept to polishing.

Leather-shod steps came up onto the porch, reached porch-edge and stopped. She looked up at a blurred outline of a man in uptorn clothes standing there above. Blinked and saw the daylight catch the hair and hover there.

M'God.

M'God. She sheathed the knife, dropped the stone and got to her feet in the well, staring up at the elegant man on the porch, the man who took the ladder-rail and came down it to step off onto the slats of her well.

He looked all right. He stood there as if he no longer knew his balance on a skip. Pretty sword at his side. Nice clothes.

You get along with Kalugin all right, then, Mondragon?

"Jones—"

All pretty again. You got an eel's turns, sure enough. Woman breaks her heart over you and you come back smelling like an uptowner, and no mark on you.

"Got room for a passenger?"

"Hey, I ain't loaded. You going somewhere's in particular, dressed like that?"

"Jones, dammit."

She pushed her cap back and resettled it, wiped her fingers on her sweater. "You're looking all right."

"I'm all right."

"You leaving town?"

"No, I—" He gestured vaguely toward uptown, motion of a lace-cuffed hand. "I'm staying in Boregy. Till I can find somewhere else. Moved late last night. Boregy's boat delivered me down at the corner—" His voice trailed off. "I'm late, aren't I?"

"Hell, not much." Her eyelashes prickled with damp when she blinked. Damnfool man. Can he tell I was crying? Did he see me? "You look real nice."

"You too." He came close to her, all perfume-smelling, all clean and fancy lace-front and wool coat, and she backed and held her knife-blacked hands out of the way as her leg hit the half-deck. "Jones, let's go somewhere."

She stared at him. "You in hire to Kalugin, are you?"

A little tautness came to his mouth. "I have a patron. That's the way a foreigner lives in this town."

"Damn, you trust that—"

"He's very likely to be governor someday. I know his kind. They often win."

"Yey. They do."

"I haven't got a choice, Jones."

She drew several quick, short breaths. "Huh." She wiped her hands again. "Well, that's another thing, ain't it?"

"You want me to untie?"

She blinked, flung up a bewildered gesture. "Hell, uptowner don't do the work." She edged past him, went her barefoot way forward and jerked the tie. Looked up at Ali standing there on the porch rim. At Jep behind him. "Dammit, ye looking for gossip?" She waved a go-away at them. "Tell Moghi I got 'im!"

"Where you going, Jones?" Moghi's voice bellowed out.

"I dunno. Ware, aft!" She unracked the pole and pushed off. "We'll know it when we get there." Pole down. The bow came about into Fishmarket shadow, for up-Grand.

"And don't you dare open them letters, Moghi! I know how I tied them knots!"

APPENDIX

Of Union, Alliance, and Merovin
A Concise History of Merovin

THE history of Merovin is a history of mistake. There was from early in Alliance and Union history (2530 AD) a proclamation colloquially known as the Gehenna Doctrine: it declared as a matter of policy that no Terran genetic material should be introduced into any compatible alien ecology; and that humanity should not contact any alien species onworld, and should not land on any planet unless invited by a dominant sapient species. The practical sense of it was this: that humanity would keep to space and leave developing worlds free to develop without contamination traveling in either direction; and that humanity would contact no species that had not advanced into spaceflight. The theory behind this was that such a species had (1) avoided blowing itself up with advanced power systems and (2) learned enough about its own planetary ecology to devise protections against contamination at critical levels.

The Gehenna Doctrine guided humanity in the twenty sixth century; by the twenty seventh, it was suffering some erosion. Humanity spread out not in a coherent sphere from Earth, but outward from Tau Ceti and in the general direction of Vega and Sirius in thin threads of lanes along routes ships could use, to stars humankind could use; and the lack of centralization spelled lack of central control.

Of the two human superpowers, Alliance (near the center of human space) was more nearly a coherent territory and actually had a coherent government. Union spread outward in a series of threads that more resembled a network of corridors of diminishing cohesiveness: Union realized early on that it was never going to *be* a coherent, compact government, that it was doomed to sprawl. It had taken certain educational measures with its citizens to assure an underlying conformity (Alliance called it mind-washing) and simply shrugged as the lines of colonization extended outward beyond its reach or understanding. Union asked peace of its component parts; and violated the Gehenna Doctrine not as collective policy (it had none) but locally. In effect Union applied the Gehenna Doctrine to humanity more than to alien contacts: it cared very little what went on within a local unit, down an isolate star lane, or on a particular world—as long as what exited that unit and came into another unit's space left its neighbors alone and generally obeyed Union law.

Merovingen was an example of the kind of accident Union was prone to: a wildcat colony launched in 2608 by someone far from Union's capital at Cyteen, at a little G-class star with an earthlike planet—just too attractive for certain economic interests to resist. It was a general period of expansion, and in the confidence of new science, worlds were no longer exempt.

The expedition moved in haste at all levels, worried about attracting attention from upper levels of the Union super-government (under the general apprehension that the Government tended to take interest in anything that went on too long and with too much local disruption). This haste had a foreseeable consequence: hasty geologic reports, hasty climatological studies, objections from field officers stifled by superiors whose superiors might be distressed if schedules were not met. Hasty zonal survey.

And a very illegal coverup of what the colonial officials tried to call a natural formation; fracture patterns. A geologist objected and found himself grounded. No archaeologist was consulted at all; it was quite evident that whatever it was, was deeply buried, thoroughly abandoned, and of no consequence to the colony. Someone a long time ago had colonized the world and abandoned it. That was the opinion behind the most securitied doors in the survey mission. And *basaltic formation* was the word that got beyond those doors. Listening scan of nearby stars picked up no aliens and no activity. The world had none. It was all very safe. The people and the higher echelons did not have to know, until, well—later. *After* the colony was in place.

Things went quite smoothly—like a fall over a cliff. The colonists debarked, built and built, the crops thrived, the colony achieved level II industry, the space station added new sections, the shuttle port enlarged its perimeters, the promoters became rich, and the companies back at the parent star were all smiles and complacency.

Then the former landlords showed up.

Sharrh was the name they called themselves. They communicated with humans in 2652: they permitted no contact from the other direction, and used their (quite excellent) command of human language to deliver an ultimatum. The colony at Merovin was to be removed. Or they would remove it.

This was a disturbance that promised real trouble. The central government might be involved. The companies scrambled to disentangle themselves, which compromised any defense that might have been made; and in the scramble, all in the hasty tumble of events that brought Cyteen kiting in with warships—some minor functionary whose head was on the block had stolen some microfiches and spilled the whole business to interested Cyteen officials. Other heads rolled—figuratively. And the government at Cyteen realized that the whole colonization effort was a monumental series of coverups that meant *no* records could be trusted.

Now the colossus that was Union central government could move with amazing dispatch in crisis. Around this time Union's attention was on another discovery, in that period of prosperity just preceding the Mri/regul Wars. It wished to be rid of an embarrassment to prevent a souring of its relations with the Alliance. So it simply advised the sharrh that the colony was not authorized and resurrected the Gehenna Doctrine to assure the sharrh that if the sharrh wanted no contact, no contact would occur. End of statement. No sharrh to enter human space. No humans to enter sharrh space. They were dealing with xenophobes and an alien government with unknown parameters and exigencies; and dis-contact was the operative word. Discontact; disengagement; dismantlement.

Human warships arrived with transports, stripped the space station, stripped the cities onworld of all documents that might benefit the sharrh; and ordered the colonists to board shuttles for transport to human space.

Colonists rushed the spaceport, and with the first few loads, there was more difficulty restraining the boarders than coaxing them.

Then it came down to the colonists who had other ideas. Troops landed to scour them out. Cities were torched. Independent-minded colonists took to the hills and fired back.

That was the end of it. Union had another policy: not to spend the lives of its troops protecting people who shot at them. Union ordered its forces offworld in 2655, pulled its ships out of that region, packed up and left, with a final word to the sharrh that humanity would accept a peaceful contact but would regard that contact henceforth as the sharrh's business—if the sharrh cared to make it.

Union effectively slammed the door on that corridor and went on about its affairs, carefully skirting the whole region thereafter, but not without listening in that direction. The sharrh were territorially smaller than Union. Union might win a war. But there was no percentage in fighting it. If there was one lesson Union had learned, it was that its component parts tended to erupt in internal disturbance whenever the central government was tied down to a prolonged problem in some other area; and Union simply avoided conflicts unless it was cornered or its authority was questioned. It chose to regard this incident not as a questioning of its authority but as a chance to chastise a few companies which had gotten beyond themselves. The blame went to them. And Union, the central body of the octopus that was Union, simply grew a little and controlled that corridor of access a bit more tightly.

Merovin's problems, alas, were only beginning.

Chronology

Note: Some dates are given for general reference and time frame; Merovin-pertinent dates are asterisked.

AD	LOCAL EVENT	
2600*		Erosion of Gehenna Doctrine.
2608*		Merovin colony lands.
2623		First Alliance/Union contact with majat of A Hyi II (Cerdin). Crew eaten.
2652*		Sharrh demand removal of colony from Merovin.
2653*		Union/sharrh treaty cedes Merovin.
2654*		Union troops remove colonists.
2655*		Merovin exodus complete.
2657*		The Scouring of Merovin.
2658*	1 AS	Sharrh withdraw; elsewhere the first Gehennan to leave his world reaches Fargone.
2659*	2 AS	Minor quake in Det Valley, Merovingen.
2672*	14	Calendree of Nev Hettek organizes Det Valley militias: beginning of Re-Establishment.

2679*	21	Merovingen defies Nev Hettek.
2680*	22	Merovingen joined by other militias rejecting Nev Hettek rule.
2690*	32	Great Quake in Det Valley.
2691*	33	Flood in Merovingen.
2695*	37	Flood in Merovingen.
2698*	40	Flood in Merovingen.
2699*	41	Flood in Merovingen.
2700*	42	Flood in Merovingen; Angel of Merovingen found.
2701*	43	First contact of Alliance with the regul and the mri; dike breaks in Merovingen.
2702*	44	Flood in Merovingen.
2703	45	The Mri Wars begin: generally throughout this period, since the regul/mri assault came from a side of Alliance not involving Union, the Alliance fought alone. The Alliance, moreover, in its long distrust of Union, feared an attack on its flank from Union, The Alliance security organization (AlSec) founded 300 years previously by Signy Mallory proved all too powerful against the constitution framed by Damon Konstantin. Alliance became a police state on the home front, repressive and suspicious. Union, while worried, was not able to intervene across Alliance space until the war worsened.

2710*	52	Adventist riots on Merovin; Nev Hettek intervenes in Merovingen and the original Angel is lost.
2712*	54	The Angel of Merovingen is set on the bridge. Nev Hettek is expelled from Merovingen.
2720*	62	Merovingen's harbor destroyed in major quake; sea gates jam open; boats are sunk. Miraculously the Angel continues to stand. A sandbar forms above the wrecked boats, completing the devastation.
2721*	63	The New Harbor is begun in Merovingen.
2722	64	Alliance government center removed to Haven from Pell, to bring the government center closer to the war zone and improve reaction time. Pell is reduced to a regional capital, but remains the cultural, if not the administrative, center of the Alliance.
2724*	66	The Faisal Rebellion; ends Re-Establishment.
2730	72	Fall of Haven to the mri: Alliance finally appeals for Union help. The help is debated in the Union Council while Haven falls, and Union forces when they do arrive are met with distrust and anger by Alliance forces who do not understand what restraints have operated on the home front. It has been AlSec policy to keep the war out of the home territory at Pell; but there is now intense economic suffering and the loss of life can no longer be concealed.

2743	85	End of the Mri Wars: Haven retaken.
2748	90	Regul reach internal crisis because of human contact and go totally xenophobic.
2749	91	The Alliance suffers revolution as AlSec is curtailed and the Konstantin constitution is restored. Union observes prudent silence during this period.
2779*	121	Earthquake in the Chattalen.
2805*	147	Minor Det Valley quake.
2907*	249	Major flood in Merovingen.
3141	483	Massacre of the Meth-marens of the Hydri Stars.
3187	529	The Hanan break from the Alliance in a minor fracas limited to a narrow string of stars, but the struggle will last a thousand years. Union is not involved.
3241*	583	Altair Jones born on Merovin.
3243*	585	Minor quake in Merovingen.
3253*	595	Retribution Jones dies in flood.

Religions of Merovin

Sharrists

Sharrists believe that if humans can become more like the sharrh the sharrh will relent and let Merovin back into space. The sharrh, of course, are not supposed to be bothering the humans of this world at all, except that there are some of their number with piratical inclinations and no scruples whatsoever about using their worshipers.

It should be noted that the humans involved with the Sharrist cult range from denominations which have no religious aspects, to those which have very metaphysical beliefs that they can *become* sharrh physically, or be reborn as sharrh, by becoming more and more like the sharrh.

Adventists

Adventists expect humanity to return with superior weapons and defeat the sharrh and take Merovin into the human community by force. Adventists have an aggressive outlook and are often involved in forbidden technology and plots. They give their children tech-names or star names; or names like Hope or Retribution. By this can be seen their philosophy. Those of mystical inclination hope to hasten the day of Advent by prayers and believe in a God of retribution. They do in general believe in karma, but view karma as a collective karma of all Merovans, which must be purified to enable the Retribution. A subcult, the Immaterial Adventists, often known as the Preachers, believe that the Retribution will be more metaphysical and look for human life to improve only after humans have acquired virtue enough to atone for their past sins of greed and corruption. Another subcult, the Sword of God, trains its members in martial arts and devotes its energies to gaining temporal power, obliterating sharrist influence, and preparing for war, and in the belief that God will subject the world to a second Scouring before the Retribution, and will reward only those humans who join in obliterating the sharrh all the way back to their world of origin. From these two subcults various other cults depend, each differing in some point of dogma; but these are the two extremes of Adventist thought.

Many governments have laws restricting Adventists, but they are officially recognized in Soghon and Nev Hettek.

Revenantists

This religion believes in reincarnation, that Merovin is a testing-place for souls or a place of punishment (denominations differ on this point) and that by virtue it is possible to win rebirth higher up the scale of society on Merovin and ultimately to another human world, in a long progress of karma acquired and ties to Merovin diminished.

Revenantism is the most formal of Merovan religions, and the most widespread. It is the majority religion of Merovingen and Canbera.

It has elaborate rituals and ceremonies, particularly revolving around birth, death, and majority.

Church of God

This cult claims to follow the old human ways of worship based on revelation and documents rescued from the Scouring. They are mostly a Wold entity, but maintain a religious seat at Gothhead and are strong among the Falkenaers. They are divided into numerous denominations. Most believe in an afterlife of all species, sharrh as well as humans.

New Worlders

This cult is an offshoot of the Church of God, which maintains that true belief has been lost and that God must be reapproached and rediscovered without reference to documents or cult objects. The New Worlders have three denominations: the Scholiasts, who believe this approach should be intellectual; the Ecstatics, who seek revelation; and the Revisionists, who try to apply both theories. They are predominant in Megar.

Janes

Followers of Althea Jane Morgoth, generally polytheists who practice magic and healing rituals. Jane Morgoth was a farmer from the Upper Ligur who convinced a large following of her powers and led the Ligurian Riots until she was arrested and executed in 432. Her followers believe she became a spirit of two sorts: healing for believers and retribution for nonbelievers. This belief was encouraged by the deaths of three of her judges in the same year; and it is said that no member of the jury lived beyond the decade. Detractors claimed that this was due to assassination by members of the cult, and in three cases by heart failure which may have been attributable to harassment.

Janes are predominant in the rural Liger but not unknown in Suttani and the Isles of Fire.

Seasons and Time

The concept of time on Merovin is based on twenty-seventh-century practice, which looks back to military timekeeping of old Earth, all of which was modified by the exigencies of the Scouring.

The result is a twenty-four-hour clock and a twelve-month year.

The months are (from a numerical origin modified by history and agricultural practice): Prime; Deuce; Planting; Greening; Quartin; Quinte; Sexte; Septe; Harvest; Falling; Turning; Fallow.

The months have twenty eight days, excepting Fallow, which has twenty nine. There is also the Day of the Turn, which serves as an intercalary unit to trim up the irregularity of the year. This *day* may actually be more than one day in length; and is set by the Astronomer of Merovingen, decreed by the governor, and by all other governors. In practice however, it is well known in advance that such a decree will be made, so the event is virtually simultaneous despite the slow speed of communications, there being more than one Astronomer in the world. This Day is celebrated variously: Revenantists consider it a time of meditation; Adventists consider it a day without record, and no act without permanent consequence is forbidden: it is a carnival in Adventist cities. In Merovingen it is said among Adventists that the Angel sleeps on that one day; Revenantists call this heresy.

The weeks are a uniform seven days excepting the last week of Fallow, which has eight. The days of the week are Sunday; Monday; Tuesday; Wensday; Thursday; Friday; Satterday. The origins of the names are forgotten.

The days have twenty-four hours on the civic clock; but popularly (going back to the Scouring and the Restoration when time was reckoned without the benefit of precise clocks) the day consists approximately of hours between six or so in the morning and runs down to the eighteenth hour or so, until dark, after which a variety of regional time descriptions take over. A Merovingian speaking other than officially will describe the dark hours as Watches, of which there are six before the dawn—as, for instance, the top of the first watch is the beginning of full dark; the bottom of the fifth is a couple of hours before dawn; the bottom of the sixth is the first perception of sunrise.

The most universal holidays are 24 Harvest, which is the date on which the Scouring began, and 10 Prime, which is the generally accepted date of its ending. The 24th of Harvest is a day of mourning and sober reflection for all religions. The 10th of Prime is a day of celebration, sometimes of licentiousness. The 24th of Harvest is a particularly tense time for police in cities where there is a strong Adventist presence, as the *melancholy* as Merovans refer to it, may result in overindulgence, which in turn leads to hallucinations or to religiously-inspired and quite cold-blooded decisions on the part of groups or individuals to take direct action against real or imagined enemies. On one famous occasion a band of twenty Adventists from Soghon set out to destroy the sharrh ruins at Kevogi and fought their way through three companies of militia from Soghon and Merovingen who set out to stop them. They cost a hundred and fifty-two lives before the last of them was subdued. The sole survivor of the action was a twenty-two year old man named Tom Caney, wounded in the final assault and later hanged at Merovingen. The incident is generally referred to as the Faisal Rebellion, after its chief instigator.

Other holidays are pertinent to certain religious groups and are celebrated in certain locales but not in others; still others commemorate local events, such as the Festival of the Angel on 20th to 25th Fallow, in Merovingen, which unites a number of reglious observances in a mutually agreed date. The general tenor of the festival is a purification and absolution in memory of divine intervention; but sects differ considerably in interpretation. The practice among almost all sects involves the giving of gifts and the mending of broken friendships and lapsed vows before the year's end: there is a belief in Merovingen that this festival is pre-Scouring; and that therefore it is the one festival which intervenes in the period between 24th Harvest and 10th Prime. There is even a legend that in the Det Valley, during the darkest day of the Winter, when sharrh were hunting humans up and down the valley, a band of starving humans decided to celebrate this ancient festival, and in a cave deep in the hills, with the attack going on in the valley, they gave each other gifts that became a miracle— since each of them had secreted things that, brought into the open, helped the whole company survive. The story is perhaps apocryphal; but the festival is observed by all sects and across sect lines throughout the Det Valley in some form; and the practice and the legend have been picked up by the Falkenaer, who devoutly insist that the site of the miracle was the Falkenaer Isles.

The Angel of Merovingen

The Angel, which is a copy of one which did predate the Scouring, was set in its present position in the year 55 After the Scouring, precisely on the 25th Fallow, in a civic ceremony. The original, discovered in about 22 AS in the ruins of Merovingen, disappeared when it was stolen by the governor of Nev Hettek in the intervention during the Adventist riots of 53 AS; the barge transporting it sank in the Det, some believe as a result of Adventist sabotage;

some say that the barge was struck by lightning during a storm; and the implication is that the lightning was divinely directed.

Legend states various things about the Angel, which is a gilt figure twice lifesize, of a winged figure in flowing robes either drawing or sheathing a sword. Adventists say that the Angel's name is Retribution, and that he is in the act of drawing. Some say that the sword advances and retreats into the sheath by tiny degrees at each act of humankind that either advances or retards the day of Retribution. Of course this is immeasurable because of the number of people in the world, but some Adventists insist there has been measurable movement.

Revenantists state that the Angel's name is Michael and that he is sheathing the sword which caused the earthquake.

The Church of God agrees in the name and says that he is a divine witness to human affairs, and will remain to guard the world from the sharrh until the Church is restored to its former purity.

The Janes and the New Worlders incorporate him into their own beliefs as an entity of divine wrath which defends humanity from the sharrh: Janes call him the Watcher and New Worlders call him simply the Angel. Replicas of the Angel are venerated in Suttani, the Falken Isles, the Goth, and Kasparl.

The Scouring and Re-establishment

There is an event referred to as the Little Scouring, which was the purposeful demolition of structures and removal of dangerous information offworld by human forces in the face of the sharrh advance and in compliance with the sharrh-human treaty. This demolition was also designed to compel surrender of the holdouts.

It did secure some further compliance. It further and accidentally ensured human survival by driving the colonists into the hills to escape arrest; it also hardened the attitudes of the most determined resistance, the hard core of which was convinced (after repeated betrayal by authorities) that the whole alien threat was concocted by either the companies or the government to take their land.

But on 24th Harvest in the year 2657 of the old reckoning (still used for religious purposes and in official documents) the sharrh came down to eradicate the last remnant of human settlement on Merovin.

The first strike took out the space station, which by then was only a ransacked and stripped hulk. It also hit the major cities with C-fractional strikes, not, fortunately for the ecology and the remaining survivors, with atomics. Subsequent attacks were at close range with beamfire and finally with demolitions and air-to-ground missiles or with rifles as sharrh hunters carried out a site by site search for survivors, and perhaps, though sharrh motives remain obscure, a search for records.

Humans lost ground steadily, and finally devoted most of their energies not to attack but to evasion. This continued through the Long Winter of 2657–58, during which humans suffered from exposure and starvation.

By a time generally accepted as 10th Prime, the sharrh stopped shelling the hills and withdrew their patrols. After that, the sharrh left the world.

It was not until full spring that the first humans ventured out into their former lands. Some of these were true resistence fighters; others were human predators who were as apt to turn on other humans as on the sharrh. And for the next several years, that was the condition of the Det Valley and Megar and Kaspar River.

Eventually places like Kasparl sprang up, freewheeling trading posts founded on ruin; and places like Merovingen, Soghon and Nev Hettek, where farmers and traders reestablished themselves; and the hardy Falkenaer, who stripped their isles of trees in the making of boats of quite different sort than they had used in colonial days; but they had been fisherfolk from the founding of the colony.

This period of rebuilding is called the Re-establishment. It stretched on over fifty years before human life on Merovin achieved any feeling of permanence. These were rough

years in which there were numbers of locally notorious
bandits and leaders and would-be leaders who rose and fell
and left little legacy. Noted in the area around Susain was
the bandit Sager, whose band faded away into the elusive
desert-dwelling folk who live mostly by trading and by
petty theft in the outback around Susain; while in the Det
Valley, Nev Hettek took its militia and marched south in
2672, sweeping up local militias by persuasion and threat
until they reached the sea and Merovingen, using the Det
as a highway for supply and communication which the
bandits could not prevent. Generally this military action
was hailed with relief, and it gave the Det Valley settlements the earliest start of any in the world in the Re-
establishment of human trade and culture. Nev Hettek
thereafter made a bid to be capital of the whole valley, but
Merovingen refused to bow to its authority, and Merovingian
resistance encouraged the militias to remember their regional loyalties, which more than any other factor served
to put term to Nev Hettek's dream of being the world
capital.

The Earthquake

Among disasters associated with the Scouring was the
Great Earthquake. Merovan opinions differ as to whether
the sharrh activated the Det Valley fault, or whether the
calamity was merely a spectacularly unlucky natural disas-
ter. In any case, quakes were known from the year after
the Scouring, but subsided by 2662.

Then in 2690, an earthquake of great magnitude caused
severe damage the length of the Det from Nev Hettek to
Merovingen, with less disastrous effect for Merovingen,
which had been among the most prosperous post-Scouring
cities, building on the ruins of the Ancestors. There was a
tidal disturbance and flooding in Merovingen, while Nev
Hettek suffered extensive damage, but Rogon was com-
pletely leveled and abandoned.

The stubborn survivors rebuilt; but nature reserved a particularly cruel turn for the inhabitants of Merovingen. Less troubled by the aftershocks than Nev Hettek and certainly than miserable Soghon, they sent aid north to the relief of Soghon and the survivors of Rogon even in the midst of their own flooding.

But the area remained prey to seismic upheaval for years afterward; and there were floods in Merovingen in the summer of 2691, in 2695, in 2696, in 2698, 2699, and 2700, generally just a flooding of the streets, but in 2696 and 2700 the floods came high enough to cause extensive damage. The early floods were attributed to slight subsidence and unseasonal rains, which had indeed been known during and after the sharrh attacks. It was theorized the fires which attended the quake denuded the land and prevented the retention of water upland. Minor diking and sandbagging took care of the problem in most years.

And there was one curious incident, when floodwaters revealed the Angel of Merovingen, which appeared from forgotten (some said miraculous) provenance, washed to light in the clearing of rubble from the original governor's residence. It was seized upon as a sign of hope by the desperate citizens and contributed to the resolve of Merovingians to stay on the site of their city.

But in 2701 the dikes broke and the floodwaters stayed into winter, shallow enough to wade in most districts. Desperate Merovingians filled basements with rubble, built bridges, and in general survived as best they could.

So Merovingen began to be a city of bridges, but the full extent of the calamity was not evident until 2702, when flooding became worse. Merovingians, prevented by fear of Nev Hettek and by inhospitable conditions to either side of their harbor, stayed put.

Conditions grew worse gradually, then seemed to stabilize by 2710, when Nev Hettek intervened in a flooded Merovingen and proved unable to hold it.

Nature, however, was not through with Merovingen, for in 2720, a quake and a subsequent storm combined to alter the contours of the harbor, which had been undergoing silting and which already had numerous difficulties. Many ships in the harbor were swept from moorings and ground together to their destruction, forming a sandbar that finished the harbor in the years that followed. A new, deeper anchorage was established on the other side of Rimmon Isle. The construction of massive dikes and the eventual lessening of the rate of subsidence helped stabilize both city and harbor.

Legends persist that drowned dead rise from the harbor in the worst storms and crew the ships buried in the shallows of the Dead Harbor, which are occasionally said to rise and sail in particularly bad storms. Further superstitions say that the dead recruit sailors to their midst; that all who die at sea are bound to sunken ships, and that at the final departure of the last human from Merovin, the Ghost Fleet will follow.

The Dead Harbor remains the refuge of the lost and the desperate, the outcasts of every city up and down the Det.

Merovan Names

Generally Merovan names reflect the frequency of names in the area of space from which colonists came: that area itself was a frontier and had, like most frontiers, a fairly polyglot and polyethnic population.

Many original place names honored a discoverer, for example the name Merovin itself: or were the whimsy of mapmakers or colonists; or were historical referents to geographical features of other worlds; and finally, some were sharrh names attached only after the initial terse communique identified certain sites in evidence of sharrh claims.

During the Re-establishment two forces operated within the language: first, a breakdown of formal education and the fact that a few groups were bilingual, using the ground-based equivalent of ship-speech: some small, remote areas were actually dominated by these family-languages, derived from Terran origins. Second, there was a realization in the latter part of the Re-establishment that a great deal had been lost, and there was a conscious attempt to restore original forms both in nomenclature and in speech and to adhere to them.

At the ordinary rate of linguistic change in a society without telecommunications, deepteach, or even minimal literacy in a great deal of the population, six hundred years of life on Merovin might have seen Merovin a patchwork of regional dialects so divergent that average citizens from widely separated regions could not understand each other. But to this tendency of language to change rapidly there was a counterbalance: the profound interest of Merovans in regaining contact with humankind, or in preserving their culture against these changes which Merovans of the Re-establishment saw accelerating in their own time.

The influence of religion on this preservation is extreme but varied: Adventists, believing that humankind will come to rescue them, believe that there is a very substantive reason to preserve the original language, so that they can comprehend instruction from their deliverers, who, they trust, will speak something unchanged: they preserve a recollection of deepteach. Revenantists on the other hand do not believe in an intervention, but believe that preserving the ways of the Ancestors gains merit and that a sort of collective karma or sympathy toward the rest of humanity increases the likelihood of rebirth on another world.

In practice, the priests and the wealthy religious speak an educated, conservative language of forms current six hundred years ago; while there exists even among the upper class educated a vernacular which changes much more rapidly, new words which pepper a more conservative speech and which generally disappear as out of vogue. There is therefore change, but it is slow. The trades, on the other hand, have evolved a vernacular of their own to handle work and business with implements the Ancestors knew only in principle. And the illiterate (or the functionally illiterate, since some learn their letters for religious motives but cannot read with any skill) have a vernacular which is held to the conservative mainstream only by the necessity to communicate with the upper classes. As operative within the illiterate community is the tendency of alienated populations to develop jargon or cant specifically designed to shut out unwanted listeners. In some areas this has become impenetrable dialect; and in others, where Terran languages have compounded the problem, there might be said to exist new evolved languages. An example of this is the Falken Isles, where the original neo-Terran language and the creation of an entire new wooden-ship technology have created a language no outsider can understand.

Likewise a canaler from Merovingen or a farmer from the upper Det can lapse deliberately into an accent so extreme that an outsider might hear few intelligible words; and might misunderstand the contextual meanings of those.

Generally personal names and family names have withstood changes far better than place names. This link with personal Ancestors is a tie which few Merovans will abandon, particularly in the surname. More flexibility appears in the personal name, which is religiously influenced; but even many sharrists are reluctant to abandon the advantages of an Ancestor-name: some names in particular have social or financial advantage, establishing ties to wealthy families or heroes of the Re-establishment, or establishing ties to privileges which have attached to certain names. In Nev Hettek the Schuler name entails the right to the first booth in the main row of the autumn fair. and in Merovingen the Ebers have the right to direct petition of the governor without going through the Justiciary.

Merovin and Money

In general the world runs on the gold standard, each bank or city able to mint its own coin.

Merovingen and other cities of the Det have a basically standard monetary system, although the coinages differ in imprint.

Examples of such, their colloquial names, and their

values in ounces are as follows; and reckoning gold at
$425 and silver at $8 an ounce, a comparison in late 20th
century coinage is appended.

Merovingian Coinage

gold coinage

sol (dek)	1.60 ounces	$680
demi (dem)	.70 ounce	$297
dece (tenner)	.35 ounce	$148.75
gram (piece)	.035 ounce	$14.87

silver coinage

lune (silver)	1.60 ounces	$12.80
half (half)	.70 ounce	$ 5.60
dece silver (silverbit)	.35 ounce	$ 2.80.
gram silver (libby)	.035 ounce	$ .28

bronze coinage

(bronze and copper are reckoned as portions of a silver
lune, and fluctuate with the value of the lune.)

penny	1/10 lune	$1.28
halfpenny (pennybit)	1/20 lune	$ .64
cent	1/100 lune	$ .128

copper coinage

copper (bit)	1/10 cent	$ .0128

Chattalen Coinage

gold coinage

credit (cred)	1.60 ounces	$680
demis (demi)	.80 ounces	$340
dekas (dek)	.16 ounces	$ 68

silver coinage

standard (round)	.35 ounces	$2.80
silver penny (skimmer)	.035 ounces	$ .28

copper coinage

penny (flor)	1/10 standard	$ .28
halfpenny (half)	1/20 standard	$ .14
cent	1/100 standard	$ .03

   Some idea of the true value of currencies may be gained by knowing the value per ounce of gold and silver on the current market; but where living standards vary widely or where there is a great difference in technological level or a wide gap between rich and poor, a good measure is the cost of a staple such as a day's supply of bread.

   In Merovingen 2 cents will buy a loaf of bread or a decent fish; but you would pay 2 or 3 lunes for a pound of imported meat; and while a sweater on a canalside (a better measure than a pair of shoes, since shoes are a luxury there) might sell for a halflune, the very same sweater might go for 8 lunes in an uptown shop; and a silk scarf (imported fabric) could go for a gold dece or 4 lunes silver. There is a vast difference between luxury and necessity in Merovingen.

Banking

Each city stamps its own coinage, in gold, silver and base metal. There is also scrip, as traders and bankers exchange letters of credit which are very like banknotes—transferable with appropriate seals and signature—to avoid physical shipment of gold and other valuables from city to city with attendent risks of loss. But a clever thief with a good fence can manage to steal and negotiate letters of credit: corruption does go high up. The common thief, unless well-placed, does not receive near face value: this is the principle deterrent to theivery of such paper. It does *not* stop those high enough to wash it illegally through cooperative agencies.

Manufacturing and Trade

There are some heavy manufacturing centers on Merovin. Most such industry is located well away from population centers. Some few industries such as the iron and steel mills, the few refineries and the small plastics industry are well organized with permanent employment of skilled staff, but it is considered a hazardous occupation and there are fewer people anxious for employment in what might become prime targets in another Scouring—than might be imagined. Cities generally will not tolerate such centers near them, so they are isolated, which further diminishes the number of job-seekers.

In Merovingen as an example, there are traders, there are cottage industries and small operations like goldsmithing; there are services like taverns; a small iron foundry; there are tiny breweries and distilleries and importers and exporters. There are those who move freight on the canals. There are the bankers and rich landlords and there are the latecomers and the victims of disasters like flood or political upheaval. And in this economy many transient and many poor live from hand to mouth, in the tradition of their spacefaring ancestors who well understood the benefits of recycling. Anything thrown out is sorted and claimed down the line until very little is actually thrown away.

Merovingen exports fish, salt, and what comes in by sea; artworks, crafts, lace and leatherwork, some drugs and medicines, and many cottage industry items; some weapons; fine metalsmithing; fertilizer.

It imports: petroleum products, some drugs, textiles, grains, meats, leathers, raw metals.

In various adjustments for local abundance (Nev Hettek, for instance, is in the grain belt for the whole Det Valley and has grazing animals, but imports some fish and produces some little amount of petroleum) this is representative of Det Valley trade; and quite representative as a unit of other areas.

The tropics produce other items which arrive at Merovingen, among them raw materials and exotic luxuries and exchange is for the petroleum the Chattalen totally lacks.

Clothing and Fashion

Since the technology of Merovin was mid-27th century gone backward, Merovan technology is a hodgepodge of the modern and the makeshift. Merovin has forgotten a great deal that it once knew; certain areas of the globe remember things that other areas have forgotten due to the presence of a particular group of individuals who retained the knowledge, due to the preservation of records, or due to the prevalence of an industry elsewhere in disuse—an example of the latter being the petroleum industry in a few areas around the globe.

It is an advanced technology reduced to an earlier technology and hindered by an artificial cap, ie, that advanced technology is frowned upon.

The tendency in furnishings and dress and even in manufacture is toward the baroque: ornament for ornament's sake, but founded on a Classic age (the 27th century) which was austerely simple and high-tech. So in many respects this tendency to the baroque wars with the Classic ideal, and the result is a combination of 27th century pragmatic simplicity—for example the idea that clothes and furniture should be comfortable above all else; and the tendency of Merovan craftsfolk to embellish and complicate what they produce. Fashion exists in a few larger cities, and particularly in the Det River cities, where the river affords more than usual movement of ordinary citizens (as opposed to traders) from one city to the other, and where there exists considerable social division. In the Det Valley and also (but differently) in the tropic Chattalen, exists a concept of modishness, with all the attendant expenditure on changing fashion.

There is, underlying all of this concept, that persistent Classic ideal, which looks back to the sleek, simple comfort of 27th century dress which relied on advanced materials, and which had no particular gender-distinction. So whatever local dress has become, it is worldwide from the same origin. Since the prosperity of the Colonial period established itself in the popular mind as the epitome of human development, the tendency was to preserve the basic garments and to add accouterments and ornament.

In Merovingen-below, certain economic factors bear on style of dress. There are terrestrial cattle on Merovin, imported along with humans, but the term also includes native animals down to some the size and habits (but not the taste) of swine. There is no refrigeration except such amenities as rootcellars and springhouses, ice in the southlands being a very rare commodity. Most meat is smoked, dried, or preserved in brine or by canning. A city like Merovingen, with abundant fish, imports little meat, except for the palates of the rich; a few small towns to the north supply Merovingen with the little amount of fresh meat it gets. The fact that both Nev Hettek and Soghon are cattle-raising areas which supply most of their own needs combined with the problems in refrigeration and Mero vingen's own reliance on local beef, tend paradoxically to discourage the development of any major cattle industry in the north of Megon. *If* refrigeration were common it would be a different matter. As it is, the only animal product which does come downriver from that industry in any great abundance is leather; but again, scarcity, relatively high price, and the very mundane realities of a city on canals dictate that the majority of Merovingians who live on the canalsides go in wooden clogs for work, even though they will keep a pair of leather shoes for going *off* the premises or otherwise go barefoot more acceptably than wearing clogs onto the noisy bridges and balconies of Merovingen-above. Canalers on the other hand go barefoot in all but the coldest weather, simply because footgear is more often soaked than not: the worst weather usually sees an amazing variety of footgear, which varies from leather boots to (more commonly) ropesoled canvas. The only leather item a canaler will generally possess is a belt. Middletowners wear practical, heavy leather articles which are expected to last for years; and only the very rich remain to keep the cobblers well-to-do. But the rich as a class are not enough against other difficulties, to encourage a vast meat and leather industry to the north—all of which serves as a very small example of the intricacies of economics, trade, and Merovingian style.

A great deal of knowledge of textiles survived the Scouring. There is no industry supporting synthetics and in the abundance of local natural fibers and materials, and the universal fear of technology, there is no driving impetus to create a large plastics industry. In the Det Valley, as an example, there is some wool industry, the majority of which is used in the colder north; there is abundant cultivation of a local flax-like plant which produces a very serviceable linen or cotton-like material; and on one occasion angry Revenantist farmers burned a barge of a Nev Hettek refinery which experimented with sheet plastics, which they saw as a threat to their livelihood and a Provocation against the sharrh.

Weaving is a very advanced art, using some power looms; jacquards and corduroys are not out of reach. There is a very tough sailcloth-derived weave called chambrys. Chambrys is dyed a variety of colors (mostly indigo and brown and black) and is universal among working classes: of a fiber tougher and more resilient than cotton, it resists abrasion and takes amazing abuse. The same linen fiber is also widely used, though differently prepared, for knitting. There is silk, imported from the Chattalen, of high quality. There is felt and fur; and there is (another import) an airy vegetable-derived fiber very like fine combed cotton which is rarely seen in the lands of the Sundance. Waterproofing is accomplished generally by oil and wax, though the Wold is beginning a rubber industry which has met several setbacks similar in nature to the incident of the Det Valley farmers.

The mode of dress almost universal in the Det Valley is a pair of durable trousers and a sweater, be it Merovingian canal-rat or hightowner from the uppermost ranks of society, or a citizen of industrial Nev Hettek. But while the northern lands favor knee-high boots in all seasons, the Merovingian poleboatman will go shod as a rule, and have his trousers no longer than mid-calf; and wear black or brown stockings which show no effects of an occasional wetting or of dirt. The skip-boatman will go barefoot; the canalsider will dress much the same except for stockings and clogs or occasionally leather shoes; while the uptown resident will maintain a certain flair of fashion, fine knee boots, a scarf, a sweater designed to expose an embroidered high collar, or one flared silk sleeve, always with a certain coordination of color, usually dark, which distinguishes one of the gentry going casual: and not uncommonly accompanied with a very utilitarian sword-belt or belt-knife. A scarf for the head, tied bandanna-fashion, is not improper in Merovingen, where seasonal fogs wreak havoc with careful coiffure; and not uncommonly this is crowned with a hat, usually of sweeping brim which serves a practical purpose in inclement weather. Hats are a practical development in which a great deal of local character manifests itself; a few are of traditional form, like the canaler's cap; but vanity runs rampant among the gentry.

There is one gender distinction which was present in the

Classic period and which still remains, in the Det Valley
and in most other places: women of the upper classes
particularly, but generally of all classes, use cosmetics.
There are communities particularly among those dominated by certain Revenantist sects, where this is not the
case. Cosmetics among both men and women are common
in the Chattalen. Jewelry ranges from elaborate (the Chattalen
and the Suttani region) to the stylishly restrained (Merovingen). In Merovingen, finger rings are vitually universal, a solitary earring is not uncommon in either gender,
and necklaces for formal occasions are a throat-encircling
collar sometimes worn over a shirt's self-collar (either
gender) but among the truly elite the jewelry is actually
stitched to the collar—so that one is obliged to have quite
a lot of jewelry to maintain a wardrobe. Many an aspirant
to the upper society may tax his or her servant in the
constant transfer and re-arrangement of jewelry to a variety
of shirts.

The ordinary dress of the Merovingian hightowner is
boots and close-fitting trousers, usually dark but not always; and a shirt of white (or in some years, almost any
color) linen or silk usually hiplength and belted, having
flaring sleeves embroidered about the cuffs and about the
high, throat-circling collar with floral patterns; in modification this is also the pattern of the workman's shirt,
which is of more durable fabric.

There are, more formally, two other styles of shirt, both
designed to be tucked in, one wide-sleeved, by conven-
tion, with the collar open to the third button—often worn
with a bright scarf somewhere about the person; such shirts
are frequently of bright colors or of patterns; a second type
with more conservative but still generous sleeves, serves
as an undergarment for a sweater; or if made of silk,
frequently has lace cuffs and lace up the front, concealing
the buttons. (It is a peculiar circumstance that Merovingians
wear very little of the lace for which their craftspeople are
famous, though it is a staple of Nev Hettek fashion—in
Merovingen it is mostly used in table linen and curtaining,
except for a very few fine pieces.) This more tailored shirt
is worn in society in those seasons where a coat is re-

quired; and that in Merovingen means a tailored waistlength coat with lightly padded shoulders; or more rarely, a kind of frock coat appropriate even for the most formal occasions. For daytime wear any fashionable footwear is acceptable; for evening wear the trousers must be long and the footwear light pumps which currently have a moderate heel.

All of this keeps the clothing industry in Merovingen quite busy: fashion can be set in an evening by the tiniest change by the governor's tailor, who naturally makes such changes minute but frequent, and who in the case of the current governor has an elegant but aging client whose figure needs increasing flattery: thus go the cycles of style in Merovingen, from the daring and experimental to the conservative and more concealing in periods dictated by the aging and eventual replacement of the chief trend-setter.

Additional garments are the poncho worn by the canalers and by the poorest of the poor, often manufactured out of a blanket or tarp which has had a number of years of service. Finer ones are made of oiled wool or canvas and have some water repellent qualities.

A variety of cloaks are common among the middle and upper classes, ranging from utilitarian oiled wool to very fine grades of wool which are light and flowing.

Clothing is a fairly accurate indication of social class and, among the working classes, often an indicator of occupation. There are few uniforms: the notable exception is the uniform of the local police or militia. (See: Uniforms and Blacklegs)

Uniforms and Blacklegs

The uniform of the police or militia (in many cities the terms are interchangeable) in Merovingen, Nev Hettek, and traditionally throughout the Det Valley, is a brown waistlength coat over a black shirt, brown trousers down to the knee, and black stockings and black, lowcut shoes—hence the name blacklegs.

Originally this was the militia which during the Scouring saw to guerrilla operations and food procurement. The uniform (and the tradition and rules on which modern police departments are organized) arose during the Reestablishment when there was some inter-human conflict and a need to protect citizens against banditry. It was based on what was actually worn in the hills—knee length trousers were less readily soaked in dewy grass; and boots or even socks and shoes were a luxury in those hard days. The knee socks and the uniformity of color arrived when Calendree of Nev Hettek organized the first formal militia/police force and swept down the Det clearing the region of bandits and establishing local defense regions.

The militia was not well-equipped: the black socks were cheaper than bootleather and the brown uniform in those days was of every shade and every fabric, the accompanying weaponry whatever the individual militia member could come up with on his or her own. Joining the militia in those days was a way to eat regularly. It remains such: the blacklegs enjoy a good salary, and still purchase their own uniforms and weapons, which are now dictated by statute, except in the small towns, where the militia may consist of a handful of individuals who are far less formal; or in villages, which may have a single officer who deals with the local characters more by force of personality than by force of arms, and whose uniform is a matter of his or her own discretion.

The equipment of the modern police is regulation: usual on the street is a rapier and a stick and a pair of handcuffs. Guns exist but are brought out only on certain occasions: public executions, state funerals, and in times of unrest. Guns have a certain ceremonial mystique, partly due to fear of the gun and partly due to fear of the sharrh; and even more attributable to the dread of cult violence. That police go armed is a public and solemn reminder of authority of last resort.

Weaponry

There are no restrictions on carrying weapons in Merovingen, and likewise in most settlements and cities throughout Merovin: it was an armed populace who formed the cities, a good portion of the Det Valley's citizens in particular are Adventist and believe with religious passion that they may have to take up weapons on the Day of Retribution (See: Religions), so they would resist disarmament with armed force. So might some Janes. In fact, there are not many citizens of Merovin who would agree to be disarmed, whatever their religion, since some are nervous about the sharrh, some are nervous about the thieves, some about the law, some about fanatics, and many others are just not willing to give up any advantage to their survival should there be a second Scouring.

There are: guns, mostly revolvers; some antique muzzle-loaders from the Scouring; some rifles; occasional explosives. Swords, mostly of the style of the terrestrial epee, rapier, or occasionally cutlass; and knives that range from the stiletto to the shortsword, depending on locale and opportunity. The art of fence is one-handed or two-handed (rapier and main-gauche in some cities, the devotees of which do travel). The reason for the reinvention of the sword as a weapon is the same reason as other low-tech options: ease of production, silence, and the general fear among the populace of all persuasions that the sharrh might intervene if the tech level should grow too ambitious. Swords and daggers have popular acceptance because they are "nonprovocative" weapons, with reference to the sharrh.

There are rumors of Old Weapons, but rumors of this kind have never proved valid.

There are also poisons, garrotes, and various martial arts, particularly among Adventists and Janes, and the Sword of God in particular.

The river and canal and sea-craft of Merovin have an array of tools and implements readily turned to mayhem:

barrel- and boathooks are particularly deadly; there are also knives, marlin spikes and belaying pins, cutlasses and occasional firearms, and now and again a springloading grenade launcher that substitutes for cannon. The "grenade" may be anything from a firebomb to real explosives on a variety of fuses.

Government

The Governor lives in in the Signeury (original spelling: Signeurie), which is a large fortified isle on the Grand Canal. His position is sometimes hereditary, often usurped, often won by political connivance, assassination, coup or other upheaval, including the bribery of the keeper of the Seal, who once forged a will.

Sentences are carried out inside the Justiciary, and occasionally at the Hanging Bridge, which is not named for its architecture. The blacklegs are the officers of the Signeury and are its police: they carry guns. See: Weaponry. The court is in the Signeury, executions in the Justiciary, with rare exceptions.

Over all is the governor; and directly responsible to him are the Keeper of the Seal and the Astronomer.

Responsible primarily through the Keeper of the Seal to the governor are the heads of house and the Chief Justiciar, who heads the Justiciary. Likewise the heads of the trade associations are responsible through the Keeper of the Seal; but the harbormaster is independently responsible to the governor and to the Astronomer.

The Justiciar has under his or her authority the Executor, who runs the prison; the council justiciar, or parliamentarian and legal aide to the council; and the advocate justiciar, who is the attorney general; likewise the Justiciar is over the chief of records of the Council; and of course, all functions within the Justiciary.

The Priest of the Revenant College is a religious figure not responsible to any of the above but supporting them in their offices and through the services of the College, notably the keeping of relics and records, advising on cleric law, and investigating instances of Provocation. Directly under the Priest is the Advocate of the College, the legal arm; and the Librarian, who is the archivist. All operations within the College rest under Priestly authority.

The Chief Militiar (Mi-LI-ti-ahr) is responsible to governor and council, and governs the militia, commonly called the blacklegs. He or she is therefore both military and police chief; and has some independent functions in crisis. Beneath the Chief Militiar are the Chief Armorer, in charge of weapons and quartermastery; the chief of works, who is the chief civil and military engineer (the chief of works also reports to and from the harbormaster and the astronomer); and there is finally the legal arm, the Advocate Militiar, who handles military justice.

The legislative branch is headed by the chief councillor, who is chosen from among the Council; which is in turn composed of the heads of houses and trades and whatever other interests have been voted a seat.

Either governor or council may invoke the Chief Militiar, whose responsibility is only to the Governor or the Council, but not to the Chief Councillor.

Heads of houses may appeal to the Governor and own position within the Council.

The Chief Councillor is elected biennially from and by the Council.

The Chief Militiar is appointed by the Council and approved each five years, though it is usually *de facto* appointment for life.

The Governor chooses his own successor but the succession must have the approval of the Council, the Chief Militiar, and the Astronomer. The Governor holds office for life or until resignation or impeachment, the latter of which must originate in Council and command an 80 percent majority vote of both Council and Militia rank and file.

No document of law is official without the Seal; the Keeper of the Seal is *de facto* vice-governor, and functions for the governor in many capacities.

Merovan Boats

Sea-going

The sea freighters are by and large sail-craft with diesel
engines which they use sparingly. The most common routes
are coastal, up and down the Chattalen or the settlements
of Canbera and Savajen; a few cross the Cape of Storms to
Wold; and a great variety of craft ply the the Inner Sea of
Wold. The Falkenaers are the most daring seafarers of
Merovingen and Falkenaer ships carry a great deal of freight
and most of the passengers willing to commit themselves to
sea travel. The rocky isles of the Falkenaers are only the
port-of-convenience for these sailors, the focus of loyalty.
Falkenaer crews are born to their ships and may live birth to
death never having set eyes on the Falken Isles, to which,
nevertheless the Falkenaers maintain a staunch devotion.

The Praesi of Wold South and the Jakkinin of Sirene are
noted also among sea-farers: but the livelihood of the
Praesi is fishing, and their months-long voyages return to
their home ports.

Navigation on the Sundance south of the Chattalen is
rare, except for coastal craft. The southern Sundance is
given to contrary winds and typhoons.

Riverboats

The boats that ply the Det vary from small blunt-bowed
barges about 25 feet in length, used by locals, to the big
passenger packets, of which the most famous are the
Obligation and the *Sundancer:* triple-decked, hollow-hulled,
screw-driven, about 250 feet in length and 30 feet beam to
beam, they offer cabin space and deck passage. The ill-
fated *Det Star* was larger, at 300 feet and 35 feet beam;
and relied on sail as well as engines.

The majority of Det freight moves on motor barges,
many of which also accept passengers.

The felucs of the Goth River of Nevander are similar,
but use a triangular sail.

The smaller waterways of Wold and Megon use craft of similar design but smaller size.

The Boats of Merovingen

Some Det-river craft can come beyond the Harbor; most freight, however is transferred to small canalboats, which are of design too eclectic to set forth here: but the notable types are:

1. THE SKIP: a flat-bottomed, blunt-bowed craft about 5 feet by 22 feet, with a very small inboard engine.

   The living arrangement is often a tarp awning set with a couple of poles and guys, but it is not practical to have up while using the pole, which requires a lot of walking back and forth.

   The bottom is slatted for water drainage; the rear has a cubbyhole forward of the engine mount under a sort of raised quarterdeck on which the poler can walk. It is common to shelter in this place, though it is tight quarters. The cubby (canalers call it the hidey) is about 5×5 with 1.2 feet of engine wall to the rear and about 1.5' overhead clearance. So there is about 16 feet of free cargo room on the slats to the front plus the deck surface. A good deal of gear is stowed to the sides of the cubby, which makes the centerspace quite tight.

   The deck has a shallow rim that keeps things from going overboard and the pole, about 12' long, with the boathook, lies along the rim in a special rack. Other large items are stored in the open and shifted about at need. Ropes and tackle are stored along the sides of the forward well and down in the well, where needed.

   The bow is not truly square but rather a blunt rounded affair. This type of boat is the most common craft in Merovingen.

2. The CANALER: about a third larger than the skip, confined to the main waterways and used for heavy cargo.

3. The POLEBOAT: a motorless gondola-like craft, long and slim and used commonly for hire, the taxi of Merovingen.

4. The CATBOAT: catamaran, a boat confined to the bay and usually propelled by paddle or sail, for small fishing and harbor freight.
5. The LONGBOAT: a 10-oar gondola-style craft used for state occasions and funerals.
6. The COASTER: one of the fisher-boats, high-sided and broad of beam for its length. It sails the edge of the Sundance.
7. The FANCYBOAT: a motor launch for the rich, generally used only in the uptown area.
8. The YACHT: a large motor-sail vessel used primarily by the wealthiest for transport either on the river or along the coast.

Canaler's Slang

The Ancestors of Merovin were not spacers, but station-dwellers and employees of the founding corporations some of whom were planet-based. The original Merovans were polyglot, with some influence of spacer-culture, with which they worked.

Events combined to break down linguistic conformity: the Scouring and the lack of formal education.

Other factors tended to prevent breakdown: the religions.

And there was the necessity of coping with new professions and new environments, which meant new vocabulary.

Old French, Italian, Turkish, English, Russian, Hindi, German and the Slavic-influenced Union Standard station-speak of Fargone were among the predominant influences.

Add to that the abbreviated grammar and musical lilt of shipspeak.

Merovan languages vary considerably, particularly the trade-languages, the languages of profession, which deliberately seek to exclude outsiders to the trade.

An example is the jargon of the Merovingian canalers, which, like many unwritten languages, is highly contextual: one word may have a dozen implications depending on situation and tone of voice.

Ware!	Look out!
Ware hey!	Calamity! Alarm!
Ware port	Watch boat's left.
Ware starb'd	Watch boat's right.
Ware deck!	(sometimes just *Deck!*) Hit the deck.
Scup!	Object about to roll overboard. May be combined with direction, as aft, port, starb'd.
Bow a-port, a-starb'd!	Turn left, right.
Hin	Put the pole on the bottom.
Ya-hin	You put the pole in.
Hey-hin	I put the pole in.
Hup	Lift the pole from the bottom.
Yoss	Steady as she goes.
She's a wash	There's a washout (hole) here.
Double pole	Two people poling: (starboard poler sets pace and starts call).
Tie-up	Any tie made to shore or boat; (2) a metal tie-ring for mooring.
Night-tie	Mooring fore and side for stability.
Full-tie	Same procedure as night-tie.
Jury-tie	A quick tie to one point.
Hof	Off! Back away!
Haw	Stop! hold it!
Get aslant of	Take objection to; blockade; oppose
Ne (neh)	(1) Now. (2) Wait.
Ney (nay)	No.
Yey	(Expresses agreement, consent acknowledges an order or request).
Yey and haw	(lit. yes and stop) Give yey and haw: tell someone what to do.
Not know hin from hey	(lit. not know turn-signal from collison-warning) Varies according to application: (1) of a canaler: he's stupid; (2) of a landsman: he's ignorant.

Merovan Sea Life

The Merovan oceans cover a great portion of the globe and abound with life both bathic and free-swimming. Some of the creatures are legendary, such as the many-armed Kraken, alleged to inhabit the deeps of the Sundance. Others are merely rare, such as the seaflower, which spreads jelly-like polychrome veils over a good three meters of surface.

Certain areas such as the Falken Isles and the Wold Sea and the Black Sea support major fishing industries.

The Det estuary is heavily reliant on fish but does not export much in the way of fish products. Known in Merovingen are, of sea fish caught by Merovingian coasters:

The *whitetail*: a slender, silver fish with a notable white streamer flowing from its topmost tail fin: delicate of flavor, rare, and expensive. Rarely tops five kilos in weight.

The *silverbit*: a prolific breeder and common foodfish with a rich, oily flavor. About a handspan in length and caught by trawling in great abundance.

The *sailfin*: a green to silver cartilaginous-skeletoned fish two to three meters in length, caught by hook. The meat is flavorful but has a toxin requiring care in the preparation.

The *sea eel*: as the name implies, an eel-like creature with impressive teeth, brown to black in color, edible, but difficult to take. Top size is two meters, top weight 13 kilos.

The *whale*: a slender-bodied, large mammal with a cat-like face and numerous teeth. General color is ink black. It is forbidden to hunt this creature, which occurs primarily in antarctic waters, but in some seasons ventures to the equator. It is predatory toward other sea mammals and fishes. It is not known to attack humans. Top size, reported 100 meters. Weight unknown.

The *sherk*: a quick-moving, primitive fish known to travel in schools. Up to 15 meters long, but most specimans are from two to five meters, and a known hazard to fishermen. The sherk will attack anything less than its own size. Its general color is green to black. The meat is palatable if heavily seasoned.

Estuary

An estuary fish travels freely between salt and fresh water. The Det River has a wide variety of such fish perhaps due to the complex nature of its estuary, which ranges from still, almost stagnant shallows, to deep harbor.

Notable are:

The *freshwater eel*: brown to black and about a meter or less in length, flourishing in the worst water. A food staple among the poor.

The *razorfin*: a voracious, spiny, needle-toothed fish needing careful handling. Top weight is 5 kilos. It is lively on the line and a destroyer of nets. A good food fish with a white, delicate meat.

The *yellowbelly*: a mild toxin in the fins and a painful bite makes this fish another difficult one to handle. Sometimes taken in nets, it tops 10 kilos and provides a bland if pleasant meat.

The *prickleback*: bony, with a good assortment of spiny fins which lay flat until grasped. A fat, toothless bottomfeeder of about 3 to 6 kilos, excellent food fish if properly filleted.

The *fathead*: a big bottomfeeder with a conspicuous fleshy prominence above the eyes, toothless but voracious and omnivorous. It may top 30 kilos and tends out to sea past its first few years, where it grows above 100 kilos in weight.

The *redfin*: named for its beautiful red-orange tail and dorsal fins, this small fish (about two handspans in length at maximum) is an excellent but troublesome foodfish. Its bite is notoriously painful.

The *deathangel*: most beautiful of estuary fish, with trailing fins of black on a yellow and silver body, the deathangel is aptly named. The three banner-spines and the

ventral spine carry a toxin so lethal and so long-lasting that
the dried spine of a deathangel can kill a victim weeks
afterward, if the poison sac at the ventral side of the spine
is intact. If the spines and the internal glands are removed,
the deathangel, about a kilo of platter-shaped fish, is deli-
cious and mildly intoxicating, though overindulgence can
lead to toxic reaction. In a few sensitive individuals this
reaction comes much sooner, and one fatality from the
meat alone has been recorded in Merovingen.

Merovingian Music

Music on Merovin has the same roots as language, [see
Language] both ethnic and popular. It is also influenced by
the spacer-chanteys, which are both ethnic and varied, and
which are a ship's living history.

Some songs survived the Scouring; others are hero bal-
lads out of the Scouring and the Re-establishment [QV]
which relate tales of the resistance and the rebuilding.

There are love songs and a rich and varied liturgical
music; marches and work-songs and working sea-chanteys
and popular ditties which come and go by fashion, many
of which are disguisedly political.

Principle instruments are: the *horn*, a brass, lip-modulated
instrument of increasingly complex shapes and tones.

The *drum*: drummers are a popular holiday street enter-
tainment; and drums also signal executions and solemn
occasion.

The *gitar*: a stringed, long-necked instrument

The *sither*: another variety of gitar but much larger,
having drone-strings and a round sounding-chamber: this
instrument is Merovan in origin, by extensive modification
of a Terran instrument. Common in the Chattalen, and
known in the north and in Nevander, it plays often in
accompaniment to drums and chimes.

The *harp*: a vertical stringed instrument of ancient origins,
reproduced on Merovin in imitation of traditional description.

Chimes: all sorts of bells.

Index of Isles and Buildings by Regions

THE ROCK: (ELITE RESIDENTIAL)LAGOONSIDE

1. The Rock
2. Exeter
3. Rodrigues
4. Navale
5. Columbo
6. McAllister
7. Basargin
8. Kalugin (governor's relatives)
9. Tremaine
10. Dundee
11. Kuzmin
12. Rajwade
13. Kuminski
14. Ito
15. Krobo
16. Lindsey
17. Cromwell
18. Vance
19. Smith
20. Cham
21. Spraker
22. Yucel
23. Deems
24. Ortega
25. Bois
26. Mansur

GOVERNMENT CENTER

THE TEN ISLES (ELITE RESIDENCE)

27. Spur (militia)
28. Justiciary
29. College (Revenant)
30. Signeury
31. Carswell
32. Kistna
33. Elgin
34. Narain
35. Zorya
36. Eshkol
37. Romney
38. Rosenblum
39. Boregy
40. Dorjan

THE SOUTH BANK	THE RESIDENCIES
Second rank of elite	Mostly wealthy or government
41. White	51. North
42. Eber	52. Spellbridge
43. Chavez	53. Kass
44. Bucher	54. Borg
45. St. John	55. Bent
46. Malvino (Adventist)	56. French
47. Mendelev	57. Cantry
48. Sofia	58. Porfirio
49. Kamat	59. Wex
50. Tyler	

WEST END	PORTSIDE
Upper middle class	Middle class
60. Novgorod	78. Golden.
61. Ciro	79. Pauley
62. Bolado	80. Eick
63. diNero	81. Torrence
64. Mars	82. Yesudian
65. Ventura	83. Capone
66. Gallandry (Advent.)	84. Deva.
67. Martel	85. Bruder
68. Salazar	86. Mohan
69. Williams	87. Deniz
70. Pardee	88. Hendricks
71. Calliste	89. Racawski
72. Spiller	90. Hofmeyr
73. Yan	91. Petri
74. Ventani	92. Rohan
75. Turk	93. Herschell
76. Princeton	94. Bierbauer
77. Dunham	95. Godwin
	96. Arden
	97. Aswad

TIDEWATER (SLUM)   **FOUNDRY DISTRICT**

 98. Hafiz (brewery)   109. Spellman
 99. Rostov   110. Foundry
100. Ravi   111. Vaitan
101. Greely   112. Sarojin
102. Megary (slaver)   113. Nayab
103. Ulger   114. Petrescu
104. Mendez   115. Hagen
105. Amparo
106. Calder
107. Fife
108. Salvatore

EASTSIDE   **RIMMON ISLE**
(LOWER MID.)   **(ELITE/MERCANTILE)**

116. Fishmarket   124. Khan
117. Masud   125. Raza
118. Knowles   126. Takezawa
119. Gossan (Adventist)   127. Yakunin
120. Bogar   128. Balaci
121. Mantovan (Advent.)   129. Martushev
     (wealthy)   130. Nikolaev
122. Salem
123. Delaree

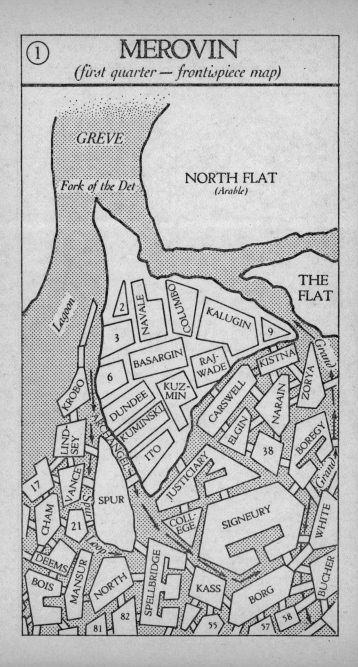

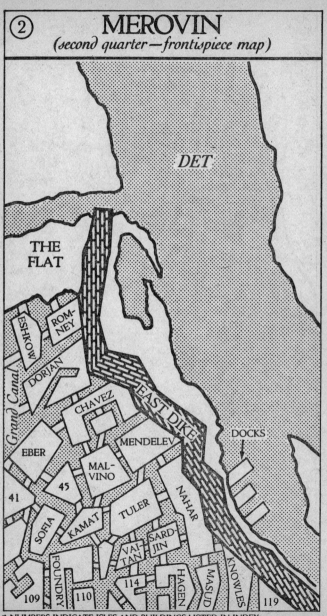

② MEROVIN
(second quarter—frontispiece map)

DET

THE FLAT

ESHKOW

ROM-NEY

DORJAN

Grand Canal

CHAVEZ

EAST DIKE

EBER

MENDELEV

DOCKS

MAL-VINO

45

41

SOFIA

KAMAT

TULER

NAHAR

VAI-TAN

SARD-JIN

FOUNDRY

109

110

114

HAGEN

MASUD

KNOWLES

119

❋ NUMBERS INDICATE ISLES AND BUILDINGS LISTED IN INDEX

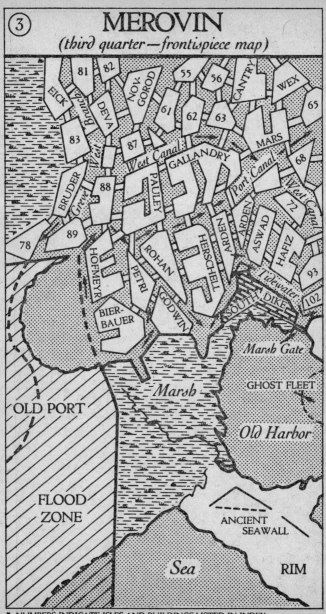

MEROVIN
(third quarter—frontispiece map)

EICK

81

82

Brana

DEVA

NOV-GOROD

55

56

CANTRY

WEX

61

62

63

65

83

West

87

West Canal

GALLANDRY

MARS

68

BRUDER

88

PAULEY

Port Canal

West Canal

Grevel

72

78

89

HOFMEYR

ROHAN

HERSCHELL

ARDEN

ARDEN

ASWAD

HAFIZ

93

PETRI

GODWIN

SOUTH DIKE

Tidewater

102

BIER-BAUER

Marsh Gate

GHOST FLEET

Marsh

OLD PORT

Old Harbor

FLOOD ZONE

ANCIENT SEAWALL

Sea

RIM

* NUMBERS INDICATE ISLES AND BUILDINGS LISTED IN INDEX

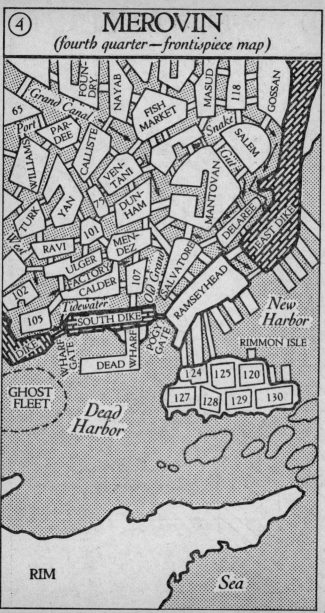

MEROVIN
(fourth quarter — frontispiece map)

④

65

Port Williams

Grand Canal

FOUN-DRY

NAYAB

FISH MARKET

MASUD

118

GOSSAN

PAR-DEE

CALLISTE

VEN-TANI

Snake

SALEM

Gulf

TURK

YAN

75

DUN-HAM

MANTOVAN

West

101

RAVI

MEN-DEZ

SALVATORE

DELAREE

EAST DIKE

102

ULGER

FACTORY

CALDER

107

Old Grand

105

Tidewater

SOUTH DIKE

RAMSEYHEAD

New Harbor

DIKE

WHARF GATE

DEAD

WHARF

POGY GATE

RIMMON ISLE

124

125

120

GHOST FLEET

Dead Harbor

127

128

129

130

RIM

Sea

✱ NUMBERS INDICATE ISLES AND BUILDINGS LISTED IN INDEX

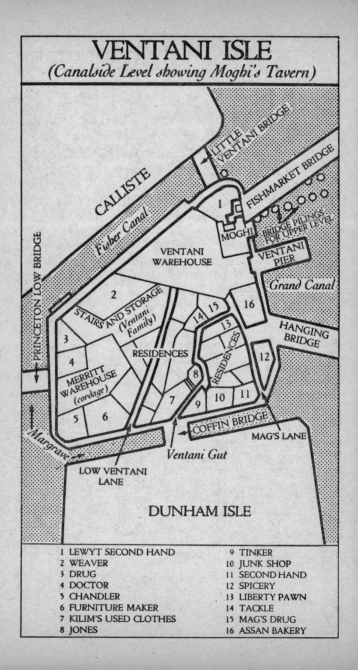

VENTANI ISLE
(Canalside Level showing Moghi's Tavern)

LITTLE VENTANI BRIDGE

CALLISTE

FISHMARKET BRIDGE

Fisher Canal

PRINCETON LOW BRIDGE

1

MOGHI

BRIDGE PILINGS
FOR UPPER LEVEL

VENTANI
WAREHOUSE

VENTANI
PIER

Grand Canal

2

STAIRS AND STORAGE
(Ventani
Family)

15

16

14

HANGING
BRIDGE

3

RESIDENCES

13

RESIDENCES

4

MERRITT
WAREHOUSE
(cordage)

8

12

7

9

10

11

5

6

COFFIN BRIDGE

MAG'S LANE

Margrave

Ventani Gut

LOW VENTANI
LANE

DUNHAM ISLE

1 LEWYT SECOND HAND	9 TINKER
2 WEAVER	10 JUNK SHOP
3 DRUG	11 SECOND HAND
4 DOCTOR	12 SPICERY
5 CHANDLER	13 LIBERTY PAWN
6 FURNITURE MAKER	14 TACKLE
7 KILIM'S USED CLOTHES	15 MAG'S DRUG
8 JONES	16 ASSAN BAKERY

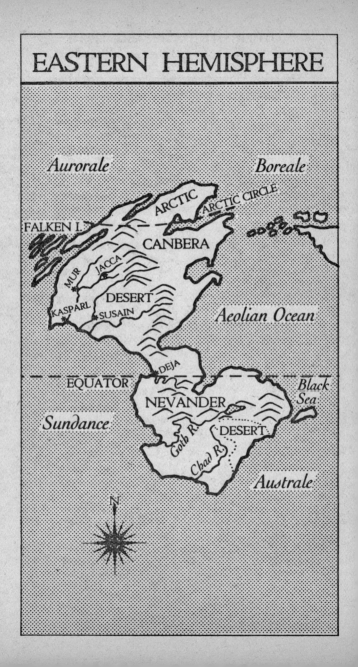

VGSF, Cash Sales Department, PO Box 11, Falmouth, Cornwall.

Please send cheque or postal order, no currency.

Please allow cost of book(s) plus the following for postage and packing:

UK customers – Allow 60p for the first book, 25p for the second book plus 15p for each additional book ordered, to a maximum charge of £1.90.

BFPO – Allow 60p for the first book, 25p for the second book plus 15p per copy for the next seven books, thereafter 9p per book.

Overseas customers including Eire – Allow £1.25 for the first book, 75p for the second book plus 28p for each additional book ordered.

NAME *(Block letters)* ....

ADDRESS..

....

....